BOARD STIFF

"Great dialogue and characters enhance this cozy mystery. Starting with the first scene, the book is laugh-out-loud funny, and the strong humor continues throughout."

—*RT Book Reviews, Top Pick*

LUCKY STIFF

"Annelise Ryan has done it again! Her heroine, Mattie Winston, has a way with a crime scene that will keep you reading, laughing and wondering just what can possibly happen next in this entertaining romp. Wisconsin's engaging assistant coroner brings readers another winning mystery!"

—Leann Sweeney, author of the Cats in Trouble Mysteries

"*Lucky Stiff* is a roller-coaster ride of stomach-clenching action, sizzling attraction, belly laughs, and a puzzler of a mystery. Annelise Ryan has created a smart and saucy heroine in Mattie Winston, who you just can't help but like, especially as she endures what is possibly the worst road trip ever. What a thrill ride!"

—Jenn McKinlay, author of the Cupcake Bakery Mysteries and the Library Lover's Mysteries

FROZEN STIFF

"Ryan mixes science and great storytelling in this cozy series. . . . The forensic details ring true and add substance to this fast-paced and funny mystery. Good plotting and relationship drama keep the mystery rolling, while Mattie's humorous take on life provides many comedic moments."

—*RT Book Reviews*

"[Mattie's] competence as a former ER nurse, plus a quirky supporting cast, makes the series intriguing. Ryan has a good eye for forensic and medical detail, and Mattie gets to be the woman of the hour in her third outing."

—*Library Journal*

"Absorbing. . . . Ryan smoothly blends humor, distinctive characters, and authentic forensic detail."

—*Publishers Weekly*

SCARED STIFF

"An appealing series on multiple fronts: the forensic details will interest Patricia Cornwell readers, though the tone here is lighter, while the often slapstick humor and the blossoming romance between Mattie and Hurley will draw Evanovich fans who don't object to the cozier mood."

—*Booklist*

"Ryan's sharp second mystery . . . shows growing skill at mixing humor with CSI–style crime."

—Publishers Weekly

WORKING STIFF

"Sassy, sexy, and suspenseful, Annelise Ryan knocks 'em dead in her wry and original *Working Stiff*."

—Carolyn Hart, author of *Dare to Die*

"Move over, Stephanie Plum. Make way for Mattie Winston, the funniest deputy coroner to cut up a corpse since, well, ever. I loved every minute I spent with her in this sharp and sassy debut mystery."

—Laura Levine, author of *Killer Cruise*

Books by Annelise Ryan

WORKING STIFF

SCARED STIFF

FROZEN STIFF

LUCKY STIFF

BOARD STIFF

STIFF PENALTY

Published by Kensington Publishing Corp.

Stiff Penalty

Annelise Ryan

KENSINGTON BOOKS

http://www.kensingtonbooks.com

KENSINGTON BOOKS are published by

Kensington Publishing Corp.
119 West 40th Street
New York, NY 10018

All Kensington titles, imprints and distributed lines are available at special quantity discounts for bulk purchases for sales promotion, premiums, fund-raising, educational or institutional use. Special book excerpts or customized printings can also be created to fit specific needs. For details, write or phone the office of the Kensington Special Sales Manager: Kensington Publishing Corp., 119 West 40th Street, New York, NY, 10018. Attn. Special Sales Department. Phone: 1-800-221-2647.

Kensington and the K logo Reg. U.S. Pat. & TM Off.

ISBN-13: 978-1-61773-408-3
ISBN-10: 1-61773-408-X
First Kensington Mass Market Edition: March 2015

eISBN-13: 978-1-61773-409-0
eISBN-10: 1-61773-409-8
First Kensington Electronic Edition: March 2015

10 9 8 7 6 5 4 3 2 1

Printed in the United States of America

Chapter 1

I find it ironic that I'm sitting across from a psychiatrist discussing the dichotomy of life and death, not only because I hate shrinks and once swore I'd never go to one, but because I came here voluntarily, at least this time. My name is Mattie Winston, and I deal with life and death on a regular basis these days: death because it's a part of my daily job, life because there is a new one growing inside me.

I'm pregnant . . . very, very pregnant at the moment. And while being in this condition is something I had planned for at some point in my life, getting here the way I have has been as well planned as a train wreck. I've been imagining my future since I was twelve years old, sitting in my bedroom acting out scenes of domestic bliss with Barbie and Ken, and cutting pictures out of bridal magazines with my sister, Desi, who was ten at the time. My future was crystal clear in my mind: a loving husband, two adorable children, and a life full of comfort and fun in my Barbie Dreamhouse, with occasional family vacations in our Barbie camper.

Things appeared to be progressing according to the Big Plan when I snagged a husband who seemed to fit nicely into the Ken/Prince Charming mold I'd carved out for him. His name was David Winston, and he was a surgeon I met at the hospital where I worked. At the time I was an ER nurse, but I quickly transferred and became an OR nurse so I could be closer to him. I missed the ER like crazy, but I figured a little job unhappiness was a worthy sacrifice to be near the man I loved. After a whirlwind courtship, David and I managed a few years of marital bliss. But that starry-eyed, fairy-tale future I'd imagined as a child crashed and burned when I found David performing exploratory surgery on one of our coworkers late one night in an otherwise deserted operating room. Unfortunately, the only surgical instrument he was using at the time was his penis.

Crushed, humiliated, and hurt beyond belief, I fled my job and my marriage. My neighbor and good friend, Izzy Rybarceski, who is the medical examiner for our county, gave me a place to hide by allowing me to move into the mother-in-law cottage behind his house. It was nice to have a place to run to, but the location of the cottage meant I was only a stone's throw away from the home I had shared with David. I know this because I've thrown stones at it a time or two.

Izzy let me sit and stew for a couple of months while I came to terms with the end of my marriage and the tattered remains of my childhood dream. My money ran out about the same time Izzy's patience did, and when I emerged from my cave of self-pity, he offered me a position as his assistant. The job description entailed dissecting dead bodies and investigating any crimes involving deaths, so I felt reasonably qualified for the work, given my OR experience at the hospital, my insatiable curiosity, and my general nosiness.

It turned out to be a good fit, and it's a job I love more than any other I've ever had. But it came with a curveball named Steve Hurley, a tall, dark-haired, blue-eyed homicide detective who had arrived in town a few months before I started working for Izzy.

Hurley and I hit it off in a big way, and I began to consider David a mere misstep in my planned future, a fork in the road that I had to take in order to meet up with Hurley. It turned out there were many other forks in that road—like the fact that Hurley and I met over the dead body of the woman David had had his affair with, like the fact that both David and I were prime suspects in her murder, and like the fact that Hurley had a wife and child he didn't know he had. I suspect there are many more forks to come. In fact, given that my relationship with Hurley thus far has had more ups and downs and more ins and outs than a porno movie, I expect to get thoroughly forked over in the months and years to come.

The psychiatrist sitting across from me—Maggie Baldwin, or Dr. Naggy as I like to call her—is someone I was forced to see months ago when Hurley and I experienced the latest speed bump on our road to happiness. Because of a non-fraternization rule that came up when the ME's office and the police were tasked with oversight duties for one another, Hurley and I couldn't be a couple and work together. After much agonizing, I decided to quit my job with Izzy and go back to work in the hospital ER. I wasn't happy about the decision—I loved my job with Izzy—

but I loved Hurley more. Plus, returning to the scene of David's crime wasn't something I looked forward to. Small towns like Sorenson thrive on gossip, and I'd been the primary topic more times than I liked of late. I knew everyone at the hospital would be whispering and gossiping behind my back, watching like vultures for any chance encounters David and I might have, eager to pick at the bloody remains left behind.

As it turned out, my worries were for naught. Because our town is a small one, the hospital has trouble attracting physicians at times. Many of them prefer larger city hospitals, where there are more resources, more amenities, more cohorts to share on-call hours with, and more earning potential. So when David basically blackmailed the hospital administrators by threatening to leave if I came back to work there, they decided at the last minute that I was no longer welcome. Nurses were a dime a dozen, but David was the only surgeon on staff at the time, and the hospital couldn't afford to lose him.

My job with Izzy had already been given to someone else, but my settlement in the divorce left me with a nice cushion of money to tide me over for a while. I was fine with the career setbacks because at least I had Hurley, or so I thought. Unfortunately, there were two other women who popped into Hurley's life at exactly the same time, and their hold on him was much stronger than mine. One was Kate, the wife Hurley thought he'd divorced years ago—a wife I never knew he'd had. The other was a teenage girl named Emily—Hurley's daughter—a daughter that until then, Hurley never knew he had.

The forks kept coming. A bit of bad luck for my

newly hired replacement turned out to be good luck for me. I was able to return to my job with Izzy and found myself once again working side-by-side with Hurley, determined to put him and his newfound family behind me. But Hurley and I are drawn to one another the way a metal oxygen tank is drawn to an MRI, explosive results included. Before long we were sneaking rolls in the hay whenever and wherever we could.

Then Hurley found out the true reason why his not-really-an-ex-wife had suddenly come back into his life, and that discovery led to him and his new-found daughter leaving town and staying gone for two months. The road truly forked me that time because shortly after Hurley left I discovered I was pregnant.

It is now mid-September, almost a year since I first met Hurley, and the road has recently forked me again. I am days away from my projected delivery date, and my huge, hormone-addled body has my brain so muddled that I can't think straight. I am about to embark on the biggest journey ever in my life, but every time I try to focus on it and the future, my thoughts go flying off in a million different directions like a burst of fireworks. In an effort to douse this incendiary state of mind, I made the decision to come back to Dr. Naggy after a six-month break. I was hoping she'd give me a quick fix, some brilliant bit of insight that would make everything feel right. Instead, she is insisting on knowing everything that has happened to me during the six months since I last saw her, a portion of my life she has labeled "the inciting events," as if they somehow led to a riot.

"So tell me what happened when Hurley came back to town," she says to me.

I ponder the question for a moment, wondering how to summarize six months of chaos during an hour-long appointment.

"Well, it all began around the start of May," I tell her. "That's when Hurley returned to Sorenson and his job. And once again our meeting took place over a murdered body. That seems to be a recurring theme in our lives."

"That's not too surprising, given your line of work," Dr. Naggy says.

"Yeah, but this time it was different because I wasn't there to investigate the death. This time I was there because I was the killer."

Chapter 2

The events that led to me being tagged as a killer started on a beautiful spring evening at the start of May. Tulips and daffodils were in bloom everywhere; the landscape had shed its winter mantle of white and was once again bedecked in green, a favorite hue in Wisconsin because it signals winter's end and it's half of the Packers' traditional colors.

I was entering into my fifth month of pregnancy by then, and so far I'd managed to hide my condition from my friends and family, a subterfuge aided by the fact that I'm six feet tall and a well-rounded person . . . and I mean that in terms of body habitus as opposed to experience or mental health.

Hurley had been gone for just over two months, but we had talked on the phone regularly, keeping one another updated, talking about current events, and occasionally having some mind-blowing phone sex. These phone calls were kept as secret as my pregnancy, which I hadn't yet mentioned to anyone—including Hurley—for several reasons. One reason I hadn't told Hurley was because he was tending to something of a very emotional and personal nature, and I didn't want to distract him from that. Another reason was because he was still recovering from the shock of discovering he already had a child he never knew about, a bright, personable fourteen-year-old girl named Emily who would be living with him when he returned. Heaping the news on him of yet another child he hadn't planned for seemed cruel. My third reason, perhaps the strongest one of all, was my recollection of all the things Hurley had said when he'd learned about Emily, about how he never wanted to be a father, wasn't suited for the job, and hadn't asked for it.

The final reason was because I wanted to have time to talk with Hurley about our relationship before the added pressure of knowing there would be another child came into play. I had some doubts about Hurley's feelings for me, and the last thing I wanted to do was force him into a proposal simply because he felt obligated.

There was never any question in my mind about whether to keep the baby. In fact, I'd fantasized numerous times in the past about what a child of ours would look like. Certain aspects of my mental image changed from time to time—hair color, overall build, gender—but the two things that stayed consistent were height and the color of the eyes. I'm fair-haired with a fair complexion and have blue eyes, and Hurley has black hair, a somewhat ruddy complexion, and blue eyes. We're both tall, so I felt certain the child inside me would be also, and the blue eyes were a given. But Hurley is tall and lanky, whereas my body type is the sort made for keeping one's innards warm during the long, cold Wisconsin winters. Animal lovers call it blubber on seals, whales, and walruses, but I prefer to call it insulation. I've managed to trim some of my insulation over the last couple of months by working out regularly at a nearby gym and altering my diet to one that is healthier for both me and my baby. But I don't think I'll ever be at risk for freezing to death.

While I'm determined to keep the baby regardless of what happens between me and Hurley, I also know it means I might end up as a single mother. And that means once again being fodder for the Sorenson gossip mill.

At the start of May I was looking forward to Hurley's return, but I was also dreading it. Despite my gym efforts, I knew I couldn't hide my pregnancy much longer. Not only was my tummy starting to show—something I might have been able to pass off as weight gain for a little while longer—something weird was going on in my hips, and I was starting to waddle like a penguin. Plus my already large bosom was popping out of every bra and blouse I owned. Even with the best sports bra money could buy, my personal trainer, Gunther, said watching me run on the treadmill was like watching the Harlem Globetrotters play while on LSD. I started to ask him if he meant the players or the watchers were on LSD, but then realized it didn't matter.

The changes in my figure weren't the only problem. People were starting to notice other things, too. In my third month, I was plagued with terrible bouts of morning sickness that had Izzy wondering if I was still suited for the job. It didn't help that I was assaulted by strange and often nasty smells on a regular basis, everything from formaldehyde to body parts that were long past their expiration dates. I told Izzy it was just nerves, and that I was seeing a doctor about it. He was visibly relieved when I quit having to leave both death sites and the autopsy suite to make a mad dash for the restroom to barf, although this respite only lasted about two weeks. That's when the child inside me decided that my bladder was a punching bag. Once again Izzy became concerned about my frequent bathroom runs, and once again I assured him I was seeing a doctor about the problem, and that it was probably nothing more than a bad bladder infection. The first part of that excuse was true: I was seeing a doctor. The last part, however, was a lie. I knew it wasn't a bladder infection that was making me pee every half hour.

I was also much more cautious about using personal protective equipment whenever I was on-site or in the autopsy room, and Izzy hadn't missed this change in my behavior, either. Several times I saw him eyeing me with that curious, quizzical expression he often got right before he figured out some deep dark secret of mine that I had hoped to keep hidden. I passed this one off by saying that my eyes had been opened by Jonas Kriedeman's life-threatening allergies to the chemicals we use. This was an unfortunate situation for Jonas, the person who took my position when I turned in my ill-fated resignation, but a fortunate one for me since it enabled me to get my job back. And it had worked out okay for Jonas, too, because he was able get his old job back, working as an evidence tech for the police department.

Despite my efforts to hide things, my days of keeping my condition a secret were numbered, and I knew it. I had hoped to keep it under wraps for at least another week or two, because juicy gossip seeps through our town like the scent of manure does in the early spring when the surrounding farmers fertilize their fields. In fact, manure and gossip have many things in common. The more they reek, the better people think they are. The fouler the stench, the faster people want to spread them. And both items tend to linger long after some people wish they were gone.

Because of this, both Maggie and the OB doctor I was seeing for my pregnancy were in a neighboring town nearly a half hour away. Despite the fact that HIPAA laws are supposed to prevent people from disclosing confidential medical information about the people they care for, certain things have a way of getting around. In fact, people in small towns are masters at innuendo. There is an entire subculture built around the ability to reveal information about someone without actually saying it. Facial expressions and vocal fluctuations are easily interpreted by those familiar with small-town gossip in the same way twins who make up their own language understand one another. The big reveal would go something like this: "Hey, I saw Mattie Winston at the grocery store the other day, and she had such a glow about her." Then the speaker would arch an eyebrow and in a suggestive tone, add, "You know what I mean?" If asked later, the person who said this could truthfully deny telling anyone I was pregnant.

I knew Izzy would likely figure things out before anyone else, although his partner, Dom, and my sister, Desi, were equally probable front-runners. My mother, on the other hand, is much too self-absorbed. I'm not sure she'd pick up on the fact that I was pregnant if I was giving birth on her dining room table, an act that would probably give her a stroke, not because I was giving birth, but because of all the germs I'd be distributing across the surface of her table. My mother has issues, and to say that she is a bit of a germophobe is like saying the Pacific Ocean has a bit of water.

Getting pregnant when I did hadn't been intentional—no one could have been more surprised than I was—and it happened the first time Hurley and I ever slept together. I was on birth control pills, but while investigating a case with ties to a local casino, I'd gotten caught up in the gambling scene and found myself making frequent trips to the place to play some blackjack or poker. Once inside the casino, day and night became indistinguishable, and I often lost all sense of time. As a result, I didn't take my birth control pills with the regularity I should have, and apparently that, combined with a course of antibiotics I took for a sinus infection, was the perfect cocktail for conception.

I was eager for Hurley to return because I didn't want anyone to find out about my pregnancy before he did, and I didn't want to tell him over the phone. In order to fully gauge his reaction to the news, I needed to see his face and body language when he heard it. Would he be angry that I hadn't told him sooner? Would he be angry that I'd let it happen in the first place? Would he feel duped, tricked into something he didn't want? Would he feel trapped, forced to do the "right" thing?

These questions circled through my mind constantly, and when I finally learned that Hurley would be coming home, they became a major distraction. I practiced imaginary scenarios in which I delivered the news to him in a hundred different ways. I fretted over his possible responses and agonized over what the future might hold. I obsessed over how things would go, and I think that contributed to what happened. My mind was so focused on Hurley and my situation that I didn't pay enough attention to my surroundings. Otherwise I might have realized that I was being stalked by someone who wanted to see me dead.

All my role-playing and fretting turned out to be a giant waste of time because fate wasn't done forking with my life's path yet. Never in my wildest dreams could I have imagined how the moment of revelation would actually go down.

Chapter 3

As I try to bring Dr. Naggy up to date, I realize that my original claim about things starting at the beginning of May isn't altogether true. I think the trouble actually began back at the beginning of March. While Izzy and I were trying to investigate the case we were on at the time, Emily's mother, Kate, left town for what was supposed to be a few days, leaving Hurley to look after Emily. Through a series of unfortunate events, Emily ended up staying alone at my cottage one evening while Hurley and I tried to carry on with an investigation that had more suspects than the Agatha Christie section of the library. While at my place, Emily got spooked when my dog, Hoover, started barking at windows and prowling restlessly around the house. When Emily saw a strange man actually peeking in through my windows at her, she got much more than spooked.

Hurley and I hurried back to my place, but whoever had been skulking around outside—and there definitely had been someone because there were footprints in the flowerbeds, and both Emily and

Dom had seen the guy—was gone. Emily is a very talented artist, and she managed to draw a sketch of the man, a sketch that seemed vaguely familiar to me. When my mother saw the picture, she identified the man as my father. This left me with a mixed bag of emotions because my father had disappeared from my life just before I started kindergarten, and I haven't heard or seen anything of him since. I have no idea why he left, and my mother claims not to know either. I suspect her obsessive personality, chronic hypochondria, and overpowering narcissism had something to do with it. Whatever it was, it made Mom mad enough that she threw away all his pictures, tossed out any personal items he had left behind, and refused to ever discuss him with me when I was growing up.

I didn't much care what had happened between my dad and my mother. I know she is not an easy person to live with, and given that I spent most of my life waiting for the day when I could get away from her, it was easy for me to understand how she'd managed to go through four husbands so far. The thing I did care about, the thing I struggled to understand, was why my father had left me. Had I done something to earn the same disdain he had for my mother? Or was he just an irresponsible cad who'd buckled under the pressures of fatherhood? Part of me was angry at this vague memory of a man who had abandoned me at such a young age. But another part of me was curious. I wanted to see what he looked like, hear what he sounded like, and ask him a million questions.

The idea that my father might have been spying on me intrigued me. Thoughts of him lingered in my mind after that first sighting, but they quickly took a backseat to the news of my pregnancy, the possibility of Hurley leaving me, and obsessive worries about my future.

The first phone call came two days after Hurley left town. It came on my work cell phone, which did double duty as my private phone since I didn't have a landline in the cottage. When the phone rang, I hoped it was Hurley calling, but no caller ID came up in the window. I answered it with, "Hi, this is Mattie Winston with the ME's office," not knowing if the call might be work-related. All I heard on the other end was the static of an open line for a few seconds and then the quiet nothingness of what I assumed was a dropped call. Thinking the caller might try back right away, I waited a few minutes with the phone in my hand. But nothing happened.

The second call came a few days after that, and the third about a week later. This time I was at work, sitting in the library space that doubled as my office, finishing up some paperwork. Once again there was no caller ID displayed, and once again I was greeted with the hiss of an open line and another noise that sounded like someone breathing into the phone on the other end. I tried a few tentative hellos to see if anyone answered, but once again the call went dead.

I happened to mention the odd calls to our office receptionist, Cass, and she shed some light on the mystery. A few days after the spying incident, she had taken a call from a man who claimed to be a lawyer from Milwaukee. He told her he needed to talk to me right away about some testimony I was scheduled to give in a case he was trying the following week. It was a ruse because there was no case—I had yet to testify in court, though Izzy was training me for it— but Cass didn't know that. She fell for the sound of authority and urgency in the man's voice and gave him my cell number. When I checked the office phone log to see when the pretend lawyer had called, it turned out to have come in minutes before my first mystery call.

The calls continued, and they came more or less weekly after that third one, though there didn't seem to be a pattern with regard to day or time. While I had no proof of the caller's true identity, in my gut I felt certain it was my father. It was the only answer that made any sense. I pondered the question of why he would call me and then just hang up, like some pranking middle-school kid yearning to play a practical joke on someone. I told myself that it was likely because he was nervous about what he had done, and worried about the sort of reception he might get. Maybe he just needed some time to work up the courage to speak, or to work up a good story to explain his neglect and abandonment. Whatever it was, I was willing to play along for a while, content to let him have as much time as he wanted.

Things came to a head on a Saturday night at the start of May when I was on call, bored, and having a major jones for some cheesecake or ice cream from one of our local restaurants, Dairy Airs. My torturer, Gunther (I know he calls himself a personal trainer, but I'm not fooled), has made me very aware of just how much exercise is needed to burn off the calories in most of my favorite foods. Granted, most of my favorite foods aren't on anyone's recommended list for dieters, things like macaroni and cheese (actually, almost anything with cheese; I am from Wisconsin, after all), pies, pasta dishes, and cakes . . . especially cheesecake, which combines two of my favorite foods:

cheese and cake. This leaves me constantly at war with myself, my common sense and newfound awareness of nutrition battling my cravings and my body's constant efforts to insulate itself against a Neptunian winter.

Being pregnant has made it easier for me to be good in some ways; I'm not only eating for two, I'm behaving for two. I've kept my OB doctor informed on a regular basis, and both she and Gunther have been monitoring my exercise and diet program closely. I'd definitely been striving for more balance in what I ate, and my efforts had garnered me a mere four-pound weight gain by the time I reached my fourth month of pregnancy. But I was also battling some horrendous food cravings, and on this particular day, the enemy won.

My gym time meant telling Gunther the Torturer that I was pregnant, but I swore him to absolute secrecy. And the fact that he knows the actual weights of most of the women in town leads me to believe he knows how to keep a secret. You're risking your life if you ever reveal a woman's true weight, and if the judge hearing the case happens to be a woman, odds are it will be ruled a justifiable homicide.

Much as I hated to admit it, the gym time was working. My legs and arms were stronger and more toned, my energy levels were up, and I felt better than I had in a long time. I wasn't losing weight, but I wasn't gaining tons either, and my OB doc assured me I was right on target. There was one interesting consequence of this newfound body image and energy combined with the hormonal surges of pregnancy: a crazy sex drive. And Hurley, my only outlet for such things at the time, was hundreds of miles away.

It occurred to me that my food cravings might be

substitutes for the carnal yearnings I had. I didn't think that was the case with my cheesecake jones on the night in question, however, because I had just spent an hour on the phone with Hurley indulging in phone sex. I tried to wait the craving out, thinking the desire might dissipate, but it not only remained persistent, it got worse. After an hour of trying to ignore mental images of every kind of cheesecake one could imagine, I gave up, blamed it on the pregnancy, and got in the car to drive to Dairy Airs.

I suppose I might have been followed other times before this—in retrospect, I think I must have been—but this was the first time I became aware of it. I'm not sure what it was that clued me in during my six-minute drive to the restaurant. Maybe it was the fact that I had just gotten another one of those mystery phone calls with a ghost on the other end. Maybe it was some hormonal version of paranoia triggered by the headlights I saw in my rearview mirror when I turned onto the road at the bottom of my driveway. Headlights alone wouldn't necessarily have attracted my attention, but these headlights turned onto the road from a driveway, just as I had. And the driveway they exited from was right next door, the one that led up to the house I used to live in with my ex. It was being rebuilt after a disastrous fire that basically gutted the place, and when it was done, David intended to share it with his new girlfriend, our insurance agent, Patty Volker.

Given that it was after eight in the evening on a Saturday, and the construction workers weren't typically there on the weekends, much less this late at night, I wondered if the car behind me might have been David, Patty, or both. I kept glancing at my rearview mirror, expecting to see the car turn off at some point and give me a glimpse of its make and model, but it stayed behind me. Only when I pulled into the parking lot of Dairy Airs did it veer off, and then only after hesitating, as if the driver had considered pulling into the lot but decided against it.

I did get a glimpse of the car as it pulled away, but it was too dark to tell what make and model it was, or to even be certain of the color. All I knew for sure was that it was a basic sedan, a little boxy in shape, and dark in color. I knew it wasn't David's car; he had recently bought himself a new BMW in a pearly gray color to replace the one that was destroyed in the fire. And I knew it wasn't Patty's car since she owned an SUV. I saw it the day I discovered her helping David move out of the Sorenson Motel and into her house.

Given all my rule-outs, I deduced the car either wasn't following me and I was just being paranoid, or that the car belonged to my father—who was most likely my mystery caller as well—and for whatever reason, he was as yet unwilling to make contact or meet face-to-face.

I ordered my cheesecake to go and headed back home, hearing the voice of Gunther the Torturer in my mind, lecturing me on how long it was going to take me to burn off those calories. I tried to ignore him, but Gunther was not only annoying, he was persistent. Finally, halfway into my drive, I mentally sat on him to shut him up.

It was then that headlights once again loomed in my rearview mirror. I glanced at them and wondered if it might be the same car, but it was too dark to tell.

And when I turned onto my street the other car went straight, so I dismissed it from my mind.

I had barely shut the door of my cottage when my cell phone rang. I saw it was Izzy and knew it was most likely a death call, which meant my cheesecake would have to wait.

"Hey, Izzy," I said, answering the call. "What's up?"

"I see you just pulled in," he said. Izzy's house and mine are quite close given that mine is in his backyard. "We have a call. Your wheels or mine?"

"Mine," I said quickly, wondering why he bothered to ask.

Lately whenever we went out on calls together, I was adamant about driving my car. No doubt Dr. Naggy would interpret my need to drive as some sort of power play or need for control. But it wasn't the driving I insisted on as much as it was the vehicle, and it wasn't a power play but rather a simple matter of comfort and survival. Izzy's car is a refurbished Impala from the sixties, and it has a bench front seat. Since I'm six feet tall and Izzy barely clears five feet, he needs to have the front seat up as far as it will go. Put me in that front seat beside him and the kid in my belly has more room than I do. Of course, I could offer to drive Izzy's car, but he'd never let me. It's his baby, and he won't let anyone else drive it, Dom included.

Given all that, it made much more sense for me to drive us in my car: a retired hearse in a lovely midnight blue color. It has a bench front seat, too, but I can push it back far enough to accommodate my long legs, which leaves Izzy looking like a toddler in need of a booster seat. Granted it might seem a bit callous to drive a hearse to the scene of a death, but I figure it's more appropriate than, say, an ice cream truck, which at one time was my dream car, right after I figured out Barbie and her life were a myth.

"Meet you outside," Izzy said, offering me no details. There would be time for him to fill me in along the way.

I put my cheesecake in the refrigerator and checked in on my two cats, Rubbish and Tux, who were sleeping on top of my bed, oblivious to my presence or lack thereof. I then gave a pat on the head to Hoover, who more than compensated for the cats' indifference by following me around and watching my every move with those big, sad, brown eyes that let me know he, at least, would miss me.

I met Izzy outside and we climbed into the hearse. "Where to?" I asked.

"The hospital. They have a death in the ER."

I made a face at this. I'd been avoiding the hospital because of the David-doing-surgery-with-his-penis debacle, and the recent job fiasco. "I really don't want to go there," I said.

"Why? Because of that thing with David and Molinaro giving in to his blackmail?"

I gave Izzy a *duh!* look.

Izzy shook his head and sighed. "Mattie, you have to quit judging yourself based on other people's opinions. Besides, in this case it isn't you who looks bad, it's David. The guy was a jerk to do what he did. And I'm guessing everyone at the hospital knows it."

"I suppose, but I'm still pissed that he and Molinaro got away with it."

"Not much you can do about it except stew over it," Izzy said. "And all that's likely to do is give you an ulcer. Wisconsin is an at-will work state, which means they don't have to give you a reason for not hiring you. Even if you took them to court over it, you'd never be able to prove anything. It's a he-said-she-said kind of thing."

I pouted and started up the hearse, knowing he was right, but still feeling the sting of it all.

"Besides," Izzy said, fastening his seat belt, "it worked out for the best, didn't it?" He didn't give me a chance to answer. "You were able to come back to work with me. In fact, I think we should thank David and Molinaro, because their timing was serendipitous."

"That still doesn't make it right."

"No, it doesn't. But I have to confess, I'm glad it happened. I missed you, Mattie. We make a good team."

There was the faintest hitch in his voice as he spoke, and I was genuinely touched by this rare show of emotion. Izzy has always been stoic, down-to-earth, and not prone to displays of affection—public or private. I envy his ability to keep his emotions so controlled and in check, and wish I could be more like him. But lately it seems my emotions are hanging on my sleeve like a collection of dangerously loose threads, constantly at risk of being snagged by the slightest provocation, after which they would unravel with terrifying speed, exposing parts of me I'd rather keep hidden.

In fact, such was the case at that moment. My appreciation and affection for Izzy—for his friendship, support, and faith in me, and for everything he had done for me—bubbled up inside. Then the bubbles came out in a burst of tears.

Izzy stared at me, looking concerned and confused. "Did I say something wrong?"

"No," I blubbered, trying desperately to get a handle on my emotional surge. "In fact, you said everything right. I love you, Izzy."

I had a strong urge to lean over and hug him, and might have done just that if he hadn't said, "You do know I'm gay, right?"

I knew his comment was meant to break the tension and introduce some levity into the moment, and it worked. A chortle escaped me, and then my tears turned into riotous laughter. Izzy looked relieved but still a bit wary. "I'm sorry," I said, struggling to rein in my laughter. "My emotions have been extremely labile lately."

"Yeah, I kind of noticed that, along with some other things. Are you okay to drive?"

"I'm fine." As if to prove my point, I shifted the car into reverse, backed out of my parking spot alongside the cottage, shifted into drive, and eased my way down the driveway, relieved to feel the emotional knot in my chest start to loosen up. As I pulled out onto the road, I saw a flash of headlights behind me, a car pulling out from the same place the earlier one had—David's driveway.

"Is it Hurley's?" Izzy asked.

I looked over at him with a bemused expression. "How could it be? He's not even in town." I was approaching the stop sign at the end of our road, so I slowed and signaled for a left turn. I stopped and waited longer than necessary given that no traffic was coming along the intersecting road, and I stared into my rearview mirror, trying to make out the face of the driver in the car behind me. The car stopped several feet back, its headlights shining into my window, so I couldn't make out a face. But in the light reflecting off the car's surface from my taillights, I could tell the edges of the vehicle were boxier than Hurley's sedan. "Even if Hurley was in town, I'm certain it isn't his," I concluded. "I think it's my father's."

I turned left onto the main road and watched as the car behind us turned right. As I turned my focus back to the road in front of me, I slowly became aware of Izzy staring at me with a befuddled, slightly frightened expression.

"What's wrong?" I asked him.

"You think it's your father's?" he said, swallowing hard.

"It's the only thing that makes sense," I told him. "I think he wants to try to start up a new relationship with me."

Izzy looked away for a few seconds, shook his head, then looked back at me. "What are we talking about?"

"The car," I said, enunciating slowly and casting a worried sidelong glance at Izzy. Was he having a stroke or something? How could he have forgotten what we were talking about just seconds before?

"What car?" Izzy asked, looking even more confused.

"The one behind us . . . or at least the one that *was* behind us. When we turned left, it turned right. I've seen what I think is the same dark car behind me fairly often lately, and twice now it has emerged from David's driveway at a time of day when no one should be there. At first I thought it might be following me, but now I'm not so sure. Maybe I'm just being paranoid."

Izzy twisted around and tried to look out the rear window, but the seat back was too high for him to see.

"You were talking about a car," he said, with a tone of sudden comprehension. He chuckled and shook his head. "Thank goodness. Now your answers make much more sense."

I replayed our conversation in my mind and came out puzzled. "You asked me if it was Hurley's car. What else could we have been talking about?"

"I didn't say car."

"You lost me," I said, shaking my head. "What else could belong to Hurley?" In the millisecond before he answered, I got it.

"Your baby, of course," Izzy said, and that's when the world began to spin.

Chapter 4

"Watch out!" Izzy yelled.

I'd been staring gape-jawed at Izzy instead of at the road ahead of me. When I glanced back at the road, I saw that I was in the left lane and instinctively jerked the wheel to the right and slammed on the brakes, triggering a frightening fishtail. Had I been going any faster, we would have likely been the cause of a great deal of scrambling and chaos as someone tried to figure out who was going to do the autopsies for the accident that took the lives of the medical examiner and his assistant. But I was able to get the hearse under control, and in the wake of an angry blare from a passing motorist's horn, I pulled the car off onto the shoulder and parked.

After a few seconds of near-death silence in which the only sound was the quiet hum of the engine and the settling of the dust I'd kicked up, I looked over at Izzy. "You know? Who told you? Was it Gunther? Because if it was, I'm going to chain his legs into that exercise machine he keeps putting me on and spread that sucker until he splits like the wishbone on a turkey."

"Nobody told me. I'm gay, Mattie, not stupid. And while I realize that my patients are typically a little riper than most, I *am* a doctor."

I didn't say anything for several seconds. I just stared out the windshield. For lack of any better comeback I finally said, "What gave me away?"

"A number of things. Your sudden interest in using all the personal protective equipment was one. I didn't buy that lame excuse you gave about Jonas for one minute. I figured you either inherited your mother's germophobia and it was just now manifesting itself, or you had some other reason for the sudden interest in your health. Then there was the vomiting, and having to pee all the time. Not to mention your boobs."

"My boobs?"

"Yeah, your boobs. Hell, they probably qualify for their own zip code by now."

"I know, right? They're freaking huge! No one I've talked to has looked me straight in the eye for weeks now, and that includes women. And they ache all the time," I added, rubbing the side of the right one.

"Well, they are rather hard to ignore," Izzy said, and even he was staring at my chest with an expression of awe.

I sighed and shook my head. "I should have known you'd figure it out."

"How far along are you?"

"About sixteen weeks."

"I guess that means you're keeping it."

I nodded.

"And is it Hurley's?"

"It is. It happened when we . . . while . . . it was

right after Christmas, when I quit my job," I added quickly. This was the truth based on the dates the doctor came up with using what a one-time patient of mine, who was pregnant for the eighth time, had dubbed the wheel of misfortune, a little cardboard dial that calculates the date of conception and esti- mates the date of delivery. I didn't want to tell Izzy that Hurley and I had rendezvoused several other times after that, and hoped my answer would keep him from asking, since such liaisons were forbidden if I wanted to keep my job. And now that I was on the verge of having two mouths to feed, I needed my job more than ever, not to mention the maternity and child-care benefits that came with it.

"What does Hurley have to say about it?"

"He doesn't know yet." I admitted, wincing.

Izzy sighed and shook his head. "When are you planning on telling him?"

"As soon as he comes back. He said he should be home on Monday."

We sat through several seconds of silence, both of us staring straight ahead, both caught up in our own thoughts.

It was Izzy who finally broke the silence. "So what are your plans?"

"My plans?"

"With the baby."

"I intend to keep it and raise it. If it means being a single working mom, so be it. I won't let Hurley marry me just because it's the right thing to do."

"That's all very heroic and noble," said Izzy, his tone laced with sarcasm. "But what about what Hurley wants?"

I shrugged. "I'll deal with that when I get to it. I'll

have to wait and see what he says when I talk to him." I turned and faced Izzy then, my expression imploring. "I'm determined to make this work, Izzy, whatever it takes. I promise you I will do whatever I need to in order to keep my job. I not only like it, I need it. I need the income, and I need the benefits."

Izzy gave me a solemn look. "We need to discuss this some more, but clearly this isn't the best time. For now, let's just keep it business as usual, and we'll figure out a time to talk later, okay?"

I nodded, too afraid to say anything.

"We should get to the hospital."

I looked over my shoulder to check for oncoming traffic and waited as a single car passed. Then I eased the hearse back onto the road. Less than five minutes later, we were heading into the hospital. I hoped our case would be a simple, straightforward one that we could finish up within the hour. I forgot that my basket of hopes is overrun with forks.

The ER was its usual bustling craziness. My good friend Phyllis—aka Syph to those of us in the know—directed us to the room that held our victim. Inside the room, behind a curtain, we found Bob Richmond standing at the bedside, one hand cupping his elbow, the other pulling at his chin as he stared at the dead man.

Bob Richmond is a semiretired detective with the Sorenson PD who was covering in Hurley's absence. He had gotten shot while working a case with me back in the fall, a case in which Hurley appeared to be the primary suspect. No cop wants to get shot, but in Bob's case it turned out to be a good thing, in a way. At the time of the injury he weighed north of four hundred pounds and was a heart attack waiting to happen. But after getting gut shot, having several surgeries, and acquiring a new outlook on life and death, he had lost over one hundred pounds and counting. Prior to the shooting, his main form of exercise was shoveling food into his mouth, but nowadays he works out at the gym regularly. The change in him is so dramatic that many people who know him don't recognize him anymore.

Richmond's desire to get healthy and his dramatic success inspired me. Back before he was shot I'd agreed to go to the gym with him in support of his efforts, and while I have taken a few short sabbaticals, the two of us have stuck with it, for the most part. Richmond is much more dedicated and determined than I am, however; there have been times when he has had to drag me along kicking and screaming. I hate hanging out with women who are thinner than my fettuccine.

As Izzy and I entered the room, Richmond glanced over at us and nodded. Then he looked back at the victim without saying a word, letting us absorb the scene for a minute or two.

The room looked like a tornado had blown through it. The floor was littered with torn wrappers from all the equipment and supplies that had been used, and a crash cart was parked nearby with several of its drawers partially opened. There was blood on the stretcher and the railings, and a smeared puddle of it on the floor, along with a trail of bloody footprints that meandered around the room. IV tubing, catheter tubing, and several types of monitoring cords snaked their way from various poles and machinery to the bed.

After taking in the room, I let my gaze shift to the

dead man, who was lying on his back on the stretcher, a sheet covering him from the waist down. The first thing I noticed was undoubtedly the first thing everyone else noticed because it was the elephant in the room. Sticking out of the man's chest was a two-foot-long, wooden-handled implement, the base of which was wrapped in a huge bundle of white gauze. I glanced at an X-ray hanging on a light box on the wall and saw that the handle was part of a large barbecue fork, the tines of which, judging from its position on the X-ray, had ended up in the victim's heart.

The fact that a fork played a role in this murder should have been my first clue that this wasn't going to be a quick and easy case.

When I was able to take my eyes off the fork long enough to look at the dead man's face, I saw thinning blond hair, blue eyes that stared sightless at the ceiling, and pale skin, though I couldn't tell for sure if the coloring was due to nature or exsanguination. His nose was swollen, and there was dried blood crusted in both nostrils. His left eye had a dark purplish area beneath it, and I could see the start of a bruise along his lower left jawline. When I shifted my focus away from specific injuries and took in the whole face, I realized I knew him.

"That's Derrick Ames. I took care of him once in the ER when he cut his hand on a table saw. Isn't he a math teacher at the high school?"

"Correct," Richmond said. "He also teaches German. His parents are German nationals who came over here just before he was born."

"What happened to him?" Izzy asked. "Aside from the obvious."

"Not sure," Bob said with a shrug. "According to

EMS, he came stumbling out of his house around seven-forty with the fork in his chest, and scared the crap out of two boys who were skateboarding in the street. One of the kids stayed with Ames, and the other one ran home and got his mother. She called 911 at seven forty-nine and then went outside to see if she could help."

"Was he still conscious?" I asked.

"Barely. The woman said she could tell the fork was in his heart because it was jerking with every one of his heartbeats. Ames told her to pull it out and tried to do it himself, but she wouldn't let him."

"Smart woman," I said. "Leaving the fork in there plugged the holes it made. Pull it out and you get uncontrolled bleeding and a swift death."

"Not that it made a difference in the end," Richmond said, reaching over and pulling the sheet down. On Ames's belly was a large wad of bloody dressing pads. Then Richmond, who was wearing gloves, lifted the pads and revealed a large stab wound about three inches below the sternum and a couple of inches to the right of Ames's navel. "It turns out the fork was unnecessary. Ames was also stabbed with what was likely a large knife, judging from the size and shape of the wound. The doc says it nicked his aorta. He was bleeding internally even without the fork."

"You said he was conscious when the woman got to him," Izzy said. "Did he say anything to her? Like who did it?"

"Junior Feller is at the scene, and he's been talking to the witnesses there. Let me find out what he's got so far." While Richmond took out his cell phone and stepped out of the room to make the call, Izzy and I took a closer look at Derrick's body and snapped some photos. Then we took out a body bag in preparation for moving him to our morgue.

Richmond returned just as we were zipping up the body bag—though we had to improvise some to work around the fork—and told us what he'd learned. "It turns out Derrick did say something to Janet Calgary, the woman who was with him in the street, though it wasn't much. She said he muttered the word *payday,* let out a long sigh, and then went unconscious."

"*Payday?*" I said. "That's an odd thing to say."

Richmond shrugged. "Maybe he was trying to say it was a payback of some sort."

"I take it the knife wasn't in him when he came out of the house, or when he arrived in the ER?" Izzy asked Richmond.

"Nope. According to the Calgary woman, Ames was covered in blood, but the only injury she saw was the barbecue fork."

"That doesn't mean he didn't have another one," I said. "That fork kind of rivets one's gaze."

The three of us stared at it for several seconds as proof of my claim.

Finally Izzy asked, "Any idea where this knife is?"

Bob nodded. "Junior is inside Ames's house, and he said there's a bloody knife on the kitchen floor. They're waiting for Jonas and someone from your office to get there before they start collecting anything. So far all they've done is look around, make sure the scene is safe, and chat up some of the neighbors."

Izzy and I headed out to the main part of the ER so Izzy could talk to the doctor who had treated Ames to see if there was any other useful information that might help with the autopsy, and to request a copy of the medical record. He charged me with calling one of the local funeral homes to come and transport the body back to the morgue. As we approached the nurse's station, I stopped short. There, sitting in a chair at one of the computers, was David.

He looked up, saw me, and frowned.

I gave back as good as I got, leaning in close and keeping my voice low. "Hello, David. Looks like your shenanigans couldn't keep me out of the ER after all."

"Shenanigans?" he said with a tone of amusement that suggested I was dumber than a box of rocks. "What the hell are you talking about?"

"I'm talking about your attempts to keep me from coming back to work here. You know, that threat you made to leave if Molinaro gave me a job? You knew the hospital couldn't afford to lose the only general surgeon they had left on staff. And you used that to screw me. Which shouldn't surprise me since it's well known that you screw anything that walks by."

"Who told you that?"

"That you screw anything that walks by? No one had to tell me. I kind of figured it out on my own when I caught you playing hide the snake with Karen Owenby, remember? Thanks to that debacle, everyone knows what a skank you are."

I saw that some nurses who were standing nearby were listening in on our conversation, though they were making a valiant effort to look like they weren't.

Apparently David noticed them, too, because he lowered his voice and moved his head a tad closer to me. "That's not what I meant and you know it," he said just above a whisper. "I meant who told you that I didn't want you working here?"

"Oh, that was Molinaro."

David glared at me, his lips tight. "That's bull," he grumbled. "Why would I do that?"

"Good question," I shot back. "Why did you do it?"

"I didn't," he said, biting his lip and shifting his gaze away from me.

I knew he was lying. Judging from the scoffing sounds I heard from the eavesdropping nurses, they knew it, as well. Too bad I wasn't as good at picking up on his deceptions when we were still married.

"Liar," I hissed.

I heard someone behind me clear their throat and turned around to see Nancy Molinaro herself standing there, scowling. She wasn't a tall woman—I towered over her by nearly a foot—but there was something about her stocky build, fearless stance, fierce eyes, and hirsute body that scared the hell out of me. I had no doubt she could take me in a fight . . . me and four other people. A rumor about her had been circulating for years, that she was an ex mob moll—or perhaps a mobster who had undergone a very bad sex change—who had been placed in the witness protection program and sent here to hide. I don't think anyone actually believed this story, particularly since a small town like Sorenson is the worst kind of place to hide. Nothing interesting happens here that remains a secret for long. But that didn't make Molinaro any less scary.

In her raspy whisper of a voice, Molinaro said, "If you two kiddos can't play nice together in our little sandbox here, I'll be forced to take action."

"We're fine," David said in an amiable tone that was the polar opposite of the one he'd been using moments before. It almost made me laugh because I realized David was as frightened of Molinaro as I was. "Mattie and I were just catching up."

"Is that so?" Molinaro rasped, turning her death-ray gaze up at me.

"It is," I lied. "I was just asking David how the construction was coming along on his new house. I saw him pull out of the drive when I was on my way here and was wondering how much progress had been made."

"Did you now?" Molinaro asked, narrowing her eyes at me.

I stared down at her and nodded vigorously, spooked by her intense stare. I probably looked like a bobblehead doll.

"Why would you need to ask David about the progress on his house?" she asked me. "You live right next door to the place, don't you?"

I felt myself start to sweat beneath her laser glare, and when I realized I was shifting nervously from one foot to another, I forced myself to stop. "I haven't been over there, and I can't see the house from my cottage now that the trees have leafed out. The woods between us are thick."

The part about the trees blocking my visibility was true, but it wasn't true that I hadn't been over there. I had sneaked through the woods several times, curious to see what the new place was going to be like. It was coming along nicely and would make a decent addition to the neighborhood. And despite David's claim some time ago that the new house would be smaller than the old one, it appeared to be just as large as the original.

Molinaro harrumphed at my answer, and after giving both David and me one last death glare, she turned and left. I breathed a sigh of relief and looked over at David, who was shaking his head at me.

"I've been here for the past three hours doing an emergency appendectomy," he said in a low voice. "And as soon as I finished that, I was called down here to be on standby in case Derrick Ames needed surgery. So your claim that you saw me pulling out of my driveway a short time ago was a dumb one. Molinaro knows I've been here the whole time."

I didn't much care about Molinaro at this point; I was more interested in David's timeline. "If you've been here for the past several hours, who did I see pulling out of your driveway twenty minutes ago? I know your construction guys don't work on the weekends, and I also know what Patty's car looks like. It wasn't her, and I definitely saw a car pull out of there. In fact, it followed me."

David shrugged. "Maybe it was the construction supervisor. I don't know. As to someone following you, I think you're being paranoid. This *is* a small town. Cars don't have many options." He gave me his own version of a harrumph and added, "Or maybe this job of yours is finally getting to you."

My job with Izzy had been a bone of contention with David from day one, though I've never been sure why. Had he been hoping I'd flounder when I left him and my hospital job, forcing me to come crawling back to him? Was he angry that I managed to find a new job and survive just fine without him? Did the job embarrass him for some reason? Was he angry that I was doing something he had no control over? Was he jealous over the fact that I met Hurley on the job? Maybe it was all of those things . . . or none of them. I scowled at him and tried to come up with a witty comeback, but before I could, Izzy walked up to us.

He nodded at David but didn't say anything to him. Instead he looked over at me and said, "Have you called the funeral home yet?"

"No, sorry. I got distracted." I shot David an irritated look.

"No problem," Izzy said. "I'll do it. Why don't you and Bob go to the victim's house and process the scene while I take the body back to the morgue? I'll ride back with the funeral home."

"That's fine," I said.

Izzy took out his cell phone and headed back to Derrick Ames's ER room. Richmond walked up to me and said, "Did I hear you're coming with me?"

"I am."

"Need a ride?"

I shook my head. "I have my car here. If you don't mind, I'll just follow you."

"That'll work," Richmond said. "I just need to hit the can quick before we go. Meet you out front?"

"Sure." With that, Richmond hurried off to find a bathroom.

"Charming company you keep these days," David sneered.

I bent down to whisper in his ear. "Any company is better than spending time with you. Be careful, David. Karma has a way of coming back and biting you in the ass."

With that I walked away, feeling the burn of his glare in my back as I went. Little did I know that my warning would prove fortuitous, though not in the way I'd imagined.

Chapter 5

Derrick Ames's house was in one of the older neighborhoods in town, a dozen square blocks filled with an eclectic mix of home styles that ranged from 1950s-era ranch houses to sprawling Victorians built in the early 1900s. The houses were close together, and most of the backyards, including Ames's, were surrounded by privacy fencing.

Despite the darkness of the hour, the neighborhood was well lit between the street lamps, the flash bars on the police cars, and the glow from porch and interior lights in nearly every house on the block. Ames's house was easy to spot, thanks to the yellow police tape strung between towering old oaks to cordon off the property and a police car parked in the driveway. Huddles of neighbors were gathered in nearby front yards, whispering and talking in low murmurs, their expressions curious and concerned. Several were on their cell phones, no doubt assuring that the latest town gossip spread as far as it could as fast as it could. Derrick's house was a large Victorian with gingerbread trim, the outside of which had recently been painted in shades of blue, yellow, and white. The glass in the front windows had a wavy look to it, making me think Ames had preserved the original panes.

Richmond and I met in the street in front of the house and ducked under the police tape. As we headed for the house, we heard a ruckus behind us and turned to look. A woman with short, white-blond hair was standing a few feet away, staring at all the vehicles and police tape.

"What's going on?" she said in a soft, slightly hoarse voice. I couldn't tell if the hoarseness was her norm or if it was because she was being strangled with emotion. "What's going on? Oh my God, what's going on?"

One of the other neighbors, a heavy, fiftyish woman in a terry-cloth bathrobe rushed out into the street, put an arm over the first woman's shoulders, and tried to pull her away, but the blond woman shrugged her off.

"Mandy, come with me," bathrobe woman said. "Something bad has happened."

Richmond and I ducked back under the tape and approached the two women. The blond woman switched her focus from the cars and flashing lights to first Richmond, then me. "What happened? Is Derrick okay? Are the boys okay?"

"Who are you, ma'am?" Richmond asked.

"Mandy Terwilliger. I'm Derrick's . . . he and I . . ."

"She's been dating Derrick," the neighbor woman said. "And the boys are with their mom."

Derrick Ames had good taste. Mandy was a beautiful woman with skin as pale as her hair, a slender build with legs that looked fabulous in a pair of red, peep-toe high heels, and huge green eyes. Her features were delicate, her nails—hands and feet—were manicured and painted a color that matched her shoes, and her lipstick was the same shade, a color my sister calls hooker red. She was wearing a tight-fitting, black pencil skirt with a low-cut, white silk blouse.

"When did you last see Derrick?" I asked Mandy.

"Did something happen to him?" she asked, avoiding my question.

"Yes," I said. "He's not here at the house."

This seemed to finally divert her attention. "Where is he?"

"He was taken to the hospital," Richmond said.

"The hospital? Is he okay?"

"No, ma'am, he isn't," Richmond said. "Mr. Ames died."

"Oh, no." Mandy Terwilliger's body sagged, and if the neighbor lady hadn't been standing next to her, she probably would have gone to the ground. As it was, the neighbor lady caught her and pulled her back to her feet. "What happened?" Mandy repeated. "Was it a heart attack?"

"When did you last see him?" It was Richmond who asked this time, and he returned the favor by ignoring her question. Finally we got an answer.

"Um, yesterday, at the school."

"Are you a teacher, too?"

"No, I volunteer in my son's classroom three days a week. I work part-time at the florist shop downtown on the weekends, noon to around eight-thirty or nine, depending on how many deliveries there are. I . . . I just left there."

"How long have you and Derrick been dating?" Richmond asked.

"Not long, a couple of months. We've been keeping it kind of quiet because we weren't sure how our kids were going to take it. Are the boys okay?"

"They are," I said.

"What happened to Derrick?"

"Somebody killed him," the neighbor woman said, apparently tired of our avoidance games. Richmond shot her an angry look, but she either didn't see it or chose to ignore it. "Someone stabbed him in the chest with one of those big forks," the neighbor woman continued.

Mandy seemed dumbstruck by this information, and she looked at Richmond with an inquisitive and disbelieving expression.

Richmond stepped closer to the neighbor woman and said, "Your name, ma'am?"

She wasn't the least bit intimidated. She straightened up to all of her massive, bathrobe-clad glory, nearly sticking her boobs in Mandy's face. "Rose Carpenter. I live two doors down from Derrick. He taught both my boys when they were in school. Who are you?"

"I'm Detective Bob Richmond, with the Sorenson Police Department. This is Mattie Winston with the ME's office."

Rose dismissed this with a wave of her hand. "I know who she is," she said, casting me a dismissive sideways glance. She turned back to Richmond and eyed him from head to toe. "Are you really Bob Richmond?"

"Yes, ma'am."

"You look good. You've lost a ton of weight."

"Not quite a ton, but a decent amount."

"Hunh," Rose said, giving him a second head-to-toe look.

"And how do you know Ms. Terwilliger?" Bob asked.

"I know her all kinds of ways," Rose said, sounding pompous. "I've known her since she went to work down at the florist's shop after her divorce because I send something to my mom in Arizona every month. Plus we serve on the PTA together, and my youngest, Tina, is in the same grade as Mandy's oldest boy, Ian. And I've seen her with Derrick a few times. This *is* a small town, you know."

Boy, did I.

"Can you give me a number where you can be reached, Ms. Terwilliger?" Richmond asked. "I would like to talk some more with you later."

Mandy provided the requested information, and then Rose steered her away. As they reached the steps to Rose's porch, Rose cast one last appraising look back at Richmond.

"I think Rose likes you," I said to Richmond.

He gave me a skeptical look, shook his head, and then stepped beneath the police tape. I followed suit, but when he headed inside the house, I hung outside, took out the camera I had in my scene kit, and started snapping pictures and a video or two, beginning with some scenes of the street and house. I also made sure to include as many of the neighborhood lookie-loos as I could, knowing that perpetrators often return to the scene of their crimes out of curiosity, to see what the police are doing. After finishing the general scene shots, I switched to focus on a pool of drying blood in the street that had its own police tape perimeter—presumably the spot where Ames had collapsed after exiting his house.

As I snapped my photos, I was aware of the people

who were watching me doing the same thing. Everywhere I looked, someone was holding up a phone, and flashes of light kept firing from every direction. No doubt news of Derrick Ames's demise would hit the news on Facebook and Twitter long before the TV stations or newspaper got wind of it.

Once I finished shooting my outdoor pictures, I paused at the bottom of the porch stairs to don gloves and shoe covers from my scene kit before proceeding. I snapped both distant and close-up shots of the stairs, the porch, and the entryway and foyer of the house, taking care to sidestep the blood-spotted trail pointed out to me by the uniformed cop who was standing guard. Once inside, I shut the front door behind me and took a moment to breathe and take in my surroundings.

I knew Derrick Ames had been in the area for more than a decade, and judging from what I saw he had spent a good portion of that time restoring this place. Many of the original details of the house— stained-glass windows, a polished wood staircase with carved newels, narrow-board hardwood floors—had been lovingly restored.

The style of the house may have been Victorian, but the furnishings were all contemporary, mismatched, and basic. There was no froufrou anywhere; the place had a definite masculine, utilitarian feel to it. I sidestepped the trail of blood droplets that led down the hallway to a room at the far end— which I assumed was the kitchen, based on the side of a refrigerator I could see—and veered left into the living room, where I found Richmond and Junior Feller, the uniformed officer in charge. Junior was on his cell phone, and he acknowledged me with a little nod. He held up a finger to indicate he was almost done, and we waited for him to hang up.

As soon as Junior disconnected his call, Bob said, "Tell us what you know so far."

Junior, like most cops, carried a small notebook that he used to keep track of information. He flipped it back a few pages and started filling us in.

"It looks like Ames was stabbed in his kitchen. There's blood all over the floor and cabinets in there, and we found a bloody knife that appears to have been taken from Ames's own knife set. I've got some guys coming in to help Jonas process the place. He's out in the kitchen now getting set up. None of the neighbors claim to have seen anyone enter or leave the house around the time of the murder other than when Ames came stumbling out of his house with the barbecue fork in his chest."

"Was Ames married?" I asked.

Junior shook his head. "He was, but he and his wife, Wendy, underwent a rather contentious divorce a little over a year ago. The neighbors said it used to be every time they saw the two of them together for any reason, they were fighting. She lives over on Wilson Street with their two sons: Jacob, who is sixteen, and Michael, who is twelve. According to some of the neighbors, the boys split their time between the two parents, one week here, one week there."

All the streets in this older part of town were named after U.S. presidents. Since Ames lived on Truman, his ex-wife's house couldn't be more than a few blocks away.

"I sent a couple of guys over to Wendy Ames's house to inform her of Derrick's death," Junior went on. "I asked them to give her and the boys some time to adjust to the news, and then to bring them down to the station so you can talk to them."

"Learn anything else from the neighbors?" Bob asked.

"Yeah, apparently Derrick's eldest son, Jacob, exchanged some heated words with his father earlier this afternoon. Neighbors overheard them yelling at one another and then they saw Jacob storm out of the house, swearing a blue streak. Apparently Derrick's girlfriend, Mandy Terwilliger, was here at the time and left a short time later. I haven't had a chance to talk to her yet. One of the neighbors said she works at the florist shop downtown, but when I tried to call there, I got a recording saying they closed at eight. Aside from that, I haven't found any other issues or potential motives."

"That's interesting because we just talked to the Terwilliger woman," Richmond said. "She told us she hadn't seen Derrick since yesterday. So either she lied to us, or the neighbors are mistaken."

"If the neighbors are mistaken, it's several of them," Junior said. "More than one person said they saw Terwilliger leave the house this afternoon."

"Have you talked to anyone from the school yet?" I asked.

"No, at least not directly. A couple of the neighbors here are parents of kids that attend the high school, and they said that as far they know Ames was a well-liked, popular teacher. He's active in the PTA, has received numerous teaching awards, and has mentored a number of students."

"I guess we're going to have to talk to the family sooner rather than later," Bob said, glancing at his watch. "So far, the ex and the older kid sound like the only ones with motives, although the girlfriend lying certainly looks suspicious." He turned to me. "Do you want to stay here and help with the evidence collection, or come with me to talk to the family?"

"Let me check with Izzy and see what he prefers." My personal preference was to go with Bob. The interrogations and interviews were always more interesting to me than the tedium of evidence collection, particularly when there is a lot of blood evidence. Every sample of blood has to be swabbed, labeled, mapped, and tagged so it can be sent for analysis. Often DNA evidence is found that might pinpoint the killer, but it takes time on both ends. Another reason for my preference—one I couldn't share with the others—was that I wanted to minimize my exposure to any pathogens that might be present in the blood. But, given my earlier discussion with Izzy, I felt he should be the one to make the call.

I took out my phone, stepped aside, and dialed Izzy's number.

"Hey, Mattie," Izzy answered. "What's up?"

I explained the situation, and Izzy must have been reading my mind because he said, "Why don't you shoot the scene photos and then go with Bob. I'll have Arnie come down and help Jonas and the others with the evidence collection. You always do a good job with the photography, and you're skilled at reading people, so it makes sense to do it that way. Besides, it's probably safer for you, under the circumstances."

"What about Ames's autopsy? Who's going to help you with that?"

"I can manage on my own."

"Are you sure? Maybe you should wait and do it in the morning."

"I've done autopsies on my own plenty of times before. It will take me a little longer, but I'll get it done. If it was a routine death, I'd wait. But since it's a homicide, I want to get on it right away. If I run into any problems and need help I'll give you a call."

"Do you want me to call Arnie, or will you do it?"

"I'll do it. He's here in the office already anyway. But you and I still need to sit down and talk later."

"I know."

I glanced over at Bob and Junior, afraid they might be able to overhear. To give myself a little more privacy, I meandered my way out of the living room and into the hallway as Izzy said, "Why don't you come over for dinner tomorrow night? Dom is making pesto fettuccine with Italian sausage."

I winced, knowing the conversation wasn't going to be an easy one, but it wasn't like I had a choice. And my decision was made a little easier knowing what was on the menu and that Dom would be cooking. Not only is Italian my favorite food group, Izzy's partner is a phenomenal cook, which is probably why Izzy is nearly as wide as he is tall. "Okay. What time?"

"Let's shoot for six. If you get caught up in something in your investigation that runs longer than that, let me know."

"I will."

"Good. See you then."

"Izzy, wait," I said, hoping to catch him before he disconnected the call.

"What?"

"Does Dom know?"

He hesitated just long enough that he didn't have to answer, but he did anyway.

"He does. In fact, he was the one who picked up on it first."

It figured. If straight men could read women as well as gay men do, the divorce rates in our country would probably plummet.

"He's very excited about the whole thing," Izzy went on. "In fact, he's hoping you'll let him babysit."

Babysitters. It was one of the many complications that had been lurking in the back of my mind since I'd decided I was going to have the baby. I hadn't dwelled on it much yet, figuring I had plenty of time and several options. Dom was definitely on the list, as was my sister. But bringing it up now made me realize just how fast time was slipping by.

"Of course I will," I said. Then, eager to get off the subject, I said, "We can talk about it more tomorrow at dinner. Right now I've got Richmond waiting."

"Call me if anything significant comes up."

"I will," I assured him.

I disconnected the call and headed back into the living room, where I filled Richmond and Junior in on the plans.

"Works for me," Richmond said. "I'm glad to have you in on the interviews, Mattie. You're good at reading people. The officers at Wendy Ames's house know to call me when they're ready to bring the family in. Let's go take a look at the kitchen while we're waiting."

Junior led the way to the kitchen, which was in a state of disarray. There were broken dishes on the floor, a silverware drawer had been pulled out of its sliders, its contents spilled onto the floor, and a chair had been knocked over. It looked like Ames had put up one hell of a fight. The blood on the floor was smeared in some places, and there was a large, partially congealed puddle in one spot that suggested Derrick had lain there a while. On the counter I saw a butcher-block knife holder with one empty slot, and a large butcher knife that matched the description the ER doctor had provided was on the floor, smeared with blood.

Jonas Kreideman stood in the doorway of a mud and laundry room built off the back of the kitchen. He was dressed in a paper body suit, booties, and protective glasses, and he held a mask and gloves in his hands. Jonas had put on a lot of weight in the past two months, compliments of the steroids the docs had put him on to help him deal with his allergies. It left him pale and puffy-looking, and with the protective glasses and the white body suit, he looked like a nerdy version of the Pillsbury Dough Boy.

At his feet was a box filled with cotton-tipped swabs that were used to collect blood, DNA, and other fluid samples, and a bag filled with small, flattened cardboard containers that could be formed into an elongated box shape with a flap closing on either end. The swabs were placed in these boxes once they were used, and then the boxes were closed and both ends were sealed with evidence tape. Each sample also had to be numbered, labeled, and logged. It was a tedious, time-consuming process, and before any of it could begin, the scene needed to be photographed as it was found.

"Hey, guys," Jonas said, nodding at us as we entered.

Then he focused his gaze on me. "This one's a doozy, Mattie. You can start shooting pictures whenever you're ready. It looks like we'll be here a while."

"I'll do the photography," I told him, "but then I'm going with Richmond to talk to the family. Izzy is sending Arnie here to help you with the evidence collection."

Jonas rolled his eyes. "Why can't you stay here?" he whined. "I'd much rather work with you."

"What's wrong with Arnie? He's quick, he's thorough, and he knows his stuff."

"I know, I know. It's just that all he does the whole time he's collecting evidence is talk about how the world is filled with all these secret societies and evil conspiracies."

"Arnie does have some crazy ideas, but they're harmless. Some of them are even entertaining."

Jonas sighed and shook his head. "They may be harmless, but after a while the rhetoric gets old. The last time I worked with him he was spouting some garbage about how the wingdings font is actually a secret code that was invented by the Nazis for passing along top-secret messages, and later installed on computers by Middle Eastern fanatics to use in the same way. He said he can prove it because if you type the letters NYC using the original wingdings font, the resultant symbols predict the 9/11 debacle."

While the rest of us laughed this off, Junior took out his smartphone and started tapping keys. "Holy cow," he said a moment later. "Arnie might be on to something. If you type NYC using wingdings, you get a skull and crossbones, the Star of David, and a thumbs-up picture. Look."

He showed us his phone screen. On it was a table showing what wingdings symbol would result for each letter typed.

"Don't be ridiculous, Feller," Richmond said, shaking his head.

"Hey," Junior said with a little shrug, "just because you're paranoid doesn't mean someone isn't out to get you."

Though I couldn't have known it at the time, this line would prove fortuitous and fateful for me.

Richmond started whistling the theme song from *The X-Files*, and I would have joined in, but my cell phone rang. I answered it without looking at the caller ID, assuming it was Izzy with some sort of update or change in plans. But it wasn't, and that *X-Files* music turned out to be prophetic.

Chapter 6

"Hello?"

All I heard was static.

"Hello?" I said again. I realized everyone in the room was staring at me, and after listening to the crackling silence for a few more seconds, I disconnected the call. "Must have been a wrong number, or a dropped call," I said with a shrug and a smile. My tone was light-hearted and dismissive, but the truth was the call spooked me. I chalked it up to the contagious paranoia triggered by the discussion about Arnie's conspiracy theories and tried to put it out of my mind.

As I slipped my phone back into my pocket, a thought occurred to me. "Why did Derrick Ames go out into the street for help?" I said to no one in particular.

"What do you mean?" Bob said.

"Why didn't he just call 911?"

Everyone in the room exchanged looks for a few seconds, and then Richmond said, "A phone. He must have had a phone." We looked around the kitchen and then ventured into the living room, and from there through the rest of the first floor. On the second floor, which had three bedrooms—two with twin beds that were clearly set up for Derrick's boys when they stayed with him, and a master bedroom—we found a phone charger on the bedside stand beside Derrick's double bed. But there was no phone. "No landline, and no cell," Richmond said.

"Maybe it was with his personal belongings at the hospital," I suggested. "They gave Izzy a bag with his clothes and shoes in it. Maybe the phone was in there, too."

Richmond took out his own cell and placed a call to Izzy, who said he would look and call him back.

In the meantime, we headed downstairs to join the others. When we were back in the kitchen, Jonas pointed toward the knives in the holder on the counter. "I'm guessing that's where the murder weapon came from. And I'm betting the barbecue fork was in that silverware drawer that's been spilled all over the floor."

Richmond nodded, frowning. "That makes it harder for us since we can't connect the weapons to someone from outside the house. Looks to me like whatever happened here was an unplanned, heat-of-the-moment thing, and the killer just grabbed whatever was handy."

I started snapping photos of the room and its contents, including the blood spatter and several close-ups of the knife before Jonas bagged and tagged it. A few minutes later, Richmond's phone rang. He looked at the caller ID and said, "It's Izzy."

We all watched as he listened to what Izzy had to say, curious about the phone thing. When Richmond's look of hope faded to one of curious disappointment, I knew what the answer would be.

"There was no phone with Derrick's personal belongings," he said once he disconnected the call. "Where the hell is it?"

"Maybe the killer took it?" I posed.

"Why?" Richmond said, shaking his head. "It doesn't make sense."

"Maybe not now," I said, "but if the killer took it, I'm sure they had a reason. And if they still have it, maybe it will help us find whoever it was."

That made Richmond brighten a little, and as the rest of us went back to our separate duties, he gave Junior a list of tasks that included digging up a cell phone account and number for Derrick, seeing if the phone could be tracked with GPS, and looking into the man's bank accounts. "Look for any unusual transactions," Richmond said. "Since the last thing Ames said was the word *payday*, maybe there's money involved somehow."

I was taking pictures of some blood smears on a low cabinet by the refrigerator when something in the crack between the cabinet and the fridge caught my eye. The space was about four inches wide, and something with a shiny circle on it was wedged a few inches in. I stuck my gloved hand in sideways, and after a bit of maneuvering, I was able to push the item out.

"Look at this," I said, holding up a small, handheld camcorder. I pointed to the area between the cabinet and fridge. "It was wedged into this space here with the lens pointed out toward the kitchen."

No one looked particularly excited by my news until I told them the next part. "And there's blood on it."

"I don't suppose it's turned on," Richmond asked.

I shook my head, and after making sure there was no blood evidence on the power button, I pushed it. Nothing happened. "It won't turn on. I wonder if the battery is dead," I said. "Maybe Derrick was using it when his killer was here. How else would it have ended up stuck between the fridge and the counter?"

Richmond said, "Maybe it was sitting on the edge of the counter and got knocked off during the struggle. Maybe it's not a dead battery, maybe it's broken."

Junior said, "I'm pretty sure it's new. I saw a box for it in the trash out there in the laundry room." He pointed to the room off the back of the kitchen.

"Did anyone see a charge cord for it?" I asked.

Everyone looked around the kitchen, scanning the outlets above the countertops, but there was nothing there. Jonas walked back into the laundry room and said, "I'll bet this is it."

I tiptoed my way through the spilled silverware and the blood smears over to the entrance to the laundry room. There, on a table against the wall, was a cord plugged into an outlet. I picked up the other end and examined the adapter, comparing it to the plug-in notch on the camera. "Looks like a fit," I said.

"Stuff like that often comes with some charge on the battery, but they have to be plugged in for twenty-four hours before they're fully charged," Jonas said. He rummaged a little deeper in the trash bin and pulled out a piece of paper. "It looks like it might have arrived today. Here's the box and the receipt. The camera was ordered two days ago from a company in Massachusetts." He then looked at the box and smiled. "And it was delivered via UPS."

"Good news for us," Richmond said as Jonas slid the receipt into a plastic bag, sealed it, and handed it over to him. "We should be able to find out exactly when it was delivered." Jonas then handed the box over to Richmond, who snapped a picture of the labels on it with his phone's camera before handing it back to Jonas for packaging, labeling, and sealing. Then Richmond stepped out of the room, presumably to make a call to UPS.

I resumed my picture taking, and Jonas resumed his evidence collection with some help from a trio of uniformed officers. A few minutes later Richmond returned and said, "You were right, Jonas. UPS delivered that package at ten this morning."

"Should we plug the camera in to charge it up?" I asked. "Maybe there's something on it that's relevant to the crime. Maybe Ames filmed whoever was here."

Richmond considered this and then said, "It's not a bad idea, but for the sake of securing our evidentiary chain, I'd rather just bag and tag everything as it is for now and let Arnie or the lab in Madison deal with it."

Jonas did just that with the camera and the power cord, adding them to the box of growing evidentiary specimens he had on the floor of the laundry room.

I had finished taking pictures in the kitchen, so I moved on to snap the rest of the house. I carefully walked the length of the front hallway, taking shots of the blood trail. I took some general pictures of all the rooms off the hallway as I went, and while none of them appeared to offer any evidentiary value, I did find the color schemes and architecture interesting. Every room had high wooden baseboards, crown molding, and wide window trim with decorative rosettes at the corners. All the trim was painted in a bright, glossy white that beautifully framed the vividly colored plaster walls. The living room, entryway, and hallway were painted in a rich, dark, forest green, the dining room was done in colonial blue, and plum was the color of choice for a front room that had probably served as a parlor at one time but was now a TV/family room, complete with a game system. Judging from the controllers sitting on the coffee table, I surmised that the game system was used a lot, or at the very least had been used recently.

I headed upstairs to the bedrooms and snapped the two boys' rooms first, poking around as I went. From there I moved into the master bedroom and took some more shots, including one of the phone charger. In the closet I found two items of women's clothing hanging along with all the men's stuff: one white blouse and a pair of gray dress slacks. I didn't know how Derrick's wife was built, so I couldn't be sure these weren't left over from her, but the tiny size of the clothing made me think they might be Mandy's.

Richmond came up a few minutes later and found me peeking into Derrick's dirty clothes hamper. With a gloved hand I reached in and snagged the black lacy thong that was lying on top and showed it to Richmond. "Either Derrick had a secret fetish, or Mandy was here recently."

"I'm going to hope for the latter," Richmond said. He peered closer at the undies and said, "How does someone wear those things?"

"It's a thong." I held them up by the waist and showed him the back part. "This part goes up your butt crack."

Richmond made a face. "I know what it is. I just don't get how anyone could wear it. It looks like it would be really uncomfortable."

"I wouldn't know," I told him, tossing the thong back in the hamper. "I've never been much into butt floss, and to be honest, most of the panties in my size are boring old granny panties. Apparently the lingerie makers figure that if you aren't a size zero or two, you wouldn't want to strut around in sexy undies."

Richmond was staring at his feet and shifting uncomfortably from one to the other.

"Sorry," I said, giving him an apologetic look. "Was that too much information?"

"No, it's not that. It's just a topic I don't know much about. I don't have any sisters, I've never been married, and I never dated much. Most of the girls I knew weren't too keen on going out with someone who looked like Jabba the Hutt."

My heart ached for the guy. I realized then what a lonely existence he must have had prior to his weight loss. "You don't look like Jabba the Hutt anymore," I said. "In fact, you're looking pretty darned good these days, Richmond."

"Too bad I didn't lose the weight when I was younger. Things might have been a whole lot different."

"It's never too late to start."

"I'm going to be fifty in June, Mattie."

"So?"

He sighed and shook his head. Then he switched topics on me. "Our dispatcher just called and said the officers are bringing Ames's wife and kids down to the station at ten, which gives us about twenty minutes."

"Is Arnie here yet?"

"He is. In fact, he's in the kitchen as we speak trying to convince Jonas that Elvis Presley isn't dead, but rather that he faked his death and had a wax body buried in his coffin so he could escape from the music business and go off somewhere private and live in peace."

"Poor Jonas," I said, shaking my head and smiling. "I just hope all those steroids he's been taking don't trigger any 'roid rage in him or we may end up with a double homicide to investigate."

"Junior might have saved the day. He loaned Jonas his iPod and some earbuds so Jonas can tune Arnie out."

"Ooh, I don't know if that's a good idea," I said with a grimace. "Just the other day Arnie was telling me about the latest conspiracy theory circulating on the Internet regarding iPods."

Richmond gave me a puzzled look, opened his mouth as if to say something, and then snapped it shut again, shaking his head. "I don't want to know," he grumbled under his breath.

"Wise choice. Is it okay if I meet you at the station? I want to stop by my office and download these pictures first."

"No problem. I'll see you there."

I exited the house and headed for my hearse, which I had been forced to park a few houses away because of all the other official vehicles on-site. It was dark outside, but the weather was warm, the sky was clear, and there were so many lights on in the neighborhood that it looked like daylight. The neighbors were still out in force, talking among themselves about what had happened. They all stared at me with wistful expressions, no doubt hoping I would share a juicy tidbit or two with them. From the corner of my eye I saw one woman separate herself from a group and head my way at a fast clip. It was Alison Miller, Sorenson's ace reporter and photographer. I ramped up my pace, hoping to outrun her, but she was too close and too fast for me.

"You know I can't tell you anything, Alison," I said as she caught up to me.

"Oh, come on, Mattie. Give me something. Anything. Any kind of quote will do."

I kept going and said nothing, but if Alison is anything, she is persistent.

"Please, Mattie?" she said, a bit breathless as she kept pace at my side. "Just a little something for old time's sake?"

I stopped then and whirled on her. "For old time's sake? Seriously?" I said, looking askance. "You've done everything you can to embarrass me in that stupid rag you work for, publishing pictures of me half naked, and writing stories about how my divorce left me, and I quote, 'unable to face the living so I decided to go work with the dead.' And don't even get me started on that whole business with Hurley a while back. How can you possibly think I'd want to help you after all that?" I turned away from her to continue my march to my car, but her next words stopped me short.

"My mother's dying," she said.

"What?" I turned back to her, unsure if I'd heard her right. The sad, overwrought expression on her face suggested I had.

"You almost got rid of me," she said with a painful smile. "Do you remember that fiasco with the Heinrich family?"

I remembered it all right. A car accident had led to the death of multimillionaire Dietmar Heinrich and his second wife, Bitsy, who had been an exotic dancer prior to marrying Dietmar. Determining which of them had died first dictated who inherited the money—Bitsy's kids or Dietmar's—and the two families had engaged in some very public and ugly warfare. Because Dietmar Heinrich was a well-known public figure, news agencies from all over the country had descended on Sorenson to cover the case and the subsequent fallout. Alison found herself front and center, with a starring role in it all, and it had given her the kind of exposure most small-town reporters can only dream of.

"Of course I remember it, Alison. That picture you took of me in my underwear at the Heinrich's crash scene not only made it into the local paper, but into some national tabloids as well."

"Yeah," she said with a wince. "Sorry about that, though technically it wasn't my fault that the pictures got published."

She was right about that. It was a freakish sequence of events that led to the pictures getting out, but that didn't mean Alison was off the hook. "If you hadn't taken them in the first place, they never would have been published anywhere," I said.

"Yeah, like I said, I'm sorry about that," she repeated, sounding genuinely sincere. "Anyway, after all the coverage from the various news outlets, the *Chicago Tribune* offered me a job. I was all set to accept it when my mother had what we thought at first was a stroke. Two days later she was diagnosed with ALS."

Now it was my turn to wince. "I'm so sorry to hear that," I told her, and I meant it. ALS is not a kind disease, slowly robbing its victims of every last bit of dignity before it kills them. I wouldn't wish it on my worst enemy.

"Anyway, my parents split up eight years ago, and my dad moved out to California and married some hottie who's younger than I am. I'm the only family my mother has left, and I didn't feel I could leave her here alone, so I had to pass on the job offer." She sighed. "For now I'm stuck here with this job, and I'm just trying to do the best with it that I can. So give me a break, okay?"

She stared at me with pleading eyes that tore down any remaining defenses I might have had. "I'm truly sorry about your mom and your job, Alison. But I have to be careful. Besides, the police are the gate-keepers for releasing facts when they feel it's appropriate and won't compromise the investigation. You really should be after them, not me."

"But they never tell me anything. I thought it might get easier when Steve Hurley left town, but Bob Richmond isn't any better. In fact, if anything, he's even more tight-lipped than Steve was. If I have to rely solely on them for information, I might as well quit my job. I need someone who will open up to me more. I was hoping that would be you, Mattie."

I saw Bob Richmond exit the Ames house and glanced at my watch. "I have to go, Alison. I'll do what I can for you, but I'm not making any promises."

"Thanks, Mattie. I knew I could count on you."

I turned away from Alison and walked the rest of the way to my car, feeling like a heel. I was truly sympathetic to her plight and felt bad for her and her mother, knowing what lay ahead for them. I would do what I could for Alison, but I feared she might be expecting more than I was willing or able to give. I wasn't going to do anything that would compromise my job or any of our cases.

Normally the drive to my office would have taken five to seven minutes, depending on whether the two stoplights on Main were red or green. But on this particular night it took me a little longer because I noticed a car that fell in behind me as soon as I turned off Truman Street.

As a test, to see if the car really was following me, I detoured from my usual route and drove up and down some residential streets, turning aimlessly, with no set destination in mind. Sure enough, the car behind me followed me turn for turn, though it did fall back some.

After a half dozen random turns, I tired of the little cat-and-mouse game and headed instead for a nearby strip mall that had a small, well-lit parking lot. At least that way, if my pursuer continued to follow, I'd get a good look at the car and maybe even the driver.

I headed down River Street—aptly named since it runs along the river that cuts through town—and approached the strip-mall parking lot. The car behind me continued to follow, closer now, and I flipped on my indicator and turned, only to watch with disappointment as the car revved up and passed me by.

I caught a brief glimpse of the vehicle, but it was of little help. All I could tell was that it was a dark-colored sedan. I wasn't even sure if it was the same car I'd seen earlier. That the car had been tailing me, I had no doubt. There was no other rational explanation for why it had followed the same zigzag route I'd driven. And after that pointless meandering through the neighborhood, I figured whoever was behind the wheel—and by now I was convinced that it had to be my father—had probably figured out I was on to him. Clearly he didn't want to reveal himself yet for reasons only he knew, but I figured that eventually he'd make face-to-face contact and offer an explanation.

Some other niggling part of my mind suggested that maybe the person making the calls and tailing me in the car wasn't my father at all, but I rejected the thought almost immediately. At the time it was the only answer that made sense.

As it turned out, I was wrong, and it was a mistake that nearly cost me my life.

Chapter 7

I drove to my office, parked in the attached underground garage, and headed for the library, which did double duty as my office. It took me a few minutes to launch the appropriate software and hook the camera up to the computer to start the download. I glanced at my watch and saw it was only a few minutes before ten, and even though I knew it meant I might end up running late, I went looking for Izzy.

He wasn't in his office, so I made my way to the autopsy suite and peeked in through the window in the door. Izzy was there, his back to me, working alone on Derrick Ames's autopsy. He was doing something down by Derrick's legs, and I could see that he hadn't cut the man open yet, but the barbecue fork had been removed from his chest and was sitting on a nearby stainless-steel table.

I pushed the door open and said, "Hey, Izzy." He startled, nearly falling off the stool he stands on in order to adequately reach the table. He clapped a hand over his chest and looked over his shoulder at me, eyes wide.

"Oh, geez, sorry," I said. "I didn't mean to spook you. Are you okay?"

"I will be," he said, turning back to Derrick's body, "just as soon as my heart rate slows down. You'd think that after all the years I've spent cutting open dead people that I'd be beyond getting the heebie-jeebies, but sometimes when I'm here alone, my imagination gets the better of me."

"I'd be more worried if it didn't bother you," I told him. "Any building at night when you're alone can be scary. Throw in a few dead bodies and you've got the makings of a Stephen King novel."

"I've never read any of his stuff," Izzy said. "All my reading time gets spent on professional journals."

"It's probably just as well. That man cost me a few nights of sleep before I started this job. I don't know if I'll ever read him again now. Anyway, I just dropped off the camera and hooked it up to download the pictures. Come up with anything yet?"

"Nothing surprising. Derrick has a black eye and a broken nose that looks like it bled a lot, so I'm pretty sure he took a hit in the face from something. He also has a number of fresh bruises on his arms and a linear bruise on his back just below his waist that I'm thinking must be from being pushed up hard against the counter. The arm bruises are most likely from the struggle he put up against his killer. Maybe I'll come up with something more once I open him up."

"Need me to help you with anything?"

"No, I'm okay. Just don't sneak up on me again."

"You got it. I'm heading over to the police station to meet up with Bob Richmond and interview Ames's family. After that I'll probably head home. Should I pick you up when I'm done?"

"No need. I'll give Dom a call, and he can come and get me."

"Okay, but let me know if you change your mind."

"I will. Thanks. I'll talk to you sometime tomorrow."

"Good night."

"Good night."

I left through the front door of the building and walked over to the police station, which was only a block away. Both buildings are located on the edge of the downtown area, and the streets are always well lit. Still, I couldn't resist looking over my shoulder a few times. I chalked my nerves up to pregnancy hormones and talk of Stephen King as opposed to any real-life threat, but I was still glad when I reached the police station and was safely inside.

Stephanie, the evening dispatcher, was behind the desk, talking on the phone. She gave me a little finger wave and buzzed me through to the back.

I found Richmond in Hurley's office, sitting at Hurley's desk. The sight of him there instead of Hurley made my chest ache.

"Junior found a number for Derrick's cell phone," he said when he saw me.

"And?"

"And nothing," he said with frustrated shake of his head. "When he tried to call, it went straight to voice mail. He had the phone company see if they could pick up a signal or activate the GPS on it, but they got nothing. They told Junior that it had to have been deactivated."

"Meaning?"

"Meaning that either someone took the battery out of it, or they destroyed the phone."

"That's strange."

"Yes, it is."

"You can still get his call records, though, right?"

Richmond nodded. "Junior's working on getting them now. We'll have to wait until Monday to get the financials. In the meantime, I suppose we should go talk to the Ames family. You ready?"

"I am. Sorry if I kept you waiting."

He took the papers he was working on and tossed them atop a huge pile of folders. "I kept myself busy. That's one thing about this job that never changes. There's always paperwork to be done." He stood, pushed his chair back into place, and said, "And the officers kept the Ames family busy getting finger-printed. Wendy apparently balked at first, but when the guys explained that we needed the prints for elimi-nation purposes, she relented. They just finished a few minutes ago, and I had them put Ames's ex-wife in the interview room. The two boys are back in the break room with Brenda Joiner. I'd like to talk to the boys individually, and ideally without their mother present, but I'm not sure Mrs. Ames will be on board with that."

"I'm surprised she allowed them to be separated from her at all."

"Brenda suggested that some of the things we needed to talk about might not be suitable for her sons to hear. Mrs. Ames made Brenda promise that her boys wouldn't be questioned about anything without her knowledge and presence. Brenda agreed and then left Mrs. Ames in the interview room mak-ing phone calls."

"Isn't that risky, letting her make phone calls before you talk to her? What if she's working up an alibi or something?"

"I had Brenda turn on the recording device before she left," Richmond said with a wink. "So anything Wendy Ames says while talking on her phone will be recorded."

"Ah, very clever of you."

"I have my moments."

I updated Richmond on what Izzy had found so far as we headed for the interview room, which doubled as a conference room. There were no tiny interrogation rooms with small wooden tables and uncomfortable chairs here. The Sorenson PD did all of their interrogations at a large table that had eight plush chairs around it. It was the same table where they held most of their meetings. The room was carpeted and decorated, although the décor was hideous enough to drive the most determined suspects to confess, just so they wouldn't have to look at it anymore. Despite the quasi-cozy décor, the room did have audio and video recording capabilities, and an observation room. The only other hint that the room served a dual purpose was a ring in the floor by the middle seat on the far side of the table. It was there so the cops could hook ankle cuffs to it in case anyone truly dangerous was brought in, though I've heard rumors that a rookie or two has been cuffed to it in the past as part of a hazing ritual.

Wendy Ames looked to be in her late thirties or early forties. I gathered there was some Asian blood in her family tree based on her glossy black hair, small build, somewhat sallow complexion, and slightly almond-shaped eyes, which at the moment were red-rimmed and smeared with runny eye make-up. She was about the same size as Mandy Terwilliger, so I was still unsure who the clothes in Derrick's bedroom belonged to.

Wendy's cell phone sat on the tabletop in front of her, so apparently whatever calls she was making were done for now. She looked up at us as we entered and blew her nose. When she was done, she tossed the tissue onto a pile that had accumulated on the table beside her. Then she sucked in a deep breath and straightened up in her seat, visibly gathering herself together for our talk.

Richmond took a seat directly across from her, and I settled in on his left.

"Good evening, Mrs. Ames. I'm Detective Bob Richmond, and this is Mattie Winston, an investigator with the medical examiner's office."

"Please, call me Wendy," she said, her voice hoarse. "I don't suppose you allow people to smoke in here?"

"Sorry, no," Bob said.

"Didn't think so." She yanked another tissue from the box beside her and blew her nose again. "Just as well," she said when she was done. "I'm trying to quit anyway."

"First of all, let me say that we are very sorry about Mr. Ames's death," Richmond said.

"Thank you."

"Were the two of you close at all?"

Wendy snorted. "I don't think anyone would call our relationship a close one. When we first split up, things were pretty tense. But these days we make an effort to get along for the sake of the boys."

"I understand that the two of you share custody, is that right?"

Wendy nodded. "I wanted full custody at first, but we reconsidered the arrangement when our boys said how much they missed their dad. I realized I was being selfish and considering my own needs over theirs." She shrugged. "So I relented and let Derrick have them half the time." She paused and gave us a wan smile. "The boys keep trying to get us back together, no matter how many times we tell them it won't work. I've tried to tell them that . . . well, that it's complicated."

Something in the way she hesitated made me think there was more to the story. "Are you seeing anyone else?" I asked.

She hesitated long enough before answering to let me know I was on the right track. "There is someone," she said. "But the boys don't know about it. It helps that this other person doesn't live here. You know how small towns can be when it comes to gossip."

"A name please," Bob said, pen poised over his notebook.

"Why?"

"Because he's a potential suspect. We need to talk to anyone who has a connection to your husband, particularly people who may have a motive for wanting him out of the picture."

"He's my *ex*-husband," Wendy said irritably. "And the idea that the person I'm seeing has any motive for wanting Derrick dead is utterly ridiculous."

"That's your perspective," Richmond said, making Wendy's frown deepen.

Wendy chewed on her lip, and I could tell she was scared. Why? Did she think the guy might have done it? Or was he married, perhaps?

"Is this really necessary?" Wendy asked in a voice that was half whiny, half angry. "There's a marriage at stake here."

I gave myself a mental pat on the back for figuring it out, but soon learned that I was only partially right.

"It is, unless you want us to arrest you on obstruction charges," Richmond said.

"Fine," Wendy snapped, clearly irritated. "It's Blake. Blake Sutherland."

"And how can we get hold of Mr. Sutherland?" Bob asked, scribbling down the name.

Wendy bit her lip again, rolled her eyes, and then sagged in her seat. "It's Mrs. Sutherland," she said finally, looking away in embarrassment. "Blake is a woman."

Richmond stared at Wendy, his pen poised over his notebook. There were several seconds of awkward silence as we digested these pieces of information, which clarified the issue about the woman's clothes in Derrick's bedroom. I suppose Wendy might have left a blouse and some slacks behind, but the underwear was on top of the laundry pile. They had been left there recently, which meant they must have belonged to Mandy.

Richmond said, "Are you referring to the wife of John Sutherland, the owner of Sutherland Enterprises?"

Wendy nodded. I gave Richmond a questioning look. I had no idea who John Sutherland was, but clearly he did. Richmond must have sensed my confusion, because he leaned into me and explained. "Sutherland Enterprises is a real estate and building company that specializes in top-end, luxury houses.

John Sutherland is one of the richest men in Madison."

Now I understood why Wendy didn't want to get Blake involved. No doubt a breakup of the Sutherland marriage would impact Blake's, and perhaps Wendy's, lifestyle.

Wendy started sobbing, and this time I wasn't sure who her tears were for: Derrick or Blake. Or maybe she was crying for herself.

Richmond said, "I'll try to be as circumspect as possible in questioning Mrs. Sutherland. But I do need to talk to her. If she wants to come here to talk, I'll do my best to see to it that her specific involvement with this case doesn't come out, assuming of course, that I can rule her out as a suspect."

Wendy plucked several more tissues from the box and swiped at her tears. She nodded her understanding, and when she had herself somewhat together, she gave Richmond a cell phone number. Then she said, "I'll talk to her and see if she can come by tomorrow. Will that do?"

"I'll contact her myself," Richmond said. "In the meantime, can you please account for your whereabouts today?"

"Seriously?" Wendy said, glaring at Richmond. "You think I'm a suspect, too?"

"Everyone is a suspect until we can rule them out. The more people we can rule out early on, the faster and tighter our investigation will be."

Wendy shook her head and sighed. "I was at the grocery store around nine or ten this morning. I went home, put the groceries away, and then I took the boys to the noon matinee at the movies. After that I left the boys and went to a friend's house for an hour or two. Then I went home and stayed there."

"What was the movie?" Richmond asked, and Wendy told him, naming the latest action flick that was showing in town. "What time did you get home and when did you leave for your friend's house?"

"I think it was between one-thirty and two when we got home. I left maybe ten or fifteen minutes after that."

"And your friend's name?" Richmond asked, scribbling again.

"Donna Martin. We got together to discuss plans for the costumes we're making for the middle-school play. I suppose you're going to have to question her, too?"

Richmond nodded. "Where were your boys during the time you were at Donna's house?"

"At home."

"How do you know they were there the whole time?"

"Where else would they be?"

Either Wendy had been a well-behaved child who spent her teenage years being a goody-two-shoes, or she was a naïve parent. Somehow I suspected the latter. And since the neighbors had seen one of the sons leave his father's house earlier in the day, I knew Wendy's belief or insistence—whichever it was—was incorrect.

"Both boys were there when I got home around four," Wendy insisted. "My oldest boy, Jacob, went to a friend's house for dinner later, but other than that and the movies, he was home."

"The friend's name?" Richmond asked, his pen poised.

"Sean Fitzpatrick," Wendy said, looking annoyed.

"And what time was he there?"

"From four-thirty until around eight, I think."

Richmond wrote down the information, set his pen aside, and folded his hands on the table in front of him. "Mrs. Ames, I need to talk to your boys to verify their timelines, and I'd prefer to do it individually."

Wendy gave him a *whatever* shrug, nodded, and blew her nose. "And I'd prefer to do it alone," Richmond added when she was done honking.

Wendy gave him a puzzled look. "You mean without me here?"

"Yes."

"Why? You're not going to tell them about Blake, are you?"

"No, but I do need them to tell me where they were today, and where you were, since they are part of your alibi. And I don't want them to have a chance to conspire and fabricate something."

"My boys wouldn't fabricate anything," Wendy snapped. "They have no need to."

"Then it shouldn't be a problem if I talk to them," Richmond said. "As I mentioned before, the sooner we can rule out the innocent people, the quicker we can get on to the real killer."

Wendy took half a minute or so to consider the request. I could see her mentally weighing the pros and cons. Finally she said, "You can talk to them individually, but I insist on being in here with them."

Richmond gave her a half-hearted shrug of acceptance, then tossed out his own ultimatum. "That's fine as long as you stay here while I have each of them brought in, and you remain quiet while I talk to them."

Again Wendy took her time answering, and when she did, she leaned across the table and pointed a finger at Richmond. "I can live with that as long as I don't think you're asking them things you shouldn't be. But if I hear something I don't like, I'll stop you dead in your tracks."

I arched my brows at her choice of clichés, and she saw my reaction. A few seconds later she realized why. "Oh, for Christ's sake, it's just a saying!" she snapped. "You people . . ." She left the rest of her opinion hanging, and I spent the time it took Richmond to fetch the first of the Ames boys filling in the blanks.

Chapter 8

Richmond brought the younger boy, Michael, in first. He had his father's wispy blond hair, but his mother's dark, almond eyes and slight build. Derrick Ames had been of average height—around five-ten or so—but with thick, tree-trunk legs and a broad chest. His son Michael, on the other hand, was short and skinny with a narrow, slightly concave chest and stick legs that looked lost inside the baggy, knee-length shorts he was wearing.

"Have a seat right there beside your mom," Richmond said, directing the boy with his hand. At first I was surprised by this, thinking it would be better to put some distance between mother and son, but the more I thought about it, the more I realized how smart Richmond's seating arrangement was. With his mother nearby, the boy would feel more comfortable and willing to talk. And with the two of them sitting side by side, it would be impossible for Wendy to give her son any looks or mouth any words to him that we might not see. It did allow for some under-the-table hand or foot stuff, but at the moment Wendy had both of her hands on top of the table, shredding the last tissue she had ripped from the box.

Michael looked sad, and I could tell he'd been crying. I felt for the kid, and hoped Richmond would be gentle and tactful with him. I hadn't interviewed a child with Richmond yet, so I had no idea how he would handle it.

"Hi, Michael," Richmond said, settling into his seat. "My name is Bob, and this is Mattie. We're trying to figure out who hurt your dad. I'm so sorry about what happened to him. You must be very sad."

Tears welled in Michael's eyes, and as he nodded, one of them coursed down a cheek that I saw was still covered with down. It stirred something deep in my gut, and oddly enough, it also made my boobs ache. I pushed aside my curiosity over these sensations for later contemplation, assuming they were probably related to my pregnancy.

"Are you cops?" Michael asked, sniffling.

"I am," Richmond said. "Mattie works with . . . with the coroner's office."

Michael looked at me with a curious expression. "What's a corner office do?"

"Not corner, coroner," I corrected gently. "We help the police when someone dies by figuring out how it happened and whether or not a crime has been committed."

Michael frowned at that. "Is that because someone killed my dad?" he asked.

"Yes," I said, giving him a sympathetic look. "And I'm so very sorry that that happened. I know you must be very sad right now, but it's important that we find out who might have wanted to hurt your dad."

Michael's tears welled again, and as he nodded they rolled down his cheeks and fell into his lap.

Richmond continued in a soft, friendly voice. "We have to ask you some questions about where you, your mom, and your brother were today. It might sound like we think you had something to do with what happened to your dad, but the main reason we need to ask these questions is so we can figure out where everyone was when your dad was hurt. It helps us to focus on the right people. Does that make sense to you?"

Michael nodded again, staring at his hands in his lap. His mother grabbed a used tissue and reached over to try to wipe his nose, but Michael shied away from her and swiped his nose with his arm.

"Can you tell me how you spent your day today?" Richmond asked. "Start around lunchtime."

"Mom took us to the movies for lunch."

"What movie did you see?"

Michael named the same movie his mother had.

"Did you like it?" Bob asked.

Michael nodded.

"What did you do after the movie?"

"We came home. I played some video games, and Jacob went to his room."

"Was Jacob home with you all afternoon?"

Michael's eyes shifted toward his mother for a second and then, just as quickly, back to his lap. He reached up and started pulling at a lock of hair at his nape. "Yes," he said, but he wouldn't look at us when he answered, and I felt certain he was lying.

Even his mother shot him a look, her brows drawn together with worry. "Michael? Did Jacob go out somewhere this afternoon while I was at Donna's?"

Michael looked at her again but quickly averted his gaze. He squirmed in his chair. "He was there. We both were home all afternoon. Nobody went anywhere." His answers came out rapid-fire, as if he was trying to convince himself as much as us.

Richmond leaned across the table and stared at the boy, who refused to look at anyone. "Michael, you know how important it is to tell the truth, right?"

Michael nodded, still staring at his lap.

"Was your brother really with you all afternoon?"

Michael didn't answer, and after a long period of silence, Wendy said, "Michael David Ames, you need to tell the truth. Did Jacob leave the house today while I was gone?"

Tears flowed down Michael's cheeks, and my boobs were practically throbbing. *What the hell?*

"Michael!" Wendy yelled. "Tell the truth!"

"Jacob's gonna get mad at me. He told me not to tell."

"Tell what?" Richmond pushed.

"He went out this afternoon for a little while. He climbs out his bedroom window all the time. He doesn't think I know it, but I do, and I knew he was gone because I went to his bedroom to see if he wanted to play Mario Brothers with me and he was gone. When he came back, he came out and pretended he'd been in there the whole time, but I told him I knew he'd gone out. He got really mad and went back in his bedroom and slammed the door."

Wendy leaned back in her seat and squeezed her eyes closed. She ran a hand through her hair and sighed. Then she sat up and looked at Richmond. "Derrick was killed this evening, correct?"

Richmond nodded.

"Then it shouldn't matter where Jacob was this afternoon." Wendy said, looking relieved. Her reprieve didn't last long.

"Though it does show his propensity to lie to you," Richmond said.

He gave her a moment to digest this, and after a few seconds, Wendy's eyes narrowed, and she leaned forward with that fierce mother-bear-protecting-her-cub look that moms seem to come by naturally. "We're done talking until I can consult with a lawyer," she said, trying to sound stern, though I heard a definite quaver in her voice.

Richmond sighed and leaned back in his chair. Michael started sobbing, his shoulders shaking, while I struggled to resist an urge I had to massage my aching boobs.

Wendy stood abruptly, yanked Michael out of his chair, and dragged him toward the door. She exited the room and steered a tearful Michael down the hall into the break room, where Jacob was waiting with Officer Brenda Joiner. "Let's go," Wendy said to the older boy, her lips and voice tight.

Jacob Ames was a big boy, with his father's sturdy build and height but his mother's dark hair and eyes. As we entered the room, he looked from one person to the next, his expression one of surprise initially, then suspicion. "What happened?" he asked, settling his gaze on his mother.

"I said let's go," Wendy repeated.

Jacob shifted his attention to Michael, and his eyes narrowed. "You squealed, didn't you, you little weasel."

Michael hiccuped a sob and stuttered, "I'm . . . s-s-sorry . . . J-jake."

Jacob walked over and cuffed Michael behind the

ear. "You stupid little brat! I should have known better than to trust you."

"Shut up, both of you!" Wendy snapped. "And move it, Jacob!"

I watched Jacob shuffle his way toward the hall. His stonewashed jeans were baggy and long on him, the backs of his hems worn and frayed from being stepped on and dragged along the ground. They swished with every step he took, marking the group's progress down the hallway, through the door to the front public area, and out the front door.

Richmond, Stephanie, and I watched as Wendy herded the two boys across the parking lot and into her car, nearly getting hit by a sporty little convertible that was pulling in. As soon as the two boys were settled in the backseat of Wendy's car, Jacob punched Michael in the arm, Michael shoved back, and seconds later the two of them were going at it, wrestling and punching one another in the backseat while Wendy screamed at them loud enough for us to hear her inside the police station.

Richmond turned to me and said, "That went well," in a sarcastic tone. Then he stomped from the front area into the back hallway.

I followed him into the break room, where Brenda Joiner was still sitting at the table where she'd been with Jacob. "I take it things didn't go so well?" she said with a questioning look.

"That's putting it mildly," Richmond grumbled. "I don't suppose the kid said anything to you that might be helpful?"

"Afraid not," Brenda said with an apologetic shrug. "But then, I didn't ask him anything related to the crime. I didn't want to jeopardize any formal statement he might make."

Richmond huffed his frustration.

"If you don't need anything else from me, do you mind if I split?" Brenda asked.

"That's fine," Richmond said. "Thanks for babysitting."

"No problem." With that, Brenda got up and exited out the back door to the rear parking lot where all the squad cars are parked.

Richmond turned and looked at me with a frown. "Well, at least we know the older kid has a habit of sneaking out of his house. But the time we know he did it doesn't help us. We'll have to verify his alibi for later on, see if he was actually at this friend's house when he said he was."

Stephanie came back, wearing her headset. "That Terwilliger woman you told me to call just got here."

"Send her on back," Richmond said.

As Stephanie went to fetch Mandy, Richmond turned to me and said, "This ought to be interesting. Let's see if we can find out why Ms. Terwilliger felt it necessary to lie to us."

Chapter 9

Mandy Terwilliger's eyes were bloodshot and red-rimmed, and her short, white-blond hair was all spiky, as if she'd been running her hands through it. She looked frail and wounded, though it might have been her diminutive size that gave that impression, particularly since she hadn't come alone. Walking beside her, dressed in slacks and a blouse rather than a bathrobe, was Rose Carpenter, Derrick's neighbor. As the two women strolled down the hallway toward us, Stephanie hollered to Richmond.

"Sorry, I tried to get the other woman to wait up here, but they insisted on coming back there together."

Richmond dismissed her concerns with a wave of his hand and then shifted his attention to Mandy. "I have no interest in talking to your friend," he said.

Rose pouted, and I noticed she'd put on some makeup since we last saw her: mascara, eye shadow, blush, and a sexy red shade of lipstick. I bit back a smile, certain that the makeup had been applied for Richmond's benefit. Lest I had any doubts, Rose's flirtatious eye flutters and coquettish posturing confirmed my thinking. Unfortunately, I don't think Richmond was aware of it. Mandy said, "She's not here to talk, she's here to provide me with moral support."

Richmond frowned and looked over at Rose, who broke into a broad smile. Richmond quickly averted his gaze back to Mandy. "Some of the questions I need to ask you are intimate, private ones," he said. He then looked back at Rose. "You need to go wait in the lobby area."

"And if I don't?" Rose said, straightening up and looking ready for a fight.

"If you don't, I'll find something to charge you with and have you arrested," Richmond shot back irritably. I suspected it was an empty threat, but it was also a wasted one.

Rather than looking intimidated, Rose looked intrigued. "Would you have to handcuff me?" she asked in a hopeful tone of voice.

"I might," Richmond said gruffly, and once again I had to bite back a smile because it was obvious he was clueless about Rose's sexual innuendo.

Rose looked over at Mandy and said, "I'll wait out front for you."

Mandy nodded, and as soon as Rose was back in the lobby area, we led Mandy into the conference room, where Richmond directed her to sit across from us.

As soon as we were settled, Richmond flipped on the audiovisual equipment and recited the date, the time, the case this interview related to, and Mandy's full name. He then informed Mandy that everything was being recorded. Once Mandy indicated her under-standing of the situation, Richmond got right down to business.

"Ms. Terwilliger—"

"It's Mrs. Terwilliger."

Richmond looked surprised. "You're married?"

"I'm a widow."

"Oh. Sorry," Richmond said with an apologetic smile. Mandy smiled back, but her smile disappeared in a blink with Richmond's next sentence. "*Mrs.* Ter-williger, I'm interested in knowing why you lied to us earlier this evening when we asked you when you had last seen Derrick Ames."

Mandy blinked several times very fast and squirmed in her seat. "I don't know what you're talking about," she said.

"Cut the crap," Richmond said. "Several of the neighbors saw you at Derrick's house earlier today, around the same time that his son Jacob showed up. Are you saying that isn't true?"

Mandy swallowed hard. "Okay," she said, fidgeting with her fingers. "I was there this afternoon, around two-thirty or so for about thirty minutes."

"Why did you lie to us earlier?"

"Because I was working delivering flowers, and I'm not supposed to be taking time for anything per-sonal. If my boss finds out, I'll get fired. And I can't afford to lose my job. It's hard enough as it is trying to get by on a part-time salary. My husband died a year and a half ago in a car accident, and while I did get a small settlement from the insurance company, he didn't have any life insurance. The majority of the settlement money is earmarked for my kids' college fund, and we're trying to make a go of it with the rest plus my salary. As it is, we're barely squeaking by. If I lose my job, I don't know what will happen."

I sympathized with her plight, one I feared facing myself.

"If you're that tight on money, why don't you get a full-time job?" Richmond asked.

"I've thought about it," she said. "I worked as a bookkeeper full time when I first got married, but right now I need to be there for my kids. They've had a hard time of it, losing their father that way, and my youngest, Oliver, has been having some problems . . . acting out, hanging with a bad crowd, that sort of thing. That's why I'm committed to volunteering at the high school three days a week, so I can keep an eye on him. I'm hoping to return to a full-time job at some point, and I'm keeping my bookkeeping skills up to date by working as treasurer for the PTA and doing some side work for the owner of the florist shop, helping out with the books."

"You met Derrick at the school?" Richmond asked.

"Sort of," Mandy said, nodding. "The first time I met him was at a PTA meeting, and after that we crossed paths a few times at the school. We started out with a few friendly waves and hellos in the hall and cafeteria. Things didn't progress to another level until just a few months ago."

"Tell me about your visit to his house this afternoon."

Mandy glanced over at me, and her pale skin turned a fiery red in her cheeks. "I took the van home and parked it in my garage so no one would see it. Then I walked over to Derrick's for a little, um, afternoon delight," she said, looking sheepish.

"You had sex," Richmond said, putting the blunt on it.

Mandy nodded.

"And did Jacob show up while you were there?"

"He did," she said with a grimace. "We had already . . . you know . . . done it, and we were lying in bed. I said I had to go, kissed Derrick, and mentioned something about getting together for a late dinner tomorrow night. But Derrick was behaving strangely."

"How so?" Richmond asked.

"He was standoffish all of a sudden, almost cold . . . hesitant about making any future plans. I sensed something was bothering him, and I tried to coax it out of him, but he wouldn't tell me anything. So I tried a little, um, harder . . . you know what I mean?" she said, her cheeks flushing again. "And then suddenly Jacob was there, standing in the doorway to the bedroom, looking all pissed off."

"Did Jacob say anything?"

"He did," Mandy said, frowning. "I don't recall his exact words, but it was obvious he was upset."

"And what happened next?"

"Jacob ran off, and Derrick got out of bed, pulled on his jeans, and ran after him. Once they were gone, I got dressed as fast as I could and went downstairs to leave. I heard them in the kitchen arguing, and I knew that my presence there was only going to make things worse, so I left through the front door and walked back to my house. Then I finished my deliveries."

"Did you overhear any of this argument Jacob and Derrick were having?"

"Some," she said. "It was about Jacob wanting Derrick and his ex-wife to get back together. The kid's had a hard time with the divorce, and he's convinced that Derrick and Wendy can work things out between them."

"Do you think that's possible?" Richmond asked. It was a smart question, a fishing expedition to see how much Mandy knew.

Mandy pondered the question for a few seconds and then said, "Does anything I say in here stay private?"

Richmond shrugged. "It depends on whether or not anything you say becomes critical or evidentiary in solving this case. I can't make any promises. But I will tell you that we're not in the business of spreading gossip unnecessarily."

Mandy nodded, looking indecisive for a bit before she made her decision. "From what Derrick has told me, there's no chance of it," she said. "Wendy has . . . um . . . how can I put this delicately? She has other leanings."

"Meaning?" Richmond pushed. I figured he was doing so to keep Mandy unsettled since we knew exactly what Wendy's other leanings were.

"She's a lesbian," Mandy said with a roll of her eyes. "Apparently she now likes women instead of men."

"I see," Richmond said, and he scribbled something on the pad in front of him. "Did Derrick have any enemies that you're aware of?"

Mandy gave it a moment's thought and then shook her head. "No. Everybody likes him. The students like him. The other teachers like him. As far as I know, all his neighbors like him. I've never heard anyone say anything to the contrary."

"Have you dated any other men since your husband died?"

"God, no."

"Any other men show an interest in dating you?"

"Sure, there have been a few. A couple of the other male teachers made some overtures a while back, and a friend of my husband's hinted around a few months ago. But I made it clear I wasn't interested, and I never went out with any of them."

"So you don't think any of them would resent Derrick for succeeding where they failed?"

"No way," Mandy said, with an adamant shake of her head.

"Just to be sure, can you give me the names of these men?"

Mandy did so.

"Can you recall any of the specific things that were said between Jacob and Derrick during this argument they had?"

Mandy's brow furrowed in thought. "Jacob was doing most of the talking, or rather yelling," she said. "He was chastising his father for not trying hard enough to save the marriage. The usual stuff. It's a recurring theme with Jacob."

"One final thing," Richmond posed. "Did Derrick have a cell phone when you saw him today?"

Mandy frowned at this and gave Richmond an odd look. "I suppose so, though, to be honest, I can't recall seeing it. My attention was focused elsewhere most of the time."

"Did the two of you talk on the phone much, or message back and forth?"

"We did," Mandy said. "He texted me sometime after I left his house to say he wanted to see me. I texted him back around six or six-thirty, and when he didn't answer, I sent him another one an hour later, and again when I was getting off work." She paused, looked sad, and shook her head. "I knew something was wrong when he didn't answer me. He's usually so prompt."

"Do you still have those text messages on your phone?"

"I do."

"Would you mind if I took a look?"

Mandy frowned. "I guess," she said. She reached into her purse and took out her phone. Then she tapped the screen a few times and handed the phone over to Richmond.

I leaned over and read along with him. Derrick sent a text to Mandy just before four o'clock that said WE NEED TO TALK. At 6:20 she texted him back: WANT ME 2 COME BY AFTER WORK? At 7:31 she texted him again: WHEN SHOULD I COME BY? Then at 8:14 she texted him one last time: IS EVERYTHING OKAY? That was the end of any exchanges between them.

Richmond handed her back the phone and then looked over at me. "Any questions?"

I shook my head. Richmond turned back to Mandy. "Thank you for coming in, Mrs. Terwilliger," he said. "If I have any other questions, I'll be back in touch. But before you leave, would you mind letting us print you?"

"You want my fingerprints? Why?"

"For elimination purposes. Obviously we expect to find your prints in Mr. Ames's house, given the nature of your relationship with him. We're looking for prints that don't belong there, so we need to know whose prints are whose."

Mandy nodded, and Richmond used the new tablet device the department received a couple of months ago to scan her prints and upload them to a database. Once he was done, Mandy got up and left the room without so much as a good-bye.

"Did her demeanor seem odd to you?" Richmond asked me once Mandy was gone.

"I guess," I said. "It's hard to know."

Richmond cocked his head and narrowed his eyes at me. "You seem a little out of sorts tonight," he said. "Is everything okay?"

I nodded, and then, like the emotionally stable, utterly professional woman I was at the time, I burst into tears.

Chapter 10

"It sounds like it was an interesting case," Maggie says to me.

"It was."

"Lots of single parenting going on. Did that strike a theme with you?"

I pat my rotund tummy. "It did. For one thing, after watching the Ames boys go at one another in the car, I decided this child will be my one and only."

"But what about Emily? If you have any plans to spend time with Hurley, you'll also have Emily in your life, right?"

I think about that and shrug. "I suppose, but she's practically grown already."

"Don't kid yourself," says Dr. Killjoy, with a humorless laugh. "She's a teenager, one who has undergone a number of very stressful changes recently, so I wouldn't be surprised if she starts to act out at some point. And that can make a few years of child rearing seem like a lifetime."

She had that right. When I first met Emily, she had seemed like a bright, reasonable, and friendly child.

Her acceptance of me and, more important, of my romantic history with Hurley, had set me at ease. She had even shown an interest in what I did at the ME's office, and she had demonstrated an outstanding ability to draw when she made a skeleton that was hanging in our office come to life. I thought we were on a good footing and was relieved, given that the circumstances under which we met had been less than ideal. But something changed after Hurley and Emily disappeared to find her mother. Ever since their return, Emily's behavior had been the polar opposite of what it had been initially, and that made me rethink the whole idea of having kids at all. As if the child inside me registers this thought, he or she decides to act out by kicking me hard in the ribs. I wince and Maggie catches it.

"Are you okay?"

"I'll be fine," I say, rubbing my tummy. "Sometimes the kid gets a little rambunctious."

"Any regrets about the pregnancy?"

"No, at least not when it comes to my decision to have the kid."

"Meaning?"

"Well, for one thing, pregnancy is not my favorite state of being," I tell her. "Not long after I found out, it was as if someone was spinning the Barf Wheel of Fortune. I don't know why they call it morning sickness because it knows no sense of time. I could be starving hungry and grab something to eat, and halfway through it I'd have to run to the bathroom and barf it all up. Sometimes the nausea hit me in the middle of the night, in the middle of my coffee, in the middle of an autopsy . . . pretty random. I thought things would get better once the nausea went away, but then the peeing took over, and that hasn't stopped. It's like I have an army of little men in my stomach stomping on my bladder all the time. Some days I can barely wipe before I have to go again. It's even worse now than it was in the beginning because getting these pants up and down is a workout these days. And just how the hell am I supposed to be able to reach anything down there? I haven't been able to see or trim that area for months. By now it probably looks like the Amazon jungle. And I'm going to have a cadre of people staring at it any day now. I have nightmares about doctors and nurses gathered around me dressed in surgical masks, army fatigues, and pith helmets, making comments about how hard it will be to navigate through the bush."

Maggie bites back a laugh.

"It isn't funny," I tell her.

She nods and frowns as if to agree with me, but her lips are contorting as she tries not to laugh.

"I'm serious. It's no picnic, Maggie. The other day I put on two different shoes and didn't realize it until someone pointed it out to me. And then I thought it was a joke. Turns out it wasn't, but I didn't know that until I sat down and put my feet up. And don't even get me started on the stretch marks. My abdomen looks like a GPS map of downtown Chicago. Plus, it's not bad enough that I have to pee every half hour; things aren't working so good on the other end, either. Sometimes I swear this kid in here has a death grip on my colon. I'm pretty sure I now have hemorrhoids the size of walnuts, though I can't be sure since I can't see anything. All I know is there's something down there that never used to be there. I waddle like a frigging penguin, and I spend half the day wondering if that sensation I feel means I crapped my pants, or my hemorrhoid is moving."

I realize I'm rambling, so I pause and suck in a breath. Maggie, who is normally such a master of the impassive facial expression that I've wondered at times if she's a cyborg, has completely lost her smile. Now she's staring at me with a slightly frightened, wide-eyed look.

"Sorry," I say, feeling embarrassed. "That was probably TMI. I guess I went on a bit of a rant there."

"That's okay. I'm here for the rants just like I'm here for the other stuff."

"Do you have kids?" I ask her, realizing I know almost nothing about her.

"No, that one wasn't in the cards for me." There is a hint of wistfulness in her voice that tells me this is an emotional topic for her. "But I'd rather talk about you," she adds quickly, getting the subject matter back on course with a classic professional maneuver. "You've said that you always planned to have kids, but I imagine this isn't the way you expected to go about it."

"That's putting it mildly," I say with a full dose of sarcasm. "I hate to admit it, but I was as naïve and stupid as they come. All my life I've had this image of my perfect family: me, my doting, loving husband, our two kids—one boy and one girl—living out my days in heavenly, soccer-mom perfection." I scoffed. "What an idiotic dream."

"It's one that's attainable for many."

"Thanks for the reminder of what a failure I am."

"Is that how you feel, like you're a failure?"

"Well, yeah, at least with regard to that silly-assed dream." Maggie answers this with silence, another classic ploy. I'm determined to wait her out, but I buckle quickly and blame it on the hormones. "Being a single parent wasn't what I had in mind . . . ever."

"You don't know for sure if that's what will happen, do you?"

I think long and hard before I answer this one. "I don't know for sure," I admit. "But here's what I do know. Hurley griped and carried on about how blindsided he was when he found out about Emily. I believe his exact complaint was that he was 'hoodwinked and duped into fatherhood.' He said he wasn't cut out to be a father, and with the crazy hours he works, and the number of years he's been on his own, he doesn't have the time or the patience to be a father . . . or the desire, for that matter. That seems pretty damned clear to me."

"Except he said those things about Emily, a daughter who was literally sprung on him overnight, a nearly grown young woman whose childhood he wasn't involved in. She's essentially a stranger to him, and yet now he is the only parent she has. So he was going to be a parent whether you got pregnant or not."

"The fact that another woman left him feeling duped and trapped doesn't make it okay that I've now done the same thing."

"Didn't you say Hurley was not only okay with this, but that he seemed delighted?"

"Sure, at first. But I don't think the reality of it had sunk in yet. Besides, he's probably putting on a happy face for my sake. Hurley's too kind to say something he knows will hurt me."

"So you don't believe him when he says he's okay with it?"

"No . . . yes . . . I don't know." I feel exasperated and it shows.

"The situation he has with you is certainly different from what he had with Emily and Kate. At least with you he's had time to adjust to the idea. And he knows he'll be involved with the child's upbringing."

I don't say anything for a bit, and that makes Maggie suspicious. "You *are* planning on letting him be involved with the child's upbringing, aren't you?"

"Of course. He can be as involved as he wants."

"Are you prepared for what will happen if he says he doesn't want to be involved?"

I shoot her a glance, wondering if she's talked to Hurley behind my back and knows something I don't. "I have plenty of help available," I say with a tone of indifference. I sound convincing enough that I almost believe the idea of Hurley jumping ship doesn't bother me. "Dom is home all the time, he lives right outside my door, and he's dying to babysit. My sister has offered, too, though I don't think I'll use her unless Dom can't do it for some reason. She and her husband are working on their own issues with their marriage, and I don't want to complicate things by throwing a new kid into the mix, however temporary or short-term."

"How are things going with them?" Maggie asks.

"Okay, I guess. Desi says Lucien is behaving himself, and it's obvious he's a changed man. In fact, he's like a different person when I talk to him these days. But I can tell Desi is still angry. Frankly, it's all a little scary."

"What's scary, that your brother-in-law has changed, or that their marriage may be on the rocks?"

"Both," I say, wishing a second later that I could

take it back. I know where Maggie is going next, and she doesn't disappoint.

"Your personal experience with happy marriages is rather limited, isn't it?"

"Just because my mother has been married and divorced four times, and my own marriage fell apart because my ex couldn't keep Mr. Turtle in his shell doesn't mean I'm incapable of having a normal, healthy relationship."

"What's your definition of a normal, healthy relationship?"

For some reason, this question irks me. Maybe it's because I'm unsure of the answer. "It's when two people have mutual respect and love for one another," I say, taking a stab at it. "It's sticking together through the hard times. It's an unconditional acceptance of one another, both the good traits and the bad. It's sharing things, but also allowing one another room to grow. And it's trust. Trust is a big one."

"I can see why it would be, given your history with David. Do you feel you can trust Hurley?"

I consider this for a while before I answer. "I trust him with my life. And I trust him with our child's life. I'm not sure if I trust his emotions, though."

"Meaning?"

"Meaning I don't know if he wants to be with me because he loves me, or if he feels a duty to be with me because of the kid."

"You're afraid that if you trust him he'll turn around and leave you, the way your father did."

I shoot her an angry look. I have a sickening feeling she is very right about this, and I don't like it.

"Your father left when you were how old?"

"Four, almost five."

"And you don't know why he left."

"I assume it was because my mother's many idiosyncrasies drove him crazy."

"That might be why he left your mother, but what I meant was you don't know why he left *you*."

Now she's not only hit a nerve, she's plucking it. I try to fight back the tears I can feel building and burning at the back of my eyes, but it's a lost cause.

"You don't feel lovable because all of the men in your life have left you for reasons you don't understand. First your father left you, then David did the same thing. And I assume there were some stepfathers in there also?"

I nod, wiping the tears from my face with my palms.

"So who in your life serves as a strong, reliable, healthy male role model?"

"Izzy," I say with an ironic chuckle. "I know he's gay, but when it comes to being a strong, warm, loving, patient, understanding, forgiving man, he's the best one I know. He's probably the closest thing I have to a father. Not only do I adore him, he and Dom are my best friends."

"And if this child you're having is a boy, will Izzy and Dom be his primary role models for all things male?"

"Of course not," I say. "And not because Dom and Izzy are gay. There are many different types of men in the world, and I would want any son or daughter of mine to be exposed to as many of them as possible. The same goes for women."

"Do you think Detective Hurley will be a good male role model?"

"Of course he will, assuming he sticks it out and plays a part in the child's upbringing."

"You say that as if you and Hurley are no longer a couple."

"It's complicated," I say.

"Are the two of you still seeing one another?"

"Well, we see each other at work all the time."

"What about outside of work?"

"Sometimes, though not as much lately. Like I said, things have gotten complicated."

"Do you still live alone?"

I nod.

"Are you still having sex with him?"

I feel myself blush. "We were sneaking it in wherever we could up until about a month ago. I've gotten so big I feel like I should call him Ahab. And then there's the Boobzillas here," I add, waving a hand in front of my chest. "They leak if anyone so much as looks at them. Not that any of that matters anymore because Hurley has become reluctant to have sex now. He's afraid he'll poke the kid's eye out or something."

"The two of you are sneaking around because of the conflict of interest job issues?"

"No, that sort of resolved itself. But there are other issues."

"Such as?"

"Well, Emily, for one."

"Why is she an issue? Do you resent the amount of time she has with Hurley?"

"No, it's more the other way around. I think Hurley does a pretty decent job of splitting his time and attention between the two of us, but it doesn't seem to be enough for Emily. And I have a feeling that's only going to get worse after the baby comes."

"Are you concerned Hurley won't have enough love left over for your child?"

"Not at all. Hurley's a kind, generous, thoughtful man. He has plenty of love to go around."

"And yet you doubt his love for you."

"That's different."

"How so?"

"I'm not his child. The love someone feels for their child is completely different from the love they might feel for a sexual partner."

"Is that how you see yourself with Hurley? As his sexual partner?"

"No," I snap. "Not totally anyway." Maggie's probing questions feel like fingers thrust deep into a raw wound. It's making me irritable, and the kid seems to sense this. I feel a hard punch—a foot, a fist, a head butt?—and shift my position again. Then I take a deep breath and try to make myself relax. "Clearly Hurley and I have a shared affection for one another. And we also share this," I say, rubbing a hand over my Buddha belly. "But that doesn't mean we have what it takes to spend a lifetime together as a couple."

"Has Hurley asked you to marry him?"

Once again, I wonder if she has some sort of insider knowledge. "Why would you ask me that? Don't you think I would have told you if he had?"

"Honestly?" she asks, and I nod. "No, I don't think you would tell me, at least not right away."

Damn, Maggie is better at this than I realized. Either that or she has me bugged.

"So has he?"

I sigh, knowing it's no use trying to lie to her. "Yeah, he has."

"And how did you answer?"

"I told him no."

She sighs, nods, and shifts in her seat, getting comfortable. She holds her pen poised over the tablet in her lap and says, "Tell me how it happened. And don't give me the abridged version. I want all the details as seen through your filters."

I glance at my watch. "I don't think we have enough time, do we? My hour is almost up."

"As it happens, you're my only patient today," Maggie says with a smug smile. "I typically take Tuesdays off, but I made an exception for you because I know how complicated your schedule can be. So I'm all yours for as long as you want."

Oh goody.

Chapter 11

I tell Maggie how I went from interviewing the Ames family, to killing someone, to getting a marriage proposal, all in the space of twenty-four hours.

Before I left the police station on the Saturday night that Derrick Ames was killed, and after I was able to stop sobbing long enough to speak understandably, I assured Richmond that everything was fine; it was just my time of the month.

Once Richmond felt confident that I wasn't going to have a complete meltdown on him, we went into his office to make some phone calls.

"I want to speak to as many of these people as I can before our pool of suspects has a chance to get to them," Richmond said.

He placed a phone call to Blake Sutherland's cell phone number first. There was no answer, so he left a message asking her to call him back as soon as possible.

We had better luck with Donna Martin, who answered her phone in a sleepy voice and verified the fact that Wendy Ames had been at her house earlier, giving a time frame that matched the one Wendy had provided.

We were able to reach two of the three men that Mandy named as interested suitors. One of them, the family friend, was in New York for a week on business, a fact easily verified by calling the hotel where he said he was staying. The second man, a music teacher at the high school, said he had been at a band concert during the time of Derrick's death and gave the names of several schoolkids and parents who would verify this. The third man, Sam Littleton, who was also a teacher at the high school, didn't answer his phone, so Richmond left a message.

Richmond's last planned call of the night was to the home of Jacob's friend, the one he supposedly had dinner with. "I know the Fitzpatrick kid," Richmond told me. "He's a troublemaker. They busted him last year for dealing pot, and he did some time in juvey, so if Jacob is hanging out with him, heaven knows what they were up to."

Richmond put the phone on speaker, and when a sleepy-voiced woman answered, he said, "Is this Mrs. Fitzpatrick?"

"It is. I see from my caller ID that this is the police. What's Sean done now?" she asked, her tone resigned and tired.

"Nothing that I'm aware of," Richmond said, and the sigh of relief on the other end of the line was easily audible. "I'm calling to verify some information about someone else. Jacob Ames said he was at your house with your son for dinner this evening. Is that true?"

"Sort of," Mrs. Fitzpatrick said. "He came over, and

then he and Sean locked themselves in Sean's bedroom to play video games for several hours. They didn't even come out for dinner."

"What time did Jacob leave?" Richmond asked.

"Hmm, I think it was around eight, give or take."

"Mrs. Fitzpatrick, do you know for sure that the boys were there the entire time?"

"Well, I could hear the sounds of the game being played through the door to Sean's room. And I did holler at them a couple of times about dinner, and Sean kept saying they weren't hungry."

"Did you hear Jacob say anything during that time?"

There was a long pause before Mrs. Fitzpatrick said, "You know, I don't recall that I did. But then Jacob tends to be a quiet boy. He gets moody at times, but I've always found him to be a well-mannered young man. I've been hoping he might have a positive influence on Sean. Why are you asking so many questions about Jacob? Is he in some kind of trouble? Should I try to keep him and Sean apart?"

Apparently the Sorenson gossip mill hadn't made it to the Fitzpatrick household yet. Richmond skillfully avoided answering the question by saying, "Thank you for your time, Mrs. Fitzpatrick. I'll let you know if I have any other questions." Then he disconnected the call. I felt pretty sure Mrs. Fitzpatrick would sit stunned for a few seconds, staring at the phone, and then she would start making calls to find out what was going on.

"Do you really think Jacob killed his father?" I asked Richmond, trying to imagine what it would feel like to know you raised a patricidal son. Had the divorce thing messed him up that much? And if so, what chance did a kid of mine have if Hurley and I didn't end up together? It was an unsettling thought, and for an instant I had this image of my future son's face plastered across TV screens nationwide with a CNN banner running across the bottom detailing some horrific crime he'd committed. This parenting stuff was some scary shit.

"I don't know," Richmond said. "But I think it's possible." He glanced at his watch. "It's late. Why don't we pick up again tomorrow? I'll call you."

That sounded fine to me. I was tired, a state of existence that seemed to be my norm of late. My OB doctor had checked my blood and iron levels, both of which were fine, and suggested that perhaps my exhaustion was a combination of emotional stress and the physical effects of all the vomiting I'd done during the past few weeks. And since I hadn't confided half of what was going on in my life, she had no idea just how much stress I was under at the time.

As I was about to leave, Richmond's phone rang. "Hold on," he said, glancing at the screen. "It's Izzy."

He answered the call, told Izzy I was there though we were about to call it a night, and then switched the call to speakerphone.

"I didn't turn up anything more with Derrick's autopsy," he said. "It's pretty much what we expected and what I told Mattie earlier regarding the broken bloody nose and the bruises. The knife wound was the ultimate cause of death, though the barbecue fork might have done the deed if the knife hadn't since it was lodged in his heart. I've got Arnie sampling and typing the blood on the knife on the off chance that some of the killer's DNA might be there."

"So we got nothing," Richmond said, his frustration from earlier still clear in his voice.

"Not so fast," Izzy said. "Arnie has something for you. Hold on."

A few seconds later, Arnie's voice came over the phone. "I was able to lift a partial print off both the knife and the barbecue fork," he told us. "I'll run them against our suspect pool samples and through AFIS tonight to see if I get any hits. If not, I'll go back to the crime scene first thing tomorrow morning and continue processing the scene with Jonas. Maybe we can lift some prints from elsewhere in the house that will be a match."

Richmond told Arnie about the Ames family interview and the people he hoped to talk to tomorrow. "I was going to call all of them first thing in the morning," he said. "But I'll wait and see if you get a hit from AFIS. Maybe we'll get lucky and snag the killer based on a print alone."

"You may not have to call anyone," Arnie said cryptically. "I have something else that might solve the case for you. You know that camera you found between the cabinet and the refrigerator?"

"Is there something on it?" Richmond asked, his voice rising with excited anticipation.

"I'll say," Arnie said. "I found a handful of videos. Most of them are pretty mundane: pans of the rooms in the house and some outdoor clips that I suspect were test runs Derrick made with the camera to get used to using it. Then there's the last video, which starts with a shaky image and then provides a line of sight across the kitchen floor from that space where you found it. My guess is it got knocked off the counter and the fall turned it on."

"What does it show?" Richmond asked.

"Some feet and lower legs," Arnie said. "But it wasn't just what I saw, it was what I heard." Once again he paused for dramatic effect.

"Come on, Arnie, spill it," I said, growing impatient with his game. "What have you got?"

"I'm pretty sure I have video of your killer."

Richmond and I exchanged looks of disbelief that morphed into hope.

"I just e-mailed it to you," Arnie said. "I'll hold while you download it."

Richmond settled in at Hurley's desk, and I stood behind him, watching over his shoulder. It took him forever to log into his e-mail and download the attached video, so long that Arnie probably could have walked it over to us in less time.

"Okay," Richmond said into his phone. "I got it."

"Go ahead and start it," Arnie said. "It's short, just under a minute long."

I watched as a blurry image flashed on the screen, along with a time and date stamp in the lower right corner showing the current date, a time of 7:28:07 P.M., and a flashing red warning at the top of the screen that said LOW BATTERY. Within seconds the blurry image settled into a view of Derrick Ames's kitchen floor, and after a few seconds more, a close image of two pairs of jeans-clad legs and feet came into view, moving erratically. Based on the grunting and heavy breathing we could hear in the background, it wasn't hard to tell that the two people were scuffling; either that or they were the worst dance couple ever. One pair of jeans—those on the person who was backing up—were basic, straight-legged denims. The jeans on the aggressor were stonewashed, boot-cut denims, and the back hems, which were ragged and dirty, dragged on the ground. After about ten seconds the feet disappeared from view, but there was another thirty seconds or so of audio: heavy breathing, *oomph* sounds, the thud of what sounded like fists against skin, and someone—I felt certain the voice was Derrick's—yelling out "Stop, damn it!" A few seconds after that there was a loud crash. Then the video stopped.

Arnie said, "The feet you see on the right of the screen, the ones that were moving backward, belong to Derrick Ames. Those are the same pants and shoes the hospital gave Izzy when they handed over Derrick's clothing. I don't know who the second pair of feet belongs to, but those shoes are ASIC Gel Scout athletic shoes. That blue shade with the orange soles might help you find the owner."

"I can't be sure without a direct comparison," I said, "but those ragged, dirty hems on the stonewashed jeans look exactly like the ones Jacob Ames was wearing tonight."

"Did you notice his shoes?" Arnie asked.

"No, sorry."

"Can you tell what size the shoes are?" Richmond asked.

"Given that we know Derrick Ames wears a nine and the other pair of feet look to be around the same size, I'd say odds are you're looking for a nine, but they might be tens. The perspective changes from one frame to the next, and that's the closest I can come without doing the math. I can be more precise for you tomorrow, though if you can find the actual pair of shoes, I won't need to be."

"Why is that?" Richmond asked.

"If you look closely at the footage you can see a very specific scuff mark on the inside of the left shoe, just above the arch. You can see it in several frames, but it's clearest when the feet first appear. It's shaped like the Nike swoosh. Find me a shoe with that mark and we'll have a winner."

Richmond replayed the footage, advanced it more slowly, and then froze it on the frame in question. "I see it," he said. "If we play back footage from the lobby-area security camera, maybe we can see what kind of shoes Jacob was wearing. Nice find, Arnie."

"Thanks. I'm going to head home and get some sleep, but I'll be back at it early tomorrow. And if I get a hit from AFIS, I'll let you know as soon as it happens. I have the computer rigged to call my cell and forward the info once it finds a match."

"Sweet," Richmond said. "You techies are all right in my book. I don't care what everybody else says." Richmond winked at me, and the two of us waited in silence.

Arnie didn't make us wait long. "What does that mean?" he asked in what I've come to know as his conspiracy tone. "What are people saying?"

Richmond and I both laughed. "I'm just busting on you, Arnie. Nobody is saying anything."

That wasn't altogether true, given my conversation with Jonas earlier, but I decided to keep mum on that subject.

"Get some sleep," Richmond said. "We'll talk more tomorrow."

Before I left for the night, Richmond played back the station's security tape to see if we could get a look at Jacob's shoes. But the tape didn't show his feet with enough clarity to be able to tell.

Our mututal disappointment was palpable, and I sensed this case wasn't going to be an easy one, if for no other reason than because there was a fork involved.

Chapter 12

I headed home and fell into bed on Saturday night just before one in the morning. I cuddled up with my cat Rubbish at my chest, my cat Tux at my back, and my dog, Hoover, nestled alongside my legs. The four of us filled the bed quite nicely, but just before I fell asleep, I reminded them all that things were going to change once the baby arrived. The cats ignored my warning, knowing they'd sleep wherever they wanted, whenever they wanted, baby or no baby. Hoover thumped his tail twice and eyed me lovingly. It's hard to beat doggie love.

On Sunday morning, I slept in until just after eight and awoke feeling better than I had in a long time. I had a leisurely breakfast of toast, soft-boiled eggs, and orange juice. I also had a half cup of coffee despite the fact that a pregnant food Nazi named Saffron, whom I met in the waiting room of my OB doctor, said coffee was an absolute no-no. Also on Saffron's list of no-nos was nitrates (which meant no bacon, pepperoni, hot dogs, or salami), deli meats, alcohol, sugar, processed foods of any kind, cheese, and a sense of humor. I was puzzled by the cheese inclusion, and as a joke I told her I thought avoiding cheese was against the law in Wisconsin. She looked at me with this pitiful, pained expression, as if I was a drooling idiot, and then said the reason to avoid cheese is because it might not be pasteurized.

As Saffron eliminated my entire diet while warning me of all the potential hazards, she was eating something that looked like the piece of plaster that got knocked out of our kitchen wall when Desi and I were kids and decided to make a tower out of our kitchen chairs. I have no idea what Saffron eats on a regular basis, but based on her waiting room fare, I wouldn't be surprised if her kid developed a hellacious case of pica, an odd malady that makes people eat weird things, like dirt, clay, and paper. There was a kid named Hal in my third-grade class who had it, and our teacher had to resort to keeping all the chalk under lock and key so Hal wouldn't eat it.

I figured that if my mentally unhinged mother managed to have me despite the fact that she was living on a diet of coffee and wine at the time, a little coffee now and then wasn't going to hurt me or the baby. Just to be sure, I ran it by my OB doctor, who okayed it with that vague term we medical people love so much: in moderation.

Richmond called just before ten to say that Arnie had struck out with AFIS, and the Ames family had lawyered up with some hotshot from Milwaukee. They weren't going to talk to us at all that day because the soonest Mr. Hotshot could make it to Sorenson was Monday. Richmond also said he was working on getting a search warrant for the Ames house so we could look for those shoes in the video, but that it wasn't likely to come through until Monday, either.

He'd also struck out with Blake Sutherland, who wasn't answering her phone and hadn't yet returned his call. "I'm thinking she'll get back to me sooner rather than later, though," he said, "because the message I left said I needed to speak to her regarding Wendy Ames, and if I didn't hear from her today, I was going to call her husband tomorrow to track her down."

"I suspect she already knows why you're calling. I'm sure Wendy called her the first chance she had to fill her in."

"Could be, but I reviewed the tape last night after you left, and the only call Wendy made before we joined her was to her parents in California. She did text someone after that, but at this point there's no way to know who that went to."

"My money's on Blake," I said, wincing at the gambling metaphor as soon as I said it. I don't know if I've always used a lot of gambling metaphors and have only recently become aware of them after my little casino binge, or if the occasional desire to binge some more has led to a subconscious gambling fixation that is manifesting itself in my speech.

"While we're on the subject of phone calls," Richmond went on, "Junior looked over the call history for Derrick's cell. Most of the calls were to his wife and kids, and the others Junior was able to track down were to businesses, the school, and some of his coworkers. Nothing jumped out. There were a number of text messages, too, both sent and received, most of them to family and coworkers. Only five were from yesterday, including the four to and from Mandy that we know about, and one from Sam Littleton later in the evening, just before ten. Littleton is a teacher at the high school and he was one of the names Mandy gave us, the one I couldn't reach last night. I called him again this morning and explained the situation, and he offered to let me read his text message on his phone, but he's in Madison until later tonight. So I told him we'd catch up to him at the school tomorrow. We still don't know where Derrick's phone is, but I don't think the phone or text records are going to be of much help."

"Then why did the killer take Derrick's phone?"

"Maybe they didn't," Richmond said. "Maybe Derrick lost it, or dropped it in a lake somewhere, or ran over it with his car. Who knows?" I heard him sigh with frustration. "I did have one positive outcome this morning. I was able to convince Mrs. Fitzpatrick to let me come by and talk to Sean today. I'm about to head out there now. Want to come along?"

"Sure."

Half an hour later, we were standing on the front porch of the Fitzpatrick home, which was in the same neighborhood as Wendy and Derrick's houses. "Jacob could have walked to his father's house from here in a matter of minutes," I noted as Richmond knocked on the door. "It's just around the corner."

A woman with red, frizzy hair answered the door. "You the detective?" she asked in a weary voice. There were dark circles under her blue eyes, and she was dressed in gray sweatpants and a pink T-shirt with a breast cancer ribbon logo over the heart that was partially covered by a large brown stain of some sort.

"Yes, ma'am," Richmond said. "I'm Bob Richmond, and this is Mattie Winston from the ME's office."

Mrs. Fitzpatrick shot me a curious look. "Come on in," she said. "Sean is in the kitchen."

We followed her inside through a living room where a heavy, balding man in a stained T-shirt and worn jeans was sitting in a recliner aiming a remote at the TV. The kitchen was cluttered and messy: crumbs and a partially used stick of butter on one countertop, three open boxes of cereal on another countertop, three dirty cereal bowls on the table, a stack of dirty dishes in the sink, and a trail of muddy dog paw prints across the floor. The raucous sound of children fighting and playing came from beyond the room. From the backyard came the baying of hound dogs.

Sean was seated at the table, eating a bowl of cereal and studying the back of a cereal box like he was about to be quizzed on it. He had his mother's red hair, though without the frizz. Instead he had one stubborn cowlick near the crown of his head that made him look like Alfalfa.

"Sorry about the mess," Mrs. Fitzpatrick said. "With four kids, two dogs, and a husband who thinks Sundays are for sitting in the recliner and drinking beer, it's hard to keep up at times."

Sean hadn't acknowledged our presence, and his mother cuffed him on the back side of the head and said, "Pay attention, Sean. You have company."

"Company is invited, and I didn't invite them," he said, never taking his eyes off the cereal box.

"Sorry to intrude on your Sunday brunch," Richmond said, "but we need to ask you a few questions."

"Whatever it is, I didn't do it," Sean said.

Richmond shot me a look; Mrs. Fitzpatrick gave

Sean another whack on the back of his head, which earned her a surly side glare from the boy.

"They aren't here to talk about you," Mrs. Fitzpatrick said. "They're here to ask some questions about Jacob."

That got Sean's attention. For once he wasn't the one in trouble. He looked at us with curiosity, dropped his spoon in his bowl with a loud clatter, and leaned back in his chair, tossing one arm over the back of it.

"What do you want to know about Jacob?" he asked.

"He was here last night," Richmond said.

"Yeah, so?"

"So I need to know what hours he was here, and whether or not he left at any point in time."

"You guys think he offed his dad, don't you?"

"Why would you say that?" I asked.

"It makes sense," Sean said with a shrug. "That's when his dad was killed, right?"

"It is," Richmond said. "So can you answer my questions?"

"I'm afraid not," he said in a cocky tone, giving Richmond a sad look. "My memory isn't so good these days."

Mrs. Fitzpatrick had a dish towel in her hands, and she snapped it at her son. "Damn it, Sean! This is serious business. This isn't one of your pranks or little misdemeanor violations. A man is dead. So quit playing games."

Sean rubbed at his arm where the towel had snapped him and scowled at his mother. "Yeah, he was here last night," he grumbled. "But I don't recall the time. We were in my room playing video games. I don't know what time it was."

Richmond walked over and stood across the table from Sean. Then he bent down, put his hands on the table, and leaned forward, pinning Sean with his eyes. "You better be telling the truth, Sean," he said.

Sean stared back at him with an expression full of teenage rebellion. "I told you what I know," he said, his lips tight, his tone even tighter. "Next time you want me to squeal on someone, let me know ahead of time, and I'll try to keep a better timeline."

The two of them stared at one another for several seconds until Richmond finally turned away.

Mrs. Fitzpatrick said, "I know it was around eight because Kelly works a three to eight shift over at the grocery store, and she got home minutes after Jacob left."

"Kelly?" Richmond said.

"That would be Miss Goody Two Shoes," Sean said with a sneer.

"It's his twin sister," his mother said with a much-put-upon sigh.

Richmond looked thoughtful for a moment and then said, "Okay, I think we're done here. Thank you for your time."

Mrs. Fitzpatrick showed us out. We walked right past her husband again, who had not acknowledged our arrival and appeared equally oblivious to our departure. Like father like son, I thought. And then I wondered what might be different in this household if there was no father figure at all. Would it be better or worse? Was I dooming my child to a warped upbringing if I tried to raise him or her by myself? I didn't think so because there were plenty of single-parent households that produced perfectly fine kids, and I essentially grew up without a father, though I did have a few intermittent stepfathers along the way. Then again, I wasn't sure I should put myself forth as a paragon of good mental health and emotional stability either.

"Man, I'm glad I don't have kids," Richmond said as we walked back to our cars. "That was an exercise in frustration. I'm going to head to the gym and work some of it off. Want to come along?"

I did battle with myself. I knew I should work out, but I had so much on my mind with the pending dinner tonight and Hurley's return tomorrow that I felt I needed some alone time to prepare myself. "I'm going to rest for a day or two," I told him. "I've been feeling a little off. I think I might be coming down with something."

"Okay. I'll let you know if anything else comes up later today; otherwise, I'll call you in the morning."

"Okey-dokey. Have fun at the gym."

"I will. Feel better."

Too late for that. There was no cure for coming down with a bad case of pregnant.

Chapter 13

With a free day ahead of me, I settled in on the couch and put my feet up on a pillow I set on the coffee table. I tried to read a book—some heavy family drama thing I'd had on my to-be-read pile for months, but it struck a little too close to home and made my anxiety worsen. So I tried to watch TV instead, but my mind kept going back to the two things that were keeping me on edge: my upcoming dinner and talk with Izzy, and Hurley's return the next day. I turned the TV off and spent an hour mentally playing out dozens of scenarios with the two men, imagining awkward conversational moments, rehearsing my speeches and responses, and chewing on my fingernails out of nervousness, a dietary item I felt sure would give Saffron a stroke. I was hoping the mental practice would calm my nerves, but instead it had the opposite effect. Even eating the cheesecake I had in the fridge from the night before didn't help. In fact, it made things worse because now I felt guilty about not going to the gym.

To burn off some calories and hopefully some of

my nervous energy, I took Hoover for a walk. We ventured into the woods, and I let him lead me wherever he wanted to go for the first ten minutes. But after standing by and watching him sniff and then mark every leaf, stick, and clod of dirt, I started tugging him in a different direction so I could take another peek at David's new house. I thought I might see a dark sedan parked there—and realized later that I had no idea what I would have done if there had been one—but I struck out. I chalked up my car paranoia to yet another hormonal quirk of pregnancy, and after walking around the place and building up a good case of resentment over David's palatial structure, Hoover and I headed back home.

I was bored, and even after my walk my fattest fat pants were feeling uncomfortably tight, so I decided it was time to bite the bullet and pay a visit to The Mother Hood, the only store in town that carried maternity clothes. I knew I risked word getting out about my condition, but I figured I was safe given that Hurley would be back in town soon and Izzy and Dom already knew. I made a mental note to call and give the news to my sister and my mother later tonight so they wouldn't hear it from someone else first.

The Mother Hood was owned by a woman in her mid-thirties named Priscilla McDaniel, a native Sorensonian who because of her skinny genes often wore skinny jeans and looked good in them. I'd known Priscilla—or Miss Priss, as we used to call her in high school—since we were both kids. Her choice of businesses seemed like a logical progression in her life. She had earned the nickname Miss Priss because of the remain-a-virgin-until-I'm-married mantra that she'd started spouting in the sixth grade. Unfortunately, Billy McDaniel had other ideas, and Miss Priss had missed her senior year in high school because Billy got her pregnant. They got married, and Priss spat out five more kids over the next six years. Since she always managed to return to her rail-thin state after each one, I could only assume that she had elastic in places where the rest of us have skin. Sadly, I think my body is made up of something that more closely resembles memory foam.

My arrival at The Mother Hood was announced by the tinkle of a little bell over the door and the sound of Brahms' Lullaby filling the air.

Priscilla was seated behind a counter reading a magazine, and when she looked up at me, her expression was one of incredulity, as if she couldn't believe what her eyes were seeing. She blinked real fast several times and then broke into a big smile. "Mattie Winston! Long time no see." She tossed the magazine onto the counter and jumped up. She was wearing a tailored white blouse over . . . you guessed it . . . skinny jeans. Her straight, brown hair shone with high- and lowlights, and it was cut at shoulder length and tucked behind her ears. "What brings you in today?" Then she cocked her head to one side and put her hands on her hips. "Is your sister pregnant again?"

"No, I am." There. I'd said it. The news was officially out.

Again Priscilla blinked several times really fast. It was like the blinking somehow powered her comprehension. "Are you?" she said with a tone of puzzlement. "Well, congratulations! I didn't know you'd remarried already."

"I haven't."

"Oh." She dragged the word out into two syllables—oh-oo—and her eyes got really big. "You have a new beau then?"

"No, I'm not seeing anyone right now." This was basically the truth, although before he left town, Hurley and I had "seen" each other in every way possible.

"No one knows yet," I said, anxious to move on and willing to tell this little white lie. "I've been keeping it to myself up until now." As soon as the words left my mouth, I knew I'd made a huge mistake. Priscilla's eyes grew huge. Being the first person to know a juicy tidbit of gossip is like instant fame in Sorenson. I knew that the first chance she got, Priscilla would be triggering a phone tree that spread news faster than a packed room full of sneezers can spread a cold. "Please don't tell anyone yet," I begged. "Can you wait until Tuesday at least?"

She gave me a noncommittal smile and shrugged. "Who's the lucky daddy?"

Like I'd tell her that now. "No one you know," I said with a dismissive wave, thinking this one might not be a lie. I mean there was a teeny, tiny, snowball's chance in hell that she didn't know Hurley, though I suspect his arrival in town was widely known minutes after his first appearance. A handsome, single guy like Hurley would have better luck sneaking into Fort Knox unnoticed than he would into Sorenson. I was willing to bet that within days of his arrival, all the single women in town were looking at him as if they'd been starving for months and he was a huge hunk of cheesecake, all the married women in town were looking at him as a potential dalliance or some entertaining eye candy, and all the men in town were probably looking at him like they wished they could either kill him or be him.

"Well, let me show you some things," Priscilla said, letting the prying go for the time being. She propped her elbow in one hand, her chin in the other, and eyed me from head to toe. "You are so . . . tall. I might have to special order some stuff for you. But let's see what we can find." She spun around and headed for the racks of clothing. Then, proving that Priss knew a big challenge when she saw one, she said, "Let's start with some tops before we try to tackle the pants."

The first tops she showed me were made from stretchy, knitted fabrics that clung to the body. "Priscilla, I never wore clingy stuff before I was pregnant, and I don't want to start now. Don't you have something that hangs loose?"

Priscilla eyed my ample chest with a frown, and after a few seconds, she said, "Maybe we need to get you some new bras first. You always were big-busted, and being pregnant only makes them bigger."

"Tell me about it," I said, rolling my eyes. I put my arms in a chicken dance position and ran the backs of my hands along the sides of my boobs. "And they've been aching lately," I said. "Is that normal?"

"Oh, yes," she said. "And it will get worse." Priscilla dragged a measuring tape out of her pocket and proceeded to hug me as she tried to get the tape around my chest. To say it was awkward would be an understatement, but I held my breath and forced myself to tolerate it, knowing that in a few months I'd be losing any sense of privacy and dignity I ever had when I hit the delivery room.

Priscilla then steered me into a back area where there were dozens of different bra styles on display. It was quite an assortment, with materials that ranged from soft and stretchy to sleek and shiny. There were colored ones and patterned ones, and most were bedecked with tiny flowers or ribbon decorations of some type. They were very feminine and sexy-looking. Unfortunately, Priscilla zipped right past all of these and went straight for the industrial-strength, no-nonsense bras that came in basic white and looked like they could contain a nuclear blast.

"Here we go," she said, grabbing something that looked like the slingshot Goliath should have had when he met David. "You might as well invest in a good nursing bra." Then she arched her brows again and said, "I'm sorry. I shouldn't assume anything. Are you planning on breast feeding?"

"I hope to," I said.

"Oh, good." Priscilla sounded relieved. "Breast milk is so healthy for newborns. It gives them immunity and nutrition that no formula can provide." She leaned and dropped her voice to a whisper. "And nursing will help you shed those pregnancy pounds so much faster."

That alone was reason enough for me. But I hadn't sorted out all the logistics yet. "I'll be able to take some time off after the birth, but eventually I'll need to return to work, so I suppose I'll need one of those breast pump thingies."

"Got you covered," Priscilla said, and then she disappeared through a door that led into a storage area at the back of the store.

Despite all my years of working as a nurse, I've never done obstetrics other than a rotation in nursing school that lasted a few weeks. For many of my fellow students, obstetrics was the ultimate dream job. To me it was the last place on earth I'd want to work. The women in labor screamed. The newborn babies screamed. Working an obstetrics unit was an endless cycle of screaming and crotches. I did help my sister some after each of her children were born, but it was mostly a token effort. Desi seemed born for motherhood, and she took to it as naturally as I took to ice cream. Consequently, I had no idea how to use a breast pump. I knew they existed because other women I'd worked with had taken breaks to go and pump, but beyond that I was clueless.

So when Priscilla returned armed with several boxes that had pictures of scary-looking contraptions on the front that resembled miniature versions of the life-sucking machine from *The Princess Bride*, I felt more than a little intimidated.

Priscilla grabbed a box and held it out to me. "This double pump is my top-of-the-line model and the one I used with my kids. It retails for three-ninety-nine, but I can let you have it for three-seventy-five."

"Four hundred bucks for a breast pump?" I said aghast.

"If you prefer the manual type, they're less than a hundred. But they don't get the job done nearly as well."

"I think I'm getting ahead of myself here," I said. "Let's stick to clothing for now. I've got plenty of time to think about breast pumps."

"Very well," Priscilla sniffed. She looked hurt. I didn't care. "Why don't you go into the dressing room and try that bra on?"

I did as instructed and took the bra she'd given

me into the dressing room. Surprisingly, it fit quite well, although the little trap doors in the cups threw me for a few seconds. I kept it on, pulled my blouse back on, and stuffed my old bra into my purse. Then I headed out to try and appease Priscilla's hurt feelings. "This is perfect," I told her. "Do you have another one?"

"Not here in the store, but I can order you as many as you like," she said. "You might want to wait before buying too many of them, though, because your cup size is likely to change several times in the coming months."

"Oh, okay."

"Let's go look at some more tops."

She gathered up some cute tops with empire waists that had plenty of free-flowing material beneath the bust line. But by the time I found one that fit my bust, the bottom part looked like a tent. "Look at this," I said in a disgusted voice, grabbing handfuls of all the free-hanging material around my gut. "I could hide a Bedouin, his harem, and all his camels inside this thing."

Priscilla gave me a patient, tolerant smile. "It's not that bad," she assured me. "Right now it looks like a lot of excess, but by the time you get into your third trimester, it's going to seem downright snug."

Snug? Really? I stared at the billowing yards of material in horror.

I finally opted for four tents, one tight, stretchy screw-it-I'm-pregnant-and-not-afraid-to-show-it T-shirt that I wouldn't wear until my pregnancy was more obvious, and a double tank top so I could continue my workouts. I also tried on and bought one dress. I don't have too many occasions to dress up, but I thought I should have at least one option to start with.

We moved on to the pants. Priscilla had an impressively varied selection, including a number of tall sizes. She wisely started me off with some elastic-waist jeans that had the little front panel that's made to expand along with one's tummy. When I tried these on with one of the tops I'd picked out, the panel was well hidden, and the overall look wasn't too bad. Then I made the mistake of trying on a pair of dressier slacks made out of some thin, stretchy material that clung to every nook and cranny of my legs. When I turned around to look at the rear view and lifted the top I had on, I nearly cried.

I headed out of the dressing room and displayed myself to Priscilla. "I've been working out at the gym for months in an effort to manage my weight and get in shape. And this," I waved a hand around my butt, "is what I get for my efforts? My ass is so big if they shot me into space I'd trigger an eclipse."

"That's just pregnancy butt," Priscilla said with a dismissive wave of her hand. "It happens to everyone."

I looked at her with an expression of disbelief, trying not to cry.

"That particular material might not be the best choice," she admitted. "Go try the gray ones. I think they will work better for you."

I scuttled back into the dressing room and stripped off the offending pants, tossing them onto the built-in seat. I also took the top off and hung it on a hook. When I bent over to put on the gray pants, I felt a gas bubble shift in my gut. As I pulled on the second leg and straightened up, the bubble shifted again. But it felt different somehow, more intentional, more purposeful, less random. And then it hit me. I'd just felt my baby move for the first time.

Goose bumps raced down my spine, and a swell of love and amazement overcame me. Smiling like an idiot, I burst out of the dressing room and practically yelled to Priscilla, "I just felt it move for the first time!"

Unfortunately, I had forgotten to put my top back on, so all I was wearing from the waist up was my new bra. And just as unfortunate was the fact that my mind was so overwhelmed with emotion that it didn't register the tinkle of the bell, or the sound of Brahms' Lullaby playing. Priscilla was no longer alone. As I stood staring at her and the male sales rep who had just entered the store, they stared back, all of us speechless. That's when one of my bra's little trapdoors—its hook apparently loosened by all my twisting and turning—decided to fall open.

I had just created a whole new nipple incident.

Chapter 14

I quickly slapped a hand over my exposed breast, muttered some half-assed apology, and slunk my way back into the dressing room. I fixed the bra and put on my own clothes. Then I sat down on the built-in seat and waited. I wasn't coming out of that dressing room until the salesman left, even if it meant I had to live in there for a few days.

After what seemed like an eternity, and after I'd dug through my purse looking for anything I might be able to use to pee in, I heard Brahms start to play again. Moments later Priscilla hollered, "You can come out now."

Miss Priss was wearing an amused smirk on her face, but it didn't look malicious. "That's another thing you'll have to get used to," she said. "Embarrassing moments are a dime a dozen both during pregnancy and once you have the kids."

"I'm scared to do this with one kid," I told her. "How on earth do you manage things with six?"

Priscilla shrugged. "Sometimes I think kids are like dogs: it's easier when you have more than one, though

I have to admit that Billy and I might have exceeded the number where the advantages outweigh the disadvantages. And then there's the expense. It seems we can never get ahead on our budget. Just when we think things are starting to look better, one of the kids needs new clothes, or some medicine, or the car dies. I keep thinking I should close down the store, or hire someone to manage it so I can stay home with the kids, but we need the extra money the store brings in, and hiring a manager will eat all my profits."

"Aren't you supposed to make me feel better about this?" I said, picturing tired, bedraggled-looking Mrs. Fitzpatrick in my mind.

Priscilla shrugged and smiled. "Parenting is the most rewarding job you'll ever do, but don't be mistaken; the demands are never-ending, not just on your money but also on your time and your sanity. It was easier when the kids were all little because I could just bring them here for the day and let them play in the store. But now that they're all in school, they want to participate in sports and after-school activities. Every one of those requires some type of financial investment. And then there's the mechanics of just getting them all to where they need to be. My eldest just got his driver's license, so that helps a little because he can help with some of the logistics . . . not that he wants to," she added with a roll of her eyes. "But we had to buy another car so he could drive the kids around. Between trying to run this place and getting to all the parent teacher conferences, the PTA meetings, the class trips I get cajoled into chaperoning—it never ends. If it wasn't for friends and family, Billy and I would have lost our minds years ago."

"Any regrets?"

She shook her head and smiled. "Not a one. Every one of my kids is special in their own unique way, and I can't imagine my life without any of them." She nodded toward my tummy. "You felt it, didn't you? That first quickening changes the way you feel about everything."

I nodded and smiled. "A definite emotional high," I said. I handed over the stack of clothes I was holding and added, "Now ring me up and bring me back down to reality."

While Priscilla bagged my purchases, I went outside and pulled my hearse into the alley that ran behind the store. I didn't want anyone who might be driving by to see me exiting The Mother Hood with what was clearly a new wardrobe. Yes, the news would travel fast, and I had my doubts about Priscilla's ability to wait until Tuesday to start spreading it, as I'd asked, but I figured it was better to do all I could to prevent any speculation. Even if Priscilla could hold out until Tuesday, it would only be if no one asked her anything. If someone saw me leave her store and called her to ask why I was there, I knew she wouldn't be able to stay mum about me becoming a mum. Loading my purchases behind the store was my version of an antibiotic, an attempt to slow the spreading infection of gossip. Unfortunately, gossip behaves more like a virus, and my efforts were likely to be a waste of time, much as treating a virus with antibiotics is a waste of time.

Priscilla met me at the back door and helped me load everything into the back of the vehicle. "Are you going to keep this after you have the baby?" she asked, eyeing the hearse as I closed the tailgate. I could tell from her expression that she hoped my answer would be no, but I was about to disappoint her.

"Sure. Why wouldn't I? It runs well, it has relatively low mileage, and there is plenty of room inside for both a kid and a dog. Plus I like the color."

Priscilla looked a little horrified but said nothing more. After thanking me and telling me to come back anytime, she backed into her store—never taking her eyes off the car—and shut the door. A second later I heard her throw three different locks. By the time I got behind the wheel, I felt certain Miss Priss was on the phone already, spreading her news.

Chapter 15

As I was about to pull out, my cell phone rang. I saw it was Izzy and thought someone else must have died, meaning we had another call. I was half right.

"Hey, Izzy, what's up?"

"I need to cancel our dinner plans for tonight. Dom's father had a heart attack and died, so we're heading for Iowa."

"Oh, no," I said, hoping I sounded genuinely saddened by the news, because my feelings on the topic were mixed. While I could never be happy about anyone dying, particularly the relative of a close friend, my relief at getting out of dinner and The Talk with Izzy was huge. "Is Dom okay?"

"I think so, but you know how things were with his dad. Their relationship was complicated."

That was an understatement. The only person in Dom's family who was at all understanding or supportive of his lifestyle was his mother. His father and brothers didn't approve, and they made it known any time Dom and Izzy visited. The situation was made even more difficult because Dom's father had been an alcoholic who often got mean when he drank.

"Give Dom a hug for me," I said.

"I will. I've made arrangements for Gary Henderson to cover for me while I'm gone. He's a part-time assistant medical examiner in Madison, and he'll stay at the Sorenson Motel while he's covering. I briefed him on my findings in Derrick Ames's autopsy and the status of the investigation, so he should be up to speed. Will you call Bob Richmond and let him know what's going on?"

"Of course."

"Thanks. I'll check in with you once we get to Iowa and let you know what our plans are. I'm not sure when the funeral will be, but I expect we'll probably be there for the week."

"Don't worry about it. Take as long as you need. I'll stay on top of things here and make sure Henderson stays informed with our progress in the investigation."

"Thanks, Mattie. And with regard to the other thing, we'll talk when I get back. In the meantime, good luck with Hurley."

"Thanks."

I disconnected the call and then placed one to Richmond. "Hey, Mattie, what's up?"

I filled him in on Izzy's news.

"That's a bummer about Dom's dad."

"Yeah, it is. Do you know anything about this Dr. Henderson guy?"

"As a matter of fact, I do. I worked with him years ago when I was in Madison."

"What's he like?"

"He's kind of big on adhering to the rules, and he

can be a bit of a stickler for details, but otherwise he's okay."

"So is Izzy, so that shouldn't be a problem for me. I'm used to it." Despite my cavalier tone, I had concerns about working with someone new. It's never easy adapting to someone else's work style, and the only person I've worked this job with is Izzy. He and I fell into an easy rhythm early on, and we've grown comfortable with one another and with our work routines. And Izzy has been imminently patient with me as I've learned the ins and outs of my new career. Throwing someone new into the mix, someone who might be difficult to work with, was a complication I could have done without.

"I'm glad you called because I was going to call you in a little while anyway. I've got a schedule of sorts put together for tomorrow. Blake Sutherland called me back and agreed to come in and talk to me at nine. Wendy and her sons, along with their lawyer, will be coming in at ten. And at some point tomorrow I want to go to the school to talk with Derrick's coworkers."

"Is Blake Sutherland coming alone, or did she lawyer up?"

"As far as I know she's coming alone because she thinks the only reason I need to talk to her is to verify information about Wendy. Plus I'm guessing she's trying to keep her trip here as low profile as possible so her hubby doesn't find out. I'm not sure she knows she's on my suspect list, though to be honest, she isn't very high on it."

"Sounds like a busy day. Where and what time should we meet up?"

"Why don't we meet at the police station around eight?"

"Can we do eight-thirty? Given that there will be someone new in our office, I feel like I should be there first thing to make sure the transition goes smoothly."

"Eight-thirty is fine."

"Great. I don't think it will be a problem with Henderson if I work with you tomorrow, but if there is a death during the night, all bets are off." I winced again at my metaphorical slip, even as I conjured up a mental image of gambling chips being scooped off a blackjack table. I could feel the rough texture of the felt-covered table, hear the sound of cards snapping down, smell the smoke-tinged, badly filtered air. I had a sudden overwhelming urge to head for the casino, and had I not been on call, I might have caved and gone.

"Let me know if something does come up."

"Will do."

Now that I was off the hook for The Talk later today, I decided to stop in and visit my sister, Desi, and deliver my news before she heard it from someone else. At some point I would have to either call or visit my mother for the same reason, but I wasn't ready to face that yet.

I called Desi, and she answered on the first ring.

"Hey, sis, any chance you've got room for one more at your dinner table tonight?"

"For you, always," she told me. "How soon can you be here? I've got baked macaroni and cheese and a meat loaf ready to come out of the oven in about fifteen minutes."

I made it there in five.

Even though I hadn't been to my sister's house or

seen any of the family for a little over a month, when I arrived I went in without knocking. Desi's kids, Erika and Ethan, were in the living room watching the last few minutes of the movie *Independence Day* on TV with their father, Lucien. All three acknowledged my arrival, Erika and Ethan with, "Hi, Aunt Mattie," and Lucien with his standard, "Hey, Mattiekins."

I responded with a generic, "Hi, guys," and then followed the enticing aromas to the kitchen.

"Hey, you," Desi said with a smile. She set the microwave to nuke two bags of corn and then came over and gave me a big hug. When she released me, she stood back, cocked her head to one side, and stared at my chest. "Your boobs are bigger," she said, finally looking at my face.

I smiled. "Yes, they are."

Desi clapped a hand over her mouth, and her eyes grew huge. After a few seconds she said, "Oh my God. Are you pregnant?"

"Wow, you sure know how to steal someone's thunder." I watched the emotions play over Desi's face: excitement, curiosity, worry. Her hand dropped away from her mouth, and she stammered for a few seconds. Then she lunged at me and hugged me again. When she stepped back she finally managed to get one word out.

"Hurley?"

I nodded. "He doesn't know yet. I've been talking to him on the phone regularly since he left town, but I want to give him the news in person, so I can see how he reacts. He's supposed to be back tomorrow, and I'm going to tell him then."

"Are you worried?"

"A little," I admitted. "This business with Emily and

Kate really shook him up. He must have said a dozen times how he never wanted to be a father, and how if he'd wanted kids he would have had them, yadda yadda yadda."

"But that was different," Desi said. "Finding out so many years after the fact that you have a kid has to be a bit unsettling."

"True, but I don't think doubling his trouble is going to help any."

"I'm betting he'll be delighted. In fact, I can already hear the wedding bells," Desi said, ignoring my doubts.

"Oh, no, I'm not going to marry him."

"What?" Desi reared back as if she'd been slapped. "Why not?"

"I couldn't in good conscience. I'd always feel like I trapped him into it, and I'd spend my life wondering if he would have wanted to marry me anyway if not for the kid."

"That's ridiculous," Desi said, turning away in response to the timer on the oven going off. "Even with the little time I've spent with Hurley, it's obvious the guy is nuts about you. Heck, when Emily went to the waterpark with us, she even said so."

"Really?"

"Yes, really."

"But he told me he felt blindsided when he found out about Emily."

"Different circumstances," Desi said, donning hot mitts and opening the oven door. "Besides, Kate did you a favor by prepping him ahead of time for the whole fatherhood thing. I'm telling you, he'll be fine with it." She took the bubbling-hot dish of macaroni and cheese out of the oven and placed it on top of the stove. Then she went back for the meat loaf. "Have you told Mom yet?"

"No, and I'm not looking forward to the task. I still remember the histrionics she went through when you told her you were pregnant with Erika." I clapped a hand over my heart and mimicked my mother. "Oh, no," I said in classic, melodramatic Sarah Bernhardt style. "Surely my end is in sight. Being a grandmother is like having one foot in the grave. I can feel my arteries hardening and my bones creaking as we stand here."

Desi and I both laughed, and then she added, "Then there was that whole 'I hope you don't expect me to babysit' speech, followed by the list of childhood illnesses she might be exposed to." Desi closed the oven door with her foot and carried the meat loaf into the dining room. Then she came back and grabbed the macaroni and cheese. "It's a wonder you and I are normal at all," she said, setting the casserole dish on the dining room table.

The microwave dinged, so I made myself useful by taking the packages of corn out, dumping them in a bowl, and tossing a large pat of butter on top of it all. "I don't know," I said. "I think calling myself normal might be a stretch at times."

"There are days when I feel that way, too," Desi said with a smile. Then the smile faltered. "I mean I feel that way about me, not you," she clarified.

"I knew what you meant."

"Can we share your news with Lucien and the kids?" she asked.

I shrugged. "Might as well. I don't want it to get out before I have a chance to tell Hurley, but unfortunately

I went shopping at The Mother Hood today, and I'm betting Miss Priss will be spreading the word in no time. I just have to hope Hurley hears it from me first rather than someone else."

Desi grabbed me and gave me a big hug. "I'm so excited for you, Mattie!"

Her enthusiasm was contagious, and by the time we headed in to the dining room to call everyone to dinner, I had a huge grin on my face that I couldn't seem to contain. Even if we hadn't agreed to share my news, Lucien and the kids would have known something was up just from my demeanor.

I had thought we might wait until the end of the meal to make the announcement, but Desi was busting at the seams and couldn't wait. The news was met with general delight by all, especially Erika, who was eager to know if I'd let her babysit. Throughout the meal our conversation revolved around the baby: did I know the gender yet, was I going to find out, had I thought about names? Oddly, no one asked who the father was, and the subject of marriage didn't come up. I wasn't sure if that was because the answers were assumed, or because everyone felt awkward about asking. A few months ago, I would have assumed the former because there were no limits on the topics Lucien might bring up or ask about. Back then he never seemed to have any regard for politeness, political correctness, or even simple respect for someone else's feelings. He couldn't speak to me without coming out with a crass comment or some dicey bit of sexual innuendo. Nowadays, his behavior bordered on normal. Even his appearance had improved. Whereas he used to dress in wrinkled, worn, and stained clothing, and typically slicked his hair back with enough grease to lube the hearse several times over, he was now dressed in a clean shirt and khakis, and his hair looked clean and grease-free.

This new Lucien both heartened and saddened me. He was a changed man, a black-and-white version of his once much more colorful self. I knew these changes were for Desi's benefit, and so far it seemed to be working. Yet as much as I hated to admit it, I kind of missed that old Lucien. There had been something oddly endearing about him, crass and crude as he was. And that old personality was a big part of his success as a lawyer. I wondered if the new Lucien would still be as clever, crafty, and persistent.

Though the subject of fatherhood didn't come up, things still got plenty awkward. Ethan, looking all innocent and curious, stayed quiet through much of the discussion. Then, when there was a brief lull in the conversations, he said, "So you have a baby in your tummy?"

"Yes, I do," I said smiling.

"How did it get in there?"

"Um . . ." I looked to Desi for help while Erika sniggered.

Then Lucien said, "I'll explain it to you after supper."

At that, Desi and I stared at one another with matching expressions of horror. Lucien had done the facts of life talk with Erika, and while none of us witnessed the actual talk, we know he used a store-bought turkey to help demonstrate. Come prep time for Thanksgiving dinner, Erika wanted to know how we got the little package inside the turkey to come out when the long, squirty thing hadn't even been used yet.

Desi saved Ethan from a similar fate when she said, "That's okay, Lucien. I got this one."

I ate until I felt I was about to burst. Sated and happy, I wanted to stay and hang out for a while, but I knew Hoover needed to be let out soon. As I prepared to leave, Lucien took me aside.

"I am very excited for you, Mattiekins," he said. "You deserve some happiness."

"Thanks, Lucien."

"Don't let this Hurley guy get away. He seems like a good one. I never did like David."

Now he tells me. "Thanks, Lucien. And if there's anything I can do for you, just let me know."

He grabbed my hand and stuffed something into it. When I looked, I saw it was a check for two thousand dollars. "I know it's not much," Lucien said. "But I intend to pay back every cent you gave me. You don't know how much it meant to both me and Desi that you were willing to help us out."

"Lucien, you don't need to pay me back."

"Yes, I do. And don't you dare destroy that check. It's part of my new resolution to pay all my debts. I've picked up some work, and things are slowly turning around for me. So please, take it."

I could tell from his anxious, earnest expression that accepting his payback was important to him. "Okay. And thank you, Lucien."

"No, thank *you*." Then he did the most unexpected thing. He gave me a kiss on the cheek, a perfectly nice, nonsexual, brotherly type of kiss.

I left the house and sat behind the wheel of my car for a minute or two, trying to decide if I should deliver the news to my mother in person or over the phone. I didn't relish the task either way because I knew she wasn't going to be happy. It was bad enough that I'd divorced a doctor, which to her was proof of my stupidity and insanity. Never mind that fact that he cheated on me. Now I had made things worse by getting knocked up by a man who made less than a hundred grand a year, and who held a job that my mother perceived as having little to no prestige or social value. Ironically, despite her four failed marriages, my mother considers herself something of a relationship guru, spouting out her Rules for Wives, a list of behaviors and acts that she swears are the secrets to achieving a happy marriage. However, my mother's definition of a happy marriage is the polar opposite of mine. For her it's all about financial stability, social standing, and cleanliness. For me it's all about love, trust, fidelity, and friendship, which is why I had decided not to marry Hurley even if he asked. I felt I'd already betrayed his trust and friendship by getting pregnant in the first place, even though I hadn't planned to do so.

I finally opted for the chicken way out and decided it would be easier to hang up on my mother if she went berserk and launched a tirade than it would be to walk out on her. I'd call her when I got home.

My decision stayed firm long enough for me to start the car and pull into the street. Then I started thinking it might be easier to call Mom in the morning. One turn later I was seriously considering letting Desi or the town gossips inform her, thereby giving Mom time to cool down and accept things before I talked to her. But I knew it would be too cruel to let her find out the news from someone else that way, so by the time I turned into my driveway, I was back to my decision to get it over with and call her as soon as I was in the house.

I pulled up and parked in my usual spot beside the cottage, glanced at the darkened windows on Izzy's house, and thought about Dom, his father, and their difficult relationship, and me, my mother, and our difficult relationship. Family sure had a way of complicating life.

I took the keys from the ignition, got out of the car, and went around to open the back so I could unload my purchases from The Mother Hood. As I tried to juggle my purse and the hatch latch, I dropped my keys on the ground. Cursing, I bent down to get them.

That's when one of the car windows exploded.

Chapter 16

It took me a second to realize what was happening, but I recognized the sound that came with the breaking glass. Someone was shooting at me! The bullet had shattered the rear driver-side window and the ceiling light. I scrambled around on the ground, moving to the other side of the car, away from the woods and the direction the shot seemed to have come from. Then I reached into my purse and pulled out my cell phone.

I flipped it open and quickly dialed 911, listening as I did so for the sound of someone approaching. All I could hear was my own ragged breathing and Hoover's frantic barks inside. I crab-walked to the front passenger door and had a hold on the handle when the 911 operator answered.

"This is Mattie Winston. I'm at my house, and someone is shooting at me! I need help. Please hurry!" I rattled off the address and listened as the operator quickly dispatched the police. Then she came back and asked me if I knew who it was. "No, I can't see anyone. They shot at me when I was unloading the back of my hearse, and it shattered the window. I think the shot came from the woods to the south."

"I've dispatched the officers, and they should be there momentarily."

Just then another shot hit the rear fender. I felt trapped squatting beside my car, but the door of my cottage was too exposed and too far away to make a run for it. I got down on my hands and knees and peered underneath the hearse. I saw the lower half of a human shape emerge from the woods about twenty-five feet behind the car, someone wearing jeans and bright white running shoes. After some quick thought, I reached up and opened the passenger-side door, uttering a silent *thank you* to the shooter for doing in my overhead interior light. I wormed my way onto and across the front seat, keeping my body low so I wasn't visible through the windows. My hands were shaking horribly, and it took me several tries before I was able to slide my key into the ignition. I started the engine, shifted the car into reverse, pulled my feet up so that I was in a fetal position, and pushed on the gas pedal with my hand.

My parking space was a straight shot from the driveway, and I did my best to keep the wheels straight as the car roared backward and headed down the drive. Another shot fired, and I shielded my head with my arm as more glass came flying in on top of me. Then there was a loud thud, and the car jumped and bumped over something. At first I thought I'd gone off the pavement and into the dirt alongside the driveway, but the car was still moving. It seemed like an eternity until everything came to a body-jarring halt amid the screech and squeal of crunching metal and another rainfall of broken glass. The passenger-side front door, which I had left open, banged closed as my body slammed into the back of the front seat.

I lay there for a few seconds, trying to figure out if I should slink back out of the car, sit up, or just stay where I was. That's when I heard the sirens closing in. I breathed a sigh of relief and remained on my side, lying on the seat and waiting.

Moments later I heard the squeal of braking tires. The interior of the hearse was lit up with flashes of blue and red light. I heard a man yell, "Don't move!" and nearly smiled with relief when I recognized the voice as Junior Feller's.

"It's me . . . Mattie," I yelled, waving one arm up so it could be seen through what was left of my windows. "I'm here in the hearse." I didn't know if I was the one Junior was yelling at, so I figured it was smart to play it safe. I heard another male voice yell, "We're clear!" and then the passenger-side door at my feet was wrenched open. I rose up to see who it was, half afraid I'd see that shadowy figure standing there, aiming a gun at my head. What I saw instead shocked me nearly as much.

"Mattie? Jesus, are you okay?"

"Hurley? Oh my God, Hurley!" I wriggled myself out of the car and threw myself at him. I don't think I've ever been so happy to see him. He wrapped his arms around me, held me close, and I instantly felt safe, secure, and happy. "What are you doing here?" I asked, the words a bit garbled from having my face squished against his neck.

"I got home early. I dropped Emily off at the house and was on my way here to surprise you when I heard the radio call go out for shots fired at your address. What the hell is going on?"

Reluctantly, I pulled back from the warmth and security of his hold and looked up at his face. Lord, I adored this man. The mere sight of him filled me with a mix of longing, lust, and dare I say it . . . love.

"I don't know exactly," I told him. "When I got home and started unloading stuff from the hearse, I dropped my keys. Good thing I did because the first shot came when I bent down to pick them up. Had I stayed standing, I probably would have been hit."

"Why is someone shooting at you?"

"How would I know?" I shot back, sounding as frustrated and frightened as I felt. "I've been getting these strange calls lately, calls where no one says anything. And there's a car that I think might have been following me. But I don't know if those things are related."

"Someone made threatening phone calls to you?"

"Not threatening exactly. Just calls where I can tell someone is on the line but they never say anything. After several seconds they hang up."

Bob Richmond had arrived along with a swarm of officers, and they were all milling about: putting up roadblocks, congregating in my driveway, and examining the hearse. I looked around and realized that my car had gone all the way down the driveway and into the street below, crossing it and hitting a telephone pole.

Junior Feller emerged from the crowd and approached us, a grim look on his face. "Welcome back, Hurley," he said.

"Thanks. I wasn't planning on getting back into things quite this way, but . . ." He shrugged. "Did you guys get whoever was shooting at Mattie?"

"Um, no, not exactly," Junior said, rubbing his chin. "It looks like Mattie did."

"What?" I said, thinking I must have misheard him. "What do you mean?"

"There's a dead man in your driveway. A few feet away from him is a gun that smells like it was recently fired."

"He's dead?" I said, aghast. Then I recalled the thud followed by the bump-jump of the hearse as it was barreling down the driveway.

"It looks like you ran him over with that behemoth you drive," Junior said, verifying my suspicion.

I let out a hysterical little laugh triggered by my appreciation for the irony as well as my relief. Then I remembered that at one time I had thought the person making the phone calls might have been my father. Was the person following me the same person? And was that my shooter? Or were they all different people? That didn't make sense to me; it was too coincidental. But if it had been my father who was both calling and following me, was there a reason why he would shoot at me? Was he disturbed, or mean, or crazy and my mother just never told me? Was that why she would never talk about him? Had I just killed my own father?

"I need to see him," I said.

"I'm not sure that's a good idea," Junior countered.

"I don't care. I have to see him. Please."

Junior looked at Hurley. So did I, giving him my best pleading look. "Hurley, remember the night Emily was here and there was someone peeking in the windows of my cottage?"

He nodded, and then a look dawned over his face.

"You said your mother thought the drawing Emily did of that man looked like your father," he said, and I nodded.

"The weird phone calls started days after that."

"What weird phone calls?" Junior asked.

It didn't take Hurley long to make the connection. "You think your father's been calling you?"

I ignored Junior and answered Hurley instead. "I do, or at least I did. I thought it might have been him who was following me, too."

"Wait, someone has been following you?" Junior said, sounding exasperated. "Why didn't you say something?"

"I wasn't sure," I told him. "And even if someone was following me, I didn't think it was anyone dangerous. I thought . . ." I didn't finish the sentence; my horror at the obvious conclusion struck me momentarily dumb.

"You think you might have just killed your father," Hurley finished for me.

I nodded, still unable to speak.

"Oh, geez," Junior said, raking a hand through his hair.

I pushed myself away from Hurley and tried to peer through the crowd of cops standing near the top of the driveway. I could make out the vague outline of someone lying on the ground clad in jeans and bright white running shoes. I started walking in that direction.

Hurley stayed beside me and wrapped an arm over my shoulders, pulling me close. Together we climbed the incline of the driveway, and when we reached the crowd near the top, they parted and let us have a look.

"Oh, my," I said.

I didn't need any pictures to know that the dead man wasn't my father. The man on the ground was thin, blond, and didn't look much older than me. No way was he my father, nor did he bear any resemblance to the man in the drawing Emily had done. "It's not him," I said, sighing with relief.

"Then who is it?" Junior asked.

I stared at the face, searching my memory banks for any hint of familiarity. Finally I shrugged. "I have no idea." I shuddered, and Hurley pulled me a little closer.

One of the uniformed cops came traipsing out of the woods that separated my house from David's. "There's a car parked over at the next house," he said. "An older model, black Volvo sedan. We ran the plates, and they came back as stolen. I'm guessing it was what this guy was driving."

Hurley looked over at Richmond. "You want to take it?"

"Sure," he said with a shrug. He grabbed two of the other uniformed cops, and they disappeared into the woods.

Junior said, "Where's Izzy?"

"He's out of town. Dom's father died. He arranged for someone to cover for him, a Dr. Gary Henderson. He's supposed to be staying at the Sorenson Motel. I have his number in my phone, which I think is on the floor of my car. I dropped it when I hit the pole."

"I'll get it," Junior said, and he jogged back down the driveway. That left me and Hurley alone . . . if you didn't count the dead man.

"Bob looks good," Hurley said.

"Yeah, he does," I agreed. "He's been working really hard at it."

"You look really good, too," he said, switching his gaze to me. "I've missed you, Winston."

"I missed you, too." I slid out from beneath his arm. "But we still need to keep things low key. And we have to talk. In private. I need to tell you some things."

Hurley smiled and looked at me with a curious expression. "Private sounds good to me," he said.

I almost let myself slip into romantic mode, but the sound of Hoover's desperate barks brought me back to my senses . . . that and the dead man at our feet. I looked at him again. "He had to have been the one who was following me. I wonder if he was the one behind the phone calls, too. I really thought it was my father trying to reconnect with me but not knowing how." I couldn't hide the disappointment I felt . . . or the fear.

"What did the car that was following you look like?" Hurley asked.

"It was hard to tell because it was always nighttime when I saw it. It was either dark blue or black, and it was some kind of boxy sedan. Other than that, I don't have a clue. I can't even tell you for sure who was driving it. Maybe I was just being paranoid. Maybe there was no one following me."

"Well, your description of the car you thought might be following you fits the one the guys found next door. So I'd say your paranoia was justified because someone was definitely out to get you." Hurley looked at me with a soft smile and a worried bend in his brows. "Are you sure you're okay? Does your stomach hurt? Maybe we should take you to the hospital to get checked out."

I realized I was rubbing a hand over my tummy and stopped doing it, dropping my hand to my side. "Just a few lingering butterflies," I said, looking off into the woods. I didn't trust myself at that moment to look Hurley in the eye. "I'm sure it's just some left-over adrenaline. I'm fine. I was lying down on the front seat, and I didn't hit anything in the car when it stopped. I promise you, I'm okay."

From behind us a female voice said, "Oh, my, what happened here?"

I whirled around, recognizing the voice immediately. "Alison, what are you doing here?"

"Covering a story, of course," she said. Then in a chastising tone she added, "Though I have to say I was hoping you'd be a source for my stories rather than the subject." She shifted her gaze to Hurley and gave him a warm smile. "Nice to have you back in town, Detective Hurley."

"Thanks." Hurley didn't look any happier than I did to see Alison.

"Can you guys tell me what's going on here?" Alison asked, looking over at the dead man in my driveway. "I heard a call go out on my scanner for shots fired. I would have been here sooner, but I had to get my neighbor to stay with my mom first."

I had momentarily forgotten about Alison's mother and her illness. "How is she doing?" I asked.

Alison shrugged. "Okay, I guess. She has good days and bad days. Today was one of her bad days."

Given my prior history with Alison, I couldn't help but wonder if she was exaggerating the truth to garner sympathy from me. If she was, it was working. "I'm sorry," I said. Then I looked over at Hurley. "Alison's mother was recently diagnosed with ALS."

"I'm sorry to hear that, Alison," he said. "I've heard it's an unpleasant disease."

Alison nodded grimly. "That it is," she said. "Anyway, are you guys going to give me anything here?"

"I'll tell you what we know so far," I said. "That man over there," I nodded toward the dead man, "shot at me. The only reason I'm alive is because I ran over him with my hearse. Any chance he looks familiar to you?"

Alison walked over closer to the dead man and stared at him for several seconds. Then she shook her head. "I have no clue," she said. "Are you saying you don't know who he is?"

"I have no clue," I told her. "I don't know who he is, or why he was shooting at me."

Hurley said, "Look, Alison, we might need to spin this story a little bit in order to sort it out. Can we count on your cooperation?"

"Sure, if you promise to keep me in the loop."

"We can do that," Hurley said, "but you have to promise that you won't publish anything unless we approve it first."

"I can do that," she said.

I wasn't sure if we could believe her, but she seemed sincere.

Junior was approaching us. He had fetched my phone from the car as well as the bags that I'd had stashed in the back. He was hauling them up the driveway toward us and started talking when he was still a few feet away. "Since we're probably going to have to tow the hearse in as evidence, I got all the stuff you had in the car," he said as he approached. He held out my shopping bags. "These fell out of the back when you hit the pole, but it doesn't look like anything was damaged." He set them on the ground at my feet, and I swear the words *The Mother Hood* glowed in the light from the various police cars.

Alison's face suddenly lit up. "You have a lot of clothes here," she said, peering into one of the bags. "Who's pregnant?"

I bit my lip and tried to come up with a lie, but I was too rattled to think of anything that made sense. This wasn't how I wanted this to go down. Alison was staring at me with an expression that resembled one of my cats when they are watching me open a can of cat food. I knew then that she knew, and that meant the jig was up. I looked Hurley dead in the eye, braced myself, and spat it out.

"I am."

Chapter 17

"You're pregnant?" Hurley said, clearly aghast. He stared at me, his mouth hanging open like the perfect flytrap.

"Yes, I am," I said. "Four months already," I added with what I hoped looked like genuine enthusiasm.

"Oh my," Alison said, with a sly grin. She looked over at Hurley. "You didn't know?"

Junior became a nervous ball of tics, shuffling his feet, wringing his hands, looking anywhere but at me or Hurley. After what seemed an interminable amount of time, Hurley took me by the arm and said, "Let's go inside and reassure your dog. You really shouldn't be involved in this investigation anyway since you're the one who killed the guy."

I winced at the harshness of his words, however true, and bent down to gather up the bags Junior had set on the ground. As soon as I had them in hand, Hurley started hauling me toward my door, where we were forced to stop. I saw that Alison was right on our heels.

"The door is locked, and my keys are still in the

hearse," I said to Hurley, speaking through tension so thick it was like a wall between us.

Hurley cussed and said, "Stay right here." He then stormed off down the driveway.

"Who is the father?" Alison asked, as soon as Hurley was gone.

"That's really none of your business," I said irritably.

"Oh, come on, Mattie," Alison pleaded. "I'm asking as a friend, not as a reporter."

"It's still none of your business," I said. "It's personal."

"Okay," she said with a resigned sigh. "But I hope it's Hurley. It's obvious that the two of you are gaga for one another."

Hurley returned with my house key in hand, and Alison, thankfully, turned and headed down the driveway toward the cops who were standing around my car. As soon as Hurley unlocked and opened the door, Hoover came bounding out, wagging his tail furiously, whining and licking my hand. After a few seconds of this he turned and did the same thing to Hurley.

"Hey, boy," Hurley said, cupping Hoover's face in his hands. "Good to see you." Hurley then rose, looked at me, and swept his arm toward the door. "After you."

I tried to read the expression on his face, but it was all shadows. So I called to Hoover and headed inside, flipping on the light as I went. I half expected Hurley to slam the door closed behind me, but it closed with slow silence, which was actually a little scarier. I went into my bedroom to deposit my bags, knowing that both cats were likely to be there and thinking I might need to use them as my defense. Hurley is deathly afraid of cats.

As expected, both Tux and Rubbish were stretched

out on the bed. They barely acknowledged my entrance, each of them opening one eye, shifting their positions slightly, and then going back to sleep. Hurley followed me but stopped just inside the bedroom door.

"You're pregnant," he said again, but a statement this time rather than a question.

"Yes, I am. I'm sorry. This isn't how I wanted you to find out."

"How long have you known?"

"A couple of months. I found out the same day you and Emily left town."

Hurley frowned and looked away. I could tell he was thinking, calculating, and when he finally looked back at me, his expression was nervous. So I decided to answer the question I thought he was too afraid to ask.

"I haven't been with anyone except you, Hurley."

Hurley raked a hand through his hair, turned around, and took two steps into the living room, then spun around and returned to his original spot. "You and I are going to have a baby." He said it with a flat tone, and the expression on his face was equally benign. I couldn't read him at all. "Why didn't you tell me sooner?"

"I wanted to do it in person. I didn't think it was the kind of news that should be delivered over the phone. Plus, you had a lot of other things on your mind with Kate and all."

"Who else knows?"

"Izzy knows. He guessed after Dom figured it out. And I told my sister and her family tonight right before I came home. Obviously the owner of the clothing store I was at today knows, so I suspect the news will get out pretty fast now."

"What did Izzy have to say about it?"

"He said we would need to talk, about the job and such. I was supposed to join him for dinner tonight, but then he got the news about Dom's father and had to leave. So I don't know what he was planning to tell me." I paused and took a breath. Hurley was still staring at me with that benign expression. "I'm really sorry this happened, Hurley. I didn't plan for it. The doctor said the antibiotics I took back in December interfered with my birth control pills. Apparently it happened that first night . . . the night Kate and Emily showed up."

Hurley smiled and gazed off at nothing. "That was one hell of a night."

"Yes, it was." I wasn't smiling, mainly because I was recalling the humiliation and depression I felt when Kate showed up and announced that Hurley was not only married to her, but the father of her teenage daughter. It wasn't hard to guess what part of that night Hurley was remembering.

"Okay," Hurley said, refocusing on me, "when should we do the deed?"

"Do the deed?"

"Yeah, when should we get hitched?"

I stared at him, utterly dumbfounded, and didn't say a word.

"Oh, should I do it all romantic like?" He got down on one knee, and I immediately turned away from him.

"Get up, Hurley. We're not going to get married."

"We're not? Is it because I don't have a ring, because I can get one."

I turned and looked back at him. He was so damned

adorable down on one knee, his face imploring. "I don't need a ring, Hurley."

"Fine," he said, rising to his feet. "No ring. But we should still get married."

"We should?"

"Yeah. We're having a kid. It's the right thing to do."

"And that's precisely why we're not doing it," I said. "I'd never be able to convince myself that you didn't marry me simply out of some sense of duty and obligation." Hurley opened his mouth, presumably to object, but I didn't let him get a word out. I had an advantage in this debate; I'd been practicing it for the past two months. "And I have several more reasons," I added quickly. "One, I don't want to lose my job, and if you and I are married, one of us is going to have to change jobs. Two, I just killed a man . . . granted he probably deserved it, but still . . . so it really isn't the time to be talking about future plans. And three, I know you felt duped, trapped, and not ready when the whole Kate and Emily thing happened, and I'm not going to do that to you. You have enough on your hands right now with Emily. And speaking of Emily, how is she going to handle the news?"

Hurley gave me a wounded look, and his lips pinched tight. He moved closer, and I resisted the two opposing urges I had: to back away from him and to run into his arms. "Look," he said, stopping a few feet away, probably because Rubbish—who was asleep on the bed with Tux, both of them oblivious to the chaos going on outside—opened one eye and stared at him. I saw Hurley shoot the cats a wary glance before he continued. "I know I said some things when Kate showed up that implied how unhappy I was with the surprise she sprang on me . . . several surprises for that matter. But you and I . . . we're different. I don't feel trapped; I feel excited about this. And as for the job situation, we can do a justice of the peace thing and keep it quiet for now. No one has to know."

"Get real, Hurley," I said, feeling my heart break. The one thing I wanted to hear from him and didn't was that he loved me. "We live in a small town where gossip spreads faster than flesh-eating bacteria and with a similar end result. We'll both be skinned alive. There's no way we could keep something like that a secret. Not only that, you're just coming off of another relationship, and I don't want to be your rebound wife."

He let out a sigh of exasperation. "Kate and I didn't have a relationship. As for Emily, she'll do fine with it. She's a great kid." He paused and cocked his head to the side, looking at me with a sad, longing expression. "I missed you, Mattie, and I—"

Whatever he was going to say next was cut short when there was a loud knock on my door. Hoover, who up until now had been sitting at our feet, his head moving back and forth as he looked at whoever was doing the talking, barked and ran for the door.

"Mattie?" It was Junior Feller yelling from outside. "Dr. Henderson is here, and he wants to talk to you."

"See?" I said, trying not to cry. "Not a good time."

I made a move to walk past him, but he grabbed my arm and stopped me. "Look, we need to discuss this," he said. "If not now, then very soon."

"I agree. But for now, can we keep things on the down-low? I don't need any more complications in my life right now."

"Is that what I am to you? Is that what *this* is to you? A complication?"

"Come on, Hurley. You know what I mean. We'll talk more about it later. Now is not the time."

"Whatever," Hurley said a bit snidely, raking his hair with his hand again. He looked confused, shell-shocked, frustrated, and a little hurt. "But it will be soon."

He let me go then, and I hurried over to the door and opened it. Junior was standing on the front porch with Gary Henderson. Hoover took one glance at them and then promptly stepped forward and started sniffing at their shoes like they were raw hamburger. Then I realized that, considering the scene outside, it might have been something frighteningly close to that he smelled, so I grabbed his collar, pulled him back inside, and told him to sit.

Gary Henderson was a tall, somewhat gangly man with wavy brown hair, hazel eyes, and a friendly smile. He was wearing rectangular-shaped glasses and was dressed in blue jeans and a plaid flannel shirt. The lumberjack outfit seemed a sharp contrast to his otherwise nerdy appearance.

"This is Mattie Winston," Junior said, nodding toward me. "Mattie, this is Dr. Gary Henderson. I briefed him on what happened, but he still needs to talk to you."

"Of course he does," I said with a smile. "Come on in."

"Actually, I'd rather not," Dr. Henderson said. "This is your home?"

"Yes. I live here, and Izzy lives in the main house."

"Yes, well," he paused, cleared his throat, and pushed his glasses up on his nose. "Given the proximity of the . . . um . . . incident to your home, this is part of our crime scene. As such, we need to secure it until we've had a chance to investigate the matter more thoroughly."

"What? Why?" I protested. It was bad enough that my car was likely to be out of service for who knew how long. Now I was going to lose my house, too?

I felt rather than heard Hurley come up behind me. I could feel the heat from his body radiating onto my back. "I don't think that's necessary," Hurley said. "I'm Detective Steve Hurley with the Sorenson Police Department. I was with Mattie when she entered the house, and the front door was locked. Everything that happened did so outside."

"Yes, well . . ." Henderson paused and pushed his glasses up again. "You know how closely we need to guard our evidentiary processes these days after that scandal in Milwaukee. And given that Ms. Winston here works closely with all of you, I think we should bring in someone from the outside to investigate this matter, both to process the evidence and to conduct the investigation."

"Are you suggesting that we're trying to hide something here?" Hurley asked, his voice surly. I suspected he was about to vent his suppressed anger from our little chat on Dr. Henderson.

"I'm not suggesting anything," Henderson said with a forced smile. "Bringing in outside investigators is as much to protect all of you as it is to protect any evidence. I'm sure the investigation will show that Ms. Winston was perfectly justified in running over the man outside."

I winced at his blunt wording, and his equally blunt tone, which somehow belied his words.

"That man she ran over was trying to kill her," Hurley said, still angry. "The guy shot at her, for

Christ's sake. Did you bother to look at her car? Clearly this was a case of self-defense."

Henderson's phony smile grew even phonier. "Now, now, detective, I understand why you're upset about this given that Ms. Winston here is a colleague of yours."

Something like that, anyway.

"And I assure you that the investigation will be done swiftly and fairly," Henderson continued in the tone of voice a parent might use on a child having a tantrum. "If what you say is true, then Ms. Winston should be exonerated in very short order. But in order to ensure that all of the evidence is processed properly and the investigation is conducted properly, we need to be very transparent and objective about things. And if you investigate this case, and Ms. Winston's coworkers process the evidence, it will appear as if you are trying to sweep things under the rug, whether you are or not."

"Are you kidding me?" Hurley seethed.

Sensing that things might get out of control rather quickly, I spun around and put a hand on his chest. Since the angle of our positions hid my other hand from view, I slid it into the belt on Hurley's pants. "It's okay, Hurley. Let it go. If you think about it, you know Dr. Henderson is right about this. I don't want any lingering doubts when the investigation is concluded. I need to have my name completely cleared, with no shadows or gossip that might taint things in the future. You understand that, don't you?"

I said these last two sentences in a tone of voice meant to make him realize I was implying more than just my own future. Just in case he didn't get it from that alone, I tugged on his belt as I said it. My gambit seemed to work. At first Hurley's hands were closed into fists, his face looked like an overripe tomato ready to explode, and his entire body was tensed, ready to spring. But by the time I finished my little tug-and-speech, I saw the spark in his eye fade and felt his body begin to relax.

I released my grip on his pants and turned back to face Dr. Henderson. "I understand completely, and I agree with you," I said, which triggered what appeared to be a genuine smile from Henderson. "We are in the middle of investigating another case at the moment. Is it all right if I continue to be a part of that?"

Henderson narrowed his eyes in thought. "Are you referring to the case Dr. Rybarceski told me about before he left town?"

I nodded, smiling at his formal use. Izthak Rybarceski was just Izzy to the rest of us. I couldn't remember the last time he was called Dr. Rybarceski by anyone, although I imagined it happened when he had to testify in court. That was one of the job duties he'd been prepping me for of late, though I hadn't yet set foot inside a courtroom. I thought I might have to in order to finalize my divorce from David, but that was all handled by lawyers. Now it appeared as though my first court appearance might be as a defendant rather than a witness. Like everything else in my life of late, this was not the way I'd planned it.

"As long as you don't have anything to do with this investigation, I don't see any reason why you can't continue with the other one," Henderson said finally. "Although we should rule out the possibility that this incident might be related to that case."

"I don't see how it could be," I told him. "We don't have a clear suspect yet, and so far my involvement in the investigation has been limited to some photography and some interviews Detective Richmond conducted with the victim's family members and associates."

"Well, while I don't discount your interpretation of the situation, I will need to talk to Detective Richmond first before I decide, to get his take on it. If he agrees with you that this shooting isn't related, then I don't see why you can't resume work on that case. However, I should probably oversee any evidence that is handled by you or anyone in your office. I'll bring in some techs from Madison to handle the evidence from this case, and they'll be working side by side with you and your coworkers as you process any evidence from your case, at least until this investigation is closed." He paused and nudged his slippery specs back up his nose again. "I will discuss all this with Dr. Rybarceski, of course, but I believe that is how we should proceed."

I heard Hurley let out a frustrated sigh behind me, and he muttered something I couldn't make out. Fearful he would work himself into a lather again, I quickly said, "I'm sure that will be fine," even though I knew it was a lie. Like Hurley, neither Richmond nor Arnie would take well to having someone from the outside looking over their shoulders, particularly Arnie, who could find a conspiracy hiding in his underwear drawer. On the up side, since Richmond was the detective in charge of the Derrick Ames case, Hurley shouldn't be impacted much by this temporary change, which was just as well given his current demeanor.

Hurley brushed past me, and for a second I was afraid he was going to deck Dr. Henderson. But he bypassed him harmlessly, muttered, "I've got things I need to do," and stalked off. It tore me up inside to watch him go, but I shoved my emotions down deep inside and refocused on Dr. Henderson.

"I guess I need to find another place to stay," I said to no one in particular.

I briefly considered my options. My sister's place was out of the question. She and Lucien were still working things out. The last thing they needed was a pregnant, emotional, possible felon complicating things. Clearly Izzy's house wasn't going to be acceptable. My mother's place didn't even bear consideration. Even without the pregnancy issue, there was her germophobia. My mother doesn't just keep her house clean, she keeps it sterile. She wears a biohazard suit every time she has to empty her vacuum cleaner bag, which, not surprisingly, is after every use, which, also not surprisingly, is several times a day. Since I had two cats and an often messy dog to take with me, it was a recipe for certain disaster. Hurley might have been a dreamy option if not for the little problem of my pregnancy, Emily, and the current tortured state of our relationship. That left me with only one other choice.

"I'll put myself up at the Sorenson Motel for now," I announced. "I need to take some clothing and such with me. Will that be okay?"

Henderson nodded. "Sure, but I want to supervise you while you pack."

"Whatever," I said, giving him a smile every bit as phony as the one he had used on me.

Henderson didn't miss the sarcasm. "Look, I know this is awkward for you, but I'm just doing my job."

He sounded sincere, and my building anger deflated faster than Hurley's hopes for the future had.

"I know that," I said, resigned to my fate. "So let's start moving and get this over with."

Henderson sent Junior to fetch Richmond and the other uniformed officers and tell them to stop whatever they were doing and focus on securing the scene. Then he got on his phone, and as he tailed me into my bedroom so I could pack some clothes, he made the necessary arrangements to have a crew come to Sorenson to handle the investigation into my shooter's death.

When he was done, he disconnected his call, slipped the phone into his shirt pocket, and then redeemed himself some when he discovered Tux and Rubbish sleeping on my bed. "Cute cats," he said. He walked over to give Rubbish a little scratch behind the ears, and my cat rolled over and offered up his belly. Before I could warn him, Henderson went to scratch that, too, and Rubbish wrapped himself around Henderson's arm the way John Hurt's alien wrapped over his face. I anticipated blood and an angry man, but to my surprise, Henderson grabbed Rubbish by the middle and scooped him off the bed into his arms. Then he used his other hand to start scratching under Rubbish's chin. Just like that my cat fell in love. If only it was that easy for people.

"Clearly you're a cat person," I said.

"I have two of my own back in Madison." Rubbish was a ball of furry putty in his hands.

"Who's looking after them while you're in Sorenson?"

"A neighbor lady. I live in a town house, and the woman next door is an elderly retired widow with nothing better to do." He shrugged. "It works out for both of us. She's a good friend. I mow her lawn, shovel her walks, and do some fix-ups around her place, and in exchange she cooks stuff for me."

"That's nice."

I dragged a suitcase out of the closet and started throwing some clothes into it, most of which I wouldn't be able to fit into much longer. I almost told Henderson then that I was pregnant, but before I could, he said, "It's a good give-and-take; Marian makes a mean lasagna." He smiled, and I got a sudden sense that he was a lonely person. Not hard to believe, given his line of work. It's a real relationship destroyer when you tell someone on your first date that you work with dead bodies on a regular basis.

"Do you have anyone special in your life, a girlfriend, or a wife?" I asked, suddenly curious.

"Not at the moment. I was engaged once, but she ended up leaving me for someone who she referred to as a real doctor."

"Ouch," I commiserated. "I know how that goes."

"How about you?" he asked, finally putting Rubbish back on the bed. The cat looked seriously annoyed by this sudden rejection. He mewled plaintively and then hopped off the bed and started weaving himself around Henderson's feet.

"I'm divorced," I told him. Then in a tone of disgust I added, "My ex is one of those real doctors."

"Ouch," he said, and after a brief shared glance, we both broke out in laughter. I was beginning to think that maybe Henderson wasn't such a bad egg after all. He helped me get the cats into their carriers, pack up food and toys for them and the dog, and haul everything I was taking with me out to the front porch. By then a state police car had arrived, and there were two troopers on-site talking with Junior, Richmond, and the others.

"Are you going to have the state guys handle the investigation?" I asked.

"For now. It makes the most sense. They're objective enough and close enough to take over things. Wait here a minute so I can talk to them, and then I'll drive you over to the motel. We can talk more about what happened here on the way."

I stood on my front porch and watched as Henderson delivered the news to Richmond and the others. They didn't look any more pleased than Hurley had. Then Henderson went over and examined my shooter's lifeless body for several minutes. Hoover watched, too, whining impatiently and looking around. I wondered if he was looking for Hurley. I was, but he was nowhere in sight.

When Henderson was done, he had a couple of uniformed guys help him get the dead man into a body bag, and then he spoke to the state troopers, who had multiplied by then. When Henderson was done doling out his instructions, which sent two of the troopers through the woods, presumably to examine the shooter's car and get it hauled away for evidence, he came back over to me, along with Richmond. "I'll take the cat carriers," he said. "Bob, can you manage the suitcases?"

Richmond looked glum, but he didn't say a word. He simply nodded, grabbed the two suitcases I had packed, and headed down the driveway. Henderson fell into step behind him with the two cat carriers under one of his lanky arms and a smaller bag that held my toiletries under the other. That left me with

Hoover, my bag of pet food and toys, and one litter box, which I had cleaned and emptied. I had no human food with me, and I realized that since I also had no car, I was going to be hungry. The closest food source to the Sorenson Motel was Dairy Airs, whose main menu items were cheesecake, ice cream, and various cheese sandwiches. It was within walking distance, and I decided I would survive just fine on what the place had to offer. I also had my cell phone and could have food delivered if necessary, though my options there were limited to one sandwich shop, a pizza parlor, and Chinese . . . pretty much my pre-pregnancy diet.

I had Hoover on a leash. Though he was generally reliable when it came to sticking around, I didn't trust him not to run over and sniff at the dead body. I hoisted the litter box and the bag of pet stuff—which also had a container of litter in it, so it was heavy—in one arm and held Hoover's leash in the other. As expected, Hoover whined and tried to pull me over to the body as we passed it, but after a firm, "No!" from me, he gave up and fell into step at my side. I made my way to Henderson's car—an old Jeep Wagoneer with wood-paneled sides—and shoved my items in next to the other stuff.

When everything was loaded, Henderson closed the hatch, and Richmond turned to me. "Want me to pick you up in the morning?"

"That would be great since I won't have any wheels. Do you still want to shoot for eight-thirty?" I asked, sparing a mourning glance toward my hearse. The thing was built like a tank, and other than the missing windows, it didn't look too bad. Of course, that didn't mean I was going to get it back anytime soon.

I had no idea how long it would take them to process it for evidence.

"How about seven?" Bob said. "Then we can grab a bite to eat before we head out."

Richmond was a foodie after my own heart, and since I no longer felt it necessary to check into the office first thing in the morning, I readily agreed. "Good idea. See you then."

I put Hoover in the backseat of Henderson's car and then climbed into the front passenger side. Henderson had some final words for Richmond before he got in. "The funeral home should be here to pick up the body anytime. The troopers will see it back to the ME's office. And I have a towing service coming to take both cars to the police garage so they can be processed for evidence. I'll plan on doing the autopsy in the morning, but for tonight, the troopers will oversee the gathering of evidence here, including any bullets and casings. I'd appreciate it if you would see to it that your men cooperate."

"No problem," Richmond said, his jaw tight. Then he spun around and headed back up the drive.

Henderson got in behind the wheel and started the engine. Then he pulled out, driving me off into a future that was more uncertain than ever before.

Chapter 18

It took nearly fifteen minutes to get to the Sorenson Motel, a trip I can normally make in just over five. But Henderson was driving like an octogenarian, creeping along the streets at the speed of a snail. I wondered if he always drove that way or if he was purposely driving slowly to give us time to talk.

"So tell me what happened tonight," he said at the start of our crawl. "Give it to me in your own words."

This last was a quaint, odd turn of phrase that made me wonder if he thought I might speak in tongues or channel the soul of some deceased person.

"It started yesterday when I went to get something to eat," I began. Then I corrected myself. "Or maybe it started two months ago. I'm not sure." I then filled him in on the phone calls, and the car I'd seen pull out of David's driveway, and my suspicion that it was following me. He stopped me to question how I came to be living next door to my ex, and to ask if it bothered me any.

"No, not really," I lied. "I like the cottage. It's just the right size for me."

"Will it be big enough when you have your baby?"

This shocked me. "Who told?" I asked, staring at him and mentally plotting revenge on the squealer, whoever it was.

"I figured it out," he said. "I saw you packing those clothes from The Mother Hood bags, and there was one of those books on your bedside table about what to expect when you're pregnant. I asked the officers you work with just to be sure, and Officer Feller confirmed it for me."

"I think the cottage will do fine for now," I said. "My bedroom is big enough to fit a crib along with my bed. And since Izzy's partner, Dom, is eager to provide me with babysitting services, it will be convenient for whenever I have to work. As you know, the hours can be odd at times, so having Dom right there will be handy."

Henderson nodded. "So back to this car that was following you last night," he said.

"I wasn't one hundred percent sure it was following me the first time I saw it, but the way the driver hesitated when I pulled into the parking lot of the restaurant sure made it look that way. I thought I might just be paranoid, but then later, when I saw a car following me from the crime scene, I zigzagged through some neighborhoods, just driving randomly with no destination in mind, and the car kept up with me turn for turn until I pulled into a strip-mall parking lot."

"What did the car look like?"

"It was a boxy, dark sedan of some sort. I never got a very good look at it because it was dark and the headlights obscured my vision."

"The car they found on your ex's property is a

dark sedan, so it seems your instincts may have been spot on. Why didn't you report it to someone, so they could look into it?"

"Well, for one, I didn't want to look stupid if I was imagining things. And to be honest, I thought it might have been my father."

"Your father?" He shot me a questioning look, so I told him about my history, or lack thereof, with my father, the incident of the man spying through my windows, Emily's drawing, and my mother's declaration that it was my father. I then told him I thought my father might have been behind the odd phone calls I'd been receiving.

"The cops can run those calls to see where they came from," Henderson said. "The guy who shot you had a cell phone on him, but it got smashed when you drove over him, so it might take a while to figure out if he was the one making those calls."

While it didn't bode well for a quick resolution to my case, I did see a light at the end of the tunnel with regard to my being able to continue with the Ames case. "If the guy who shot at me was also the guy who was following me, then it couldn't have anything to do with our current murder investigation because I was being followed before that case existed. Right?"

"I suppose," Henderson said. "Tell me about tonight. What led up to you running that man over with your car?"

"I didn't know I was running him over. I was just trying to get away." I then gave him a detailed explanation of the events leading up to the shooter's death.

"Any idea why someone would want to kill you?"

I thought long and hard but came up with nothing. "No idea at all," I told him.

"What about your father? Do you think he would want to kill you?"

"My father?" My skepticism and horror were clear in my tone. "Why on earth would he want me dead?"

"Why did he leave?"

"I wish I knew. But he never told me or gave me any clues that he was leaving. Or if he did, I don't remember it. And my mother refuses to talk about him."

"Why is that, do you think?"

"If you knew my mother, you wouldn't have to ask that question. My father was one of her four husbands, and at the moment she's living with a man I once dated."

Henderson shot me a look of horror.

"It's not as twisted as it sounds," I said. "In fact, I'm the one who fixed the two of them up. Trust me; they're perfect for one another."

We had arrived, finally, at the Sorenson Motel, and rather than respond to my latest revelation, Henderson simply stopped in front of the office entrance, shifted into park, and said, "Go ahead and book a room. I'll wait here."

I rolled my eyes, told Hoover to stay, and got out.

The owner of the Sorenson Motel is a sixty-something curmudgeon by the name of Joseph Wagner, who is best known in town for his constant flow of letters to the editor criticizing the local government. Joseph and our mayor, Charlie Petersen, have been battling one another for about forty years now, all because of a girl the two of them met back in their heydays. Charlie won the battle, though knowing what the girl they fought over is like today, I think Joseph won the war.

I found Joseph parked behind his desk, reading a large-print issue of *Reader's Digest*. He had large, loose bags beneath his eyes, and he was wearing a pair of overalls with a worn, denim shirt underneath. His head was bald on top, but he had thick, curly, gray hair on the sides, making him look like Larry Fine from the Three Stooges.

The Sorenson Motel is nearly as old as Joseph and hasn't fared much better in the looks department. The place is clean enough, but the décor is straight out of the eighties. It's a typical sixties-era, roadside motel: a long, narrow building with two wings of units—front and back—divided by an office in the middle. Joseph does what he needs to in order to keep the place running, but not much more. The upside of this is affordable rates. And he does offer a few modern conveniences, such as free Internet access, cable TV, and pay-per-view porn.

I was hoping to snag one of the end units: suites that included a kitchenette and sitting area. It would make my temporary living situation a little more tolerable.

"Hey, Joseph, how are you?"

He lowered the magazine, squinted at me, and frowned. "Are you here to look for a killer among my guests again?"

"No, I'm here to become one of your guests."

"Really?" He dropped the magazine, and his expression turned happy.

I figured telling him I was a fresh-off-the-block killer myself wasn't going to win me any points, so I gave him a vague reason for my need. "I'm having some work done on my place, and I need somewhere to stay for a few days. Do you have one of the end suites available?"

"Just so happens I do. It's the one down on the east end. Same one your ex stayed in, in fact."

That figured.

"Some doctor guy has the one on the west end."

"That would be Dr. Henderson. He's filling in for Izzy for a while."

"Did Izzy finally take a vacation?"

"No, Dom's father died, so he went with him to Iowa."

"Oh. Too bad." I assumed he meant it was too bad that Dom's father died, but his next words clarified things. "That man works too hard."

He had a point. I couldn't remember the last time Izzy took time off for any fun stuff. He'd occasionally take a day or two over a holiday if we had someone who could cover, but other than that, he worked every day.

"How much for the room?" I asked, taking out a credit card and sliding it across the desk.

"How long you going to be needing it? You can get a cheaper rate if you go by the week."

"I don't think it will be that long." Truth be told, I had no idea how long it would be. "What's the daily rate?"

"Fifty a day."

"And the weekly rate?"

"Three hundred. You basically get a day for free."

"Is that the best you can do?"

"It is, assuming you don't have any pets or anything."

I grimaced at that. "I do have pets. A dog. And a cat."

"Is the dog housebroken?"

"Of course. And the cat is litter-trained. I brought a litter box with me."

"Pets are an additional twenty a day, or an extra fifty a week."

"That seems steep." Lord knew what he'd charge me if he found out I had not one cat, but two.

"That's my offer. Take it or leave it."

I was pretty much stuck taking it, but I didn't like it. I tried another gambit. "You know, I send business your way all the time, Joseph. Like that doctor who's staying here. I recommended this place to him. Shouldn't that earn me a discount of some sort?" I prayed that Henderson hadn't mentioned that it was actually Izzy who recommended the place, but I needn't have worried. Joseph wasn't going to budge.

"I don't do discounts for referrals," he said. "I just return the favor instead."

"Really? Well then, you make sure you refer the next dead person who tries to check in to me, okay?"

Joseph just smiled.

"Come on, can't you give me a better rate than that? I'm a local. You know I'm good for it."

"I'm trying to run a business here, you know? So the rate is what it is. If you don't like it, you can head over to that other place in town, but I can tell you that their rates are even higher. Plus they don't allow pets of any kind, and they don't have any suites."

I had one last gambit to try. "I'm pregnant, you know. Don't you think that should entitle me to a special rate?"

"You're preggers?" he said, and I nodded, rubbing my tummy and for once trying to pooch it out rather than suck it in. "Well, why didn't you say so?" Joseph said with a smile.

"I just did," I countered with my own smile.

"Well, I'll tell you what. I'll give you the special knocked-up rate then. That will be three-forty-nine ninety-nine for the week."

My smile morphed into a glare. I knew he wasn't going to budge, so I caved, but not without one last question. "If I pay the weekly rate but check out early, do I get a refund?"

"What do you think?"

We engaged in a stare-down that lasted at least fifteen seconds.

"Fine," I said, letting my irritation show. "Let me have a week." I shoved my credit card over to him, and he ran it through his little machine.

The card was brand spanking new, the first one I'd gotten since my divorce from David. All the cards I had before that were in his name, with me as an authorized signer. Prior to getting married I'd worked on a strictly cash basis, using a debit card that pulled money from my bank account. It was a good way to budget money, something I had to do in order to pay off my school loans. Seven years of living high on the hog with a well-to-do surgeon had given me a taste of how simple and, yes, fun a credit card could be. Unfortunately, I wasn't smart enough to have built any credit in my own name, so once we split I was back to working on a cash basis again. Now that I had a steady income—at least I hoped it would prove to be steady—and a healthy savings account that would have been a hell of a lot healthier if I hadn't spent so much time and money at the blackjack tables recently,

I decided it was time to apply for a credit card in my own name. It had a five thousand dollar limit on it, and I'd spent more than a fifth of that already at The Mother Hood.

When Joseph was done running my card and I'd filled in the appropriate paperwork, he slid a key over to me. I was about to head back out to Henderson when Joseph stopped me. "You didn't fill in a license plate number," he said, shoving the card back across the desk at me.

"I don't have one to fill in. My car is also having some work done, so at the moment I don't have any wheels."

"Hmph," Joseph said. "That's not very good planning, if you ask me."

He had no idea. Though I kind of wished I had the hearse with me. Parking it right out front might scare away some potential business, which would serve Joseph right.

I headed outside and got into Henderson's car. Hoover thumped his tail on the back of his seat and nuzzled my neck. "I have the suite down on the east end," I told Henderson. "Apparently you have the one on the west end."

"Yes, I do. We'll be neighbors for a spell. And listen, I put in a call to the troopers while you were in there, and since we don't know why this guy was after you, I've arranged for you to have a police guard for now. The state guys are stretched a little thin with this investigation on top of their regular duties, so we all agreed that the locals will provide the service. There will be someone from the Sorenson PD parked outside your room for the night."

"Thanks, I think." I wondered if his motivation behind this arrangement was what he told me, or if it was because he felt the need to keep a close eye on his prime suspect.

He drove me down to my room and helped me unload my stuff. As soon as we had everything inside, I let the cats out of their carriers. They were spooked and at first tried to get back into their carriers. Then Rubbish made a mad dash for the bed and tried to run under it. Unfortunately, there was no under portion because the bed sat on a wooden platform. Rubbish ran into it headfirst and crumpled into a bewildered ball of fur on the floor. Tux, who had been moved at least once already in his life, stayed put. I figured they'd both be on the bed within the hour, assuming Rubbish wasn't too dizzy to jump up. Clearly he was not pleased with the arrangement, because as soon as he was able to pick himself up and walk, he came over to me and swatted my leg with his foot. Then he went over and settled down in front of the small couch.

There was a knock on the door, and Henderson went to open it. Standing on the threshold was Brenda Joiner. "I'm here to keep an eye on Mattie."

"Hi, Brenda," I said, peeking around Henderson at her. "Thanks for volunteering to take the first shift."

"I'll do as many as I can," she said. "I owe you."

In a way, this was true. Had I not intervened when I had in the last case we worked, Brenda Joiner might be dead.

"I'll be here until Bob comes to get you in the morning," she said.

Henderson turned to me then and said, "Have you had dinner yet?"

"No, I was going to order something when I got home, but things didn't quite go as planned."

"Want to join me? I was thinking of going to that Italian place in town. Joseph recommended it."

"I'd love to," I said, salivating at the mere mention of food, not to mention Italian. Henderson turned to Brenda and said, "Is that okay with you?"

"Sure."

I looked over at my animals, who were all watching us. "Just let me get the cats settled with the litter box and their food bowls. And I should probably take Hoover for a walk. He hasn't done his business in a while."

Henderson said, "Then why don't you go walk the dog, and I'll get the cats set up for you."

Brenda frowned. "Maybe it would be better if I walked the dog," she said. "The less time Mattie spends outside right now, the better."

"Are you sure you don't mind?" I asked, thinking that Henderson's willingness to let me go outside confirmed my suspicions about his motives.

"I don't mind at all," Brenda said, grabbing the leash and hooking it up. Then she gave Hoover a vigorous rub behind his ears, which had my dog drooling in ecstasy. By the time she headed out the door, Hoover was looking up at her with the canine equivalent of star-struck eyes. I think that if Brenda hadn't ever come back that night, Hoover would have been all too happy to take her on as his new owner.

As Henderson went about filling the litter box, I went into the bathroom to freshen up. I decided Henderson wasn't such a bad guy after all. A little quirky maybe, but okay. But then, as I sat on the toilet, a thought came to me. I shook it off, thinking it was my paranoia setting in again, but the more I thought about it, the more I believed it. I finished peeing, quietly pulled up my pants, and then I put one hand on the door handle and the other on the flush handle. A second after I flushed, I whipped open the bathroom door.

Henderson was standing by the table and chairs going through my purse. He froze mid-action and blushed bright red.

"What the hell?" I said, my suspicion confirmed.

"Sorry," Henderson said. He dropped my wallet back into the purse, but he hung onto the cell phone that was in his other hand. "I had to," he said, his tone apologetic. "Part of the investigation."

"First of all, you're not a cop. And second of all, why didn't you just ask me? I would have gladly let you paw through anything you wanted to see."

"I suppose I should have," he said, blushing.

"You think?" I snapped. I walked over, grabbed my purse, and dumped its contents out on the tabletop. "There, have at it," I said. I grabbed an old tampon that I hadn't even known was in there, ripped it open, and pulled the tampon out. "Oh, darn, it's just a tampon, not a secret drug stash." I walked over and held the tampon over a trash can, letting it dangle by the string. "Oh, wait, did you want to bag this just in case?"

My reaction was crass and theatrical, intended to embarrass Henderson even more than he already was. It worked. His blush deepened and spread down his neck. Rather than let him off the hook, I pushed on, venting weeks of pent-up emotion and frustration on the poor man.

I dropped the ruined tampon into the trash and then walked back to the table and grabbed a small, round, jewel-topped pill holder. When I hit a button on the side of it, the lid sprang open, revealing several tiny white pills. "Uh-oh, maybe I'm not just using drugs, maybe I'm dealing them, too," I said in an overly dramatic voice. "Except, oh, darn, these are the nausea pills I had to have on hand when my morning sickness was really bad. Sorry to disappoint." I snapped the lid closed and stood staring at him, one hand on my hip. "Anything else you want to see? Are there any more of my civil rights you want to violate?"

"I said I was sorry," Henderson stammered. "I just wanted to be sure."

"You have no business going through my personal belongings without my permission. You're not a cop, Henderson, you're an ME. Now kindly give me back my phone."

He handed it over, looking sheepish.

I dropped the phone back into my purse and said, "I think you should leave now."

He nodded and hung his head. Then he shuffled his way out the door. Once he was outside, he turned around and opened his mouth to say something, but I slammed the door closed. Just before I shut it, I saw Brenda outside with Hoover standing in the middle of the parking lot looking wary, alert, and a little confused.

"Damn it!" I muttered.

A moment later there was a knock on the door,

and after peering through the peephole, I let Brenda and Hoover inside. "Dr. Henderson looked a little tense," Brenda said, unhooking Hoover's leash.

I looked down at Hoover, who was looking back at me with those soft brown eyes. He could tell I was upset, though I doubt he understood why. I stroked his head to reassure him.

"We had a little disagreement," I said vaguely. "The dinner plans have changed. I'm going to order a pizza. Care to join me?"

"If you're staying in, I think I'll pass," Brenda said. "The only reason I was going to go with you to the restaurant was to keep an eye on you. To be honest, I ate a short time ago and I'm not hungry. But thank you for the offer."

I thanked her for walking Hoover, and after she returned to her car I ordered my pizza: pepperoni, sausage, and extra cheese. While waiting for it to be delivered, I finished unpacking my things. My anger was slowly dissipating, but it had worked up a mighty appetite in me.

My pizza arrived, and after Brenda practically frisked the delivery boy, I settled down to eat. A few slices later, there was a knock on my door. I peered through the peephole and saw a state trooper standing outside along with Brenda.

"Mattie, can you open up?" Brenda said. "Trooper Collins needs to get a statement from you."

I opened the door and let Trooper Collins in. He was a short, bald, squat, older guy, built like a fire-plug. He made me go through the entire story again, stopping me at frequent intervals to ask a question or clarify something I said. I expected him to be tough,

maybe even a bit accusatory, but while he was annoy-
ingly thorough, he was polite, objective, and to the
point. Once he was gone, I nuked another piece of
pizza, knowing I'd need fortitude for my next task:
calling my mom.

Before the night was done, I'd eaten the entire
pizza.

Saffron would have had a stroke.

Chapter 19

Richmond showed up right on time the next morning. I was ready and waiting for him because I'd barely slept all night. Tux and Rubbish had remained restless, too, and Hoover looked lost and bewildered. I suspect he'd thought of the move as an exciting trip of some sort initially, but now that I was leaving him, he didn't understand why.

"Where would you like to eat?" Richmond asked as I climbed into his car. I was surprised by the appearance of the interior. At one time it had been littered with the detritus of his fast-food habit. Now it was spick-and-span clean and smelled faintly of some type of lemony cleaner.

"How about that little coffee shop on Main Street?" I suggested.

"Works for me." He pulled out of the parking lot, and I saw that Henderson's Jeep was gone. Clearly the spy was an early riser. "How was your night?" Richmond asked.

"Restless. The animals were all pacing and spooked. Plus I ordered a pizza and ate the whole thing. I had heartburn all night, and guilt over eating that much and not working out."

"Been there, done that," Richmond said, and I knew he had and understood. He was one of the few people I could be honest with when it came to my eating and exercise habits. "Everybody's entitled to a slip now and then."

"It's the stress. It makes me eat," I said, knowing this was a half-truth. Eating is pretty much my solution to everything in life. "I had to give a statement to one of the troopers, and after that I had to call my mother and tell her the news about my pregnancy before someone else did."

"How did that go?"

"Oh, about like you'd expect, especially when she found out David isn't the father. In her eyes I've sunk about as low as I can go. Talking to her was exhausting, and after that I had to talk to Izzy. Apparently Henderson called and filled him in."

"So did I," Richmond said. "I figured he should know and I figured it couldn't hurt to have him put in a word for you with Henderson."

"Perhaps, but that's the last thing he needs right now with all he has going on down there in Iowa. Any news on the case?"

"Which one, yours or the Ames case?"

"Mine for starters. Do they know who this guy is who shot at me? Or why he shot at me?"

"Well, we know who he is, but so far that hasn't been much help. He's a two-time felon named Roscoe Schneider with a history of rape and armed robbery. He did a double nickel down in Florida and was paroled last year. The cops down there said he's been a troublemaker since he was a kid. Apparently he was raised in the foster system and got placed in some not-so-savory homes. He did some time in juvey after he held up a convenience store. Right after he got out he was accused of raping someone, but that case never went to trial because the victim refused to testify against him. She knew him prior to the rape, and Schneider swore that the sex was consensual, and that the girl only said it was rape because her father would have beat her if he thought she'd done it willingly. Since it basically boiled down to a case of he said, she said, the case got dropped. A year later Schneider was involved in a liquor store holdup that resulted in a homicide. That's what got him put away."

"So he's killed before?"

"Not exactly, at least not in that case. The store had video cameras, and everything was caught on tape, but both men were masked and gloved, and it was only because of a lucky fluke that Schneider was caught. He was armed, but based on the video footage, he never fired a shot. The shot that killed the store owner was fired by Schneider's partner, someone who was never caught. Two things led to Schneider getting nailed. First, the store owner's daughter, who was also shot but survived, recognized Schneider's voice. She'd been raped the week before, and though she couldn't identify the man's face because he was wearing a mask, when she heard Schneider's voice during the robbery, she recognized it as that of her rapist. She didn't report the crime at the time because Schneider threatened to come back and kill both her and her father if she did, and she knew she couldn't identify the guy. But after the robbery she told the cops about the rape and her certainty that one of the robbers was also her rapist. The cops were able to tie Schneider to the robbery because one of the bullets hit a liquor bottle on the counter near where he was standing and the flying bits of glass cut him. He left a few tiny drops of blood on the floor, and the cops took a sample of it and ran it for DNA. Even though that earlier rape case against Schneider was dropped, his DNA was entered into the system, so the cops got a hit. The girl was able to identify him based on voice recognition alone from a lineup of masked men. The DA offered Schneider a lighter sentence in exchange for the name of his partner, but he opted to do the time instead. Because of that, the girl backed out of testifying against him for the rape, fearful his partner might try to exact revenge. So once again he escaped a rape charge, but he was sentenced to ten years for the holdup. He just got out a couple of months ago."

"I don't get it," I said, shaking my head. "Why did he come after me? What's he even doing up here?"

"We don't know. Near as we can tell, Schneider's never been in Wisconsin before, and he violated his parole by coming up here. As far as we know, he doesn't have any connections to any cases here, so your guess is as good as mine. I don't suppose his name rings a bell?"

"None at all."

"Maybe he wandered up here for a change of scenery, and for whatever reason, you caught his eye."

It was a scary thought that made me shudder, though the more I thought about it, the less convinced I was. "I'm not sure I buy that, Richmond," I said. "Not to knock myself, but if a rapist is on the hunt for a random victim, why would he pass up any number of attractive, petite women he could easily overpower physically for a woman my size? And if rape was what he had in mind, why didn't he try? Why did he just shoot at me instead?"

"All good questions," Richmond admitted. "Hopefully with time we'll get some answers."

"Do they think this guy was working alone?"

"All I know so far is that the car was registered in Florida in his name, and there's nothing so far to suggest a second person was involved. But I haven't talked to any of the troopers yet this morning. We'll get an update when we get to the station."

"How long do you think it will be before I can move back into my place?"

"I don't know, a few days . . . maybe a week? So far the evidence seems straightforward, and given Schneider's record, I can't imagine the investigation will take very long."

The evidence might have been straightforward, but the motive wasn't. I hoped Richmond's downplayed assessment was right, and I made an effort to put it, and my other life issues, out of my mind for now so I could focus on the Ames investigation. Unfortunately, that didn't happen because when we entered the coffee shop, Hurley was there. Richmond escorted me in, staying close behind me, so close that he bumped into me when I saw Hurley and stopped short.

I expected to see anger on Hurley's face when he saw me, but instead he just looked sad. He walked over and greeted us.

"Good morning," he said, giving me a quick glance

and then diverting his attention to Richmond. "My work plate is empty thanks to my time off and the fact that the state guys are working Mattie's case. Need any help with the Ames investigation?"

"Sure," Richmond said. "I've got a ton of people to interview, a ton of evidence to process, and, as usual, a handful of people to do it."

"Well, I'm glad to help," Hurley said, and then he finally switched his attention to me. "I really need to talk to you sometime soon. Any chance you might be free for dinner?"

I debated my options. On the one hand, I couldn't bear the thought of sitting across a table from Hurley while he was wearing the hangdog expression he had at the moment. And I didn't think our discussion would go any better than it had last night. But I also missed him terribly, and I was clinging, however futilely, to the idea that he might have some workable solution figured out.

It was then that Richmond revealed just how good his detecting skills were. "Listen, I have some news that might help you guys out. Have you eaten yet, Steve?"

Hurley shook his head. "I only came in for a coffee."

"Then join us for a bite."

I was curious, and judging from the expression on Hurley's face, so was he. He nodded, and the three of us made our way to an empty table located in a back corner near the restrooms. Richmond made me sit on one side with him and Hurley across from one another. Richmond said he wanted to face the door so he could keep an eye on things. "If I yell at you to go," he said, "run into the ladies room."

We perused the limited menu and made our choices;

since there was no waitress, Richmond offered to go up to the counter and place our orders. That left me and Hurley alone.

"I came back to your place last night to make sure you were okay," Hurley said in a low voice so neighboring diners couldn't hear him. "They had everything taped off. I take it you're staying somewhere else for now?"

I nodded. "For the moment I'm at the Sorenson Motel staying in the same suite David was in." I rolled my eyes at this. "It's not ideal, particularly since I don't have a car to go anywhere, but hopefully I can move back into my place before too long."

"It's just as well that you don't have a car because for the time being you're going to have a police escort everywhere you go."

"Great."

"Think of it as a personal car service."

"Sure, okay." I gave him a smile that I knew didn't look very happy.

"Look, last night didn't go the way it should have," Hurley said. "You caught me off guard with your news, and I didn't react very well."

"You reacted fine under the circumstances. It wasn't at all how I wanted you to find out."

"I realize that. And though I was hurt at first, I also realize why you didn't tell me over the phone. You wanted to be able to judge my reaction face-to-face."

I nodded and gave him another wan smile.

"And I understand your reluctance, given the comments I made about Kate and Emily. Having a nearly grown child I knew nothing about thrust on me out of nowhere definitely threw me. But you and I . . . that's different. I—"

"Food should be ready in five to ten minutes," Richmond said, returning to the table.

Hurley sat back in his chair, his expression grim, his lips tight. I cursed the timing, desperate to hear the rest of whatever Hurley was going to say.

Richmond settled into his seat and leaned forward the same way Hurley had moments before. "So here's what I'm thinking," he said. "The two of you have a thing going on, and it's causing problems because of the conflict of interest issues."

I opened my mouth to deny that there was a thing going on, but Richmond held a hand up and spoke before I could. "Don't bother trying to deny it, Mattie," he said. "Everyone on the force knows it. You may think you're doing a good job of hiding it, but you might as well try to hide a mansion behind a rose bush." I clamped my mouth shut and frowned. "Don't worry about it," Richmond said, seeing my expression. "No one is going to report it. We're all rooting for the two of you, and now your being pregnant adds a whole other level to this thing. Are you planning to get married?"

"No," I said before Hurley had a chance to respond, though he did make a face that communicated his displeasure.

"Okay, but clearly you plan to stay together on some level, right?"

Hurley and I stared at one another, but neither of us said anything. After several seconds of silence, Richmond rolled his eyes and said, "Trust me, you will continue to see one another. You can't help yourselves."

We both gave him sheepish looks.

"So here are my thoughts on the matter. I've enjoyed being back at work, and now that I'm trying to maintain my new girlish figure, it helps if I stay active. My early semiretirement created a vacancy that Chief Hanson never filled, hoping to trim the budget overruns. But sadly, the workload has increased, and he knows that there is too much for the current staff to handle. He did some figuring and realized that he's paying out more in overtime than what it would cost to hire on another full-time detective. So I talked to him about coming back to work on a more permanent basis, and he agreed. It means deferring my retirement income, and there are a shitload of hoops we'll have to jump through to do it, but he feels certain he can get it approved."

"That's great," I said, genuinely happy for Richmond but unsure just how he thought it was going to help me and Hurley.

"Plus, there's another piece to this. The chief applied for a grant a while back when the scuttlebutt about the evidence tampering in Milwaukee came out, and he got it. He plans to announce it this morning. Starting today, we will have a videographer on staff who will be training all of us on how to videotape our scene investigations, evidence collection, and off-site interviews. There will be enough cameras for Jonas and each detective to have one initially. The use of audiovisual evidence eliminates most of the tampering and conflict of interest issues. You'd still have to make sure no one sees the two of you handling evidence or interrogations without a video, but other than that, you should be able to work together without any problems, especially if we work as a team of three. I can function as your chaperone."

Richmond winked, sat back in his seat, and folded his arms over his chest, looking smug. Hurley and I continued to stare at one another as we digested Richmond's information. Someone yelled out Richmond's name from behind the front counter, meaning our food was ready. "Be right back," he said, and he got up to fetch our meals.

"This could work," Hurley said once Richmond was gone.

"It could," I agreed. I knew it might mean no more sneaking off for a quickie during the day, but given that we now had Emily in our lives and another kid on the way, I felt sure those episodes were coming to an end anyway. Suddenly it felt as if someone had lifted a heavy weight from my shoulders. "We can keep our jobs," I said.

"And still work together."

"It will be nice not having to hide anything anymore," I said, the relief I felt clear in my voice. While I seem to have a knack for sniffing out subterfuge, I suck at being a part of it.

"Yes, it will," Hurley agreed. "We can be open and honest and in everyone's face. Hell, Winston, we could even get married."

I sighed and gave him a weary look. "We've been over this, Hurley."

"Yeah, yeah, I know. You think I'm being trapped into something I don't want to do."

"I can't help but feel that way, Hurley. If I wasn't pregnant, would you be proposing to me right now?"

He opened his mouth to answer, and I sensed a knee-jerk response about to come out.

"Be honest, Hurley," I cautioned before he got a word out. Then I pinned him with a laser-eyed focus.

He stared back at me for two blinks, and then his mouth closed into a tight-lipped grimace.

"See?" I said.

Hurley frowned. "Just because I might not have proposed to you right now if there wasn't a pregnancy in the picture doesn't mean I wouldn't have done it eventually, or that it's not the right thing to do."

"Then there's no rush, right?" I said. "So let's give it some time. For now, and until after this kid is born, let's table the topic, okay?"

"But I—"

"Here we go," Richmond said, arriving with our meals while I again cursed his timing. He gave Hurley his egg, bacon, and croissant sandwich, gave me my garlic bagel with cream cheese, and then set down his own plate, a healthy egg-white omelet with mushrooms and onions. We all dug in with gusto, and the conversation ceased for several minutes.

About halfway through our meals, Richmond said, "So what do you guys think about what I told you? This is good news, no?"

"It is," I said. "But I'm curious. When you say everyone knows about me and Hurley, just who do you mean? Does the chief know?"

"He didn't come right out and say so, but I expect he does. All the officers and dispatchers know, so if the chief doesn't know now, he will soon enough."

"And you don't think it will cause any problems?"

"Not with the videos in play, and not if Hurley and I team up with you. It basically eliminates all of the conflict of interest issues."

I smiled at Hurley, but he didn't smile back. Apparently he was still sulking over the marriage thing. Richmond finished his breakfast and said, "I imagine the two of you have some things to discuss. Steve, I'm sure you won't mind keeping an eye on our girl here, will you?"

"Not at all."

"Good. Then I'm going to head over to the station and get things started. I already paid for the meals. Breakfast is on me today. The chief plans to announce his news at eight-thirty, and I have an interview on the Ames case scheduled for nine, and a lawyered interview with the Ames family at ten. So you guys can take some time and talk things over. Steve, when you get over to the station I'll brief you on the Ames case to get you up to speed."

"Great, Bob. And thanks, both for breakfast and the rest of it. I appreciate it."

I echoed Hurley's sentiments, and then Richmond left, leaving the two of us alone. We ate in silence for several minutes until our food was finished, leaving us with just our coffees. Hurley leaned back in his chair and looked at me with a funny smile.

"What?" I said, starting to feel uncomfortable.

"I'm just taking in the sight of you. I really did miss you these past two months."

"I missed you, too."

Hurley leaned forward, putting his elbows on the table. "Look, I get that you don't want to get married yet, and I get why. I'm willing to back off on that for now, but I want you to promise me you'll keep an open mind about it. And I also want you to promise me you won't cut me out of your life. Whether you believe it or not, I'm truly delighted that we're having a kid together. I'm excited about being a father.

And regardless of what happens between the two of us, I intend to be a big part of this kid's life. Okay?"

"Okay," I said with a smile.

"Good." He glanced at his watch. "My place is only five minutes from here, and we have nearly an hour before the chief's announcement. I don't suppose I could convince you to come by for a quick, um, re-union, so to speak." He wiggled his eyebrows sugges-tively for a second, and then his expression froze. "Wait, you can still do that, right? I mean with the baby and all."

"Oh, I can still do it," I said. And I wanted to more than anything. "What about Emily?"

"She's in school."

"They let her come back after being gone so long?"

"I enrolled her in school down in Chicago while we were there. So she didn't miss much. She'll have to do some extra stuff here to get caught up, but I think it will do her good. And since she's in school, my house is empty."

"We wouldn't want the house to get lonely," I said, feigning innocence.

"No, we wouldn't."

We were out the door twenty seconds later.

Chapter 20

"So you and Hurley worked things out," Dr. Maggie says to me. "That's great."

"You'd think so, but it didn't go as smoothly as I hoped."

"How so?"

"Well, for starters, there's the new videographer, who looks like she stepped right out of *Vogue*. She's this gorgeous, twenty-something redhead who's built like a model."

"Ah, I see. You feel threatened by her."

"Wouldn't you? I mean, look at me. I look like a beached whale. I can't take a bath anymore because I can't get out of the tub, and I haven't colored my hair in five months. I've got roots longer than Alex Haley's. Not to mention that my hormones have me vacillating day to day between a barely tamed shrew and a screaming bitch on wheels. Who would you pick?"

"Has Hurley started a relationship with this woman?"

"No, at least I don't think he has. But that hasn't stopped her from trying."

"So she's been making a play for Hurley?"

"Oh, it's been more than a play. It's more like the unabridged edition of *War and Peace*."

"Have you talked with Hurley about it?"

"No. I don't want to look like some insecure, jealous dink, even if I am one. Besides, if I bring it up, I'm afraid he'll propose again."

"Why? Did he ask again?"

"No."

"Are you sure you don't want to marry him?"

"I am, at least for now. I've already explained my reasons to him and to you. I don't understand why it's so hard for you people to grasp."

"Maybe it's because 'we people' can see how much you love the guy, and how much he loves you."

"It's not that simple," I grumble. "Things have happened. Besides, if he loves me so much, why hasn't he said so?"

"Is that what's holding you back at this point? That he hasn't told you he loves you?"

"More or less," I tell her. It isn't the only reason, or even the primary one anymore, but I'm not ready to tell her the rest of the story yet. "I mean, if he can't say that to me, it makes it all the more obvious that he's simply offering to do the deed because he thinks it's the right thing to do. That's not a good way to start a marriage."

"No, I suppose not. So what sort of relationship do you see the two of you having in the future?"

"Well, there's our working relationship, of course. And we are very good together in that regard."

"In that regard? What other regards are there?"

"Well, there's the sex. We seem to be quite good in that department, too."

"So where are the problems?"

"I think I'm in love with him, and he's in like with me," I say, verbalizing my fear for the first time.

"You're afraid."

It wasn't a question.

"What, exactly, are you afraid of? If you were to accept Hurley's proposal and get married, what would be the worst-case scenario?"

"That we'd end up hating one another. And we'd be forced to still work together, and parent together . . . it has the potential for being very awkward. I know, because it's extremely awkward with David, and we don't have a kid together."

"How would you feel if Hurley married someone else?"

I shot her a look of horror. "Why would you ask me that? Have you heard something?"

Maggie smiles. It is the same patient, beneficent smile she uses on me all the time, and today it is pissing me off because I feel as if she's treating me like a child. The fact that I may be acting like one shouldn't figure into the matter. She's a shrink. She should know better. "No, I haven't heard anything. I'm simply trying to get you to explore your feelings more deeply," she says.

"I seem to be feeling them too deeply already."

"I disagree. I think you're burying them. You're avoiding your true feelings."

I open my mouth to argue the point, but I shut it again quickly because I realize my objection would have been an automatic one with no real thought or consideration behind it. And some tiny little voice inside me says she's right. She seems to sense my capitulation and repeats her question.

"How would you feel if Hurley married someone else?"

"Devastated," I admit, tears welling in my eyes. "I would feel devastated."

"Then why don't you just accept his proposal? You love him, don't you?"

"I do. More than anything."

"Then what's the problem?"

"It's complicated," I say, exasperated.

"You won't marry him because he hasn't said he loves you?"

"In part, yes."

"What's the other part of this equation?"

"Some other things have developed."

"And they are?"

"I don't know if I'm ready to discuss that yet."

Maggie cocks her head and looks at me, eyebrows raised. I know she is hoping the silence and her expectations will wear me down, but I'm determined to do this my way.

"Okay," she says after half a minute of silence. "Let's move on, and we'll come back to this later. Tell me how things progressed once Hurley came back. What happened with your work relationship?"

"It got very interesting."

"How so?"

"Well, for one, the Ames case drove us crazy for a while. Richmond and Hurley hit a few bumps trying to figure out how to work together, and when they threw the new videographer into the mix, it only complicated things. Plus we had all these state troopers traipsing in and out of the PD, fighting for desk space, computer access, file storage, and such. The same thing was going on in my office, where new faces were popping up all the time, and those of us who worked there started to feel like we no longer belonged. Arnie became apoplectic trying to get the Ames case evidence processed after the Madison techs that Henderson brought in took over his lab space, so he finally just gave it all to the new guys and let them process both cases. I found people sitting at my desk and using my computer every time I went into the office. Things between me and Henderson remained uncomfortably awkward, and whenever we had to do an autopsy, I begged Arnie to assist since he was at loose ends anyway. I kept myself busy by switching my work hours so that I spent time in the office in the evenings when I had better luck finding my desk available."

"And then there was that guy I killed, Roscoe Schneider. I assumed that once the state guys cleared me that would be the end of it."

"But it wasn't?"

"Not even close. It turned out that Richmond was wrong when he said it didn't look like Schneider was working with someone. The state troopers found a handwritten note in Schneider's car that had my home address, my work address, and my work phone number on it."

"So this Schneider guy wrote down your address and phone number. How does that imply another person was involved?"

"Because they also found a roll of hundreds inside a bag that was in the car. There was a note wrapped around the bills that said the balance would be paid when the job was done. The handwriting on that note matched the handwriting on the other one. They also found a newspaper clipping from a few months back that showed a picture of me. So it seems there *is* someone out there who wants me dead, and I still have no idea who it is or why. My nerves are as frayed as Rubbish's scratch board."

"That has to be scary."

"It is. Hurley has people on the force guarding me whenever he can't be with me. At first he was paying them out of his own pocket, but I finally convinced him that we should share the cost."

"You mean you have guards?"

"I have someone watching my every move."

"Even now?"

"Yes, even now. There is a cop outside your office as we speak, waiting to escort me back home."

"You sound like you don't think it's necessary."

"I'm not sure it is, and to be honest, if it was just me I had to worry about, I would have ditched the guards months ago. But now I have this one to worry about, too." I rub a hand over my bulging tummy, and the kid gives me a kick. I'm not sure if it's a protest, a gesture of understanding, or simply an attempt to change positions.

"You're not still living at the motel, are you?"

"No, thank goodness. I'm back in my cottage. Only these days it feels more like a prison. I have to tell someone anytime I want to go out, and I haven't been allowed to visit any of my family because Hurley doesn't think their houses are secure enough."

"Have they visited you?"

"No. I told them not to. It's too risky. My mother hardly ever ventures outside anyway, and Desi's always busy with the kids."

"No wonder you're feeling stressed."

"And you don't know the half of it yet," I say.

"So tell me."

I glance at my watch. "Are you sure you have the time?"

"I told you I have all day. I want to hear the rest of it."

"Okay, but I have to pee first. And I'll have an escort for that, too. Fortunately, the cop with me today is a woman."

"There's a bathroom right across the hall," Maggie says. "I'll wait until you come back."

I hoist myself out of the chair, a Herculean task these days, and say, "Sure, flaunt your vast bladder capacity at me. See if I care." I lumber out of the room and find Brenda Joiner sitting in the waiting room.

"I was starting to get worried," she says, tossing aside the magazine she is reading. "You've been in there so long. If it wasn't for the fact that I could hear your voice through the door, I might have felt compelled to break in there just to make sure you were all right."

"I'm sorry, Brenda. I know it's been a while, and it's going to be even longer still, I'm afraid. I'm just taking a bathroom break." I lumber out into the hallway and to the bathroom. Brenda is right on my heels.

"If you want, you can leave, and I'll call you when I'm done," I say as I lock myself into a stall so narrow I can barely turn around in it.

"No way, José," Brenda says. "Hurley's instructions are to stay with you at all times. And I'm fine. I don't have anywhere I need to be."

"Don't you think this whole thing has gotten out of hand?" I ask her as I finish peeing. "It's been more than four months of this. If someone really wanted to kill me, don't you think they would've done it by now?"

"You're still getting those phone calls, and they're coming from a series of burner phones that change with every other call. So clearly someone has you on their radar."

I flush and emerge from the stall to wash my hands. As I dry them, I say, "I think maybe these latest phone calls have to be coming from my father."

"We know that the original calls weren't from him, so that doesn't make sense. Even if it was him, why is he being so sneaky about it? Why all the different phones? Why doesn't he just talk to you?"

"I don't know." This isn't altogether true. If the latest round of calls are indeed coming from my father, he has a very good reason for being so surreptitious. But no one knows the reason at the moment except for me, Richmond, a couple of state troopers, and a handful of federal agents. And I intend to keep it that way.

I try once again to convince Brenda to leave, but she refuses. As soon as we head back to Maggie's office, she settles in with her magazine again and says, "I'm assigned to you all day long, so take as much time as you need."

Maggie is still seated where she was when I left, and since I left the door to her office open, she has seen and heard the part of the exchange with Brenda that took place in her waiting room.

"I see what you mean," she says, once I close the office door.

I waddle back to my seat and drop into it. "I have no privacy anymore," I tell her. "Although there is an upside. It has gotten me out of going to the gym because no one thinks it's safe enough. But it's like this twenty-four hours a day. That makes it kind of hard to work on a relationship, particularly when there's a beautiful woman in the picture who doesn't wear clothes that look like tents, doesn't have boobs that leak at odd times, *does* strut around in fashionable do-me shoes, and does seem to have lots of free time to spend with whomever she wants."

"I take it that the whomever you are referring to is Hurley."

"How did you guess?"

"Let's just say it doesn't require a psychiatric degree to figure that one out. Does this videographer have a name?"

"Yeah, Charlotte the harlot."

Maggie bites back another smile.

"It's Charlotte Finnegan. She told us all to call her Charlie, because she's"—I pause and make air quotes with my fingers—"just one of the guys. Hmph! *That's* not fooling anyone."

"How do you and this Charlotte get along? I assume you've had to work with her for the past few months."

"On the surface we get along fine. Of course, many of our interactions are on film, so we both tend to be a bit restrained and on our best behaviors during those times."

"And the other times?"

"She's made it pretty clear that she's interested in Hurley."

"Are you sure about that? Is there a chance that you might be reading meanings into things that aren't there?"

"Let me tell you how our first few days together went, and then you tell me if you think I'm imagining things. If that doesn't convince you, I have plenty more."

Maggie shifted in her chair and put her legs up on a stool, getting herself comfortable. "Okay then," she said, pen poised. "Let's hear it."

Chapter 21

After we left Hurley's house and went back to the police station, Hurley walked me inside, sticking close to my backside, like a tick on a dog's ass. Once we were safely within the station's confines, I breathed a sigh of relief.

"Hey, Mattie, congratulations!" said Heidi, the day dispatcher. "I heard the good news!" She cast a wary eye around the room and then in a low voice added, "And congrats to you, too, Hurley."

It seemed Richmond was right; everyone knew about me and Hurley.

As we entered into the back area behind the security door, Hurley said, "We should try to fit you with a Kevlar vest."

I looked at him like he'd said we needed to go buy the Brooklyn Bridge. "You're kidding, right?" I eyed my chest dubiously.

"No, I'm not. It's not a guarantee of safety, but it's a move in the right direction."

"Steve's right," said Richmond, who had walked up behind us and apparently overheard.

I was about to protest, but Richmond grabbed my arm and hauled me into the office he and Hurley now shared.

The troopers had infiltrated the place, and it was obvious no one was very happy about it. Though most of the cops knew one another and had often shared a drink, a story, or a bust, you never would have guessed it from the palpable wall of tension I felt. Hurley's desk was occupied by a trooper whose name tag said SKINNER. He looked to be in his late forties, close to Richmond's age, and he was a little shorter than me, balding, and leaning toward the pudgy side.

"Good morning," Skinner greeted us. "I'll be out of your way in just a sec. I need to finish up some paperwork."

"Take your time," Richmond said, and he sounded like he meant it, even though I knew it had to aggravate him to be displaced this way. Richmond walked over to a wall cabinet, opened it, and took out a Kevlar vest that looked big enough to fit two policemen. "This is my old vest," he said. "Try it on."

"You've got to be kidding me," I said, eyeing the thing. "It's huge."

"Yeah, well, so was I."

"By the way, you look great, Bob," Hurley tossed out.

"Thanks. I've been working hard at it."

He handed me the vest, which felt like it weighed a ton. I nearly dislocated my shoulder trying to put it on. Then I nearly cried when I saw how well it fit, at least the top part of it. There was plenty of room in the bottom of it—though with time that would obviously change—but across my bust it fit just fine. It smelled like a gym locker room.

"This looks ridiculous," I said, taking the vest off and tossing it in the corner. "That's not happening."

Hurley bit back a smile. "It does look a little ridiculous," he said. "But it's the best we have for now. They don't make body armor for pregnant women."

"Then you guys are just going to have to guard me better."

Hurley and Richmond both sighed. I think they knew they had lost the battle. Richmond waved the white flag by saying, "Skinner here is in charge of the investigation into the guy who shot you." He turned to Skinner then and said, "Got anything new you can share with us?"

Skinner shook his head, but he gave me a funny look that made me think he did have something, just not something he was willing to share at the moment. He cleverly changed the subject before anyone could ask anything else. "What have you guys got going on this morning? The place is packed, and everyone is all abuzz about something."

"Yeah, the chief has an announcement to make," Richmond said. He glanced at his watch. "In fact, we need to head to the break room now because he's due to talk in two minutes."

We headed that way, leaving Skinner behind at Hurley's desk. Despite the fact that the break room was large, people were packed in like sardines. Both on- and off-duty cops had come in, and there was a lot of muttering and murmuring going on. Over in the far corner I saw Alison Miller, camera slung around her neck as usual, taking notes. She saw me looking at her and gave me a little finger wave, which I reluctantly returned. Despite her new, friendlier demeanor, I still wasn't sure I could trust her.

Chief Hanson came into the room precisely at eight-thirty. Right behind him was a woman carrying a video camera. Silence fell over the room faster than Felix Baumgartner fell to earth, and as I looked around at the others, I saw that everyone was focused on the woman who had entered with Chief Hanson. It was hard not to stare; she was glaringly, frighteningly beautiful, with fine features, porcelain skin, a cascade of thick, dark red hair, eyes as blue as an October sky, and a tall, hourglass figure that would look perfect on a pinup calendar. She showed off that figure with a pair of tight-fitting black slacks, a peacock-blue tailored blouse that complemented both her hair and her eyes, and matching blue pumps. Her makeup was subtle but there, and it looked like it had been done by a professional. I was instantly, unreasonably, and insanely envious. Of course, the fact that my ankles had morphed into cankles—a fact that wouldn't bother me quite so much in another couple of months because I wouldn't be able to see them—might have had something to do with it.

"Good morning," Chief Hanson said, smiling at the room. "I know you are all busy and have things to do and places to be, so I'll make this as short as I can. To begin with, I'd like to announce that Detective Bob Richmond has come out of semiretirement and has rejoined our ranks on a full-time basis for now. He'll be assisting Detective Hurley with all death-related investigations as well as assisting the vice squad. Please welcome Bob back into our family."

There was a general murmur of comments, and a

couple of guys slapped Richmond on the back in a friendly gesture.

After a few seconds of this, Hanson continued. "On the down side, I am sad to report that Detective Larry Johnson is leaving us to move to California. We appreciate your many years of service here with the Sorenson PD, Larry, and wish you all the best."

There was a general chorus of good wishes and a few slaps on the back for Larry, who was being forced to move to California so he could be near his kids. His ex-wife had married some rich fellow from the Silicon Valley and moved out there a month ago.

The chief waited for the murmur to die down before he continued. "I'm also happy to announce that Officer Junior Feller has been promoted to the position of detective as of this week, and he will be taking over the vice cases from Larry, with assistance as needed from Detectives Hurley and Richmond. Congratulations, Junior!"

The congratulatory murmurs in the room were louder with this announcement, and Junior got a couple of playful shoulder punches instead of slaps.

"We are actively seeking to hire on two new officers," Chief Hanson said, "and I have several interested candidates, including two new graduates and a transfer from Platteville. I hope to have the new folks in place within the month. Until they are on board, anyone wanting to work overtime shifts can see me."

This announcement was met with mixed reactions.

"And finally," the chief said, speaking a little louder to be heard over the side conversations going on in the room, "I'm happy to announce that today we will be launching a new program. We have received a grant and been approved as one of six beta sites for a new audiovisual evidentiary process. Basically this means that for the next six months we will have a full-time videographer on staff who will be accompanying the detectives to all major crime scenes so that we can film the scene, the evidence collection, and any off-site interviews that are done. Our videographer will be teaching all staff members how to operate and use the cameras to ensure high-quality videos that will be suitable for evidentiary use, as well as how to narrate when necessary as you film. This will start with the detectives and our evidence technician, Jonas, and gradually work down to all the officers. This is good news on several fronts. First, it means less paperwork for you guys because you can do many of your reports on camera rather than having to type them out."

This news was met with a mixed bag of reactions that ranged from excited and happy to wary. No one liked typing up reports, but I suspect the idea of performing in front of a camera made some folks nervous, me included.

"The other reason this new addition is good news for us is that it eliminates some of our current issues with evidence collection and our cooperative efforts with the ME's office. By videotaping our processes, we can skirt many of the problems we faced with needing to maintain professional oversight between the two agencies in order to ensure the integrity of our evidence." He looked directly at me as he said this, and I wasn't sure if it was because he knew about me and Hurley, or simply because he was mentioning the office I worked for.

Chief Hanson turned then and nodded to the gorgeous woman behind him, who stepped up and waved at everyone. "I'd like to introduce all of you to Charlotte Finnegan, our new audiovisual technician."

This time the reaction was much more positive, although a few of the guys looked dumbstruck. When Charlotte smiled and said, "Please call me Charlie. I'm just one of the guys, and I'm really looking forward to working with all of you," in a smoky voice with a hint of a Scottish lilt to it, I think every man in the room was momentarily mesmerized. I glanced over at Hurley, who was standing beside me, and was disheartened to see that he looked as awestruck as all the other men. Charlie was going to be a serious distraction.

The chief continued, though I'm not sure how much of what he said next was heard by any of the men in the room. "Charlie will be working full-time and will also be on call twenty-four seven for the first month or so. During that time she will be training the detectives and a select group of officers on filming tips and techniques, as well as the proper care and use of the cameras. Our short-term goal is to have all of you do your own filming at some point, though I'm hoping that down the road we'll be allowed to create a full-time videographer position that will include on-call time. Receiving this grant is a huge boon for us in that the cameras and Charlie are being provided to us free of charge. We were the only small-town police force that was included in the grant, so please make the most of it and make Charlie feel welcome."

Judging from the slobbering grins on most of the

men's faces, I didn't think that last part would be a problem.

Chief Hanson concluded his speech with, "That's it. Have a safe day, everyone." He then made his way through the crowd over to me and Hurley. "Steve, I've arranged for Charlie to start her training with you since you're not actively working a case right now. So if you could hook up with her once the rest of the room is done drooling over her, she'll get you started. The two of you can spend the week together getting familiar with the goods."

I gave Chief Hanson a major evil eye. No way did I want Charlotte Finnegan to get familiar with any of Hurley's goods, or vice versa. My initial excitement over the AV project and the elimination of much of the conflict of interest issues gave way to a feeling of dread and fear. I looked at Charlie as she did a meet-and-greet with various others in the room, wondering how Hurley could possibly spend a week with the woman and not want to bed her. Hell, I almost wanted to bed her.

"No problem," Hurley said to the chief. "I look forward to it."

I just bet you do, I thought, channeling my evil, snide side. I didn't want to let Hurley be alone with lovely Charlie, but before I could think up a way to insert myself into his training, Bob Richmond tapped me on the shoulder.

"Blake Sutherland should be here any minute. Are you ready?"

I didn't want to leave Hurley and Charlie alone together, but then I rationalized that it might do me good to get away from them. Blake's interview would provide a much-needed distraction. Or so I told myself. In reality, trying to get my mind off Hurley was like to trying to get one's mind off a painfully full bladder when the nearest bathroom is miles away.

Chapter 22

Alison managed to corner me and Richmond before we went in to talk with Blake Sutherland.

"Well, this new video program is certainly interesting, isn't it?"

"It is," Richmond said.

"Detective Hurley seems excited about it," Alison said with a sly look my way. "Best keep a close eye on him, Mattie."

"I don't think Mattie has anything to worry about," Richmond said.

While I appreciated his confidence, I wasn't sure I shared it.

"Any news on the Derrick Ames case?" Alison asked us.

"Check with me at the end of the day," Richmond told her. "I might have something for you by then."

"Okay, but I'm going to hold you to that," Alison said. Then she disappeared back into the crowd in the break room, looking for a photo op.

Blake Sutherland was already in the conference room waiting for us. She looked like she had just stepped out of the latest issue of *Vogue* or *Cosmopolitan*. Her chestnut-colored hair was sleek and smooth, accented with caramel highlights. Her dark brown eyes were masterfully done with shadows, liners, and mascara that magnified their color and shape without looking overdone. She was tall and slender, and dressed in tight-fitting, dark green slacks, brown pumps, and a tailored tan blouse that hugged her tiny waist and emphasized her ample bust. She was thoroughly pedicured and manicured and smelled divine. It wasn't hard to understand what Wendy saw in her. Blake Sutherland was a thoroughbred.

Her culture and manners were apparent almost immediately. She sat in a chair with her back ramrod straight, one leg crossed over the other. She folded her hands in her lap and showed us a pleasant smile that may or may not have been genuine. Richmond did the introductions and informed her that our talk would be recorded. "Of course," she said with that pleasant smile. She looked over at me as I settled into my chair and said, "Ms. Winston, you have the most amazing blue eyes. I always wanted blue eyes. Brown is so . . . earthy." Her lip curled in disgust when she said the word "earthy." Clearly it wasn't a good thing in her mind.

"Thank you," I said, wondering if she was trying to pave her way by plying me with false flattery. Frankly, I didn't care.

"Please tell me how I can be of help to you," Blake said, shifting her gaze to Richmond.

"I'm guessing Wendy Ames filled you in already?" Richmond said.

Most people would have hesitated, wondering if they should lie, but Blake answered without hesitation. "Yes, she did. She called me Saturday night right after they'd been notified. She slipped into the bathroom so she could speak to me in private. It's a terrible thing that happened to Derrick. He is . . . was a decent, kind man."

"You've met him?" Richmond said, looking surprised.

"Uh, no," Blake answered, with a guilty smile. At least she had the sense to look abashed. "But I've heard Wendy talk about him a lot. When you have two people who are caught up in an acrimonious breakup like theirs was, and they manage to set aside their own petty disagreements and differences for the sake of their children, that speaks volumes about the characters of the people involved. Derrick always put his boys first, and he's worked really hard over the past year to make the split as easy as possible for the kids. Frankly, he was much more mature about things in the beginning than Wendy was, but she came around pretty quickly."

"Did the two of them ever fight?" Richmond asked.

"I've never seen the two of them together, but based on what Wendy told me they argued from time to time, like any couple does. I think that happened more in the beginning, but over the past few months things settled down, especially after Wendy agreed to share custody."

"Have you and Wendy been involved since the split?"

"We've been involved since before the split," she said, without shame or embarrassment. "In fact, it was our relationship that led to the split. We didn't mean for it to happen; it just did. Neither of us has ever been involved in a relationship like this before, but when we met, something just clicked. It's hard to explain."

"How did you meet?" Richmond asked.

"I do some interior design work, and Wendy hired me when she wanted to remodel the kitchen in that old Victorian they lived in. The kitchen never did get done, and when Wendy left Derrick, she also left the house. She said she never liked the place, that it was Derrick who was into the older home styles. Wendy's tastes are much more modern."

"How did Derrick find out about the two of you?" I asked.

"Wendy told him. She said he didn't seem too upset until she told him she planned to move out and take the boys with her. Derrick went ballistic with that. He didn't want the divorce, but once he realized Wendy was determined to go through with it, he focused on his relationship with his boys. Wendy played hardball at first, but I convinced her to back down on the custody issue because Derrick was threatening to go to my husband about the whole thing. Once Wendy agreed to share custody, Derrick seemed to reach a level of acceptance that let him move on. After that, their relationship got much better."

"Derrick may have accepted things, but his son Jacob didn't," I said.

Blake looked appropriately concerned as she nodded. "Yes, Wendy has told me about Jacob's determination to get the two of them back together. I feel bad for the boy. I'm sure he doesn't understand how futile it is for him to want that, particularly since Wendy hasn't told either of the boys about her and me. I have to give Derrick credit. As far as I know he never trashed Wendy to his boys, nor did he rat her out."

"And I assume your husband doesn't know either?" I said.

Now she did look embarrassed. "He does not, and Wendy and I would like to keep it that way for now. At the risk of sounding like a callous gold digger, I'm not willing to give up my current lifestyle, and the money comes in handy for Wendy, too. She doesn't make much at that insurance company she works for. I hope I can count on your discretion in this matter?"

"Wendy doesn't mind sharing you with your husband?"

"It works for us for now."

Richmond and I looked at one another, and then he said, "Mrs. Sutherland, can you tell us where you were on Saturday night between the hours of six and eight?"

"Yes, I can. My husband and I were having dinner at that new French restaurant on Capitol Square in Madison, the one that just opened? We left there around seven-thirty. The maître d' is a friend of mine, and I'm sure he'll vouch for our time there."

Richmond took down the name of the maître d', and after a couple of basic contact questions, he let Blake go.

"This job never fails to surprise me," Richmond said once she was gone. "But surprises or not, Blake Sutherland seems like a dead end. Let's hope we do better with the Ames family."

"It may not be a dead end," I said. "I didn't realize Wendy Ames works for an insurance company. Makes me wonder if she took out life insurance on Derrick,

and if she did is it still active? And who are the bene-
ficiaries?"

"Good question," Richmond said. "We'll have to
ask Wendy about that, and in the meantime I'll get
Hurley to look into it, too."

The Ames family lawyer was the antithesis of Lucien—at least the old Lucien. Whereas Lucien was
typically dressed in wrinkled, worn, and stained
clothing, this guy, who announced his arrival with a
terse "Stanley Barber the Third"—with emphasis on
the Third, as if that was supposed to mean something
to us—had on a navy-blue pin-striped suit that included pants with a crease sharp enough to cut
cheese. Lucien was also known for cutting cheese, but
in his case it was a bodily function rather than any
type of fashion statement. Stanley's shirt was spotless,
and when he removed his jacket I saw the telltale
creases of a professional laundry service. His shoes
were highly polished, shiny enough that he could
have checked the status of his neatly coiffed hair in
their reflection. I couldn't help but wonder if Blake
Sutherland's money was paying for Stanley Barber
the Third.

Stanley breezed into the interrogation room with a
practiced authority and placed his alligator-skin briefcase on the table. He opened it, keeping it turned so
we couldn't see its contents, sat down in a chair with
his back ramrod straight, and folded his hands on the
table. The one thing he did have in common with
Lucien was what I call the lawyer smile. It's the same
predatory, sly smile you see on the faces of Mafia
henchmen in movies, right before they seal some-

one's feet in concrete and toss them in the East River.

Wendy looked nervous, Michael looked sad, and Jacob looked bored and indifferent. Today Jacob was wearing dark blue jeans and a red T-shirt with ZOMBIES HATE FAST FOOD written on it. I looked down at his shoes. They were high-tops, with the laces undone. I saw Richmond glance at Jacob's footwear as well, and the two of us exchanged a frustrated look when we realized they weren't the shoes we had seen in the video.

There was some juggling for seats, and when it was all done, Wendy was to Stanley's left, with Jacob and Michael to her left. As soon as everyone was in position, Stanley spoke to us with his head tilted back ever so slightly, giving the impression that he was looking down his nose at us. It wouldn't have surprised me to know that he was doing just that, if for no other reason than simply because of the way Richmond and I were dressed. Richmond was between sizes in his clothes because of the weight he had lost, and it had left him wearing baggy stuff that tended to make him look like a sloppy, shapeless blob. I was in the same situation with regard to being between sizes, but for the opposite reason. I wasn't ready to start wearing my maternity clothes just yet, and my old clothes fit snugly enough that I feared making any unusual or sudden moves lest I burst a seam somewhere and expose some part of my ever-growing body. Plus my creases, unlike Stanley's, came from being folded up inside a suitcase, not from a laundry service.

"My client, Wendy Ames, understands that you wish to question her son Jacob regarding his whereabouts on the day of his father's demise," Stanley said in a nasal, snobby tone. "You may question him at this time, but he will not answer any questions unless I tell him to." He said this with a pointed look at Jacob, making me suspect that Wendy's eldest might not want to play ball. This suspicion grew even stronger when I looked over at Jacob. He appeared sullen, angry, and ready to explode. His nose flared with every breath, his right leg was jiggling nervously, and the muscles in his jaw were twitching. I had a sense that with a little provocation he would explode like fireworks on the Fourth of July. And provocation is something I excel at.

"You may begin," Stanley said in his haughty tone.

Richmond hit the button under the table edge that started the AV recording rolling. It made me think of Hurley spending time with Charlie, and my mood plummeted. I shook it off and refocused on the task at hand.

After a brief intro to note the day, the time, the people present, and the case this interview was for, Richmond said, "Jacob, your brother told us you left the house in the late afternoon on the day of your father's death during the time that your mother was out. Is that true?"

Jacob shot his brother a nasty look, and I felt bad for the younger boy.

"You don't have to answer that," Stanley said.

"No, you don't," Richmond said. "We already know you were there. Not only did some of your father's neighbors see you arrive and leave in a huff, they heard the two of you exchange heated words." Richmond looked over at Stanley. "We have several neighbors who are willing to sign affidavits verifying this."

Stanley's pompous expression faltered just a smidge,

and he leaned over and whispered something into Wendy's ear. Wendy nodded and then looked at Jacob. "Go ahead and tell them what you told me."

"Yeah, I went over to my dad's house."

"And the two of you had a disagreement?" Richmond posed.

"I saw him in bed with another woman," Jacob said in a sneering tone. "It made me mad."

"Who was the woman?" Richmond asked.

"Ollie Terwilliger's mom, Mandy."

Richmond looked over at Wendy. "Did you know Derrick was seeing her?"

"You don't have to answer that," Stanley said.

"Why shouldn't I?" Wendy said, looking at her lawyer. "I don't have anything to hide, Stanley. And, yes," she said, shifting her gaze back to Richmond, "I did know that Derrick was seeing her."

Wendy reached over and placed a hand on her son's arm, but he immediately pulled away from her. "Jacob, honey, I've told you before that your dad and I are never going to get back together."

"What bullshit!" Jacob yelled, shooting his mother a nasty look. I could tell he was trying not to cry. "You didn't even try. Maybe if you'd put a little effort into it, he wouldn't have found himself a girlfriend."

"Your father and I did try, but it just didn't work," Wendy said with a sympathetic but pained expression. "I've explained this to you before. So has your father."

"Whatever," Jacob mumbled. He folded his arms over his chest and slammed back in his chair, grinding his teeth.

"We talked to the mother of the boy whose house

you said you were going to that night—to play some video games, I believe it was?" Richmond said.

Jacob eyed him angrily. "Yeah, so? Is it against the law to play video games now?"

"Jacob!" Wendy pivoted in her chair and faced her son. "There is no need for the snotty tone."

Richmond kept at the boy. "She said you were there, but that you and Sean didn't eat dinner. I know you were climbing out the window of your bedroom at home to sneak around. Any chance you did the same thing at Sean's house?"

"Don't answer that question," Stanley said. Then he leaned forward and eyed Richmond. "I need to confer with my client before we continue this."

I sensed that we were about to lose any advantage we had, so I jumped in. "Did you go back to your dad's house that night before you went home, Jacob?" I asked. "Were you so mad about him and Mandy Terwilliger that you went back and got in a fight?"

Jacob squirmed, and I could tell I was getting under his skin. I think Stanley sensed it, too, because he objected again, louder this time, and with a pointed look at Jacob. "Don't answer that question!"

I tried again. "Did you get so mad during the fight that you killed him?"

It was enough to push Jacob over the edge. He thrust himself out of his chair and leaned across the table, getting in my face. "Screw you!" he yelled. "I went for a walk to clear my head. You stupid police people don't know what you're talking about."

"Jacob!" Wendy yelled. She tugged on her son's sleeve, but he brushed her off angrily.

"We have you on video," Richmond said. "Your father had a video camera, and it either fell or got knocked down between the fridge and the cabinet. And it turned on. It filmed you, Jacob. It shows you struggling with your father right around the time he was stabbed."

"You assholes think you're so smart, but you don't know anything," Jacob said. Then he stormed from the room.

Stanley Barber the Third snapped his briefcase closed, stood up, and said, "We're done here." He turned to Wendy. "Let's go."

Wendy stood slowly, looking stunned. "Do you really have him on video?" she asked.

Richmond didn't answer her, and Stanley said, "I suspect it was just a bluff, an attempt to make Jacob confess, which he didn't do because he's innocent."

"It isn't a bluff," Richmond said.

"Then are you placing him under arrest?" Stanley asked. He looked far too smug, meaning he knew the answer.

Richmond said nothing, and after a few seconds, Michael started to cry. Wendy walked over and hugged him. "It will be okay, honey," she said. "Come on."

Michael stood, still sobbing. "Did Jake kill Dad?" he asked.

"Be quiet, boy," Stanley snapped, then he quickly ushered the trio from the room.

"Well, that was interesting," Richmond said once they were gone.

"Did I mess things up by provoking the kid?"

"Not at all. It showed us how short Jacob's fuse is."

"So what's next?"

"I'm hoping my search warrant for the Ames house will come through any minute now. In the meantime,

I want to look into the insurance situation and see if Junior dug up anything of interest about Derrick's finances. And we should give the lab a call to see if they've found any unexpected fingerprints or blood evidence in Derrick's house. At some point we should verify Mandy Terwilliger's alibi and confirm that she was working, but no rush on that. My money's on Jacob, and if he did it, confirming any other alibis is more a matter of eliminating reasonable doubt than it is anything else."

As we stepped out of the interview room, we ran into Hurley and Charlie in the hallway.

"Wow, you must have really pissed that kid off," Hurley said. "He stormed out of here like the hounds of hell were nipping at his heels. Think he's good for it?"

"Maybe," Richmond said. "Probably. We have video of someone struggling with the victim at the time of the murder. It only shows the feet, but the shoes are distinctive, and there's a mark on them that should make the specific pair easy to identify. The kid wasn't wearing them here today, but I bet we'll find them in his house. I don't think he's smart enough to have ditched them."

Charlie gave Hurley a gentle elbow in his ribs. "See, I told you videos are going to be the wave of the future in crime solving."

Hurley smiled back at her, which made me frown.

Richmond said, "It certainly will make a difference in this case. Let me show you." We headed into the shared office, and Richmond pulled up the video Arnie had sent. Hurley sat in the chair to watch it, and unfortunately Charlie watched it, too, standing behind and to one side of Hurley, leaning in close, and putting a hand on his shoulder.

"You're right," Hurley said when the video was done. "Those shoes are pretty distinctive."

"Plus there's some mystery surrounding the victim's cell phone," Richmond said. "It wasn't on him, wasn't in the house, and can't be found anywhere. If we're lucky, the kid will have that, too."

For the next half hour, Richmond brought Hurley and Charlie up to speed on the case and where we were so far in the investigation. A talk with Junior revealed that there were no irregularities he could find in Derrick's finances. A call to the lab offered up nothing new either. But Hurley's call to the insurance company struck gold.

"It seems that Wendy Ames had Derrick's life insured to the tune of a half million bucks," he told us when he got off the phone. "Derrick continued paying the premiums on it after the divorce. In fact, it was a stipulation in the divorce agreement. But Wendy isn't the beneficiary, the kids are."

Richmond smiled. "I'm betting Jacob knows about that policy. That gives him even more motive."

"Maybe," Hurley said. "But even though Wendy isn't the beneficiary, the policy states that if Derrick dies before the boys reach the age of eighteen, the money is to go into a trust fund that Wendy would control."

"A chunk of money like that might help convince Blake to leave her husband," I said.

There was a knock on the office door, and Heidi, the dispatcher on duty, walked in and handed some papers to Richmond. "This just came in over the fax," she said.

"Hot dog," Richmond said, flicking the corner of the papers with his fingers. "My search warrant finally came through. Let's see what Stanley Barber the Third has to say about this." He looked like a kid at Christmas who had just gotten the gift of his dreams. He took out his cell phone, called a couple of uniformed officers who were on duty, and asked them to meet us at the Ames house in ten minutes.

Charlie said, "Would you mind if we go with you when you execute the warrant and videotape the search? It would be an ideal situation for Steve's filming debut."

"That's a great idea," Hurley said.

"Then come along," Richmond said. "The more the merrier."

Yippee.

Chapter 23

"Should we all ride together, or do you and Charlie want to take a separate car?" Richmond asked Hurley.

I was about to suggest that we all ride together because the idea of Charlie and Hurley cozying up together in one car didn't make me happy. But Charlie solved the problem for me.

"Actually, I'd prefer to take my own car. I have a lot of equipment in it, some of which I might want to use, and it's a pain to have to move it."

"No problem," Hurley said. "You can follow us out there." Then he turned to me. "Want a lift?"

I breathed a sigh of relief and smiled at him. "I'd love one."

We headed out the back door to the parking lot, and I followed Hurley to his car. Once we were settled inside, we waited for Richmond to get into his vehicle and lead the way. Charlie got into an older model Toyota sedan, and Hurley motioned for her to fall in behind Richmond, allowing us to bring up the rear.

"Have you heard anything from Izzy?" Hurley asked me once we were underway.

"I talked to him last night. He's a little overwhelmed right now dealing with Dom and his family, so we kept it short and simple. He basically just wanted to make sure I was okay."

"So you didn't talk much about the baby thing?"

"Not at all since the other night when he let me know he'd figured it out. We were supposed to discuss it over dinner on Sunday, but he had to cancel because of Dom's dad's death. I wanted you to be the first person I told, but clearly that didn't go the way I planned."

"Yeah, getting shot at can really mess up your plans."

"You know what I mean," I said.

"I do, I'm just giving you a little ribbing. By the way, one of the state guys involved in your investigation is a good friend of mine. I used to work with him years ago when I was in Chicago. He promised to keep me in the loop, and after the meeting this morning he told me he thinks you'll probably be cleared in a day or two."

"That would be nice."

"Did Richmond tell you what they learned about the guy who shot at you?"

"He did, and I don't get it. Who would want to kill me, and why?"

"Who knows why the fruitcakes in the world do what they do?" Hurley said. "You don't have to worry about him anymore, but you still need to be careful since we don't know who he was working for."

I nodded, resisting a sudden urge I had to look over my shoulder. "Do you mind ferrying me around until I get the hearse back?"

"Of course not. In fact, I intend to ferry you around even after you get the hearse back to make sure you're okay. And speaking of that beast you drive, there's a good chance they'll have it back to you by next week. Jonas came in at four this morning to process it for evidence. He had to remove the back bumper, two of the tires, and the rear driver side panel because it had a bullet hole in it. The rest of the damage was all in the glass. There's a small dent in the tailgate where it hit the telephone pole, but otherwise the car is drivable. The state guys supervised the evidence collection and released the car, and Jonas had it hauled over to Marty Preston's shop to get it fixed. Turns out one of the funeral home's other hearses was involved in an accident last year, and that's why they decided to get a new fleet and bought those soccer-mom vans they drive now. The other hearse is the same make, model, year, and color as yours. It ended up in a junk yard outside of Madison, and the owner parked it out in front of the place with a sign that says, WHERE CARS COME TO DIE. They've agreed to let Marty Preston have the rear panel from that hearse to put on yours. He's picking it up today, and he said he should have it in place by the end of the week. And he's replacing the windows and tires in the next day or two."

"That's wonderful news," I said, truly excited. "I considered buying something new since I can afford it now, but I have to admit, I love that stupid hearse."

"Much as I hate to admit it, I love it, too."

Well, we're getting closer. He said he loves my car. "You do?"

"Yeah, it probably saved your life . . . yours and Junior's."

"Junior? He wasn't there until after I called 911."

"Not that Junior, this one," he said reaching over and putting a hand on my tummy. "It's going to be a boy."

"Oh, really? How do you know that?"

"I'll have you know that I come from a long line of men and women who have what we Irish call the gift."

"The gift?" I echoed, amused.

"Yeah, you know, the second sight. Sometimes I just know things."

"And to think I thought you were such a realist."

"It's real. Just you wait and see. When Junior is born, you'll be a believer, too."

I smiled and shook my head.

"Speaking of which, when is your due date?"

"September twentieth."

"Emily wanted me to ask. She's very excited about it."

"You told Emily?"

"Yeah, wasn't I supposed to?"

I thought about that and realized there was no reason for him not to tell her, though for some reason I had thought he would wait.

Before I could respond, he said, "I wasn't going to tell her right away, but she sensed there was something on my mind. She gave me an interrogation this morning worthy of the best detective. So I caved and told her. I figured she could use some lighter news for a change."

I sat in silence as we stopped at a light on Main Street and thought about Emily. My baby . . . no, *our* baby, I corrected myself, would be her half-brother or -sister.

"When do you see the doctor again?" Hurley asked when the light changed.

"Wednesday."

"Can I come along? Are they going to do one of those ultrasound things where you can see the baby?"

Hurley's request, and his happy interest in the whole matter, delighted me. After last night, I thought he might still be upset, or withdrawn, maybe even surly. But he appeared to be embracing his new role as a father with plenty of excitement and anticipation. So I said, "Sure, you can come along if you want. And yes, they are going to do one of those ultrasound things."

"So we can find out if it's going to be a boy or a girl?"

"We could, but I don't want to know."

Hurley shot me a puzzled look. "Why not?"

"Because I like surprises. I like the unpredictability of it. That's why I liked working in the ER so much. I never knew what was going to come through the door next. It's a big part of what I like about my current job."

"Well, we definitely differ on that score," Hurley said. "I like predictability."

"You were probably one of those kids who sneaked a peek at his Christmas presents early."

"Hell, yeah," he said. "One year I carefully unwrapped every present I had under the tree, easing the tape off, and unfolding the paper just enough to see what was inside. Then I just as carefully rewrapped them and put them back in their place." He frowned then and added, "It was kind of a bummer on Christmas morning. I had to act surprised even though I knew what I was getting."

"See?" I said. "Surprises do have some value."

"I suppose. I'll think about it," he said.

"And besides, I hate pink, and if it's a girl, everyone will be buying pink stuff. I don't want a bunch of pink crap."

"It's not going to be a girl."

We had arrived at the Ames house, and he parked the car in the street behind Charlie and Richmond. When he turned off the engine, I started to get out, but he grabbed me by the arm and said, "Hold on a sec."

I paused and looked back at him, expectantly . . . a veritable pregnant pause.

"Look, I just want you to know that I'm truly happy about this, Winston. Having kids wasn't on my radar at this point in my life, but I'm ready to take it on. And if I'm going to have a kid at any stage in my life, I'm glad it's with you."

My chest seized up, and before I knew what was happening, I started to sob.

"What?" Hurley said. "Did I say something wrong?"

I shook my head, unable to speak for the moment. Finally I managed to get myself under control. "No, you said everything right." *Well, almost everything.*

"Then why are you crying?"

"Because I'm pregnant," I said in a slightly exasperated tone.

"You're not happy about it?" he asked, looking confused.

"I'm very happy," I said, wiping my runny nose on my sleeve. "These are happy tears."

Hurley nodded slowly, but his expression remained befuddled. "Is it going to be like this until Junior arrives?"

"Maybe. Probably. Hell, I don't know. It might be like this for a while after Junior arrives. It's the hormones. They do weird things to me."

"Hunh."

I managed to get my sobs under control and said, "I'm sorry. It's just that this whole thing is such an emotional experience for me. My hormones are going crazy, my body is changing almost daily, and to be honest, I'm a little scared."

"Of what?"

"That something will be wrong with the baby. I don't know anything about my father, his health, or his family history. And look at the maternal genes I inherited. What if I'm a crappy mother? Or worse yet, what if I'm a mother like my mother? What if this whole thing is a huge mistake?" I looked out the car's front window and saw Richmond and Charlie, along with a couple of uniformed cops, all of them standing on the sidewalk, staring at us with curious expressions.

"We'll do tests on the kid to make sure it's okay," Hurley said. "They can do that these days, can't they?"

I nodded and took in a deep breath to try to re-center myself.

"I can deal with your hormones, Winston. Hormones are nothing. I handle killers for a living, remember?"

That made me smile, although I'm not sure he fully understood the potential damage out-of-control female hormones can do. At times I'm like a bodybuilder who's pissed off, overdosed on steroids, and armed with a chain saw.

"And I like your body no matter what it looks like," he continued. "In fact, some of the changes are very appealing." He eyed my chest and wiggled his eyebrows. I probably should have been insulted, but I wasn't. At this stage, I'd take anything. "Even if there is something wrong with the kid," Hurley went on, "we'll still raise him, take care of him, and provide him with a good life, right?"

I nodded, afraid that if I tried to speak I'd start crying again.

"It will be fine, Winston. We're in this together, okay?"

I liked the sound of that. Regardless of what happened between me and Hurley and our personal relationship, we *were* in this thing together, and I knew I'd do whatever was necessary to make sure we did the best for the child we were going to have.

"Is it too soon for me to start shopping for footballs?" Hurley asked, nudging me with his elbow.

That got a laugh out of me. I sniffed one last time, and said, "Probably, but do it anyway." I rubbed a hand over my tummy. "Who knows? By the time this critter grows up, maybe girls will be allowed to play in the NFL." I opened my door to get out. "Come on. Charlie and Richmond are waiting on us."

Chapter 24

We paraded up to the Ames's front porch, Richmond and I in the lead, Hurley and Charlie bringing up the rear. Charlie already had the camera on and aimed at the front door. "I'll shoot until we get inside, then you can take over," she said to Hurley.

Wendy Ames scowled at us when she answered the door. "What are you doing here? Stanley said not to talk to you unless he is present, so if you need something you can call him."

Richmond smiled, a predatory, self-satisfied smile that was kind of scary. "We aren't here to talk to you; we're here to conduct a search of your home."

"You can't search my house," Wendy said, frowning. She had her cell phone in hand, and she started jabbing at the screen. "I'm calling Stanley."

"Good," Richmond said. "You can read him this." He then stuck the search warrant in front of her face.

Wendy stopped poking at her phone and stared at the paper, letting the reality of it sink in. Ten seconds later, her face turned beet red, and she looked like steam was about to come out of her ears. It was easy to see where Jacob got it from. Richmond snatched the paper away and paraded past Wendy into the living room, the rest of us following.

Wendy's house was smaller than Derrick's, but the furnishings looked brand new, and the décor, as Blake had said, was decidedly modern, with lots of glass and chrome. I wondered how much of it had been paid for by Derrick and how much had been provided by Blake.

Richmond turned back to look at Wendy and said, "Where is Jacob's room?"

Wendy still looked apoplectic, but she gathered her wits together and walked past Richmond down a hallway leading off the living room. She stopped at the last room on the right and knocked on the door. "Jacob?" she hollered.

There was no answer. She grabbed the doorknob and tried to turn it, but it was locked.

"Jacob!" she yelled, sterner this time.

Still no answer.

Richmond gently pushed her aside and pounded on the door with his fist. "Jacob Ames, this is the police. Open up!"

Not a peep came from the other side of the door. Richmond looked at the knob, which had a small hole at its center, and then fished around in his pocket. He came out with a tiny Swiss Army knife, opened it to a small screwdriver, and stuck it in the hole. After maneuvering with it for a few seconds, we heard a *pop*, and Richmond turned the knob and opened the door.

There was no one in the room.

"Where is he?" Wendy asked, looking panicked.

Hurley and Charlie were shoulder to shoulder, filming everything we were doing, Hurley holding the camera and Charlie watching the screen along with him. They were practically cheek to cheek, and as Charlie passed me I shot eye daggers into the back of her head.

"Looks like he might have done another window trick," Richmond said, nodding toward the window, which was open. Richmond then walked over to Jacob's desk, which was covered with stuff: socks, an iPod, a boom box, a laptop, various personal hygiene items, some schoolbooks, notebooks, and several pieces of paper. There was also a smashed smartphone sitting off to one side. With a gloved hand, Richmond picked the phone up and showed it to Wendy.

"Is this Jacob's?"

Wendy looked puzzled and shook her head. "Jacob's phone is a flip model."

Richmond held the mangled phone up to the camera, then turned it over to show that the battery was gone.

That's when Wendy said, "That looks like Derrick's phone." The four of us exchanged looks, and Wendy didn't miss it. "What does that mean?"

Richmond didn't answer her. I grabbed an evidence bag from the scene kit I'd brought in from Hurley's car, and Richmond dropped the phone into it. I then sealed and labeled the bag.

After sifting through the rest of the stuff on Jacob's desk, Richmond went to the closet. He opened the door to reveal chaos: piles of clothes on the floor, a few items hanging askew from wire hangers, and a half dozen pairs of shoes. Right in the middle of the shoe pile was a pair of ASIC Gel Scout athletic shoes with blue trim and orange soles.

Richmond bent over, picked them up, and held them aloft for Hurley to film. On the inside of one of them was a scuff mark in the shape of the Nike swoosh. "Do these look familiar?" he said to Hurley.

Wendy looked even more panicked. "What do you mean? Why are you interested in Jacob's shoes?"

Once again Richmond ignored her question, and I could tell Wendy was getting very frustrated. I opened up a bag for him to put the shoes into. Then I sealed and labeled it.

"Would somebody please tell me what's going on?" Wendy pleaded.

"We need to find your son," Richmond said. "Do you have any idea where he might be?"

Wendy shook her head frantically. "I thought he was in his room."

From the hallway, a meek voice said, "I think he went to Sean's house." We all turned and saw Jacob's younger brother, Michael, standing there. "He goes over there all the time. He sneaks out through his window. They both do."

Richmond took out his phone, called the station, and had officers dispatched to the Fitzpatrick house to look for Jacob. Wendy started to cry. Michael started to sob, and Hurley, seeing the younger boy's obvious distress, lowered the camera. Charlie took hold of his arm and tried to raise it back up, but he shook her off and handed her the camera. Then he went over to Michael and knelt down in front of him.

"Don't feel bad about telling on your brother," Hurley said, placing his hands on Michael's shoulders. "Jacob may be mad at you for a while, and he may say some mean things to you, but you did the right thing. I promise you that someday Jacob will understand and know that, and know that you did it because you love him, even if he doesn't know that now. Okay?"

Michael nodded, staring into Hurley's eyes.

This was a new, tender side of Hurley that I'd never seen before, and I wondered if his recent and rapid induction into fatherhood—twice—had anything to do with it.

"It's important that you stay strong and tough, okay?" Hurley said.

Michael nodded, tears tracking down his cheeks. Hurley chucked him once under his chin, and Michael took that as his cue; he turned and ran from the room.

Richmond's phone rang, and he answered it with a curt "Richmond." He listened for a moment and then hung up. "They have Jacob and they're taking him down to the station." He looked over at a tearful Wendy. "Mrs. Ames, we have clear evidence that Jacob was not only at his father's house at the time of death, but that he engaged in a scuffle with him. Derrick's phone is missing, and if this phone turns out to be his, it confirms Jacob's presence. We have other evidence as well, and I'll be questioning him as soon as we get back to the station."

"Oh my God," Wendy gasped. She looked terrified, but then her face shifted, morphing into what I call the mother tiger face. "I'm going to call Stanley," she said, poking at her cell phone. "I don't want you to talk to Jacob until Stanley gets there. And I want to be there as well."

Richmond started to respond, but Wendy's call went through, and after saying, "Stanley, please help me! I think Jacob might have killed his father!" she scurried off, ranting into the phone at Stanley Barber the Third.

We spent nearly an hour going through Jacob's room, confiscating his laptop, some clothes we found in his hamper—including a pair of stonewashed jeans with ragged, dirty hems that looked like the ones in the video—and a drawing we found under some other papers on the desk that showed two male figures, one stabbing the other in the chest, blood dripping down the victim's shirt and pants onto the floor.

When we were done with the bedroom, we headed out to the main part of the house. Stanley arrived, but after he saw the search warrant, he pulled Wendy aside and did nothing to stop us. Clearly he was miffed, but most of his earlier bluff and bluster was gone. Wendy called a neighbor, who came over and picked Michael up. The kid didn't want to leave, and he sobbed all the way out to the car. It broke my heart to watch him.

After collecting several jackets and a hoodie from the coat closet, items that Wendy identified as belonging to Jacob, Richmond looked over at Charlie and Hurley. The two of them had traded the camera back and forth, taking turns filming, but they had remained linked together like Siamese twins.

"Did you guys get everything?" Richmond asked.

"We certainly did," Charlie said.

"Then I think we're done here," Richmond said. Wendy was sitting on her chrome-and-leather sofa beside Stanley. Her tears had dried, but she looked pale, frightened, and shell-shocked. "I'm sorry," Richmond said to her.

Neither Wendy nor Stanley commented, or even looked our way, so we gathered up our evidence and left, with Wendy and Stanley prepared to follow and meet us at the station.

As Hurley and I walked back to his car, both of us looked glum. I suspect Hurley was bummed because he felt bad for little Michael and what was happening to the Ames family. For me it was that, and the idea that Hurley and Charlie would be cheek to cheek again soon, bonding over the footage that documented the ruination of the Ames family.

Chapter 25

Once again we formed a caravan as we headed back to the station. As soon as Hurley and I were safely ensconced inside his car, away from other eyes and ears, he picked up our baby conversation where we left off.

"We should talk about names for the kid, don't you think?" he said as he started the car and then sat waiting for Richmond and Charlie to take off. "Do you have any in mind?"

"I hadn't really thought about it yet," I said. "But I know one name that's off the list for sure."

"What's that?"

"Mine. I wouldn't want to put any kid of mine through what I went through trying to hide from my real name. I mean what the hell were my parents thinking when they saddled me with a moniker like Matterhorn?"

"It is a bit out there," Hurley agreed. "Though I do like Mattie."

I shook my head. "I don't want the kid to have ei-

ther of our names. It's too confusing. He or she de-
serves his or her own unique name."

"Not too unique," Hurley said, pulling out behind
Charlie's car. "We need to be careful not to pick
names that will be conducive to playground jibes and
bullying. But I do like the idea of carrying on family
names. What was your father's name?"

"I don't know, and it doesn't matter because I
wouldn't use it. He abandoned me as a child, and I'll
be damned if I'm going to reward that behavior by
giving him a namesake."

Hurley shot me a look. "You sound angry."

"I am," I said, feeling churlish. "This whole pregnancy thing has me thinking about family, and it
makes me mad that my child will never know his
grandfather. Though I suppose it's just as well considering what a jerk he must be."

"When you thought it was him who was following
you, you were worried that you had killed him. So
you must have some caring left in your heart for
him."

"He's not in my life, so let's drop the matter and
move on, keeping in mind that we need to pick something that flows well."

Hurley shot me a bemused smile. "Flows well?"

"Yeah, you know, the name needs to roll off the
tongue easily and sound a little sophisticated and dig-
nified. The syllables need to feel balanced. You don't
want Ebenezer Nebuchadnezzar Winston or Jack Sprat
Winston. You want something like Susannah Marie
Winston, or Richard Allen Winston."

A brief silence followed that was palpable. "Winston?" Hurley said, his tone dark. "Why the hell would
you use that last name?"

"It's my last name."

"No, it's David's last name. The kid isn't his." He shot me another look, this one suspicious. "You're sure it's not his, right?"

His doubt pissed me off. "Of course I am," I snapped. "I told you I haven't been with anyone else but you."

"Then the kid should have my last name."

"I get why you feel that way, Hurley, but that just makes things awkward because my last name will be different."

"Not if you marry me."

"Yeah, there's a good reason to get married," I scoffed. "And even if we did get married, what makes you think I'd take your last name?"

"Why wouldn't you? Is there some reason you want to keep David's last name? Is there something you aren't telling me? Wait, is that why you don't want to marry me, because you're not over David yet?"

I let out a sigh of sorely tried patience. "Trust me, I'm long over David."

"Then what's the problem with changing your name?"

"It's a moot point, Hurley. We aren't getting married, so there's no need to change my name."

"If you think I'm going to let you slap your sleazy ex's last name on any kid of mine, you are sorely mistaken."

We rode in silence for a minute or two, a palpable tension between us, until I couldn't stand it any longer.

"Look, I get why it would bother you if our kid doesn't have your last name," I said finally.

"He doesn't have to have my last name. I just don't

want any kid of mine to have Winston for a last name. I don't want him to have any connection to David."

"Him? You seem very certain."

"I am. And quit trying to change the subject."

I sighed. I not only understood his objection to the name thing, I kind of agreed with him. "Okay," I said, folding. "We'll use your last name."

Hurley shot me a hopeful look. "Does that mean you've changed your mind about getting married?"

"No."

"So you're going to keep the name Winston?"

"For now. I'll think about it more later."

"But the kid will have my last name?"

"Yes, I just said that," I snapped, feeling irritable. "What do I have to do, put it in writing?"

"As a matter of fact, yes, when we fill out the birth certificate."

"Fine. Now that we have the last name settled, we need to come up with two more," I said, eager to move on. "Since you like the idea of using family names, what's your middle name?"

"Decker. It was my mother's maiden name."

"Decker Hurley," I said, trying it on for size. "I kind of like that."

Hurley shook his head. "Not a chance. The kids will all be calling him Decker the pecker. Trust me, I know."

"Oh. Right." We sat in silence for a while, and then I asked him, "What's your father's name?"

"Peter," he said with a shake of his head.

"I'm sensing a trend in your family."

Hurley gave me a sly smile and wiggled his eyebrows, which allowed me to let out a breath of relief. Our normal camaraderie had been restored.

Then I had a brainstorm. "I have an idea," I said. "What if we use our first names but reverse them? If it's a boy—"

"It is."

I rolled my eyes. "If it's a boy we could call him Matthew, because some Matthews are called Matt or Matty. And if it's a girl we can name her Stephanie, which is like a feminine version of Steven."

Hurley pondered that for a few seconds and then slowly nodded. "That could work. I like both names. What about middle names?"

We had arrived at the police station, so I said, "Let's think about that one for a while."

It was time to stop discussing the creation of one family and witness the destruction of another.

Chapter 26

Junior Feller was in the break room when we arrived, and Richmond handed off the evidence packages we had collected, along with a barrage of instructions.

"Compare these shoes to the ones in the video; I'm pretty sure they'll be a perfect match. Then take them over to the lab at the ME's office and have them test both the shoes and the clothing for any evidence of blood. Next, see if you, Jonas, Arnie, or anyone else can do something with this phone to determine if it's Derrick's. And there's extra credit for you if you can figure out a way to resurrect the text messages that were sent to it. Finally, have someone scour through the kid's laptop. Have them search his e-mails, any instant messages, and his browser history for anything that might be connected."

"Will do," Junior said. "And since Dr. Henderson brought in a bunch of lab folks to work on Mattie's shooting, we have some extra hands on deck and might be able to get this stuff done faster than usual."

"Nice to know the intrusion might be useful for something," Richmond grumbled. "Where's the kid?"

"He's in the interrogation room with Brenda Joiner."

"Did you read him his rights when you picked him up?"

Junior nodded. "I did, but it won't hurt for you to do it again for the record."

"Thanks." Richmond then turned to me. "Do you want to be in on this?"

"Absolutely." My interest in this interrogation stemmed from more than my need to get some answers with our case. I was also curious to watch the interactions between mother and son that were about to take place. The whole idea of raising a patricidal child both frightened and intrigued me, and I wondered if it was a nature thing, a nurture thing, or some combination of the two. I felt a need to observe and search for some kind of clue, some telling comment or interaction, some hint about what not to do when my own child finally came into the world.

Wendy and Stanley arrived, and they were escorted into the interrogation room to join Jacob. After a minute or so Brenda came out, and Richmond and I used that as our cue.

As soon as we entered the room, Richmond bent down and triggered the AV recording equipment before either of us took a seat.

Jacob was sitting in the same seat he'd been in before, with Stanley on his left and his mother on his right. He had an insolent, angry glare on his face, and his right leg bounced nervously.

As soon as he was settled in a chair, Richmond said,

"Hello, Jacob. First off, let me inform you . . . *all* of you," he stressed, glancing at first Wendy, then Stanley, "that I just turned on the recording equipment, so everything that is said or done in this room will be part of the record. You are here because you are under arrest for the murder of Derrick Ames, your father." Richmond then read Jacob his Miranda rights. "Do you understand?" he asked when he was done.

Jacob glanced at Stanley, who said, "Yes, yes, we get it. Can we move on?"

Wendy stared at her lawyer with wide, fearful eyes. "Stanley, please tell me that this is all a joke."

"I have no doubt that certain things here are a joke," Stanley said with a forced smile. "But as for why these clowns have Jacob under arrest, I can't tell you that yet."

Richmond ignored Stanley's insult and kept his eyes focused on Jacob. "We have some questions for you, Jacob," he said.

"First things first," Stanley said in his most pompous tone. "I assume you have some sort of definitive evidence against my client?"

"No," Richmond said, tearing his gaze from the boy and giving Stanley a searing look. "We just arrest people willy-nilly here whenever we feel like it."

Stanley's jaw muscles quivered like a handful of hot popcorn kernels getting ready to explode, and his face was slowly turning the color of a ripe beefsteak tomato. "Frankly, I wouldn't put something like that past you and the rest of the yahoos in this small-town police station," he said.

Richmond once again ignored Stanley's provocation and said, "We would like to ask Jacob some questions. Is he going to cooperate and talk to us or not?"

I glanced over at Jacob. Despite his attempts to display some bravado, he looked frightened and uncertain. The insolent smart-ass from two days ago was gone, and in his place was a kid scared out of his mind by an all-too-real bogeyman. I felt sorry for him and had an odd urge to walk around the table and give him a hug. Then I remembered that Jacob likely *was* the bogeyman and reined my maternal feelings back in. *Freaking hormones.*

Stanley puffed himself up and went into lawyer attack mode, his tone brisk, clipped, and aggressive. "I am asking that you reveal the evidence you are using to arrest my client. His possession of his father's cell phone—assuming it even is his father's cell phone—is hardly what I would call hard evidence. Other than that, the only things you collected from the house were some shoes, clothing, and a laptop. I know you haven't had time yet to check into the phone or the laptop, so that leaves the clothing and the shoes. No one at the house checked those items for the presence of blood, so the only assumption I can come up with is that you are on a fishing expedition. Unless you can produce something more concrete in the way of reasonable cause for this arrest, I intend to take my client home and sue everyone in this place for false arrest and harassment."

Richmond stared impassively at the other man for several seconds, and then a smile slowly stole over his face. It revealed a creepy, predatory side of Richmond that I'd never seen before. "If you want something from me, you're going to have to play nicer. I don't appreciate your insults, and they won't intimidate us small-town hicks, so my advice to you is to back off, take a deep breath, figure out what you really want out of this, and then come back and talk to me again with your best manners in place. In the meantime, I'm taking your client to jail. If you want to know what evidence we have, you can talk to the DA."

I think Stanley expected his blowhard attitude would make Richmond kowtow to him. When it didn't, Stanley's smug, self-assured expression faltered just a hair. "I'd appreciate some more time to talk with my client and his mother *in private*," he said. "Turn off the recording equipment, and please leave the room." Though this was said in a relatively friendly tone of voice, Stanley couldn't resist tossing one more barbed comment at us. "And if I find out you are recording or listening in on anything we say in here, I will see to it that this entire department is sued and all of you are fired. Understood?"

Richmond got up from his chair, walked over to Jacob, and handcuffed him. Then he pulled him to his feet and led him from the room, out into the hallway. Wendy ran out behind him, looking frantic, with Sidney bringing up the tail end. I was the last one out. When we reached the hallway, I saw Hurley and Charlie standing off to our right, the video camera in Hurley's hand. The little red light on the side of it was on, which meant the camera was filming.

"What are you doing?" Wendy cried as Richmond led Jacob down the hall toward the front entrance. There were two small lockup rooms outfitted with security cameras, along with a booking area in a part of the building that was off to one side of the dispatcher's area so it could be monitored by whoever was on duty. I figured that was where Richmond was headed. "Where are you taking Jacob?" Wendy said, her voice growing shriller. Her eyes fixed on Stanley, and she started screeching at him. "What the hell did you do? I thought you said I'd be able to take Jacob home. What's going on?"

"What's going on is I'm taking your son to jail," Richmond said. "He is under arrest for the murder of his father, he's been read his rights, and since he wants to talk to his lawyer rather than us, I have no reason to keep him here, especially since your lawyer seems more interested in insulting us than he is in doing his job." Richmond turned to address Stanley. "You can arrange to speak with your client once we have him booked."

Richmond gave Jacob, who looked even more frightened and bewildered than he had before, another nudge down the hall. But after a couple of stumbling steps, Jacob stopped and threw himself against the wall. "Hold on," he protested, his voice frantic. "You can't put me in jail. I didn't do anything. I didn't kill my father!" he yelled, tears welling in his eyes. "Yeah, I was there, and yeah we had a fight, but I didn't kill him."

"Jacob, as your lawyer I'm advising you not to say anything."

"Screw your advice! You're supposed to be my lawyer, but so far you're doing a pretty crappy job, mister. You said I wouldn't have to go to jail," Jacob whined. Suddenly he seemed much younger and more vulnerable than he had before.

Stanley flashed him an appeasing smile. "You might have to spend the night there, just until your arraignment tomorrow. Then we'll bail you out."

"The hell you will," Richmond said. "I already spoke to the DA's office, and given the evidence we have and Jacob's history of sneaking out of the house, there's no way they're going to agree to bail."

"What evidence?" Wendy said. She looked at her son as if he was a stranger. "How can they have evidence, Jacob? What's this video they mentioned before?"

"I don't know," Jacob said, shaking his head. Then he gave his mother an imploring look. "I did go back to Dad's house that night, and I did get mad at him, but I didn't kill him. I swear!"

"Shut up, Jacob," Stanley said. Then he turned to Richmond. "The kid's a juvenile."

"I'm sure the DA's office will want to try him as an adult," Richmond countered.

"What?" Wendy shrieked. "Stanley, do something, damn it!"

Stanley had lost all his puff. His eyes darted back and forth between Richmond, Jacob, and Wendy. The only person who didn't look panicked was Richmond. "Okay, let's backtrack a little," Stanley said. "Detective Richmond, I'm sorry if I was a bit, uh, rude in my approach with you. Can we perhaps start over?"

"What did you have in mind?" Richmond asked.

Stanley scratched his forehead and thought for a few seconds. "I would like to go back into the conference room and talk to my client some more. Based on what he has said out here, we might be willing to talk with you. But I need to talk to him first. Please?"

So Stanley did have some manners after all.

Richmond contemplated the request, and I suspect the length of time he took to do so was a well-calculated play. "Fine," he said at last, and there was a collective sigh in the hallway. "You may take Jacob back into the conference room for now. But he stays cuffed, and barring some miracle from heaven, he's going to jail tonight."

Stanley opened his mouth as if to object, but then, wisely, he snapped it shut. "Let's go," he said, steering Wendy back toward the conference room. Richmond led Jacob along behind them, and once they were all in the room, Richmond shut the door and stood outside in the hallway waiting.

"Nicely played, Richmond," I said. "You handled Stanley like a pro."

"Thanks. Gasbags like him are always easy to manage. You just have to find a leak, light a fire under it, and watch them explode." He looked past me then and said, "Did you get everything he said out here?"

I turned and saw Hurley and Charlie watching the playback on the video camera Hurley was holding. "We did," Hurley said. Charlie was leaning against him, her face against his arm. "Including Jacob's admission that he was at his father's and fought with him on the day he was killed," Hurley said with a satisfied grin, finally snapping the video screen closed. He looked at Charlie then and said, "I like this video stuff more and more every minute."

My feelings on the topic remained mixed. My earlier excitement over the videos making it possible for Hurley and me to work together had all but vanished. What good was it going to do me if some gorgeous redhead that came with the program ended up stealing Hurley away from me? I watched the interplay between the two of them carefully, looking for those subtle touches, the lingering glances, the flirtatious mannerisms. And judging from what I saw, Charlie was definitely interested in Hurley. I didn't see any reciprocation on Hurley's part, and that reassured me for now, but I didn't think I was out of the woods yet. Charlie was a beautiful, likable woman.

"You did much better that time," Charlie said to Hurley in a happy, atta-boy tone. Then she looked over at Richmond. "We were out here in the hallway practicing with the camera because some of the pans Steve did at the house were erratic and jumpy. I wanted him to get a better feel for keeping the camera movements nice and smooth. You guys came out right in the middle of it. I guess it was lucky we were here."

"I guess it was," Richmond said.

"Let's go download this latest bit," Charlie said, taking Hurley by the arm and steering him toward his office. I followed and watched as Hurley sat at his desk and Charlie leaned in on one side of him, her bosom practically in his face.

As Hurley hooked up the camera to start the download, I walked in and nudged in close on Hurley's other side. "Mind if I watch?" I asked.

"Of course," Charlie said, cheerfully. "The more the merrier. In fact, it's probably just as important for you to become familiar with the equipment and the techniques as it is for the cops to do so. Anyone you partner with on an investigation may need you to be behind the camera part of the time." An image popped into my head of Hurley and I making a video together, just the two of us.

The imagined end result was a video with no evidentiary value . . . unless someone happened to be investigating a porn ring.

Chapter 27

While we were busy downloading the latest video, Trooper Grimes came into the station through the front entrance. I watched from Hurley's office as he and Richmond shared a whispered conversation out in the hallway, and when I saw the two of them look over at me, I figured Grimes had an update on my case. And if the troubled expression on Richmond's face was any indication, whatever they were discussing wouldn't bode well for my future.

Stanley emerged from the conference room after about ten minutes. "Jacob is willing to talk to you," he told Richmond. "He has a perfectly plausible explanation for how he came to have his father's cell phone."

Richmond and I followed Stanley back into the conference room, and since it has its own audiovisual setup, Charlie and Hurley remained behind. Again.

As soon as we were settled in and Richmond started the tape rolling, Stanley looked over at Jacob and said, "Tell them what you just told us."

Jacob nodded, picked at a fingernail, and squirmed

in his seat. "I went to my dad's house twice on Saturday. The first time was when my mom was over at Donna Martin's house. I climbed out my bedroom window and walked over to Dad's place. I have a key, but the door wasn't locked, so I just went in. At first I didn't think Dad was home because I couldn't find him anywhere. But then I heard some noise coming from upstairs, so I went up there to look for him."

Jacob paused, swallowed hard, and clamped his hands together. "I found him in his bedroom. He was with Mrs. Terwilliger. They were . . . you know . . ." Jacob's face flushed red, but I couldn't tell for sure if it was from anger or embarrassment.

"They were what?" Richmond prompted.

Jacob swallowed hard again, and his lips pinched so tight they momentarily turned white. "They were doing it," he said in a tone of disgust. "Dad saw me and called out to me, but I cursed at him and then ran down the stairs."

"It made you mad," I said. "Your father being with another woman meant that he and your mom weren't going to get back together, right?"

"That's right," he said. "I was really mad, and I didn't know what to do. Dad came downstairs after me, and he tried to talk, but I didn't want to hear it. I just yelled at him. And the whole time *she* was up there, listening. Probably laughing."

"Oh, Jacob," Wendy said, putting a hand on her son's arm. "I've told you that your father and I aren't going to get back together."

"Why not?" Jacob snapped, shaking her hand from his arm. "You aren't running around with someone else like he is. If he just would have stopped . . . if he just would have tried. I hate him!"

He pounded his fists on the table and then seemed to realize what he had done. He shot looks at us, then at his lawyer. "I mean I hated what he was doing. I loved my dad."

"What time was this?" Richmond asked.

Jacob shrugged. "Sometime in the afternoon, two or three, I think. I'm not sure."

"Tell him the rest," Stanley said.

Everyone stared at Jacob, waiting.

"I felt bad about some of the things I said, and how I left, so I went back over there while I was at Sean's house. Sean covered for me, and I went out his window this time. When I got to my dad's house, he was in the kitchen. We started to talk, and I told him how it made me feel, knowing that he didn't care enough about us to try to work things out with Mom. He said it was complicated, and that there were things I didn't know or understand."

I shot a glance at Wendy, who was chewing on one side of her fist, tears rolling down her face. The adults in the room knew the reason why the marriage had fallen apart—though I wasn't sure if Stanley was aware—and it had little to do with Derrick or his new girlfriend, Mandy. It would have been easy for Derrick to throw his ex-wife under the bus, but to his credit, he apparently hadn't. I wondered if and when Wendy was going to come clean. Now that her husband was dead, it would be easy to keep letting him take the blame for everything, but I hoped she wouldn't do that.

"What time was it when you went over to your dad's house for the second time?" Richmond asked.

"I don't know. I think it was around six or six-thirty maybe. Anyway, we were talking in the kitchen, and I asked him to please break it off with Mrs. Terwilliger. He said he planned to do just that, but that it still wouldn't make any difference with him and Mom. Then his phone chimed, and when he looked at the text message he said he was sorry but I had to leave. That made me even madder because I knew it was probably her texting him and now he was blowing me off for her, the same way he kept blowing Mom off. I said something like, *Are you making me leave so you can be with her?* But he didn't answer me, so I walked over and grabbed his phone and looked at the message."

"Tell them what the message said, Jacob," Stanley said.

"It was from her, from Mrs. Terwilliger, and she was asking him if she could come by. See? He was making me leave just so he could talk to her. It made me so mad, and I started yelling at him, telling him that he didn't love us. And I told him . . . I said that . . . I said I hated him." Jacob's angst was clear in his voice, but now it manifested itself in fat tears that welled in his eyes and then meandered down his cheeks. "I just kept yelling at him, and he kept trying to get me to calm down. He told me to give him back his phone, but I told him no. So he tried to take it back. We ended up wrestling for it, and things got pretty physical. I . . . I punched him in the face and made his nose bleed," Jacob said, looking embarrassed and ashamed. "We knocked over a chair, and some stuff got knocked off the table and the counters, but in the end I was able to push him away long enough to smash his phone against the corner of the counter. Then I ran out, taking the phone with me. I thought Dad might try to stop me, but he didn't, and after I got home, I kept expecting him to show up and ask for the phone back, but he never did. I was so mad at him I smashed the phone with a hammer until the battery popped out of it."

Jacob paused, and the tears in his eyes welled again. "It was pretty stupid to think that breaking the phone would keep him from seeing her because all he had to do was e-mail her on his laptop or drive over to her house. It doesn't make sense now, but at the time it seemed like it did. I know I shouldn't have broken his phone, but that's all I did. When I left his house, he was fine."

I had to admit that Jacob's story and earnest pleas of innocence were very convincing, but the tale he'd just told was essentially a confession. It fit with what was on the video, and the time of the video was mere minutes before the Ames's neighbor had called 911 for Derrick, not the time Jacob had just mentioned. Between the video evidence, the shoes, and the cell phone, Jacob's future was looking rather grim. He had killed his father—a horrific crime—and yet my heart went out to him.

I wanted to feel sorry for Wendy, but the only sentiment I could muster up for her was anger. If she had been honest with her sons about the reason behind the breakup, none of this would have happened. Derrick Ames had paid the ultimate price when all he was trying to do was keep the peace and get on with his own life.

I wondered about Jacob's comment that Derrick had said he was going to break up with Mandy Terwilliger. Was it true, or was it wishful hearing on Jacob's part? If it was true, why hadn't Mandy said anything about it? Had she not known? I figured it was worth talking to her again to check out Jacob's story, though I couldn't see how any answer she might provide would change the outcome for Jacob.

That's when something else Jacob said hit me. I thought back to my walk through Derrick's house, snapping pictures of each room and its contents, and searched my memory for a particular item. When my mental search came up empty, I decided I would go back and look through the photos I had uploaded to the computer. Since the discussion in the conference room had turned to a debate over where and how Jacob was going to be detained, I decided to excuse myself, thinking I could make better use of my time following up on the question in my head rather than watching the sad, slow demise of the Ames family.

I walked out of the conference room and headed for Hurley's office, expecting to find him and Charlie still there. But the office was empty. So was the break room. Hurley and Charlie were nowhere to be found, and when I checked the back parking lot, I saw that both of their cars were gone.

That was just great. Now the two of them were off to God knew where doing God knew what with one another. I walked the block to my office, determined to put Hurley out of my mind at least until I could answer the question that was nagging at my brain.

Cass, our receptionist-slash-secretary-slash-file clerk was seated behind the front desk shuffling papers. She was very involved with a local thespian group, one that Dom also participated in, and the group put on plays in town in an old refurbished theater located around the corner from our office. Cass always had a part, and she was very serious about her roles. In order to "get into the character's head," she said she had to live twenty-four seven as that character, including altering her appearance, mannerisms, speech, and clothing. Today she was dressed in a dowdy old dress, and either she was wearing a body suit, or she had the dress strategically stuffed to give herself an overweight, dowager's build. Her hair was gray, her makeup was done to make her look soft, pudgy, and older, and she was sporting a pair of granny glasses.

"Hey, Mattie," she said. "Awful thing about Dom's dad, ain't it?" She drew the words out with a thick southern drawl.

I nodded.

"And I heard you had some excitement last night, too. Thank goodness you're okay. Dr. Henderson finished up the autopsy on that guy who shot at you a couple of hours ago. He brought in some diener from Madison to help him, saying something about how none of us could be trusted. He seems like a bit of a jerk."

While I agreed with her, I also understood why Henderson was doing things the way he was. "He's just trying to make sure everything is on the up-and-up. It's annoying but necessary."

"Yeah, well, try telling Arnie that. He's fit to be tied. Henderson has a bunch of geeks from Madison upstairs messing around in Arnie's lab, and Arnie's none too happy 'bout it, let me tell ya. He cain't even get in there to do his own stuff, so he's turned everything over to the new guys, and he's out in the field working with Jonas. He said he's afraid that if he stays here he'll say or do something that he'll later regret."

I didn't want to have to deal with Dr. Snoopy Henderson or any of his honchos, but I also didn't want anyone thinking I was poking my nose in where it didn't belong. The last thing I wanted to do was compromise my own investigation. So I said to Cass, "I need to look through the shots I took of the Ames house Saturday night. Do I need to check in with Henderson for that, do you think?"

"I don't know. But if you're planning on using your usual computer in the library, you'll have to convince the Henderson geek who's in there to let you do it."

"Someone is using my computer?" Technically it was the library computer, but the library did double duty as my office.

I started to head that way, but Cass stopped me. "Here, you have to sign in," she said, sliding a clipboard and pen toward me. "Henderson wants everyone accounted for, so y'all have to sign in and sign out. And you have a message," she said, holding out a pink slip of paper. "Alison Miller wants you to call her."

I took the message and stuffed it in my pocket. Then I scribbled my name down on the sign-in sheet and headed for the library, prepared to do battle with whoever had invaded my territory. Some subliminal part of my brain hinted that I might be looking for a hapless victim on whom to vent the frustration that had built up inside me over the Hurley/Charlie thing, but I ignored it.

Inside the library I found a woman with long black hair seated at my desk, working on my computer. She was so focused on whatever was on the screen that she didn't hear me come in. I walked up behind her and cleared my throat, making her jump.

"Oh, hell!" she said, whirling around and clapping a hand over her heart. "You scared the bejesus out of me! Who are you?" She stared up at me with huge, questioning brown eyes that looked too big for her face behind the glasses she had on.

"I didn't mean to startle you. I'm Mattie Winston. I work here. This is my desk and my computer."

"Oh, I'm sorry." She hopped out of the chair and gestured for me to take it. I hesitated and instead looked at what she'd been doing on the computer. She had the word-processing software open, and I saw she was typing a footnote at the bottom of the page, citing some kind of reference book. She saw me studying the screen and reached over to grab the mouse. "Just let me save this and then you can use the computer. It's part of my doctorate thesis," she said, clicking the save icon.

I was surprised to hear she was working on a doctorate; she looked barely old enough to be out of high school.

"I know what you're thinking," she said. I doubted it, but then she proved me wrong. "You're thinking, is she a girl genius or what because she can't be old enough to be pursuing a doctorate, right? I get that all the time. My mother says it's all the youthful genes on her side of the family. All of us women in the family look much younger than we are. How old do you think I am? Come on, take a guess."

I thought a moment, gave her a few years for her good genes, and said, "Twenty-six."

She let out a loud, boisterous laugh. "Heck, no, I'm thirty-two," she said. "I'm already working on my second career. I have a master's degree in business. Yep, an MBA. What the heck was I thinking when I did that? It turns out business is a real snore. The whole thing bored me to tears. So I decided to start over and do something I love. I figured it's never too late, you know. A lot of people thought I was crazy, and maybe I am, but I don't care because I'm happy. And happy is what it's all about, don't you think?"

It took me a moment to realize that she had actually paused. The woman talked a mile a minute and didn't seem to breathe between sentences.

"Happy is good," I said. Then, hoping to get her back on topic, I added, "I won't need the computer for very long. I just need to flip through some photos I took of the crime scene we're investigating."

"It's not the crime you're involved with, is it? Because Dr. Henderson said no one from this office can be involved with any of that. He had me install some spyware on all the computers to make sure no one accesses any files they shouldn't."

"Did he now?" I said. Clearly, trust wasn't high on Henderson's list of attributes. "Well, not to worry. The photos I want are from a murder that took place on Saturday night. You can stand here and watch over my shoulder if you want and make sure I don't access anything I'm not supposed to."

"Oh, I don't think I need to do that. I'm sure you're trustworthy. Besides, the spyware will nab you if you go where you shouldn't."

I wasn't sure if I should be insulted or flattered.

"I am trustworthy," I assured her. "But if it's all the same to you, I'd appreciate it if you'd stay. I don't want there to be any questions regarding the investigation into my own case." I slid into the chair she had vacated, minimized her document, and then logged in to the office shared drive.

"What's your name?" I asked, as I found and opened my photo file from the Ames case.

"Oh, crap. I'm sorry. It's Laura, Laura Kingston."

"Nice to meet you, Laura. I take it you're part of Dr. Henderson's group?"

"I guess you could say that. He called several of us yesterday to come here and help him out for a while. He said you guys are working with a skeleton crew as it is and that an incident had occurred that required outside investigation. I couldn't get here until this morning, and Dr. Henderson's been tied up in the autopsy suite all day, so I'm just killing time until he's done. Not to worry, though. An autopsy isn't required for killing time." She let out an awkward little laugh at her own joke, and to be polite, I smiled.

"What is it you do exactly?" I asked her as I started flipping through the pictures in the file.

"My area of study is forensic botany, with a minor in forensic toxicology. But I'm also Dr. Henderson's assistant, which basically means I'm a glorified secretary and teaching assistant."

"Henderson teaches?"

She nodded. "He's a professor in the forensic pathology program at U-Dub. I was going to become a forensic pathologist, but it turns out I don't do so well looking at dissected dead bodies. After fainting six times in the autopsy suites, I was forced to go in a different direction. I wasn't sure what field I wanted to switch to, and to help me decide, Dr. Henderson hired me on as his assistant. It proved very helpful because it gave me exposure to a number of different subfields in forensic science. I thought about forensic psychiatry or psychology, but all that criminalistics mind stuff gives me the heebie-jeebies. I'm not a fan of creepy-crawlers either, so that ruled out entomology, and some of the other subfields are just a snore, like forensic accounting and documents, though my MBA might have given me a leg up in those fields. So I settled on botany and toxicology because I don't have to deal with the bodies, but I get to be involved in the investigations and the processing of evidence. The stuff I get to study is fun and exciting."

I kept flipping through the pictures after Laura stopped rattling on, and after watching over my shoulder for a few silent seconds, she said, "May I ask what it is you're looking for?"

"Evidence."

Laura scanned the photos along with me even though she didn't know exactly what I was looking for, and when we reached the end of the file, I closed it, logged out, got up, and gestured toward the computer. "You can have it back now."

"Did you find the evidence you were looking for?" she asked.

I shook my head.

"So what does that mean?"

"It means something about this case I'm working on just doesn't fit."

"Ooh, a puzzle," Laura said, clasping her hands together and rocking on her feet. "I love puzzles. That's what attracted me to forensic science in the first place."

I smiled at her. "I like puzzles, too." My cell phone rang then, and I grabbed it out of my pocket and looked at the caller ID. It said it was an unknown number, and that made my heart skip a beat. With a mix of trepidation and anticipation, I answered the call.

"This is Mattie Winston." There was no response. "Hello?" I listened and heard the faint sound of breathing. Someone was on the line, but they were making no effort to speak to me. "Hello?" I said again. "Who is this?" Then the line went dead. I put the phone back in my pocket, forced a smiled, looked at Laura, and said, "Must have been a wrong number."

"I hate those," she said.

"Me, too." *Especially this kind*, I thought. "It was nice to meet you, Laura."

"Same here. You just let me know when you need to use your desk or your computer and I'll get out of your way."

"Thanks. I'm good for now, but I might need it later on today."

"No problem. Just holler. Dr. Henderson will probably have me doing stuff somewhere else later, anyway. He's always got lots of papers he needs filed, and reports to run and review. The man keeps me busy, that's for sure."

I escaped chatty Laura, but remained inside the building, hovering in a hallway. That phone call had unnerved me. And I realized I'd left the police station without any guard or body armor. Then my phone rang again, making me jump. I looked at the caller ID, expecting to see the same unknown caller screen, but instead it was Hurley.

"Hey, Hurley," I said, answering the call.

"Where the hell are you?" he snapped.

"At my office. I walked over here about twenty minutes ago because I needed to check on something."

"Damn it, Mattie, you know you're not supposed to be going anywhere without someone with you. What the hell were you thinking?"

"I wasn't," I admitted. "And Hurley, I just got another one of those phone calls."

This revelation was met with several seconds of silence. "You mean like the ones you had before?"

"Yes."

"But the guy is dead."

"Clearly it wasn't him making the calls."

"Stay put. I'll be over there in a minute. Don't leave, and don't go near a window or door until I get there, okay?"

"Okay," I said, disconnecting the call. Earlier, when Richmond and Hurley had made such a fuss over the whole protection thing, I thought it was an overreaction. Now I wasn't so sure. And suddenly I found that I didn't like puzzles all that much after all.

Chapter 28

My mind was a flurry of thoughts. I had assumed the previous calls were coming from the man who had shot at me, but clearly that wasn't the case with this one. Were they connected somehow? Was the person who hired the shooter the one who was calling me? Or had my original suspicion that the calls were coming from my father been right?

Hurley found me standing, or rather quaking, in the hallway minutes later. "Are you okay?" he asked, looking concerned. He was holding Richmond's old body armor, the vest I had tossed in the corner earlier.

I walked up to Hurley and hugged him. "I'm fine, just a little spooked," I said into his shoulder. "That phone call has me a little freaked."

"We'll get the troopers on it right away. Hopefully they can tell where it came from."

I nodded, reluctantly relinquished the warm security of his body, and stepped back. That's when I saw that Charlie was standing just a few feet away. She had a camera in her hand, but she wasn't using it.

Before I had a chance to ask her what the hell she was doing there, my cell phone rang again. I took it out and looked at it with trepidation, but it was only Richmond calling.

"Hey, Richmond," I said, turning my back to Charlie. I couldn't trust myself not to glare at her.

"Where the hell are you?" Richmond barked into the phone.

"At my office."

"Why the hell did you go over there?"

"I had a thought about the Ames case. Hurley is here with me. I'll tell you when I get back. See you in a few minutes."

I disconnected the call before Richmond could yell at me again, and looked at Hurley. "I need to go back to the station."

A voice that was definitely not Charlie's came from her direction. "What's going on?"

I turned and saw Henderson standing just behind Charlie, staring at us.

"We aren't doing anything we shouldn't be," I said irritably. "I came here to use my computer to review some crime scene photos I took on the Ames case. Your assistant, Laura, can vouch for me. She watched over my shoulder the whole time."

"That's all fine and dandy, but I asked what was going on because you're standing in the hallway with two other people, one of whom is carrying a camera while the other is carrying a bulletproof vest. I'm not worried about you snooping."

"Really? Is that why you installed spyware on the computers?"

Henderson sighed heavily. "The program I put on your computers is standard stuff back in Madison. It should be here, too. It's a security check for your office and protection for any evidence stored on your system. I would have put it on the computers here even if I wasn't investigating a case you're involved in. You are free to use the office as much and as often as you like. Besides, from what I've been told by Trooper Grimes, I expect you'll be cleared in the next day or so."

"She might be cleared, but that doesn't mean the case is solved," Hurley said.

"What do you mean?" Henderson asked.

Hurley explained about the phone call, the lack of any known connections between the shooter and me, and the stuff the troopers found in Roscoe Schneider's car that suggested he might not have been working alone. "Given all of that," Hurley concluded, "we're worried that someone might still be after Mattie."

"I see," Henderson said. "I guess that would explain the vest."

It did, but it didn't explain Charlie's presence, which at the moment I considered to be the bigger question. Henderson shifted his gaze to me. "I can bring in some extra security for the office, if you like."

"I like," Hurley said before I could answer.

"Consider it done," Henderson said. He then walked past us and headed down the hallway. "And be careful," he added over his shoulder. "Dr. Rybarceski will have my ass if I let anything happen to his top-notch assistant."

This last comment made me smile. I suspected Izzy and Henderson had chatted some more since last night.

"Put this on," Hurley said, handing me the vest.

"It smells, and it doesn't fit right."

"It's the best we have for now. So put it on." His tone made it clear he would brook no more protests, so I put the thing on. We headed to the main lobby area of the office, and Hurley made me stand in a corner away from the door while he signed all three of us out. Then he told me to stay and went outside. He returned a minute later and said, "Walk fast and straight back to the station, and make sure you stay close to me."

I was more than happy to oblige, and had I not been imagining some crazy crackpot assassin lurking behind every window, door, and building, I might even have enjoyed sticking to Hurley like glue while Charlie trailed behind us. As it was, I was hugely relieved once we were back inside the police station.

As we entered the break room, Hurley glanced at his watch and said, "It's mid-afternoon already. Have you had lunch yet?"

Both Charlie and I said, "No," at the exact same time.

"Well, then, I think it's time we eat something. How does Chinese sound?"

"That works for me," I said. At the moment I was hungry enough to eat just about anything. "Let's go."

"Oh, no," Hurley said. "I'll bring the food back here. In the meantime, you stay put. And I mean it. Don't you dare set foot outside this station unless you have that vest on and an armed cop with you, got it?"

I nodded, but my expression made it clear I wasn't happy about it. Had I known then how long my confinement was going to last, I'm sure I would have looked even more miserable—though a few seconds later my misery increased by leaps and bounds.

"Mind if I ride along?" Charlie asked, bestowing her gorgeous smile on Hurley.

"Not at all. We'll be back in a flash."

I had a flash in mind for Charlie, but it was more nuclear in nature. I watched the two of them leave as I shrugged out of Richmond's smelly vest, and then I stomped down the hall to Hurley's office and threw the vest back into its corner. Richmond was there, typing away on the computer at the desk that was now shared by him, Hurley, Trooper Grimes, and any other lurking trooper who might be around. Richmond spun around in his chair, took one look at me, and said, "Uh-oh, who peed in your cornflakes?"

"I don't want to talk about it."

"Fine, then let's talk about whatever it was that was important enough to make you risk your life by walking over to your office."

"Give me a break, Richmond," I shot back irritably. "I've already had the lecture once, and I don't need it again. I got focused on this idea I had, and the other stuff momentarily slipped my mind. I'm not used to having a target on my back and having to act like Jason Bourne."

"Well, until we figure this thing out, you better get used to it," Richmond grumbled.

"I got another one of those phone calls when I was in my office," I told him.

He looked puzzled for a second and then he said, "You mean the hang-up calls?"

I nodded. "So I'm thinking the calls I was getting before probably aren't related to this Schneider guy."

Richmond shook his head. "No, they're related. Grimes told me this morning that they were able to resurrect the cell phone that Schneider had on him when you . . . when he was killed. And after comparing those phone records to yours, they determined that several calls from Schneider's cell went to your cell, and they were on the dates and around the times you recalled getting those hang-up calls. Some of the other hang-up calls you had in the past were from different cell phones, but they were all untraceable burner phones with preloaded minutes and paid for in cash."

"I don't understand that," I told him. "How can the calls be related to Schneider if he's dead?"

Richmond's brow furrowed in thought. "Maybe this last call was a legitimate misdial or wrong number. Or maybe it was from whoever hired Schneider, because Schneider's phone also had several calls to Florida numbers that belong to untraceable burner phones."

"Everything keeps coming up Florida," I said, shaking my head. "I don't get it. I don't know anyone who is from there or who lives there."

"Hold on," Richmond said. He picked up his phone, dialed a number, and after a few seconds he said, "Hey, Grimes. I'm here with Mattie Winston, and she said she just got another one of those strange hang-up calls a few minutes ago. Clearly it didn't come from Schneider, so can you look into it for me?"

He listened for a minute, said thanks, and hung up. "We should hear something back from him in an hour or so. In the meantime, what was this big idea you had that made you go dashing over to your office?"

"It's something that occurred to me as Jacob was

telling us what happened when he went back to his father's place. Is he still here?"

Richmond shook his head. "Brenda took him to booking. I'm finishing up the paperwork now."

"Is Wendy still here?"

"No, she and Stanley left some time ago. Why?"

"Remember how Jacob said he knew it was stupid to take out his anger on the cell phone, as if that would prevent his father from contacting his girl-friend?" Richmond nodded and shrugged. "The rea-son he said it was stupid was because there were several other ways his father could have contacted Mandy. One of the things Jacob mentioned was that he could e-mail her on his laptop. But I didn't recall seeing a laptop in Derrick's house, or a computer of any kind, for that matter. That's why I went to my of-fice. I wanted to look through the photos I took at the house. And the reason I couldn't recall seeing any sort of computer is because there wasn't one there. And that makes no sense. Not only was Der-rick a teacher, he was the parent of a teenager. He has one whole room dedicated to gaming. He would have had some kind of computer in his house. Clearly he did or Jacob wouldn't have mentioned the e-mail option."

"You're right," Richmond said frowning in thought. "Hang on a sec." He took out his cell phone and placed a call. "Hi, it's Detective Richmond with the Sorenson PD. Have you guys had a chance to look at the laptop we turned in earlier today as evidence in the Ames case?" He listened for a minute or so, said, "Thank you, that's actually very helpful," and hung up. "So the guys that are working in Arnie's lab looked at the laptop we took from Jacob's room. It wasn't password-protected and they scanned through the basic software, browser history, e-mail, and such. They said all they found was typical teenage male kind of stuff: some computer games, some pictures of naked girls, and some schoolwork. The computer's user name is Jacob, and it looks like he has been the primary, if not the only user."

"So where is Derrick's computer? I didn't see any other laptops in the Ames house. Wendy's computer was a desktop, and Michael didn't have one."

"Maybe Jacob took it like he did the phone?"

"I don't think so. He admitted to smashing and taking Derrick's phone, to sneaking out of both his and Sean's house, and to fighting with his father. Why would he lie about the laptop?"

Richmond sighed. "Good question, and a good catch, Mattie." He took out his cell phone, rummaged through the paperwork he had in front of him on the desk, and then punched in a number. "Mrs. Ames," he said after a few seconds, "this is Detective Richmond. I'm really sorry to bother you again, but I need to ask you something."

I couldn't hear what Wendy Ames was saying on the other end, but judging from the grimace on Richmond's face, she was giving him a good chewing out. He listened, nodding silently for a minute or so while massaging his temple, and then said, "I know you're not happy with the way this has turned out. And I understand your reluctance to talk to me without your lawyer. I'm just doing my job here and following up on some loose ends. The only thing I need you to tell me is whether or not Derrick had a computer."

The answer Wendy supplied made Richmond give me a thumbs-up.

"Can you describe it for me and tell me where he normally kept this laptop?" Richmond asked. After listening again, he thanked her, told her she had been very helpful, and then disconnected the call. "You were right, Mattie. Derrick had a laptop, a metallic blue HP model with a German flag decal on the lid. Wendy said that every time she's been to his house, the laptop was set up in the game room."

"So where is it?"

"Maybe Jacob ditched it somewhere, or maybe he gave it to someone and doesn't want anyone to know. In fact, I wouldn't be surprised if he gave it to that troublemaking friend of his, Sean Fitzpatrick."

"But why take it at all?"

Richmond shrugged. "Jacob said it himself; his father could have used it to get in touch with Mandy." He made a face that told me this idea sounded as implausible to him as it did to me.

"And that's the other thing that's bothering me," I said. "Jacob said his father told him he was planning to break up with Mandy, but she never indicated that there was anything amiss in their relationship. Why is that?"

"Maybe she didn't know," Richmond said. "Maybe she thought everything was going along fine and had no idea that Derrick was going to break up with her. Or maybe Jacob just fed us a line."

"I don't know, Richmond. Jacob seemed . . . sincere, devastated, and vulnerable. What he said in there tonight rang true to me."

"Which only proves what a good liar he is. We have the video evidence, remember?"

"Which doesn't show Jacob actually killing his father."

"No, but it does show him there, wrestling with his father minutes before the 911 call. And those guys Henderson has working in your lab just told me they found blood on the shirt and pants we took from Jacob's hamper—pants that, if you recall, also match those in the video. They also found blood on the shoes. We don't know for sure yet that the blood is Derrick's, but I'm betting it will be. And they've also verified that the cell phone we found in Jacob's room was Derrick's. I'm sorry, Mattie, but the kid did it. You may not want to believe it, and I understand that, given your condition and all, but the evidence is pretty straightforward."

"My condition?"

"Well, yeah. I'm sure that being pregnant makes you more emotional. You know . . . the hormones and all."

"My *condition*, as you put it, has nothing to do with this, Richmond. I'm simply sharing my take on the case. Besides, what the hell would you know about being pregnant?"

"Just because I've never been pregnant doesn't mean I don't know what goes on."

"Who's pregnant?" said a voice behind us.

I turned to see Charlie and Hurley standing in the doorway holding bags of food from the Peking Palace.

"Is everything okay here?" Hurley asked.

"It's fine," I said, wishing it was.

"Who's pregnant?" Charlie asked again. "Are you, Mattie?"

"Yes."

"Congratulations!" She looked genuinely happy

for me, which made it all that much harder for me to understand why I wanted to wave a wand over her head and make her disappear. Forever.

"Thanks."

Apparently I didn't sound sincere enough because Charlie's broad congratulatory smile faltered. "You don't seem very happy about it," she said.

"Oh, I am. It's just that it was rather unexpected, and it kind of came at a bad time."

"Is your husband happy about it?" Charlie asked as Hurley shifted nervously from one foot to the other. Charlie's brazen nosiness made both me and Alison Miller look like amateurs.

"I'm not married," I said.

"Yet," Hurley added. "But she might change her mind."

"Ooh, I love weddings," Charlie cooed, clasping her hands together. "If you're planning one, I'd be happy to shoot a wedding video for you if you want. I've done several already."

"There isn't going to be a wedding," I said, and Hurley huffed his irritation.

Charlie looked back and forth between me and Hurley with a bemused expression. Then her face lit up with dawning. "Wait a minute," she said, pointing a finger at first me, then Hurley. "Are you the father?"

"I am," Hurley said.

"O-o-oh," Charlie said, her eyes growing big. "Well, now that I've stuck my foot in it, I think I'll pull it back out and disappear." She flashed an awkward smile, took the bag of food Hurley was holding, and backed out of the room, heading down the hall toward the break room.

Richmond shook his head in dismay. "It sounds

like you two have some things to sort out. I'm going to talk to Jacob about that computer and see what he has to say. I'll let you know." Then he, too, left the room, leaving me and Hurley alone.

"You are a stubborn, fascinating, and puzzling woman, Mattie Winston," Hurley said.

"I thought we were in agreement on this marriage thing, Hurley."

"Obviously not. I want to get married and you don't."

I sighed, cocked my head to one side and said, "Why do you want to get married?"

"We're having a kid together, aren't we?" he said, looking at me like I was an idiot.

"And it's the right thing to do?"

"Yes! Exactly," Hurley said, looking relieved that I finally seemed to get it.

I rolled my eyes at him. "I'm not getting married again simply because it's the right thing to do, Hurley. That's an obsolete and archaic social more that I don't ascribe to."

"I'm not saying we should get married simply because you're pregnant," he said, looking as exasperated as I felt. "We should get married because we . . . because I . . . because you . . ."

Silence stood between us like a brick wall for what felt like an eternity, and then Hurley blew out an irritated sigh. "Oh, hell, have it your way," he said finally, throwing his hands into the air. Then he stormed out of the room.

Chapter 29

"So maybe now you can see why I'm reluctant to marry Hurley," I say to Maggie. "He had a chance to say it; I think he wanted to say it, but he couldn't."

"You're referring to the fact that he didn't say he loved you?"

"Well, yeah." I stare at her like I would a dumb child who doesn't get the concept of the sky being blue. "It's obvious he only wants to marry me because he thinks it's the right thing to do. I don't think he has the same feelings for me that I have for him."

"Or maybe he's one of those men who has a hard time saying what he feels. Did it occur to you that maybe he doubts your feelings for him? Maybe he was waiting for you to declare your feelings."

"He knows how I feel about him," I say, frowning.

"How does he know that? Have you told him?"

"Well, no, not in so many words. But I show it all the time."

"And you don't think he shows it?"

I sigh. "He has shown me that he cares about me,

but I don't know that he's shown that he loves me, at least not the way he should if we're going to get married."

"Why haven't you told him how you feel?"

I consider my answer carefully and for a long time. I can hear the little windup clock that Maggie keeps on her desk ticking the time down. "I suppose it's because I'm afraid."

"Of what?"

"That he'll laugh at me. Or that he'll run away scared."

"Like your father did?"

I shoot her an irritated look. "You think this is about my unresolved feelings for my father?" I say askance. "That's rather clichéd."

"Perhaps, but that doesn't mean it isn't true."

"I had stepfathers who did a fine job of being there for me."

"How many of them do you see or talk to on a regular basis?"

Right now I hate Maggie. She has this uncanny ability to get right to the heart of any emotional wounds I have. Then she digs around in them, poking, and prodding, and causing me pain. "They don't live around here anymore," I tell her. "Desi's father remarried and moved to California. And my mother's third husband went back to England to be near his family."

"So they aren't a significant part of your life at this point."

"No, but I'm not at a point in my life where I need a father figure."

"What about any strong male figure? Your husband more or less abandoned you, too, didn't he?"

"That's one way of looking at it, I suppose. But I was the one who made the decision to leave him."

"Yes, you did, but not until after he abandoned you by having an affair with someone else."

"Whatever. I think you're nitpicking and getting bogged down in semantics."

"My point is that the important men in your life thus far haven't stuck around for the long haul. I want to know how that makes you feel."

At the moment it makes me feel like I want to kill Dr. Naggy. Lucky for her I've already reached my kill quota for the year. "It makes me feel like the only person I can truly rely on is me. And that's okay. Because I'm a strong woman with good intelligence, common sense most of the time, and a supportive group of family and friends."

"I'm curious, how did David react to the news of your pregnancy?"

"I think it's safe to say he wasn't pleased. Despite the fact that he and Patty have already moved into the new house together, he told me I was rushing into things headlong without enough thought."

"Does David's opinion matter to you?"

"Not really, but Lord knows what he's been saying about me behind my back."

"Why do you care?"

"Because this is a small town. People talk, and sometimes they do it in front of their kids. I don't want my kid growing up and getting teased by his friends and classmates because of some malicious gossip."

"Don't you think David's reputation and past behaviors reflect on anything he says?"

"I don't know. People like dirty gossip. They latch onto it and milk it for all it's worth. Plus, David has redeemed himself in a way. He and Patty are engaged. So he's doing things 'the proper way,' as he puts it. Humph! Like David would know proper if it jumped up and bit him in the ass."

"You seem bothered by David's progress with his personal life. Is it possible that Hurley was right? Do you have unresolved feelings for David?"

"No, it's not that. It's just that David has come out of this whole mess happy, and paired up, and living high on the hog. And I've come out of it pregnant, single, and potentially hunted by some homicidal maniac. It isn't fair."

"Life seldom is. Do you regret your choices?"

I shake my head and smile. "Not at all. I'm happy about the baby, and I'm determined to make this single parenting thing work."

"So you don't need Hurley, is that it?"

"I don't need him, but I do want him."

"Then why don't you talk to him, say what's on your mind, tell him what's in your heart. What have you got to lose? With the path you've chosen thus far, he's not a permanent part of your life, so if he tells you he's not interested, you haven't lost anything."

"It's not that he isn't interested. He is. At least for now, anyway. But I don't know if we have what it takes to make it over the long haul. And I'm feeling too vulnerable right now to risk sticking my heart out there that way. Besides, what's the rush? If we have what it takes to make it as a married couple, time will tell."

"How much time?"

"I don't know. I'll know when it's right. Right now there are too many things working against us."

"I get the sense there's something else you aren't telling me."

Once again Dr. Naggy has seen through my attempts at subterfuge, but I'm not ready to reveal my other secret yet. I may never be. So I shrug and say nothing.

Maggie sighs and sags in her chair. "Okay, enough about you and Hurley for now. You said there was something else you wanted to discuss."

"There is. It's this whole motherhood thing. I'm afraid of screwing it up. I'm afraid I'm going to be a horrible parent. It's not like I have any good role models for the job other than my sister, and she's a stay-at-home mom. I can't afford to do that. I mean, I have a decent amount saved up, but I've got all kinds of new expenses coming up. Hell, this baby stuff costs an arm and a leg. There are so many different things I've had to buy: a crib, diapers, clothing, bottles, a bassinet, blankets, baby cleaning products, a changing table, a mobile, toys . . . it's this never-ending list. And that's just the stuff I've had to buy so far. I've heard kids outgrow clothes so fast they hardly wear any one thing more than a time or two. Plus there's college to think about. By the time this kid reaches college age, it will likely cost more than a house."

"You've got plenty of time to plan for college," Maggie says.

"I'm not sure I agree. Everyone says the time goes by so fast. One day they're in kindergarten, and then, before you know it, they're talking tuition and degrees. And speaking of college, how do you sort through all these educational theories about child rearing? One book says bright colors enhance learning, and another says to go with black and white. One says singing helps kids learn, and another says singing dumbs them down. Who do you believe? How do you know if you're doing the right thing?"

Maggie smiles at me. "I think just the fact that you're so worried about being a good parent is a good sign, Mattie. You're smart, you're a nurse, you're caring, you're self-sufficient, and you're loving. That's all a kid needs. Half of it is determined by genetics anyway."

That gets a scoff out of me. "If that's true, my kid is doomed. Look at my mother. And who knows what kinds of skeletons are hiding in my father's family closet." Actually, I knew exactly what skeletons were in there. I just wasn't ready to reveal them yet.

"Hurley and his side of the family have a role in this, too, remember?" Maggie says. "And regardless of what happens between the two of you, you aren't alone in this. You said Hurley intends to play an active role in parenting your child, plus you have your extended family: Izzy and Dom."

For once, Maggie is making me feel better about things. She is right. I'm not alone in this, even though it feels that way sometimes.

"Do you have doubts that Hurley will hang in there for the long haul?"

"No, I have doubts about us hanging in for the long haul. There are so many things we don't see eye to eye on."

"Such as?"

"Sometimes it feels like he's all about what he wants out of this. He isn't listening to what I want, or what I don't want. And there are some other issues, bigger issues I'm dealing with."

"Can you give me some examples of what you mean?"

I debate whether or not to reveal my big secret and decide that it's time. "Okay," I said. "But prepare yourself. This story is more tangled than the skein of yarn my cats play with."

Chapter 30

With the Ames case seemingly resolved, Richmond wanted to let the issue of the laptop go. But after some cajoling from me—or perhaps badgering is a better term—he agreed that tomorrow we would do another search of both Wendy Ames's house and Derrick's, and pay another visit to the Fitzpatrick house, in case Richmond's theory that Jacob might have given the laptop to Sean turned out to be a viable one. Not only wasn't I yet convinced of Jacob's guilt, I was worried that Richmond might be so convinced of it that he wouldn't dig as deep as he should into any other suspects. So I decided to give Alison Miller a little test, to see if her newfound alliance was an honest one. I returned her call from earlier in the day, and learned that she knew about Jacob's arrest. I discussed my doubts with her and asked her to look into some things for me, but not to say anything or print anything without permission from me first. She agreed and I gave her an assignment.

"Look into Mandy Terwilliger for me. See what

you dig up. But do it so that no one knows you're doing it, if you can."

"Okay. What exactly do you want to know?"

"I'm interested in her finances for one thing. She works part-time, has two teenage boys at home, and she's a single mother. She told us she got a small settlement when her husband died but implied it wasn't much, so I'm curious as to how she is able to afford the sporty little convertible I saw her driving. And I'm also interested in any scuttlebutt you can dig up about the relationship between her and Derrick Ames. Some witnesses made it sound like the two of them were going to split up, but Mandy didn't give us that impression at all."

"I'll let you know," Alison said.

Trooper Grimes called Richmond back around five to report that the call I had received that afternoon had been made from an untraceable burner phone located in Florida. So it seemed the call might have been related to Schneider after all. This both frightened and disappointed me because it not only meant that I might still have someone out there hunting me; it also dashed my briefly resurgent hope that it was my father trying to contact me.

At the end of Monday's workday, Junior Feller drove me back to the Sorenson motel and hung out for a while, taking Hoover for a walk and sharing my take-out dinner. Then he went back to his car and sat outside my room until his relief showed up at eleven. I had hoped that Hurley might be the one to do all these things, but he had to get back home for Emily. Hurley did, however, pick me up the next morning and drive me in to work.

"How was your night?" he asked, as soon as we

were settled in his car. "Any more mysterious phone calls?"

"No phone calls. I didn't get much sleep, though, because the mattress on my bed is as hard as a rock. I really want to get back into my own place."

"Yeah, about that, I've arranged to have a security system installed on the cottage. I spoke to Izzy, and he's okay with it. In fact, he wants me to have them install one on his place, too."

I wasn't sure how I felt about this. On the one hand, it did seem like a nice security blanket to have, given the current situation. But it also seemed presumptive of Hurley to arrange it without talking to me first.

"Have the state guys said when they think they'll be able to release my place?"

"Not that I'm aware of. I talked to Richmond about it last night, but he was kind of cagey about the whole thing. I got the sense that something was up, but if it is, he wasn't talking. However, I do have some news on your car."

"Good news, I hope."

"I spoke to Marty about the window replacement and made a slight alteration. It means it will take a little longer to get the car back, but it will be worth it."

"What kind of alteration?" I said, giving him a suspicious look.

"He's putting bulletproof glass in all the windows."

I gaped at Hurley, slack-jawed.

"What?" he said, glancing over at me. "Did I do something wrong?"

"Don't you think that's a bit much? Hell, next you'll have them reinforcing all the side panels."

Hurley gave me a guilty look, followed by a cheesy grin.

"You didn't," I said.

"It didn't cost that much extra, and I know you well enough to know that you'll likely balk at being chauffeured around very much longer. Plus I know you don't want to wear that vest, so I did what I thought was best to insure your safety."

"You've turned my hearse into a popemobile." I shook my head and tried to figure out if I was upset or simply amused.

"Speaking of the pope," Hurley said, "what church should we use to have Junior baptized?"

Once again I was speechless.

"My parents were both practicing Episcopalians," he went on, this time clueless to my stunned state. "And while I haven't attended church much over the past decade or so, I went regularly when I was a kid. And I went a couple of times with Emily when we were in Chicago. That church was Catholic, but it's very similar to the Episcopalian Church, and I kind of enjoyed getting back into it. If you don't have a pref- erence, I thought I might get in touch with the min- ister at the Episcopal Church over on Dunkirk."

"Hurley, I don't have any plans to take our kid to church, or to have him or her baptized. I've never been a churchgoer. In fact, I'm an agnostic."

"You don't believe in God, or some sort of higher power?"

"Not really. I'm open to the possibilities, the same way I'm open to the possibility of ghosts, or Bigfoot, or life on other planets. But until I have proof posi- tive of such an existence, I remain skeptical. I don't buy into the whole superior being idea. If I'm in trouble or really want something, I might throw a prayer out there, but I don't actually believe it does anything or goes anywhere. I'm just covering all my bases. It's no different than throwing a pinch of salt over my left shoulder if I spill some."

"Huh."

"Is that a problem?"

"I don't know," he said. "Are you dead set against having our kid baptized?"

I thought about it for a few seconds. "I guess I'm not opposed to letting him or her go through the ritual if it means that much to you. But I don't see myself attending church on any kind of regular basis, and I think the kid should be allowed to make his or her own decisions in that regard, once he or she is old enough."

The rest of our trip was made in silence while I waited for a lightning bolt to strike me from above. When we arrived at the police station, I put in a call to Henderson to let him know where I was, fill him in on what Richmond had planned for the day, and see if there was anything in the office he needed me to do.

"I don't have anything pending at the moment other than your case, and unless you need to do something on the Ames case, I'm fine with having you stick with the cops today while they do their searches and interviews. If a call comes in, I can handle the on-scene stuff, but I would like you to be available to assist me if I have to do an autopsy."

"Not a problem. You have my cell number, right?"

"I do. I'll call you if I need you."

Then Hurley, Charlie, Richmond, and I had a planning meeting over coffee and donuts in the break room, mapping out our day. Richmond informed us that Blake Sutherland's alibi had checked out, eliminating her as a suspect. Then he suggested another trip to Derrick's house to make sure the laptop wasn't hiding in a desk or had simply been overlooked, and if nothing turned up there to head to the Fitzpatrick house to see if Sean had it. If that didn't produce anything, the next stop would be the high school to search Derrick's desk and the teacher's lounge, and talk to some of his coworkers. I then suggested that this would be a good time to take another run at Mandy Terwilliger.

"What useful information can we get out of Mandy at this point?" Richmond asked.

"I just feel like we need to cover all the bases. I'm bothered by Jacob's claim that Derrick told him he was going to break up with Mandy. I want to know why, and I want to know if she knew about it."

"I don't see how it has any bearing on the case at this point," Richmond argued.

"Just humor me," I said.

Richmond rolled his eyes and let out a put-upon sigh, but he agreed to talk to her.

Once all the details of the schedule were laid out, Richmond turned to me and said, "What are you going to do today?"

I stared at him in confusion for several long seconds before I answered. "I'm going with you guys."

"Not a chance," Richmond said. "It's too risky. You need to stay here. At least that way we know you aren't a target."

"You want me to hang here at the police station all day?" I said, my voice rife with skepticism.

"Bob's right," Hurley piped up. "It's the safest place for you."

"No way. Besides, you need to have someone from my office overseeing things, remember?"

"We have a videographer with us for that now, *remember*?" Richmond shot back.

Like I could forget Charlie's ever-presence. And the simple fact that she was going to be hanging with Hurley all day made me even more determined to go with them. "If I have to stay here all day long, I'll lose my mind. I might as well go home."

Richmond shrugged, indicating that was a perfectly acceptable option as far as he was concerned. I turned and gave Hurley an appealing look. Then Hurley shrugged, too.

Seeing that I was outnumbered, I came up with a new strategy. "If I agree to wear that stupid vest, will you let me go with you?"

Hurley and Richmond exchanged looks. Charlie leaned back in her chair and folded her arms over her chest, looking amused.

Finally Hurley said, "We might as well let her come. Otherwise she'll do something stupid."

"Fine," Richmond said. "But you have to wear the vest the entire time, and do everything we tell you to do."

"Okay," I said a bit petulantly.

"And before we head out," Richmond added, "I need to speak with you. In private."

With that, Charlie got up from her seat and said, "Come on, Steve. Let's go over those panning techniques again."

As Hurley followed Charlie out of the room like a dutiful dog, I glared at Richmond. "What now?" I said irritably.

"There's something I need to tell you," he said. The concerned tone of his voice worried me. "I had a little chat with Trooper Grimes earlier. They did some background research on you and came up with something that's a bit worrisome."

I fought down a frisson of panic. What had they discovered? Was that package of gum I shoplifted when I was in high school going to come back to haunt me? Did they know about that bar charge I accidentally skipped out on when Desi and I went to Chicago for a weekend a couple of years ago? Had they found something horrible and incriminating when they searched my house? I thought fast, trying to remember if I had anything embarrassing hidden away at the cottage, but I came up blank.

"They dug up some information on your father," Richmond said.

Now my mind was really spinning. I knew the state cops had scoured my cell phone records to try to trace the strange phone calls I'd been getting. Had some of those calls come from my father, as I'd originally thought? I felt a thrill of excitement, quickly followed by a throb of fear. Richmond's face told me this news wasn't going to be good.

"Do you remember the Quinton Dilles case?"

Remember it? The man's name was burned into my brain. He was Hurley's biggest enemy, and the reason Hurley lost his job in Chicago. In a way, that was a good thing since it brought Hurley to Sorenson and to me. But Quinton Dilles was also a deadly, vindictive, cruel man who had nearly cost both me and Hurley our lives.

"What does he have to do with anything?" I asked.

"There's something about his past you may not know. About five years before Dilles met his wife, the one he eventually killed, he owned one of those mailbox stores in Chicago. Some narcotics guys were working a case on a big drug ring in the area, and they thought that Dilles's mailbox store was a front for the group. They suspected Dilles was running both drugs and money through the place, shipping the stuff in packages that appeared to be from legitimate businesses. So one of the guys went undercover and started working to get proof by buddying up to the store manager, a guy named Cedric, who they thought was Dilles's right-hand man. Eventually the undercover cop, a guy named Roy Gilligan, who, by the way, was Hurley's partner at one time, let it be known that he was on the verge of getting the proof he needed. No one knows for sure what happened after that, but Roy ended up dead, shot once in the head and left in an alley. Cedric was the suspected hit man, but there was no evidence to pin it on him. Then Cedric disappeared. There were some reports of possible sightings down in Florida about a year later, but the cops down there couldn't find him, and no one has seen or heard anything of him since then."

"That's all very interesting—and tragic—but what does it have to do with my father?"

"Cedric's last name was Novak. Does that ring a bell with you at all?"

It did, but it was a very vague and distant bell. "Maybe. Why? Should it?"

"Cedric Novak was once married to a woman named Jane Obermeyer."

"That's my mother's maiden name."

Richmond just stared at me, waiting for me to put the pieces of the puzzle together. I did, and it shocked me to my core. "Cedric Novak is my father?" I said.

Richmond nodded. Then he opened a file he had on the table in front of him, a file I had thought was part of the Ames case. He slid out a rap sheet and handed it to me. On the sheet, which listed a number of crimes—mostly robberies—was the name Cedric Novak and a picture.

"That picture is about ten years old," Richmond explained. "But I think you can see the resemblance."

Indeed I could. The picture on the rap sheet was the spitting image of the man in Emily's drawing, the man who had been peering in my cottage windows one night, the man my mother identified as my father. The picture also fit with the vague image I had in my head from my childhood memories.

I stared at the picture, my brain spinning. If what Richmond said was true, Cedric Novak was my father, and he was responsible for killing a cop. And not just any cop, but Hurley's former partner. Plus he did it while working for Hurley's archenemy: Quinton Dilles.

"Does Hurley know any of this?" I asked.

Richmond shook his head. "He had already moved on to homicide by the time Roy was killed, and while he knew that this Cedric guy was suspected of killing Roy, he also knew that the order to do so had likely come from Dilles. That's one of the reasons he was so determined to nail Dilles for the murder of his socialite wife. I don't think Cedric has ever been high on Hurley's radar. He was just the henchman, and Hurley wanted the ringleader."

"You're not going to tell him, are you?"

"I don't have to. But Grimes knows. He was the one who made the connection. He was researching your background, which led him to your mother and her husbands. Cedric was her first. Grimes knew about the Chicago case and remembered the name. Once he discovered the connection, he felt he had to look into your past a little deeper."

"Is that why they aren't releasing my place yet?"

"Probably. He wants to make sure he's thorough."

"Does he think I'm in cahoots with my father or something? Because that's ridiculous. I didn't even know the man's name. I must have heard it mentioned at some point, because the name does stir some buried memory in my head, but I had no idea who it was or what it meant. My mother has always refused to talk about my father, and if she has any paperwork or pictures that mention or include him, I've never found them."

"I'm guessing that's because she figured out what he was and didn't want him connected to you in any way."

I stared at the rap sheet, which was three pages long. "You mean he was a criminal even back then?" I said, flipping to page two. My question was answered for me when I saw a handful of cons dating back to the late 1970s. I tossed the rap sheet aside and started massaging my temples. I had a sudden, throbbing headache. "It makes sense," I told Richmond. "Whenever I asked my mother about my father and why he left, she said he was nothing more than a vagabond gypsy with a black soul. I always thought she was merely venting her anger over the fact that he left us, but now I'm starting to think that every word of it was true."

"I'm sorry," Richmond said.

I stopped massaging my head and looked Richmond straight in the eye. "So am I. It is what it is, I guess. But Hurley can never know any of this. Please."

Richmond frowned, and I could tell he didn't want to agree with this, so I pleaded some more.

"If he knows that my father killed a man who was not only a cop, but also Hurley's ex-partner, and he was working with Dilles at the time, he'll hate him. He'll hate me. And what will it do when he looks at our kid? Please, Bob. He can't know."

"The information is out there. If he digs around hard enough, he'll find it."

"He has no reason to dig around if no one says anything to him."

"I think you're missing the bigger issue," Richmond said.

I looked at him, confused, unable to imagine anything bigger than the relationship-destroying information he'd already dumped on me.

"You thought your father was the one making the phone calls," Richmond said. "We now know that Roscoe Schneider made the calls that came before the shooting, but what about the one you got yesterday? Who made that call?"

"Are you suggesting that yesterday's call was from my father?"

"Schneider's calls all came from a burner phone that was purchased in Florida. Grimes looked into yesterday's call, and it also came from a burner phone that was purchased in Florida. And the last suspected sighting for Cedric Novak was in Florida."

Once again Richmond waited for me to make the connections. I did, and realized he was right. There was a bigger issue. It was starting to look like my long-lost father might want me dead.

Chapter 31

I asked Richmond if he could give me a few minutes before we left. He agreed, and I headed for the women's bathroom and locked the door so I could have a little privacy. Then I called my mother.

She answered with a cheery, "Ah, you finally found some time to spare your poor mother before she dies."

"What are you dying from this week, Mom?"

"I'm pretty sure I have a brain tumor."

This declaration didn't concern me at all. My mother has had several suspected brain tumors over the years, along with a host of other imagined ailments, all of which turned out to be nothing.

"I'm dizzy when I get up too fast, and I have this full, pressure feeling in my head. What else could it be?" my mother went on.

"It could be the cold you've had for the past few days. Have you taken a decongestant like I told you?"

"I've heard that decongestants can make your blood pressure rise, and if I have a brain tumor, that's the last thing I need. The pressure inside my head needs to remain as low as possible."

Technically, she was right about the blood pressure thing. My mother isn't your garden-variety hypochondriac; she's a well-studied one. Despite no formal medical training, she has a library most medical schools would envy, and she has read every book. Her knowledge proved useful when I was in nursing school. She would grill me on a wide assortment of disorders, diseases, and maladies, and she was as knowledgeable and well-informed as any teacher or tutor could have been. But since I was pretty sure she didn't really have a brain tumor, and I had neither the time nor the patience for her usual theatrics, I ignored this last comment and got straight to the reason for my call.

"Mom, was my father's name Cedric Novak?"

There was a lengthy silence on the other end, which gave me my answer.

"And did you know he was a criminal when you married him?"

"What has happened?" she said finally. "Has he contacted you?"

"If by contacted you mean has he tried to kill me, then yes."

"What? Don't be ridiculous. Your father wouldn't try to kill you. He loved you, Mattie. He may not have been a perfect man, and he may not have been as devoted to me as he should have been, but one thing about him that no one could deny was that he loved you."

This made my heart seize in my chest. My eyes burned as I fought back tears, and it took me a few seconds to find my voice. "Have you heard anything from him over the years?" I asked. "Has he ever been in Florida?"

Again my question was met with silence, and after

listening to it for several pounding heartbeats, I went off on a rant, propelled by my anger, hurt, and confusion. "He *has* been in Florida, hasn't he? And you've been in contact with him, haven't you? Why didn't you tell me? Do you know that the man who tried to kill me was from Florida? And do you know that I was getting strange hang-up calls for weeks before he tried to kill me? The cops traced those calls to a burner cell that the man who shot me had, one that was bought in Florida. Then I got another call yesterday, and that one also came from a burner phone that was bought in Florida. And I'm pretty sure dead men don't make phone calls. So put it all together, Mom. A man who looked like my father was peering in my cottage windows a couple of months ago, and someone tried to kill me a few days ago. I'm still getting weird phone calls, and all of this leads back to Florida."

"I can't explain what's happened to you, Mattie, but I know your father would never hurt you."

"How do you know that, Mom? What are you keeping from me?"

"I'm not keeping anything from you. I just know that your father wouldn't hurt you."

"What about other people? Has he hurt other people? Do you know that he's suspected of killing a cop?"

"Where did you hear that?"

"From the cops, Mom, where else?"

"Well, they're wrong. He wouldn't do that. Your father was not a killer. He may not have been an angel, but he was no killer."

"Did you know he was a criminal when you married him?"

"He wasn't, at least not at the time. I knew he had

done some things in the past, but he had turned his life around and wanted to start fresh."

"Then why did he leave?"

My mother sighed, and the next words she spoke came out in what Desi and I used to call her mother-knows-best tone of voice, the one that made it clear she would brook no questions or back talk. "Some things are better left alone, Mattie. That insatiable curiosity of yours always got you into trouble when you were younger, and it's still doing it today. You need to leave this alone and move on. You're starting your own family now, however misguided that may be. Let it be enough for you."

I knew she wasn't going to tell me anything more, so I hung up on her. I splashed some water on my face, hoping to cool myself down, and when I felt I had my emotions under control, I left the bathroom.

Fifteen minutes later, I was wearing a T-shirt Hurley had packed in the spare bag he kept in his trunk with Richmond's old vest over it. Over that was the top I was wearing that day, which fortunately was one of the looser-fitting new maternity tops I had just bought. As we headed out to the parking lot, the vest was already chafing me under my arms and around my hips.

Once again Charlie opted to take her own car, and I rode with Hurley, who watched with amusement as I struggled to grab hold of my shoulder belt and fasten it.

"That missing laptop was a good catch," he said as we pulled out of the lot.

"I guess," I said, finally snapping my belt into place.

Hurley shot me a look, his brow drawn into a V of worry. "Uh oh, what's wrong?"

"Nothing's wrong."

"You're lying. I can tell when something is bugging you, and right now something is bugging you. So spill it."

There was no way I was going to tell him what was actually bugging me at that moment, so I told a half-truth instead. "It's this stupid vest. It's hot, itchy, and restrictive."

"A little discomfort is better than being dead."

"What if someone aims for my head? What good is the vest going to do me then?"

"None," Hurley admitted. "But unless someone is a sharpshooter with sniper experience, the odds of them hitting you in the head are much smaller than the odds of you getting hit in the chest or gut. They're going to aim for the largest target."

"Even if they know I'm wearing a vest?"

"They won't know if you keep it hidden."

"Yeah, like no one can tell there's something strange under here," I snapped, pulling at my top. Plus it's May, Hurley. The weather is getting warmer every day. How much longer do you expect me to wear this thing? I feel like I'm in a sweatbox." I stared down at the square shape of my top below my bust. "Hell, I look like a sweatbox."

"You look fine. Now tell me what's really bothering you."

Damn the man! I quickly dug up a second half-truth. "It's this case. Something about it doesn't feel right."

"You don't think Jacob did it?"

"I don't know if it's that I actually believe he didn't do it, or if I need to believe he didn't do it. The idea of a kid killing one of his parents is kind of scary, especially now."

"Yeah, I suppose it is," Hurley said. "But just because Jacob Ames might be messed up, it doesn't mean our kid will be. If you raise them right and instill the correct values into them, they turn out okay."

"I don't know if I believe that, Hurley. I think some people are just born bad, and no amount of nurturing is going to make a difference. Derrick Ames seemed to be a loving and caring father, by all accounts, and Wendy, despite keeping her sexual identity issues a secret, seems to be a decent mother. Granted, if Jacob did this, it would seem to be a heat-of-the-moment kind of thing as opposed to some kind of personality flaw. But I can't help thinking that if it could happen to Derrick Ames, it could happen to anyone. It could happen to me."

"You actually think that our kid might grow up and kill you someday?"

The skepticism in Hurley's voice made the idea sound utterly ridiculous, and under normal circumstances, it might have been. But now I knew things I hadn't known before. Now I had to face the fact that my child was going to be the product of a genetic roll of the dice that included my law-breaking, murderous father. It was knowledge I intended to keep to myself.

"I know I'm being ridiculous," I said, trying to laugh it off. "I think it's the hormones. This pregnancy stuff does weird things to your mind and your body."

"Speaking of your body, I'm excited about this ultrasound thing tomorrow."

"Yeah, about that . . . I really don't want to know

the sex until it's born, so please don't ask, and if they offer to tell you, please decline. If you know, you'll give it away somehow."

"You don't think I can keep a secret?"

"I'm sure you can. But down the road something you'll say, or something you'll do will give it away. I just know it. So can we please agree to wait on it?"

Hurley shrugged with indifference. "Sure. I don't need an ultrasound to tell me anyway. I already know."

"Your second sight?" I said with no small amount of sarcasm.

"Go ahead and mock," Hurley said. "You'll see, and soon you'll believe."

When we arrived at Derrick's house, Richmond and Hurley bordered me on both sides as we headed inside. Wendy didn't object to our search this time, and the look on her face—frightened, bewildered, shocked—showed how much the previous day's events had devastated her.

We split into pairs: Richmond and I together, and Charlie and Hurley together. I wasn't happy about the arrangement and did what little damage control I could by declaring the upstairs as our area. At least this way I could keep Charlie and Hurley from being in a bedroom together.

Our search took a little less than an hour, and while we didn't find a laptop, we did find a thumb drive stashed in Derrick's sock drawer. We bagged it, tagged it, and then headed for the Fitzpatrick house.

Once again Mrs. Fitzpatrick was polite and more than accommodating, though she did bite back a smile when she looked at my boxy torso. "I haven't seen any new laptops here in the house," she told us. "You're welcome to look in Sean's room, or anywhere else you like. And you can talk to Sean, too, if you want. He's here because he was suspended from school for a week."

"What for?" I asked, eager to learn the warning signs of a budding juvenile delinquent.

"Smoking pot in one of the boy's bathrooms," Mrs. Fitzpatrick said with a weary sigh. "He refuses to tell anyone where he got the pot from and took the suspension instead." She shook her head and flashed us a weary smile. "He's no angel, but he's also no rat. He's always been that way, even when he was little. When one of the other kids did something, Sean would never tell on them. It's his code, I guess. And I suppose some ethic is better than none."

If Mrs. Fitzpatrick was right, Sean's code meant that even if he knew something about Jacob and the missing laptop, he wasn't likely to tell us. At first, the boy wouldn't even talk to or acknowledge us, but his mother elicited his reluctant cooperation by threatening to send him away to some camp for troubled kids. His attitude was surly initially, but that vanished when he laid eyes on Charlie for the first time. After that he was tripping all over himself to be helpful, friendly, and cooperative.

Unfortunately, our search turned up nothing, and Sean swore that he never saw Jacob with an extra laptop here, at school, or anywhere else where the two boys might have hooked up. Richmond questioned Sean for a good ten minutes, and despite the kid's starry-eyed efforts to impress Charlie, hints of his underlying, innate bad-assitude kept seeping out in his facial expressions, his body language, and some of the things he said. By the time we left, I don't think any of us felt we could believe or trust a single thing Sean had told us.

Our time at the Fitzpatrick house depressed me and made me determined to avoid a similar fate. I didn't want to spend the rest of my life exhausted, frustrated, and existing rather than living, struggling to maintain a household filled with bratty children and a TV-addicted husband who lived in a Barca-lounger, whiling away the hours of my life in an end-less cycle of cooking, cleaning, harping, and crying.

Having reached a dead end with these legs of the investigation, we moved on to the school, which was located on several acres of land on the west end of town about six blocks back from Main Street. It was a sprawling, stone, two-story building with a football field, tennis courts, and a baseball diamond on the grounds.

We headed inside and found our way to the main office. A receptionist greeted us, and as soon as Rich-mond flashed his badge and told her why we were there, she called back to the principal and relayed the information. When she was done, she hung up the phone and said, "Mrs. Knowles will be with you momentarily."

We stepped back to allow a student who had come in behind us to carry out his business. He approached the desk, handed the receptionist a piece of paper, and said, "This is my mom's excuse for missing school Friday."

"It wasn't your mom who missed school," the re-ceptionist said.

The kid stared at her in confusion. "Was my mom supposed to be here for something?"

"Never mind," the receptionist said with a little laugh, shaking her head and rolling her eyes.

The kid shrugged, mumbled something I couldn't make out, and then shuffled off to his class, the hems of his worn blue jeans dragging on the ground, his longish hair hanging in his pockmarked face.

The receptionist read the note, smiled, and lay it atop a pile of other papers in a two-tiered file tray.

I glanced over and read the note, which said:

Please excuse John from school on Friday. His girlfriend was having there baby.

So much for getting an education.

Mrs. Knowles came out of her office and walked over to greet us. She had a friendly face with a warm smile, and her gray hair and matronly build gave her a grandmotherly aura. I couldn't help but compare her to my own high school principal, Mr. Dean, a tall, skinny, bespectacled man in his fifties, who we determined developed his theories on student behavior from the Gestapo. We called him lean, mean Mr. Dean behind his back.

"I'm Jeanette Knowles, the principal here. How can I help you folks today?"

Richmond produced his badge, made the introductions, and then said, "I assume you've heard about Mr. Ames?"

"Yes, yes, a terrible thing. Is it true that you arrested Jacob?"

"Jacob has been detained, but we're still investigating the case," Richmond said, giving me a tired look. "Have you ever seen Mr. Ames carrying a laptop around?"

"Sure," Jeanette said. "Most of our teachers have laptops or tablets. Why?"

"We're trying to locate Mr. Ames's laptop. Is it here at the school by any chance?" Richmond's voice sounded hopeful.

Jeanette dashed his hopes when she frowned and said, "I'm certain he wouldn't have left it here. Something like that would be a little too much temptation for some of our students, I'm afraid."

Richmond wasn't going down without a fight. "If he was going to leave something like that here, where would it be? Did he have a desk? A locker? An office? What about the teacher's lounge?"

"None of our teachers have private offices. Mr. Ames did have a desk—all of our teachers do, but the locks are rather flimsy, so most of them don't keep anything of value in them, and we emptied Derrick's desk yesterday. There was no laptop. We do have some lockers in the teacher's lounge for our staff to store their personal belongings."

"I assume that Derrick Ames had one?"

"He did, but it's empty."

"I'd like to see it. I would also like to have a look inside the lockers of Jacob Ames and Sean Fitzpatrick."

"Sean? Why him?"

"We think Jacob may have taken Derrick's laptop from his father's house, and since he and the Fitzpatrick boy are friends, we think he may have given it to him to keep."

"Do you have a warrant?"

"I do not," Richmond said.

"Then I'm not comfortable letting you search our students' lockers. Some of our parents might get upset over such an invasion of their child's privacy."

"There is no expectation of privacy in a student's

locker," Richmond said. "The school owns the lockers, and it's up to you to decide to let us search or not. I think it would be in your best interest to let us search the lockers of these two boys, but if you disagree, I'll be happy to get a search warrant that will include every locker in this school."

Jeanette sighed and said, "We just searched Sean's locker last Friday because he was caught smoking pot in the boy's room. There was no laptop in there, and we suspended him for the week, so he hasn't been back since then."

"If you don't mind, I'd prefer to look for myself," Richmond said with a forced, plastic smile.

Jeanette sighed again, louder and more exaggerated this time. I think she sensed Richmond wasn't going to back down. "Fine," she said, heading for the office door. "Follow me."

Chapter 32

Our search of the teacher's lounge produced nothing more than stares, whispered speculations, and some strategic ducking whenever the camera was around. Derrick's locker was empty, just as Jeanette Knowles had said, and nothing turned up in Jacob's or Sean's lockers, either. So far our trip to the school was a bust, and Jeannette had a smug, I-told-you-so look on her face. She led us back to the main office, where she stopped inside the door—effectively barring our reentry—and asked, "Is there anything else I can do for you, detective?"

"Did Mr. Ames have any problems with any of the other staff?"

"No, Derrick got on well with everyone."

"What about the students? Any issues there?"

"Again, no. Like I said, he was well liked by everyone."

"Was there anyone on the staff he was particularly close to?"

Jeanette thought a moment and said, "He and Sam Littleton seemed to get on quite well. They typically lunched together and talked a lot. They're both divorced with kids, so they have a lot in common. And then, of course, there's Mandy Terwilliger, who is a volunteer rather than a member of our staff. From what I hear, she and Derrick were *very* close." Her voice was rich with prurient suggestion.

"Can you ask Mr. Littleton to come here to the office so we can talk with him?" Richmond asked.

Jeanette gave us a bemused look. "Whatever for?"

"Because I asked you to," Richmond said, clearly impatient.

Jeanette Knowles narrowed her eyes at him, folded her arms over her chest, and adjusted her stance, looking ready for a fight. The grandmotherly aura had disappeared. "I think I have a right to know why you want to talk to one of my employees," she said, her lips tight. "I heard that Jacob Ames has been arrested for the murder of his father, so I don't understand your need to go fishing among my staff for any other suspects."

"We're trying to tie up a few loose ends."

"Such as?" Jeanette said, her voice demanding. I imagined it was very effective on any students who were under fire.

Richmond sighed and smiled at her. It wasn't a particularly friendly smile. "That's really none of your business. Now can you get Mr. Littleton down here for us, or do I have to get a search warrant and disrupt the entire school day by searching this whole building and inviting all the parents to come by so I can talk to the students, too?"

I swear I saw light sabers spring out of Jeanette's eyes. Her jaw muscles clenched like a pugilist's fists. "Let me guess," she said, her voice as venomous as a rattler's bite. "You were one of those kids who visited the principal's office a lot in school, weren't you?"

"Yes, I was," Richmond said, biting back. "And as a result, I saw things. Lots of things. And that principal ended up not only getting fired, but being sent to prison." He paused for a few seconds, and Jeanette's eyes opened a little wider. "Now I'm tired of your verbal jousting." Richmond lifted his arm and looked at his watch. "You've got thirty seconds."

Though I wasn't counting, I'd wager that Jeanette used twenty-nine of her allotted seconds before she finally caved, though she never took her icy glare off Richmond. She spun around and barked out an order. "Melanie, can you please find Mr. Littleton and ask him to come to the office?"

"Sure."

Melanie got up from her chair and headed out of the office at a fast clip, head down. Since Jeanette had to step aside to let Melanie go by, Richmond took advantage of the moment and entered the office. The rest of us followed.

Jeanette scowled but wasn't done yet. She turned to Richmond and said, "I want to sit in on any interrogations you do."

"These aren't interrogations," Richmond said, his glare even icier. "They are interviews. And the only one you may sit in on is yours."

I could tell Jeanette didn't like this answer. Her lips and jaw muscles twitched with unspoken objections, but, wisely, all she said was, "You may use the conference room over there." She pointed the way, then stomped back into her office, slamming the door behind her.

"Wow," I said, looking over at Richmond with newfound respect. "It's a good thing it wasn't Jeanette who was killed because if it was, we'd have a list of suspects as long as my arm. And I have very long arms."

"She's a power-hungry bitch," Richmond grumbled.

Hurley leaned toward me and whispered, "I love your arms. They're the perfect size to reach everything they need to."

I blushed. Now he loved my arms. Surely the whole of me couldn't be too far away. Then I remembered that it really didn't matter anymore.

I noticed that Charlie, who had stood in the background silently through all of this, was staring at Richmond with a curious expression. "Did you really get your high school principal fired and jailed?" she asked.

"I did. The asshole was buying drugs from some of the students in exchange for bumping up their grades or letting them slide on their offenses. I caught on because I got sent to the principal's office a lot for getting into fights. I had a weight problem, and a lot of the kids made fun of me. I dealt with it by trying to beat the crap out of them."

"Hunh," Charlie said.

Suddenly lean, mean Mr. Dean didn't seem so bad.

We all headed for the conference room that Principal Knowles had indicated. Once inside, Charlie grabbed Hurley by the arm and hauled him down to one end of the long table that was in the room. "Let me show you how to set up the camera in order to get the best audio and video."

I watched as they bowed their heads together, and twice Charlie took hold of Hurley's hand and guided him to the appropriate holding places, which fortunately were on the video camera and not on her body.

The door to the conference room opened, and Melanie walked in with Mr. Littleton in tow.

"Hello, Mr. Littleton," Richmond said. He waved a hand toward the opposite side of the table and added, "Please have a seat."

Melanie backed out with a wary look while Sam Littleton, who looked like a young Michael Caine, made his way to the seat Richmond indicated.

Hurley and Charlie settled into chairs at their end of the table, and Richmond and I sat across from Littleton. I decided to let Richmond do all the questioning unless there was something that jumped out at me that he didn't ask.

"We'd like to talk to you about Derrick Ames," Richmond said after Charlie gave him a go-ahead nod. Hurley had the camera in hand, but Charlie was leaning into him, watching the screen.

"It's an awful thing that happened to him," Littleton said. "I don't know what I can do to help, but I'm willing to try. You said on the phone that you were interested in a text message I sent Derrick on the day of his death?"

Richmond nodded, and Littleton took a smartphone out of his pocket, tapped the screen a few times, and handed it to Richmond.

"He never answered me," Littleton said as Richmond read the text. When he was done, he handed the phone to me, and I read the message, which said, WANT TO GET A BEER AFTER SCHOOL TOMORROW NIGHT? before handing the phone off to Hurley so he could film what it showed.

Richmond turned his attention back to Littleton. "Were the two of you pretty close?" he asked.

"We were friends," Littleton said with a shrug. "We have . . . had a lot in common. We both have German parents, we're both divorced with kids, we both like to play darts."

"Darts?"

"Yeah, we belong to a league down at the Anywhere bar. It meets every Thursday night."

"Do you know if Mr. Ames had any enemies?"

Littleton shook his head. "No, everyone liked him. He was an easygoing, friendly guy."

"No fights with anyone down at the bar?"

"Fights? No," Littleton said, dismissing the issue with an expression that suggested the idea was ludicrous. "It's a friendly bunch down there."

"Were there any problems you were aware of between him and any of the other teachers? Or any of the students or parents?"

Littleton looked as if he was thinking hard, and after a few seconds, he shook his head again. "Nope. He was active in the PTA and held regular parent-teacher conferences. And he got along great with the kids, though he did have some problems with his own from time to time."

"Such as?"

"Well, the divorce thing. That's always hard on kids. He and Jacob would argue a lot."

"About what?"

"About whether or not Derrick and his wife were going to get back together, about Jacob's behavior, Jacob's choice of friends . . . all the usual teenage stuff."

"What sort of behaviors did Jacob and Derrick argue about?"

"Jacob has a tendency to lash out without much provocation. His fuse is a short one. And Derrick didn't like some of the kids he was hanging out with."

"Which kids?"

"Well, that Fitzpatrick kid, for one. Sean is a troublemaker, and he and Jacob seem to feed off one another."

"Can you give some examples?"

"Well, back around the holidays, they started a fire in the boy's bathroom just to get out of a math test they didn't want to take because they hadn't studied. Then Derrick caught Jacob and Sean smoking out in the parking lot and went ballistic. Two weeks ago, the boys broke into the biology lab late one night during a basketball game and set free all the fruit flies that were being bred in jars for a genetics study the kids were doing. There were seven periods' worth of fruit-fly colonies, with probably two dozen jars of flies for each class. Not only did it mess up the whole study; we had to close down the cafeteria for two days to get rid of the damned things. We still find them in the teacher's lounge from time to time if someone leaves a piece of fruit sitting out for more than an hour."

Richmond's cell phone chirped, and he took it out of his pocket and cast a quick glance at the screen. "Excuse me," he said. "I need to take this."

He got up and walked to a far corner of the room to take the call. As much to satisfy my own curiosity as to provide some privacy for Richmond, I took over the questions with Littleton. "What about Derrick's social life? Was he seeing anyone?" I asked.

"Oh, yeah, he recently hooked up with one of the moms who volunteers here, Mandy Terwilliger. She's a looker," he said, his eyes growing big. "A couple of the other men around here have made plays for her, me included. But she never gave any of us the time of day until Derrick came around. They hit it off, though they were trying to keep things under the radar—for the kids' sakes, I suppose."

"Did Derrick talk to you about his relationship with Mandy?"

"Some, yeah," Littleton said with half a shrug.

"Did he say anything recently about breaking things off with her?"

Littleton shook his head. "No, in fact, things between them seemed to be pretty good. Although, last Friday when we had lunch he did say that he might have to cool things down with her for a little while if Jacob didn't come around soon. He always put his boys first."

Richmond disconnected his call, returned to the table, and said, "Thank you, Mr. Littleton. I think that's all we need for now, but if you think of anything else, please call me." He slid a business card across the table, and Hurley walked over and handed the man back his phone.

Littleton nodded, took both items, got up from his chair, and left the room.

"What's up?" I asked Richmond.

"They found Derrick's laptop."

Chapter 33

"The laptop was in a Dumpster behind the high school," I tell Maggie. "A student who was smoking in the back parking lot saw it when he went to dump his butts and recognized the German flag decal. He called it in to the police, and Junior Feller went out to recover it. He knew that Richmond and the rest of us were at the high school already, so he called Richmond to have us come out back and film the recovery."

"Did it turn up anything?" Maggie asks.

I shake my head. "The hard drive had been wiped clean, and there were no prints on it. Just to be thorough, Richmond did get copies of e-mails that Derrick sent from his Internet provider, but they didn't offer up any new clues. The fact that the laptop was tossed behind the school pointed the finger even more firmly at Jacob as the culprit, so Richmond declared the case closed."

"And how did things in your own case progress?"

"Well, after five days of living at the motel, my cottage was finally released back to me, and I was able to move back in. It's a good thing I didn't need an entire week at the motel because once the story broke in the paper and Joseph learned the real reason why I was staying there, he wanted me gone. He said he didn't want to develop a reputation for housing killers. He was so glad when I finally moved out of there that he even offered to refund my unused days. Izzy came home on Sunday, Henderson went back to whatever rock he crawled out from under, and life resumed something of a normal pattern, if you can consider having someone guarding you twenty-four hours a day as normal. I also got my car back, and I'm now more secure than the president when I'm driving it, which is hardly ever since I have a police escort of some sort everywhere I go."

"Your work life has returned to normal then?" Maggie asks.

"Better than normal, as it turns out. Henderson was appalled at how little staffing we have, and he said we needed more help. When he got back to Madison, he spoke to some folks there, and we eventually got some additional positions approved. Arnie is happy, because he's going to get help in his lab. In fact, he's more than happy because he and Laura Kingston, Henderson's assistant, hit if off in a big way, and she's going to be his new assistant. The two of them have been dating for three months now."

"That's nice," Maggie says.

"Yes, it is. And there's been romance in the air for Richmond, too. It turned out I was right when I told him Rose Carpenter had a thing for him. She's been a divorcée for four years, and I guess she was tired of it because she went after Richmond the way my dog Hoover goes after squirrels. They've been hot and heavy for a couple of months now, too. It seems everyone is happy in romance except for me."

"Has Hurley found out about the connection between your father and this Dilles guy?"

"Nope, and I hope to keep it that way. I swore Grimes and Richmond to secrecy, even though they still think it's possible the phone calls I'm getting are coming from my father and that he wants me dead for some reason."

"You're still getting the calls?"

"I am. I get one about every other week or so, and it's the same thing each time: no one answers, but I can hear background noise or breathing that tells me the line is open and someone is there. After a few seconds they hang up. The cops have been tracing the calls, determining the general area they're being made from, and for the last few weeks it's always been somewhere in or around this part of Wisconsin. The calls have bounced off towers in the Chicago area, the Madison area, the Milwaukee area, in Waunakee, in Eagle River, in Sheboygan—like whoever is making them is circling ever closer. Hurley thinks it's some crazed stalker, like one of those nutty women who wants a baby. He thinks they're just waiting for me to get far enough along in my pregnancy that they can kill me but have the baby survive if they take it."

Maggie frowns at this. "What do you think?"

"I don't know," I say, shifting in my seat in a futile effort to get comfortable. "Even if Richmond and Grimes are right with their theory that it's my father calling me, I can't come up with any reason why he would want me dead. Regardless of who it is, the evidence suggests Roscoe Schneider wasn't working alone and someone out there wants me dead."

"That must be scary."

"It is," I admit. "Even though I grumbled about the changes Hurley had them make to my car, I do feel safer having the reinforcements. The security system on my house is nice, too, although I'm driving Izzy and the cops crazy because I've accidentally set the alarms off several times."

"Speaking of Izzy, how are things between you and him?"

"It's been good. He and Dom are both so excited about the baby, you'd think it was their grandchild. They bought a playpen, a high chair, and a crib for their house, and they've gone through and child-proofed the place. Izzy and I have our old working relationship back, and other than the security issues, things have been pretty much the way they were before. And since the videographer thing has eliminated the conflict of interest issues, Hurley and I have been able to continue working together."

"So what's the current status of your relationship with Hurley?"

"It's been a bit strained. He's clearly worried about the phone calls and the stalker thing, and I can tell he's upset about my refusal to marry him. To be honest, I think he might have worn me down had it not been for this thing with my father and some issues we've had with Emily. But how can I possibly marry him now, knowing what I know? He'd hate me if he knew about my father's past. And I'm afraid he'd hate our child, too."

"You can't know that. Don't you think Hurley's a smart enough guy to separate the two things?"

"I'm not sure enough to want to risk it. If I was the only one involved, I'd go for it and take what comes.

But I don't want to jeopardize the relationship Hurley will have with our child. Besides, he's under enough strain these days dealing with Emily. He's had to learn how to be a father through Crash Parenting 101, and for a man who wasn't sure he ever wanted to be a father, he's had a lot to deal with. Right now what Hurley needs is space and friendly support with no added pressures."

"So where do you go from here?"

"I don't know. If Hurley and I were meant to be together as a couple, the universe wouldn't be obstructing us in so many ways. I think we are meant to be parents, just not husband and wife."

"Are you comfortable with that?"

"What other choice do I have?"

"If Hurley ever starts a romantic relationship with someone else, are you afraid he'll pull away from you and your child?"

I think about that, long and hard. Finally I say, "I guess I am a little. I know he feels pulled in a lot of different directions right now. He's trying to find a happy balance, and it isn't easy. And while I feel confident he'll be a significant part of our child's life no matter what, in some ways he's already pulling away."

"Such as?"

"Well, his decision to pull out of the birthing classes. for one. But in order for you to understand how difficult that was for him, I should first tell you about the ultrasound appointment, because I think that best reflects his frame of mind before everything started getting messy."

And then I tell Maggie about one of the happiest days of my life so far.

Chapter 34

On the Wednesday after Hurley's return, the two of us walked into the office of my OB doctor. We had the waiting room to ourselves, and after leaving my name with the receptionist behind the glass window, I sat down next to Hurley and leaned over to see what he was reading in the magazine he was holding. It was an article on preventing stretch marks, and with it was a picture of a huge belly with ugly tracks on both sides of it, and a dark stripe that ran from the navel down to the pubis. The look of horror on Hurley's face didn't do much for my ego.

"We're not that far into this," I said, taking the magazine from him. "Don't get psyched out about things that haven't happened yet."

"What has happened to you so far?"

"Well, for a while I was vomiting at odd times of the day with little to no warning, but that seems to have passed. Now I pee all the time instead. My boobs have gotten huge—"

"So I noticed," he said, arching one brow.

"And they ache."

"Oh." Hurley looked disappointed, and his eyebrow resumed its original position.

"I'm also dealing with a long list of foods I'm not supposed to eat, which pretty much rules out anything that tastes good."

"So this pregnancy stuff isn't a fun thing?"

I considered his question for a few seconds, and as if the child inside me had heard him, he or she kicked. I smiled. "It definitely has had its high moments," I said, rubbing my tummy. "I just felt the baby move."

"Really?" Hurley stared at my belly with a mix of fascination and awe. "Can I feel it?"

"I don't know. It's been pretty random so far, and it's subtle. At first I thought it was a gas bubble."

The nurse came out then and called my name, so Hurley and I followed her into the examination area of the office. Unfortunately, we detoured at the scale.

"Step on up," the nurse said, not realizing I'd rather strip naked and parade down Main Street than let Hurley know my weight. Fortunately, Hurley seemed to sense my hesitation, and he wandered over to a plastic model of a uterus with a baby in it. The nurse was kind enough to record my weight on a slip of paper without announcing it, and with that trial passed, we moved on to the exam room.

After taking my blood pressure, temperature, and pulse, and announcing that these figures all looked good, she handed me a paper-thin gown that had been used and laundered so many times the print on the material was faded into near oblivion. "Please strip off everything and put this gown on," she said. "If you need to pee, it's best if you hold it for now. It will make it easier to see things when we do the ultrasound."

I stripped, feeling a little self-conscious about Hurley seeing me naked in the harsh, clinical lighting of the exam room, and tried to make the gown wrap around me, which it refused to do. With my butt cheeks hanging out, I sidled up onto the exam table and laid the sheet the nurse had left out over my lap. I glanced over at Hurley, who was staring at the tray the nurse had set up with the vaginal speculum, lubricant, and gloves.

"Have you ever seen a pelvic exam done before, Hurley?" I asked, tucking the sheet in around my thighs.

He shook his head.

I then gave him a brief description of what was about to happen. "I think it will be better if you sit up here by my head. Some things just aren't meant to be seen."

"I've seen it before," he said, wiggling his eyebrows.

"That's different. Trust me."

He nodded and scooted his chair up to the head of the table. His mouth was hanging partway open, and his eyes were huge; he looked like a fish out of water.

Dr. Rita Carson came into the room, looking all efficient and professional in her crisp white lab coat, tailored gray slacks, and sensible shoes. Her brown hair was pulled back into a neat little bun that made her face look a little taut, but when she smiled, she looked warm, friendly, and approachable.

"Hello, Mattie," she said. She shifted her gaze to Hurley. "And I assume this is the father, Mr. Hurley?"

"It is."

Hurley looked a little surprised that Dr. Carson knew his name, so she explained. "Mattie and I have discussed the situation between the two of you, so I'm familiar with your history. Congratulations on becoming a dad."

"I'm already a dad," Hurley said.

"Ah, right. I forgot. The teenage daughter you didn't know you had."

Hurley shifted uncomfortably in his seat and shot me a frown. "You are very well informed, it seems," he said.

"I'm sorry," I told him. "For the past two months, Rita has been the only person I've had to talk to about this pregnancy, so she's been my confidant."

"I get it," Hurley said. He didn't sound angry, but he still looked annoyed.

"Shall we get on with the exam?" Dr. Carson said. "Any issues or questions since the last time you were here?"

I shook my head. "I did experience my first quickening," I told her.

Hurley looked panicked. "What is that? Is the baby's heart going too fast? Is Mattie's?"

"No," Dr. Carson said with a smile. "*Quickening* is a term for feeling the baby move."

"Oh," Hurley said, still wearing his fish-out-of-water expression. I found it amusing. Up until that day, Hurley had always seemed so self-assured and confident. It was sweet seeing this vulnerable, unsure side of him.

Dr. Carson had me slide down on the examining table and put my feet up in the stirrups. She positioned herself between my legs, lifted the sheet, and grabbed the speculum. Hurley reached up and took my hand. It was a sweet gesture that nearly brought me to tears.

"Mattie tells me you're a homicide detective," Dr. Carson said as she started her exam.

"That's right," Hurley said. He was leaning to the side ever so slightly, trying to see what was going on beyond the sheet.

"Your cervix is thick and closed," Dr. Carson said next, an odd conversational segue.

"Is that good?" Hurley asked.

"Yes, it's very good," Dr. Carson said. She wheeled out from behind the sheet, placed the used speculum back on the tray, and said, "You can put your feet down."

I lowered my legs from the stirrups and repositioned the sheet.

"Let's take a listen to that kid's heart, shall we?" Dr. Carson said next, grabbing a small handheld Doppler device—used to magnify the sounds of pulses and, as in this case, heartbeats—and a bottle of gel. She lowered the sheet to below my belly and raised the gown up. Then she squirted a big glob of the gel onto my stomach a few inches below my navel and pressed one end of the Doppler device into it. After she moved the device around a patch of skin about four inches square, the sound suddenly came through loud and clear.

Thumpa-thumpa-thumpa-thumpa-thumpa . . .

"Sounds like a healthy heart," Dr. Carson said with a smile. "Everything seems to be progressing as expected."

She pulled the Doppler device away and started to set it down, but Hurley said, "That was my kid's heartbeat?"

"Yes," she said, her smile broadening.

Hurley looked awed and amazed. "Can we listen to it a little longer?"

"Sure."

She returned the device to the same spot, and once again the sound echoed through the room: *thumpa-thumpa-thumpa-thumpa-thumpa-thumpa-thumpa-thumpa-thumpa-thumpa* . . .

"Is it supposed to be that fast?" Hurley asked, looking a little worried.

"Yes, it's absolutely normal," Dr. Carson assured him. She let him listen a little longer, and when I felt Hurley squeeze my hand, I looked over at him. His eyes were brimming with tears. He looked over at me, and with the biggest grin I've ever seen on his face said, "We're having a kid, Winston! That was our kid!"

His enthusiasm and excitement were contagious. "If you think the kid *sounds* great, wait until you see how it looks," Dr. Carson said. "The ultrasound tech will be in with you in a few minutes. See you both next time?"

Hurley nodded hard and fast, like a bobblehead doll, and as Dr. Carson turned to leave the room he said, "Thank you!"

"You're very welcome." She winked at me and then left the room.

"That was amazing," Hurley said. He popped up out of his chair, kissed me on the forehead, and then sat back down again.

I started to say something to him, but the door to the exam room opened and a young girl wheeled in the ultrasound machine.

"It's about to get even better," I said.

Hurley fidgeted in his chair, occasionally squeezing my hand, as the ultrasound tech—who introduced herself as Amber—explained what she was doing. She got the machine in place, squeezed more gel on my belly, and then placed the ultrasound wand on top of the gel. She pressed down a little, moved the wand a couple of times, and then reached over and turned the machine toward us so we could see the screen.

"There's your baby," Amber said.

Hurley and I both stared in awe at the tiny, human-shaped figure on the screen. Amber pointed to a tiny blinking light. "That's the heart beating," she said. She left the wand there for a second or two, then moved it slightly. "Would you like to know the sex?" she asked.

"Yes!" Hurley said.

"No!" I said at the same time.

Hurley and I turned and looked at one another. "Hurley, we discussed this," I said.

"And disagreed." We stared at one another a little longer. "Fine," he said. "You win. Besides, I told you I already know it's a boy."

Amber arched a brow at him. "And how do you know that?" she asked.

"I have the second sight," he said.

"You're Irish?" Amber asked.

"Irish enough," Hurley said.

"Interesting." Amber printed out a picture and handed it to me; then she printed out a second one and handed it to Hurley. "Your baby's first picture," she said.

Hurley held that picture in his hand like it was the most precious thing he'd ever seen. And the grin on his face when we left the office was bigger than any I'd ever seen.

He drove me back to the motel, escorted me inside, and minutes later we were in bed together. But there was no hanky-panky that day. Instead we lay there, side by side, Hurley's hand gently caressing my stomach. We didn't speak, we didn't even kiss. Yet I'd never felt as close to him as I did that day.

An hour later when he got up to leave, I wanted to ask him to stay. But I didn't. Instead I made myself a sandwich for dinner, watched some TV, and then cried myself to sleep.

Chapter 35

Jacob Ames was arraigned and held without bail for the murder of his father. Stanley Barber the Third would be in charge of his defense, and I was pretty sure the money for his fees was coming from Blake. Jacob's situation depressed me, but I wasn't sure if it was because I truly didn't believe he was guilty, or because I just didn't want to believe he was guilty.

Saturday was my birthday, and while I hadn't planned for any sort of celebration short of being able to move back into my cottage, Hurley had other things in mind. He still didn't want me out in public any more than I had to be, so he came up with an alternate plan. "Emily and I are going to cook you dinner at my house," he said. "We're even going to bake a cake."

This summoned up an image of a father and daughter together in the kitchen, both of them covered with a dusting of flour, laughing and sharing this bondable moment as they stumbled through the process. It was a heartwarming picture that gave me hope for the future. It was also an example of just how much of a dreamer I can be.

Hurley picked me up around two in the afternoon, and after helping me move back into the cottage and get the animals settled, he drove me over to his place. Things started going bad almost as soon as I arrived. Hurley warned me on the way over that Emily had been very moody all week and hadn't wanted to go to school. An argument had ensued every morning, and while Hurley had always managed to get her off to school, when she came home she locked herself in her bedroom and wouldn't come out.

"She stays in there all evening watching TV, drawing in her sketchbook, or writing in her diary. She hasn't tried to hook up with any of her friends from before, she isn't participating in any social networks that I know of, and whenever I go in there and try to talk to her, she says she needs her privacy and asks me to leave. When I do, she slams the door behind me."

"Maybe she's going through some female stuff, Hurley. Maybe she just got her period for the first time."

Hurley shot me a terrified look. "What am I supposed to do for that? I don't know anything about women's periods beyond the fact that there's blood and moodiness involved."

"I'll talk to her when we get there and see if I can figure out what's going on, okay?"

"That would be great. Thanks."

When we arrived at the house, Hurley headed into the kitchen while I made my way upstairs where Emily was, as predicted, in her bedroom. I knocked on the closed door.

"Emily? It's Mattie. Can I come in and talk to you?" There was no answer, so I tried again, knocking a little louder this time, thinking she might have earphones on that were interfering with her ability to hear. When I got no answer the second time, I stood there for a moment, trying to decide what to do. Finally I reached down and tried the doorknob. It turned easily, so I slowly pushed the door open, knocking on it again and announcing my presence loudly.

"I heard you the first two times," Emily said. She was sitting on her bed, a sketch pad propped up against her bent knees, scowling at whatever she was drawing.

"I'm sorry," I said, walking over to her. "I don't mean to intrude, but—"

"But you're doing it anyway?" she said, still not looking at me.

Her demeanor saddened me. Back before she had left town with Hurley to find her mother, I felt she and I had bonded. We had spent some time together in my office, where Emily demonstrated some kick-ass drawing skills by successfully rendering the face of the woman whose skeleton was hanging in our office library, all without knowing that the woman was someone known to us and that her picture was hanging in another part of our office. Emily had even seemed accepting of—in fact encouraging toward—my relationship with her father. No doubt the death of her mother had had a devastating effect on her, but at the time I didn't realize just how devastating.

I peeked at her drawing. "That's your mom, isn't it?"

She shrugged.

"It's very good. I'm sorry about what happened."

"Are you?" Her tone was surly, challenging, a little shocking.

"Of course I am. I can't imagine what it must feel like to lose your mother that way. It must be really hard for you."

"What would you know about it? What would any-one know about it?"

I thought about sharing my own childhood with her, and telling her how for many years my mother's hypochondria had me living in fear from one day to the next that I would end up an orphan. But wisely I didn't, knowing it really wasn't the same thing.

Emily was angry, and understandably so. Not only had she lost her mother, she was now forced to live in a strange town with a father she barely knew. Add to that the fact that I threatened her relationship with her father, both because of my romantic interest in Hurley and because I was introducing another child into the picture, a child who she probably saw as a competitor for her father's affection. It was also a child Hurley would have the chance to know from day one, and that was a privilege Emily had never had the chance to enjoy. I knew it had to make her uneasy, and angry that her mother had first lied to her and then left her, however involuntarily. But she couldn't very well direct that anger toward her mother, so I was the next most likely target. Clearly this wasn't going to be easy.

I thought for a minute and then decided to skip any more platitudes and get right to the point with her. "Hurley said you've been acting a little strange lately. Is there anything I can do to help you?"

She finally looked at me, and I wished then that she

hadn't. "I think you've done enough already," she sneered. "Please go away."

"I'd feel better if you'd tell me what it is I've done," I tried.

She threw the sketch pad down on the bed and held the pencil in her fist. Then she hopped off the bed. For one terrifying second I thought she was going to stab me with that pencil, but instead she stormed over to the door and held it open. "Please leave," she said, her face a dark storm.

"Okay, but I want you to know that I'm here to talk to if there's anything you want to discuss." I walked toward the door, stopping just over the threshold. "I want to be your friend."

"I don't need any friends," she snapped, and then she slammed the door in my face.

"How did it go?" Hurley asked as I entered the kitchen.

"Not well."

"I heard the door slam."

"Yeah, I don't think I'm high on her list right now, unless we're talking about a hit list."

"Not funny," Hurley said. "Did you get any feel for what's bothering her?"

"Isn't it obvious?" I said. "She misses her mother like crazy, and not only is she dealing with that, she's dealing with all the uncertainty of her future and her relationship with you, the fear that she is about to be usurped and replaced by our baby. Right now she needs time to grieve for her mother, and all the attention, love, and reassurance you can give her."

Hurley shook his head and sighed. "I wish this parenting stuff came with a user manual."

We went about fixing dinner, or rather Hurley

went about fixing dinner. He insisted that I sit and watch.

"Want a glass of wine?" he asked.

I shook my head. "That's on the list of no-nos, I'm afraid."

"Oh." He looked at me for a moment and then shrugged. "There's no reason why I can't have one, is there?"

"Not at all. Have two, one for me and one for you." I looked toward the ceiling and added, "I suspect you're going to need them."

When it came time to sit down to eat, Hurley went to the foot of the stairs and hollered for Emily to come down.

"I'm going to skip dinner," she yelled back.

"No, you're not," Hurley yelled back. "Get down here."

Emily came, but it was obvious from her expression and her body language that she didn't want to be there. She remained silent and pouty through the entire meal, and a couple of times I caught her looking at me when I was talking with Hurley. The venom I saw in her eyes as she watched me was scary. I told myself that I was overreacting and still sensitive from the whole Jacob Ames debacle. When we were through with dinner, Emily asked to be excused, but Hurley told her she had to stay for cake and presents. I could tell she didn't want to, and I felt sorry for her. Clearly she was in pain. So I spoke up and said it was okay with me if she wanted to go upstairs. I should have saved my breath.

Emily glared at me, pushed herself back from the table, and sneered, "You don't have any say in what I do or don't do. You're not my mother."

"Emily," Hurley said, his voice on edge.

"Well, she's not!" Emily yelled at him. "She's just some bitch who's trying to trick you into marrying her by having some brat who has no business even being born. I'll bet it's not even yours. She used it to steal you away from Mom, and now she wants to steal you away from me so she can have you all to herself."

"Emily, that's enough!" Hurley yelled.

Emily shoved herself back from the table, got up, and ran to her room, once again punctuating her emotions by slamming the door.

Hurley and I sat at the table, staring off into space. After several minutes of silence, I said, "That went well. At least now we know what's bothering her."

"I wish you hadn't interfered when I told her she needed to stay down here for dessert."

I gaped at Hurley, not believing what he'd just said. "Don't you turn on me, too," I told him.

"I'm not turning on you. I'm just giving you feedback."

"I've had all the feedback I can handle for one day, thank you very much."

"I'm sorry she went off on you like that."

"Sorry doesn't make it better, Hurley. She needs help. You need to get her to a counselor or shrink of some sort, sooner rather than later."

"I know."

"And it might be a good idea if you and I spent a little less time together. Right now she needs your full attention."

"You need my attention, too," Hurley countered. Then he gave me his trademark eyebrow wiggle. "And I need *your* attention. Lots of it."

"I'm serious, Hurley. We need to help Emily as

much as we can right now. The best way to do that is for you to give her as much time and attention as you can spare, and get her some professional help."

"She'll get over it. She just needs more time."

I shook my head vehemently. "No, this is serious. Trust me. You need to make her your only focus for now."

"I can't," he said, looking at me like I was clueless. "I have a kid coming."

"Like it or not, you have a kid who's already here, Hurley, a kid who's hurting badly, a kid who desperately needs your attention. If you're going to be a father, you have to be one all the time and in all circumstances. You can't pick and choose who your kids are, or when you're going to parent them. Emily is the urgent need right now. My baby isn't."

"*Your* baby?" Hurley said tersely.

"Our baby," I quickly corrected.

"You're not going to cut me out of this, Winston."

"I'm not trying to, Hurley. I already told you that you can be as involved as you want, and I meant it. But there's nothing you can do for our kid right now. That one," I pointed toward the ceiling, "needs you, all of you, one hundred percent of you, right now. And if you can't see that, then you've got a long ways to go before you'll make a decent father."

As soon as the words left my mouth, I wished I could take them back. It wasn't that I didn't mean them, because I did. But they came out harsher and meaner than I meant them to, and that was the last thing Hurley needed. "I need to go," I said.

Hurley's face was a storm of emotion, and I thought he was going to insist that I stay. Instead, he simply nodded and picked up his cell phone to call

Brenda Joiner, who was doing my guard duty for the night. When he hung up, he said, "Brenda will be here in a few minutes. She'll drive you home." He got up from the table, walked over to the counter, and picked up the card and gift that were sitting there. "You might as well take this with you," he said, setting them on the table. Then he turned and headed upstairs.

I fought back tears as I struggled to come up with something to say to him, but before I could he hollered to me from the foot of the stairs. "Make sure you lock the door when you leave."

That last sentence was spoken with a frightening dead calm that upset me more than yelling would have. I swiped at the tears on my face, and looked at the gift and card on the table. I was tempted to leave them there and never open either one. But when a knock came a few minutes later, my curiosity won out. I grabbed them both and headed for the door.

Chapter 36

After Brenda drove me home, I went inside and set the card and gift on the kitchen table. I gave Hoover a hello kiss on the head, and then handed him off to Brenda so she could walk him. When she was done and brought him back, I thanked her and said good night. But instead of leaving, she cocked her head to one side and stared at me.

"Is everything okay?" she asked. "Hurley sounded upset on the phone, and you look like you've been crying."

"The birthday dinner didn't go quite the way we planned," I said.

"You had a fight, didn't you?"

"Something like that," I said with a humorless laugh.

"Don't let it get you down too much," Brenda said. "Fights are inevitable when people care a lot about one another. And it's pretty obvious that you and Hurley are nuts about each other."

If only it was that simple.

As soon as Brenda went back to her car, I walked

over and stared at the gift. There was a part of me that didn't want to open it, but I knew I couldn't resist it for long. I went for the card first.

It was a humorous one, telling me that the EPA was going to come after me because of what the heat from the candles on my cake was doing to global warming. There was a neatly printed, handwritten note at the bottom:

GIVEN RECENT AND COMING EVENTS I THOUGHT THIS WOULD BE THE PERFECT GIFT FOR YOU . . . FOR US.
LOVE,
HURLEY

He still hadn't said he loved me to my face, but this was pretty darned close. The fact that it happened at a time when it seemed like we couldn't be further apart made me want to cry. I set the card aside and opened the gift.

It was a video camera. I stared at the box for the longest time, sorting through a whirlwind of thoughts and emotions. It was definitely a thoughtful gift, given that we had a child on the way. But I couldn't help making the connection between him and Charlie and the whole videography thing. Had the camera been her idea? Had she helped him pick it out?

Finally, after staring at the thing for nearly half an hour, I decided I was being petty and small with my thoughts. It was a great gift, one I was sure would get a lot of use. I opened the box and took the camera out. There was a quick-start sheet that showed the basic components of the camera, and after turning it on and discovering that the battery had nearly a full charge on it, I aimed it at Hoover, who was sprawled out on the floor at my feet.

"Hoover, wake up," I said. "Let me take your picture."

Hoover dutifully snapped out of his snoring sleep and got to his feet, tail wagging, tongue lolling, eager to please even before he knew what he was supposed to be doing. I played with the zoom button, closing in on his huge brown eyes and then backing out just far enough that his big yellow head filled the screen. I had him sit and then fetch a tennis ball I tossed across the room, all the while filming his every move. I'd had a little practice with the cameras at work during the week, thanks to my attempts to interject myself between Charlie and Hurley, so my technique wasn't as bad as it might have been. But when I played back what I'd done, the images were often jumpy and shaky.

That's when I noticed the time and date stamp displayed in the lower-right corner. Puzzled, I glanced at my watch, then back at the time stamp. A lightbulb went off in my head. I grabbed the owner's manual and flipped to the back pages. The company that made the camera was located in California. And the time stamp on my screen read two hours earlier than the current time.

I tossed the camera aside, grabbed my cell phone, and called Richmond.

"Hey, Mattie, what's up?"

"I think Jacob Ames might be innocent," I told him.

He sighed, and I could almost see him rolling his eyes. "I thought we'd discussed this."

"We did, and you had me convinced until today.

But I just discovered something that might change things."

"Such as?"

"Where are you?"

"At home."

"Can you meet me at the station in ten?"

He hesitated. "Do I have to? Can't you just tell me what it is over the phone?"

"No, it will be better if I show you."

"Fine, but this better be good."

"If nothing else, it's reasonable doubt for Jacob, so it needs to be addressed."

"All right," he said in a much beleaguered tone. "See you in ten."

I loaded up the camera and went to ask Brenda to drive me to the station. We arrived eight minutes later and went in through the back entrance. Stephanie the dispatcher was in the break room, wearing her headset.

"Hey, Steph, how are things?"

"It's a quiet night so far," she said.

"Let's hope it stays that way."

"What brings you here on a Saturday night? I thought you were having some kind of birthday celebration over at Hurley's."

"I was, but we had to cut it short." I left it at that, and Brenda shot me a look. Then she excused herself to use the restroom.

I started to head for Richmond's office, but Stephanie stopped me. "Hey, can I ask you something?"

"Sure."

"What's going on with you and Hurley? I mean, are the two of you going to get hitched?"

"No plans for that, I'm afraid."

"I'm sorry."

"Don't be," I said with a dismissive shrug.

"So are the two of you still seeing one another?"

Good question. "Why do you ask?"

"Because that camera girl, Charlie, said she's interested in Hurley and wants to ask him out, but she doesn't want to step on any toes. She said she's gotten some mixed vibes regarding the two of you and wanted to know what was what."

"What did you tell her?"

"That it was complicated."

That made me laugh, perhaps a little louder than I should have. "That it is, Steph," I said. "If she asks again, tell her that Hurley has all he can handle for now and leave it at that."

"Okay," Stephanie said, eyeing me curiously. Then she headed back to her desk up front. I made my way to Richmond's desk and settled in. My feet hurt, my heart hurt, and I was fighting a headache. I sat a minute, rubbing my temples, and replaying the night's events in my head. I heard someone come in through the break room door and thought it was Richmond. But instead, Junior Feller appeared in the doorway to Richmond's office.

"Hey, Mattie, what are you doing here?" he said. "I thought you and Hurley were celebrating your birthday tonight."

"We did." I left it at that even though I could tell Junior wanted more. A second later, Charlie stepped into view.

She saw the camera I had in my hand and said, "Oh, good. I see you got your birthday present. I told Hurley it would make a great gift."

That answered that question, much to my dismay. "It *is* a great gift. Did you help him pick it out?"

"I recommended some features and a couple of places he could buy from," she said. "But he made the final choice and paid extra to get it delivered in time. Why? Is there something wrong with it?"

"No, at least not so far. Do you know where he bought it from?"

"He ordered it online from a company out in California. But it's a reputable place. If there's a problem I'm sure they'll back it up."

"Back what up?" Richmond said as he joined the group.

"My new video camera," I said, showing it to him.

"That's nice," he said. "Now what was so important that I had to come in here?"

"This is," I said, nodding toward the camera.

Richmond's eyes narrowed. "You had me come down here so you could show me your new camera?"

"Basically, yes. Not the camera per se, but rather what I filmed on it tonight, right after I took it out of the box."

I turned the camera on, put it in playback mode, and showed him the screen. He watched Hoover do his tricks, watched me zoom in and out, and shifted anxiously from one foot to the other. I could tell he was getting impatient. "Don't pay any attention to what I filmed," I told him. "Look at the time and date stamp."

Richmond stared at the screen for several seconds and then said, "So?"

"So it says I filmed this at 5:18 P.M., but I filmed it literally minutes before I called you. That was, what, twenty minutes ago at most. And that means that I really filmed it at 7:18 PM. The reason it says 5:18 is because that's the time the manufacturer set and they're located in California."

Richmond looked away, staring off into space. "Holy crap," he said. "Derrick Ames ordered his camera from the East Coast."

"Yes! And it had just arrived. If I remember correctly, Jonas said he found the box on top of the trash, and the owner's manual was sitting on the table, still folded up. Odds are Derrick did exactly what I did when I took mine out of the box. He started using it without changing any of the settings."

"And that means that the video of Jacob fighting with his father happened an hour before the time of death."

Junior and Charlie were listening to our conversation, and Charlie piped up and said, "Does that mean the kid didn't do it?"

"No," Richmond said, frowning. "But it does mean that our best piece of evidence may be useless."

"I don't think he did it," I said. "There was something about the way he looked and talked that day in the conference room. I think he was telling the truth. He fought with his father, but then he left, and his father was still alive. That means someone else came by the house after Jacob left. And that someone is the person who actually killed Derrick."

"Or Jacob just stayed there for an hour and argued with his father before killing him," Richmond countered.

"But that doesn't explain why he took the laptop, or why he wiped the hard drive, or Derrick's last utterance, that *payday* thing. None of the evidence fits well with Jacob as the culprit. I think the killer is still out there."

"But what about the blood on Jacob's clothes and shoes?" Richmond posed.

"He admitted that he had a fight with his father. He also admitted to punching his father in the face, and we know from the autopsy that Derrick had a bloody, broken nose."

Richmond sagged into a nearby chair. "Damn," he said. "We're back to square one."

"I've been thinking about that laptop. If the killer isn't Jacob, and the killer took the laptop, why? There had to have been something on that computer that would have pointed to the killer."

Richmond shook his head. "We got copies of all his e-mails from his ISP, and he had an online calendar, too. There was nothing in any of that to point a finger at anyone else."

"Then maybe it was something else he had saved on that computer, like a document."

"Or a financial sheet of some sort," Charlie suggested. We all turned and stared at her. "You said he uttered the word *payday*," she said with a shrug. "To me, that suggests something to do with money."

Much as I hated to admit it, Charlie's idea was freaking brilliant. I looked over at Richmond. "What about that thumb drive we found? Was there anything on that?"

Richmond stared at me blankly for several seconds. "Now that you mention it, I don't remember seeing anything about that thumb drive. I think I put it out of my head once we determined Jacob was good for it."

"Did somebody look at the contents?"

Richmond chewed on his lip, looking guilty. "I'm not sure, but I'll look into it right now. Do you want to help?"

I shook my head. "I've got something else I want to do. It is my birthday, after all."

"Right," Richmond said. "Happy birthday."

"If you find something, give me a call."

"Will do."

"I'll help you," Charlie said to Richmond. "It will be kind of exciting, like a treasure hunt."

With that, Charlie and Richmond headed for the evidence locker, which was in the basement of the building. I headed back to the break room and asked Brenda to take me to my office. I'd had an epiphany of sorts, a new idea that might or might not pan out. Either way, I intended to follow up on it.

Chapter 37

Brenda drove me the one block to my office—insisting that it was safer than walking—and pulled into the underground garage. After making sure the garage was secure, we got out, and I let us in with my key fob. The place was dark and empty, which used to spook me when I first started working there but no longer did. The dead don't frighten me anymore; only the living do.

We headed for the library, though I did stop and sign us in at the front desk. I got on my computer, accessed the shared file system, and pulled up the record for Derrick Ames. Once I had his file open, I navigated to the demographic page. Then I took out my cell phone and dialed a number I found there.

The woman who answered spoke English but had a thick German accent. "Hallo, dis is Gertrude Ames speaking."

"Mrs. Ames, this is Mattie Winston. I work for the medical examiner's office in Sorenson, and I've been involved in the case regarding your son's death."

"*Ja,*" she said.

"There is some new information that has come up, something that sheds new light on the case. Would you mind if I asked you a question or two about your son?"

"Is dat really necessary?"

"I wouldn't be asking if it wasn't. And it might mean your grandson is innocent." I knew this last bit was taking a big leap, and a potentially dangerous one if it turned out I was wrong, but I felt it necessary to be honest about things if I had any hope of enlisting her help.

"Vat do you vant to know?"

"I understand that you and your husband came here from Germany just before your son was born. What language did you speak around the house when he was little?"

"Vee spoke Deutsch . . . German mostly, but we learned English before we came and we taught it to Derrick when he was still young."

"So Derrick's primary language was German?"

"I guess so, *ja*."

"When your son was waiting for the ambulance, just before he died, he uttered the word *payday*, or something that sounded like that. Does that mean anything in German?"

"*Payday*? *Nein*. I do not know dis word in Deutsch."

My hopes sank. Then Gertrude added, "I would think maybe he was spelling something because *pay* is how you say the letter P and *day* is how you say the letter D, but those letters don't spell anything."

I ran the letters through my mind, trying to connect them with something, but came up empty. Then an idea flashed. "Mrs. Ames, would you do me a favor and run through the alphabet in German for me? Slowly, please."

She did so, no doubt thinking I was crazy when I made her repeat the first letter three times. But by the time she was done, I was more convinced than ever that Jacob Ames was innocent. And I had a whole new direction to go to find Derrick's killer.

My next call was to Alison Miller. When that was done, I looked up an address and told Brenda, "I need to go to the Ames house."

"Should we call Detective Richmond?"

"No, no need. He's busy anyway. And I'm not actually going to Derrick's house. I just need to talk to his neighbor to clarify something."

"Okay," she said, but she looked worried.

Ten minutes later we were in Derrick's neighborhood. "I need to go with you," Brenda said. "Hurley made me promise not to leave you alone or to let you walk around outside by yourself."

"Sure, come on then. I'm going to talk to Janet Calgary, the woman who heard Derrick's last utterance."

We got out of the car and walked up to Janet's house, which was right next door to Derrick's. As we approached, I noticed that the two homes were separated in the back by six-foot privacy fencing. I rang Janet's doorbell, and when she answered she looked at us with a puzzled expression.

"Can I help you?" she asked.

"I'm Mattie Winston with the ME's office, and this is Brenda Joiner, a Sorenson police officer. May we come in for a minute? I'd like to ask you a few questions about the night Derrick Ames was killed."

"I've already talked with someone else and told them everything I know," she said.

"I realize that, but I need to clarify something."

She considered this for a few seconds and then stepped back, waved us into the house, and closed the door.

"I wanted to ask you about what Derrick said right before the ambulance and the police arrived," I explained. "When you found him in the street."

"Like I said before to the other officer, all he said was the word *payday*."

"Yes, Officer Feller told us that. He also said that Derrick let out a sigh right after he said the word *payday*. Is that correct?"

She nodded.

"Can you tell me how he sighed? Do it the way he did it."

Janet Calgary looked at me like I was crazy.

"Please, humor me," I said.

She rolled her eyes, shrugged, and said, "Okay." Then she mimicked Derrick's sigh. "Aah."

"Great!" I said. "Now I want you to listen very carefully to what I'm about to say and tell me if it sounds like what Derrick said." I paused for a beat, and then said, "*Pay-tay-aah.*"

She nodded. "Yeah, that's about right."

"Thank you. Now I have one other request. May we look at your backyard?"

"Sure, I guess." She made a face that suggested she thought we were eccentric if not full-out crazy, turned, and took us to the back of her house where, as in Derrick's place, the kitchen was located.

I walked over to her back door and opened it.

"Mattie," Brenda said in a cautionary tone.

"It's okay, I'm not going outside." I reached over and switched on the backdoor light. "You have a gate at the back of your fence."

"Yes, the utility companies made us put one in. Something about an easement."

"So Derrick's fence has one, too?"

"Sure, everyone in the neighborhood does."

"Great, thanks." I shut the door and looked over at Brenda. "That's all I need. You can take me home now."

As we left, Janet Calgary was watching us through her front window. By now I'm sure she was convinced we were crazy.

"What was that all about?" Brenda asked.

"I have an idea who killed Derrick Ames."

"I thought the son did it?"

"I don't think so." I then filled her in on the discovery I'd made with the video camera.

"So who did do it then?" she asked when I was done.

"I don't want to say yet. I'm not absolutely sure, and there's been enough false finger-pointing in this case already. I need to wait for Richmond to look over the thumb drive they found in Derrick's house. If we're lucky, it will contain the evidence we need."

I took out my cell phone and called Richmond to let him know what I was thinking.

"I have an idea, and I want you to hear me out," I told him. "Janet Calgary said that Derrick's last word was *payday*, and that he sighed right after that and then passed out. I talked to Derrick's mother earlier to see if the word *payday* or something like it meant anything in German. She said no, but then she said that it could be letters. *Pay* is how you pronounce the letter P in German, and *day* is how you pronounce the letter D. But *tay* is how you pronounce the letter T and if you say *pay-tay* really fast, or really breathless like Derrick was, it could sound like the word *pay-day*."

"Okay, but if he was saying the letters P and T, what does that give us? The P. T. Barnum Circus? It doesn't spell anything, and I can't think of anything relevant it stands for."

"I know, but here's the other part of it. The letter A in German is pronounced *aah*, like a sigh."

It took Richmond two seconds to put it together. "PTA? Of course! He was involved with the PTA."

"Yes, and so is Mandy Terwilliger. In fact, if you remember, she told us she's their treasurer. She said she once worked as a bookkeeper, remember?"

"Okay, but I'm still not seeing where you're going with this."

"Derrick Ames was a math teacher. He knew numbers, and he would have known basic accounting. What if he discovered there was money missing from the PTA's fund? Who's the most likely candidate for taking it?"

"Mandy?"

"Yes! She's living above her means. I had Alison Miller look into her finances, and the settlement Mandy got when her husband died was for fifty grand. That amount of money won't last long or go very far because she has half of it set aside for a college fund and only works part-time. How can she support herself and two kids on that kind of money? How does she afford that fancy little convertible she drives? What if she siphoned money from the PTA fund and hoped no one would find out? But then Derrick did. Maybe he saw something when he was at her house, or maybe she said something during the time the two of them were dating. Whatever it was, he figured it out. That's why he told Jacob he was going to break up with Mandy. It also explains the text message he sent to Mandy that said they needed to talk."

"Okay," Richmond said slowly. "I'm with you so far. But how is it that no one saw her leave Derrick's house?"

"Well, we already know that Mandy could sneak over there any time she wanted to when she was supposedly doing deliveries for the florist shop. What if she came over there a second time that evening, thinking Derrick was looking for another round of afternoon delight, but instead he confronted her with what he discovered? They argued, he threatened to expose her, and she grabbed what was handy and stabbed him. Maybe she went for the knife first, and when that didn't kill him right away, he tried to grab her. They wrestled, and that's when she stabbed him with the fork. That silverware drawer got dumped when Derrick fought with his father. You can hear it on the video. So the fork was likely easy to grab."

Richmond said. "I like it. Keep going."

"Derrick probably collapsed after that—there was that pool of blood on the kitchen floor that suggests that—and Mandy thought he was dead. She took his laptop, thinking there might be incriminating evidence on it and ran out the back door. All the houses in Derrick's neighborhood have gates at the rear of their backyard fences. Someone could easily sneak in or out that way without being seen. Then she sent a text message to Derrick to make it look like she was at work and didn't know anything about what happened. She showed up at the crime scene to see what we discovered, and maybe to find out what we were thinking, and she put on that whole woe-is-me show for us. Remember how scared she looked when she heard he'd been taken to the hospital? We assumed it was because she was worried about him, but maybe she was worried about herself. She needed to get rid of the laptop, so she wiped the hard drive, cleaned her fingerprints off it, and tossed it in the Dumpster behind the school. She was at the school three days a week, so she would have known the Dumpster was there and had easy access to it without rousing suspicion. And if she heard that Jacob had been arrested, disposing of the laptop in the school garbage would point the finger at him as much as at anyone else."

"Okay," Richmond said. "So how does the thumb drive figure into it?"

"I'm hoping it will have evidence of the missing money, either some financial sheets or receipts, or something that proves there is money missing."

"It's a reasonable theory," Richmond said when I was done, "but we're going to have to wait until tomorrow to get a look at that thumb drive. Jonas sent it to the lab in your office, and the tech guys aren't there now. I called Arnie to see if he could get hold of it, but he's afraid to go in there and mess with anything since the evidence from your case is in there, too. So I called Henderson, and he agreed that until your case is officially closed, it would be better not to have Arnie mucking around in the lab when his guys aren't there. Henderson said he'll have someone come in tomorrow and look at the thumb drive, but his tech guys are commuting here from Madison, and he doesn't think it's necessary or important enough to make any of them drive here tonight."

"Damn."

"Yeah, damn. But we have time. If you're right, Mandy thinks she got away with it. She's not going anywhere. So get some rest, and we'll tackle this again tomorrow. I'll call you once I hear back from the tech guys."

"Okay."

Brenda drove me back home, and as soon as I had some privacy, I called Hurley to check in and see how things were going, hopefully mend the wound we created earlier, and bounce my theory about Mandy off of him.

"I'm sorry your birthday was such a bust," he said. "I'll make it up to you."

"No need. I'm sorry you're having such a hard time with Emily. Did things get any better after I left?"

"I suppose," Hurley said, sounding totally unconvincing. "Her mood improved, she talked to me some, and she promised to try to do better."

"That sounds encouraging."

"Except the mood change didn't happen until after I told her you were gone."

"Oh."

"Yeah. Oh. You were right, she needs help," Hurley said. "I'm going to talk to the school and see if they can hook me up with a good counselor for her."

With that out of the way, I switched to the subject of the Ames case. Hurley knew where I was headed with my idea before I had explained even half of it, and he agreed my scenario was not only possible but highly plausible. His enthusiasm for my idea and our ability to easily get past the earlier spat and move on had me feeling better about things.

After we hung up, I got ready for bed and had to struggle to get into my pajamas, which had gotten painfully snug. I looked down at my stomach and swore it had grown overnight. I finally settled for sleeping in my underpants—which were also getting a bit snug but were stretchy enough to accommodate me for now—and a baggy T-shirt. Clearly my wardrobe needed a bit more updating.

I was beginning to think pregnancy wasn't the glowing, glamorous state some women had led me to believe it was.

Chapter 38

Though I was exhausted, I had a hard time sleeping. After tossing and turning most of the night, I finally fell asleep around two in the morning and slept until nine. I would have slept later than that except Hoover's whines forced me to get up.

"Okay, boy," I said. "Just a minute."

I got up, peed, and then went to the front door. I peered out the peephole and saw a police car parked outside as usual. But it wasn't Brenda Joiner any longer, it was Junior Feller. I threw on my robe, opened the door, and waved to him.

"Good morning," Junior said, climbing out of the car.

Hoover was apparently too impatient to wait. He bounded out the door, ran to the edge of the woods, lifted his leg, and peed. Then he peed some more. I knew how he felt.

I handed Junior the leash. "Do you mind keeping an eye on him?"

"Not at all."

"Thanks. I want to hop in the shower, so here's my key. Just let him back in when he's done."

"Will do."

"And one other thing. Would you mind driving me to The Mother Hood this morning? I really need to get some more stuff. All of my clothes are so tight all of a sudden, I feel like a sausage."

"Not a problem."

"Thanks, Junior. I really appreciate you guys doing this for me. I'm sure it has to be a pain."

"I don't mind, and to be honest, I can use the extra money. Not that we wouldn't want to make sure you were safe without the money, but you know how it is."

"I do. I've been broke before."

I shut the door and headed for the bathroom. Half an hour later, I came out and got dressed, donning a pair of my new pants and one of my new tops. Underneath it all, I wore my new bra but my old panties. Junior had let Hoover back inside, and my key was sitting on the table at the end of the couch. Also on the table was a small bottle of orange juice, a decaf coffee, and a maple bar. I fed myself, Hoover, and the cats, topped off the animals' water bowls, grabbed my key, and headed outside.

As soon as I was in Junior's car, my cell phone rang. My heart skipped a beat, wondering if it was going to be one of *those* calls, but the caller ID said it was Richmond.

"Hey, Richmond, got some news for me?"

"I do, and it isn't good. Derrick's thumb drive has nothing but pictures on it."

"Are you sure?"

"Well, I haven't seen it with my own eyes, but the tech guy who had to drive all the way here this morning to look at Derrick's family photos is pretty damned sure. He's also rather annoyed."

"Darn it! I was so hoping we could find something to point the finger at her."

"Your theory is still a good one," Richmond said. "We'll just have to get the information another way."

"But that probably means waiting until tomorrow."

"Maybe not. I'll make some calls and see if I can find someone with the right connections."

"Okay, let me know."

I disconnected the call and dropped the phone into my purse with a frustrated sigh.

"The thumb drive didn't pan out?" Junior said.

"No. All it had on it were photos."

"Bummer."

We had arrived at The Mother Hood, and Junior snagged a parking place right in front. It was early enough that many folks were in church, so the Sunday shoppers hadn't hit the Main Street shops in force yet. "I'll wait out here," he said. "That's not a store I'd feel too comfortable in."

"I don't feel all that comfortable in there myself," I said with a chuckle. "And by the way, thanks for the breakfast."

"You're welcome. I saw that you didn't have much in your kitchen, so I had one of the guys make a run and grab some stuff."

"You're a sweetheart. I'll try to make this as quick as I can, okay?"

"No rush. I brought along a bunch of magazines to help me pass the time."

I got out of the car and headed into The Mother

Hood. The bell tinkled, and Brahms' Lullaby announced my arrival, but Priscilla didn't need them. She'd seen me get out of the car.

"Hey, Priscilla," I said.

She countered with a "Good morning," but she didn't look or sound all that cheery. "Is something wrong?"

"No, not at all. In fact, I love the stuff I got here the other day. It all fits great, and I'm here to get some more items."

"Oh, good," she said, clapping a hand over her heart. "What are you interested in looking at today?"

"Underwear, for starters, and some pajamas, a new bathrobe, and maybe a few more pants and tops. Did the bras I ordered last time come in yet?"

She shook her head. "They'll probably be in tomorrow. Let's start with the nightwear. I have some great items I think you'll like."

I followed her to a back area of the store, where there was a rack of bathrobes that ranged from petite to Orson Welles size and shelves covered with a variety of two-piece pajama sets and nightgowns. She grabbed several items and handed them to me.

"Go try these on," she said. "I'll dig up some more stuff in the meantime."

I went into the dressing room, and as I stripped off what I was wearing, my cell phone rang. Again I had a moment of trepidation, and again it was only Richmond.

"Hey, Richmond, what's up?"

"I called that witch Principal Knowles and asked her about the PTA. She gave me the name of the president, the vice president, and a few other members. I called the president, a woman named Marsha

Hatton, and she has access to the books. She said she can get a copy of the financials for me today."

"That's great," I said, standing in my undies and eyeing my expanding frame in the mirror. "I'm willing to bet there's money missing somewhere."

"I hope so. Your theory does make sense. But I haven't given up on Jacob yet."

"Jacob didn't do it. I'm sure of it. The PTA connection makes the most sense. Derrick was a math teacher, so he'd be familiar with accounting. And he was involved with the PTA. If he discovered there was money missing and said something to her about it, there's your motive. She said money was really tight, and that it was a struggle to raise the kids on what she makes, and as the treasurer, she had access to all those funds."

"Okay, okay, you've convinced me."

"Get with this Hatton woman and get the proof we need."

"I hope it's all those crazy hormones of yours that are making you so bossy."

"You wish."

I disconnected the call, tried on a pair of pajamas, and stepped out of the dressing room. Priscilla was standing just outside the door with a disapproving look on her face.

"What? Do they make me look too fat?"

"Those are all wrong," she said. "Try these." She thrust a pile of new stuff into my arms and then pushed past me into the dressing room. She gathered up the other pajamas that were in there and carried them out.

I went back into the dressing room, set down the

new pile of clothes, shut the door, and gave myself another appraising look in the mirror. I didn't think the ones I had on looked that bad. Maybe Priscilla wanted to steer me toward more expensive stuff. I glanced at the price tag on the ones I had on and compared it to the others she had given me. The set on top of the pile was actually cheaper. So I took off the first set and put on the cheaper one. When I went to open the dressing room door to see what Priscilla's opinion was on this set, the knob turned but the door wouldn't open. I tried again, pushing harder, but the door wouldn't budge.

"Priscilla?" I hollered. "There's something wrong with the door. I can't get it to open."

"That's because there's a chair in front of it," she said. Her voice came through the door crystal clear. I could tell she was standing just the other side of it. "I heard what you said in there on the phone. How did you figure it out?"

I frowned, not knowing what she was talking about at first. Then it started to come to me. I flashed back on my previous conversation with Priscilla, and how she'd also said that money was tight and she and her husband were struggling to raise all their kids. She'd also said she was involved with the PTA.

I thought fast and said, "Derrick didn't die in his house. He was still alive after he was stabbed. He managed to stagger out into the street, and some neighbors helped him. He wasn't able to say much, but he said enough to let us know that it had something to do with the PTA."

I waited for a response, but I didn't get one.

"Priscilla? Are you still there?"

"I'm sorry, Mattie. I wish you hadn't figured it out, but now that you have, I need to do whatever I can to get away."

"How did Derrick figure it out?" I asked her.

"That damned Terwilliger woman," she said. "She couldn't get the books to come out right, so she asked Derrick to help her with it."

"But how did you get access to the money?"

"It's easy enough when you're the treasurer. I have a business degree, you know, and I've learned how to cook the books over the years with this damned store."

"I thought Mandy was the treasurer."

"She is now, but she just took the job over a few months ago. I was the treasurer for four years before that."

I tried the door again, but it wouldn't budge. Then I heard an odd sound, some kind of splashing noise. "Priscilla? Please open the door. I'll talk to the DA and explain that you didn't mean to hurt anyone. Maybe you can work out some kind of deal. Pay restitution or something like that."

I heard Priscilla scoff. "Pay restitution? And just where the hell would the money come from? Do you have any idea what a sinkhole for money kids are? It's never-ending."

I could still hear the splashing sound and then a strange smell came to me. When I realized what it was, panic set in.

"Priscilla, I smell gasoline. What are you doing?"

"Creating a diversion. I need time to get away from here."

"You're going to set the store on fire, aren't you?"

No answer.

"Priscilla? Please, let me out of here. I'll give you time to get away, I promise. But please don't leave me in here and burn the place down. I'm pregnant, remember? You don't want to do that."

"I don't have a choice, Mattie. I'm truly sorry. This is the way it has to be."

I remembered my phone then and whirled around to grab it. My purse, and the phone that was in it, was gone. Then I realized that Priscilla must have grabbed it when she did the switch with the clothes.

My panic rose, and I threw myself against the door. It didn't budge. My baby seemed to sense my panic because suddenly I felt a flurry of movement in my belly.

"Damn it, Priscilla, don't do this," I pleaded.

I listened, waiting for a response, trying to figure out what she was doing next. She didn't answer me, and then I heard the sound of the back door closing. Seconds later I smelled smoke.

Frantic, I kicked at the door to the dressing room and yelled at the top of my lungs. Junior was parked out front in the street. Maybe he would hear me. I yelled louder and kicked harder. The smoke smell grew stronger. I screamed and screamed as loud as I could. And then I thought I heard a pounding noise.

After that, everything went black.

Chapter 39

"**O**bviously you got out," Maggie says to me.

"I did. All my screaming and panic made me hyperventilate. Add being pregnant on top of that and you have a good solid faint. As it turned out, Junior had to pee, so he got out of his car right around the time Priscilla was blocking the dressing room door with the chair. He walked up to the front door, found it locked, and peered inside. Priscilla was too preoccupied with the chair to see him, but he knew right away she was up to no good, so he got on his radio and called for help, and then went around to the alley by the back door. The minute Priscilla came out, Junior grabbed her, but she tried to run, and in the scuffle the back door closed. The only way to open it is with a key, and fortunately Priscilla had it with her since it was on the same ring as her car and house keys. By the time Junior got the keys, other cops had arrived, and someone was trying to beat the door down. That was the pounding noise I heard, I think. Anyway, by the time I knew what was happening, I was outside in the fresh air, lying on the ground in a pair of brand spanking new pajamas. And I kept them. I figured that was the least Priscilla owed me. The fire was blazing pretty good at that point, but it was mostly toward the front of the store. They were able to get it under control before it destroyed the whole place."

"It's a good thing Junior was there."

"Yes, it was. And I've decided to quit hating my bladder because of that day. The need to pee may have saved my life—even if it wasn't me who needed to do the peeing—so I've come to terms with my bladder's need to empty itself every hour and decided to forgive it."

"I'm sure your bladder is grateful," Maggie says with a smile. "I take it Jacob was exonerated as a result of all this?"

"He was, and both he and his mother were very grateful. They insisted on thanking me publicly and tried to do an ad in the local paper, but Alison Miller convinced them to participate in a large article about the whole case instead. I think she did that so she could slip the fact of my pregnancy in there somewhere, but it was something that was becoming more obvious with each passing day anyway. To be honest, I was more bothered by the fact that the article made me out to be some kind of hero when in actuality I was wrong about the whole thing."

"Not the whole thing," Maggie insists.

"Okay, I stand corrected. I was wrong about who the killer was, and it nearly cost me my life. I later learned that Mandy Terwilliger really is struggling financially. That car she was driving, the sporty little convertible? It belongs to an uncle of hers who is helping her out. He loaned her the car while hers was being repaired." I shake my head. "Sometimes I wonder if I'm cut out for this job, and lately I keep wondering if having this child might be a mistake."

"Why would you think that?"

"Well, the questionable genetics for one. My family history is a hot mess of mental health issues and personality disorders, and given that I keep getting myself into dangerous situations when it comes to work, I'm not sure I'm cut out to be a mother."

"Did you have genetic testing done?"

I nod. "The baby appears to be healthy, with no major flaws, at least physically. There are no prenatal tests for stupidity, insanity, and personality disorders."

Maggie leans forward, rests her arms on her knees, and looks me in the eye. "Mattie, I have some concerns about you, but they are minor and have nothing to do with your ability to be a good mother. In fact, I think you're going to do great. It will be challenging, no doubt, but one of the things in your life that has remained consistent is that you always rise to the challenges. Being a single mother isn't going to make it any easier for you, but you have a reasonably good support system in place, so I think you'll be fine."

"Thanks for that. Now tell me what your concerns are."

"Well, I think you're afraid to commit yourself to a relationship with Hurley because so many of your previous relationships with men have gone badly. You're not willing to open up and let yourself be vulnerable."

"That may or may not be true, but it's so much more than my willingness to commit or be vulnerable at this point. There's this whole mess with my father, and Emily is proving to be a huge obstacle. She's not only become very disturbed, she's also wily and determined to make it as difficult as possible for Hurley and me to be together. It's ironic, in a way, because now that we can be together publicly without having to worry about our jobs, we're still forced to sneak around so that we don't upset Emily."

"I'm not surprised Emily is acting out," Maggie says. "I'm sure she's having a hard time with all the changes in her life. She lost her mother, the only real family she'd had all her life, and now she finds herself thrust into this new life with a father she barely knows, a potential stepmother she's bound to resent because you're competing with her for her father's love and attention, and a new baby on the way, who she probably fears Hurley will love more than he loves her."

I stared at Maggie with newfound respect. "Well, you nailed that one," I told her.

"She resents you," Maggie says.

"Boy, does she," I say, my eyes wide with the memory of that birthday night. "I hoped with time she would become more accepting, but if anything she seems to be less so. I've tried reasoning with her several times, trying to get her to see that I'm not the enemy, but she wants nothing to do with me or my child, who she insists on calling the brat."

"Trying to reason with her was your first mistake," Maggie says, interrupting me. "Teenagers are often short on reason and high on emotion. And those are the ones who haven't gone through the kind of emotional traumas Emily has. And despite being a teenager, Emily is still a child, with all the hurt, bewilderment, and sensitivity that go with that."

I frowned. "I know she's been through a lot, but I'm seriously concerned about her. This has been going on for several months now with no sign of improvement. I've even tried talking her into counseling, either with or without me and Hurley, but she refuses to go, and Hurley isn't convinced that it's necessary or that it will be helpful."

"Do you think Hurley will make a good father?"

"I guess, but Emily's behavior has only gotten worse, and that's made him a little crazy."

"Is she doing something more than trying to ostracize you?"

"Heck, yes. She's been sassing back at Hurley a lot, and rebelling against any rules he tries to implement. For instance, he gave her a nine P.M. curfew on school nights, and ten on the weekends, but Emily ignores him and frequently stays out hours later than she should. Several times Hurley has had to go looking for her. To make matters worse, she has a new boyfriend, one with a driver's license. Hurley has tried to talk to her about sex, and birth control, and all that sort of stuff, but she always cuts him off and says she doesn't want to discuss it. Half the time she acts like she doesn't want anything to do with Hurley, but if she thinks he's off doing something with me, she'll have a crisis of some sort and call him to come help her. That's why Hurley had to back out of attending the birthing classes. Emily found out about it, and every time we had a class, she would create some sort of drama so that Hurley had to leave. One time she called him and said that if he didn't come home she was going to kill herself. Another time she called 911 and said someone was trying to break into the house, but when Hurley and the cops got there, there was no evidence of that at all. By the third or fourth incident, we started to catch on to her timing, and that's when Hurley regretfully backed out of the classes."

"If Emily is threatening suicide, then it's imperative that she get some counseling," Maggie says, looking concerned.

"I know," I say with a sigh. "But Hurley is even more anti-shrink than I am. Nothing personal," I add with a sheepish grin.

"I'm not offended," Maggie assures me. "Does he have a reason for this bias?"

I nod. "He's convinced that the shrink his boss made him see when he was working in Chicago and harassing Dilles for killing his wife is the reason he lost his job there."

Maggie gives a grudging shrug. "Understandable then, I suppose. But for the sake of Emily, you need to keep on Hurley about it."

"I intend to. If I can't convince him, maybe I'll kidnap Emily and bring her to you myself."

"To me?" Maggie says with a smile. "I'm flattered."

Now I'm the one who shrugs grudgingly. "I confess I may have been wrong about the benefits of professional counseling."

To Maggie's credit, she doesn't gloat. "Is Hurley planning on being there for the birth?" she asks.

"He wants to, but I have a backup plan in case Emily screws that up, too. I've arranged for my sister to be my birth coach, and she finished out the classes with me. Dom offered to do it, but then Izzy got hold of a film that shows childbirth, and Dom passed out trying to watch it. So for now it's me and Desi. And given the way Emily has been lately, I wouldn't be surprised if Hurley doesn't show up at all for the birth."

"I wish I had some great words of wisdom to offer you with regard to Emily, but the teenage years are notorious for being challenging under the best of circumstances. Think of it as training and practice for when your own child reaches that age."

"Great," I said with a roll of my eyes. "With any luck I can film it all with that stupid birthday present Hurley got me."

Maggie frowns. "What's wrong with the video camera? It helped you solve your case, and it seems like a great gift for an expectant mother, something to mark your child's milestones."

"Sure, except now Hurley wants to film the birth, both for the memories and in case he can't be there." I wait for Maggie to comment, and when she doesn't I give her a questioning look and say, "Hello-o?"

Maggie shrugs and shakes her head, looking clueless.

"He wants to film the birth, Maggie. I've seen women in childbirth, and it isn't pretty. At some point, they all turn into Linda Blair in *The Exorcist*. Camera-ready they are not. They are all sweaty and messy-haired and red-faced. And Hurley wants the actual birth on video, you know, the head coming out and all that. He plans to have either Desi or himself aim that camera at my hoo-ha when I'm leaky, and sweaty, and all stretched out like the universe during the Big Bang."

"So?"

"So?" I echo with disbelief. "Nobody wants to see that. Hell, it's mine, and I don't want to see it."

"As Hurley once reminded you, he *has* seen it before," Maggie says with sly humor.

"Not like that, he hasn't. Men are sometimes damaged after seeing that. Sex lives have shriveled up and died after seeing that."

"I think you're blowing this out of proportion. Don't you think it's sweet that Hurley wants a record of what will probably be one of the biggest moments in his life?"

"Yes, it's sweet, but we can film it all from the head of the bed. No one has to be down there . . . all in it."

Maggie bites back a laugh.

"It may sound funny, but the reality of the situation isn't. I have to admit, it will break my heart if Hurley isn't there when this baby comes. After seeing his reaction to the ultrasound, I know he wants to be there. There's a part of me that wants to get angry and demanding and insist that he put me first, at least with this issue. But I don't want to complicate his life any more than it already is. So for now I'm going to back off and give him the space he needs to sort things out with Emily, even though I'm afraid she's going to be a major obstacle for me and him, and for him and this baby."

"What about Charlie? Is she still an obstacle?"

"Down the road, maybe, but right now Hurley has so much going on in his life I don't think he'll have the time or the emotional energy to start up any sort of new relationship."

"Thinking that way is a gamble," Maggie warns me, and I'm glad she is the one who uses such a reference for once rather than me.

"I know," I tell her. "But right now it seems that Hurley having a relationship with any other woman is going to be a problem for Emily. Given that, I don't think Hurley is likely to start dating anyone else until things are resolved."

"Have you considered that it isn't necessarily another woman in his life as much as it is *you* in his life? You're the one who was there when Emily and her mother came back into his life. You're the one who is having the child that Emily may or may not perceive as a threat to her relationship with Hurley. So maybe it isn't another woman as much as it's you."

I shot her a perturbed look. "Aren't you supposed to make me feel better?"

"Not necessarily," she said with a smile. "I'm here to help you figure things out, to help you feel comfortable with your decisions and the impact they will have on your life, and to help you deal with your insecurities and doubts."

"Telling me I'm the root of the problem doesn't exactly make me feel secure or comfortable."

"But it may be a reality you have to face. You need to be aware of that and figure out how you're going to deal with it."

"I know my limits. I know Hurley needs some time with Emily to sort things out, but I don't want that to interfere with his relationship with our child. I don't want my child growing up without a father the way I did. A part-time father is better than none at all. If Emily is too insecure in her relationship with Hurley to share him with another child, that's just too bad. I'm not going to succumb to her emotional blackmail if it starts to compromise Hurley's relationship with our kid."

"And exactly how do you plan to handle it?"

I have no idea and tell Maggie so.

"Let's talk about your father some more. Maybe exploring your feelings on that topic more deeply will help you gain some understanding with the other situation."

"But they're totally different."

"Are they? Granted, you had some time with your father when you were very young, and Emily didn't have even that, but you've told me your memories are few and distant, so I think your experiences are more or less parallel to hers. And not only did you grow up without a father, you now have discovered that he's a criminal. So take your feelings on the father issue and think about how you would feel if you didn't have your sister, suddenly lost your mother, and then found out that your father had another whole family out there somewhere, a wife with kids who spent their entire childhoods with him."

I thought about it and realized I'd feel envious, insecure, and a little angry . . . okay, more than a little angry. Damn Maggie anyway! Sometimes it's like the woman has a tiny periscope implanted in my brain. Every time she takes a peek she finds another flaw, another emotional turmoil, another embarrassing thought I have stashed away in there.

"I get it," I tell her, feeling irritable. "I understand why Emily is struggling. I understand why she's angry. I understand why I'm angry. I'm mad as hell at my mother for not telling me the truth about my father all these years. And I'm mad as hell at my father for being who and what he is."

"Do you think your mother knew about your father's past the entire time?"

"I don't know what to think anymore," I say, shifting in my seat in a futile effort to get comfortable. My back is aching something fierce, and it's magnifying my already high level of irritation. "She claims my father had her hoodwinked in the beginning, that he was her first and one true love, and that once she did find out and confronted him, he swore he'd left his past behind and had turned over a new leaf. By the time she realized he was lying, they'd been married for five years, and I was already four. I know my father had to leave because he was in some kind of trouble, but she claims he didn't say what the trouble was, and that he told her he'd only be gone for a short time until he could straighten things out. Then she didn't see or hear anything from him for two years, and when she did finally hear something, it was divorce papers some lawyer sent her. Supposedly my father offered to make child-support payments, but after one payment, the money stopped coming. My mother tried to find him but couldn't. A short time later she met and married Desi's father, who adopted me. I took on his last name: Fjell, which is the name I grew up with."

"I'm sure none of this was easy for your mother," Maggie says, as my back stabs at me again.

"Must you always play the devil's advocate?" I snap at her. "Do you always have to interject other people's feelings into these discussions? Why can't you just let me wallow for a little while in my self-pity, or anger, or whatever the hell it is I'm feeling at the moment?"

"Because I don't feel it's productive or beneficial to your mental health."

"If you believe that, then you've never had yourself a good old-fashioned pity party. Granted it's not a good long-term strategy, but in the short term it can do wonders for one's soul."

Maggie wisely says nothing.

"Anyway," I continue, "the thing that makes me the maddest about all this is that my mother not only didn't tell me the truth, she went out of her way to hide it."

"Maybe she was trying to protect you."

"Well, if that's the case, it didn't work."

A few seconds of silence pass between us. Eventually Maggie sets her notebook aside and says, "You are about to embark on parenthood for the first time. There will be an endless parade of painful circumstances that will come up, difficult decisions you will need to make, and awkward situations you will react to. Do you think you will always make the right decision, or react in the appropriate way, or say the best thing?"

"No," I admit with a huff of irritation.

"Then is it fair to hold your mother to such a standard?"

"Okay, I get it," I say, shifting my position again.

"So where do you go from here?"

"I don't know. What do you think I should do?"

Maggie shakes her head. "That's not for me to say. They have to be your decisions. But from everything you've told me, Hurley seems like a smart, straight-thinking guy who cares about you a lot, and that's worth trying to keep and preserve."

"I know, but I just don't know if that's enough." I push myself up from my chair and wince as my back aches. "I have to pee again and I guess I should be getting back to town. Thanks for making time for me and hearing me out today. I appreciate it."

"I'm happy to help. I'm here anytime you want to

talk. Let me know what you decide, and let me know when the little one puts in an appearance."

"Will do. What do I owe you for this marathon session?"

Maggie smiles and says, "This one is on the house. Consider it a baby gift."

"That's sweet of you," I tell her, fighting back tears. "Thanks again, Maggie, for everything."

I hurry out, or at least I go as fast as my lumbering body will carry me, afraid that if I stay any longer I'll start to cry and have another one of my hormonal moments. It seems that the tiniest act of kindness makes me cry these days. I got teary-eyed last week when someone yielded to my car at an intersection, and I wasn't even driving—Junior was. And I burst into full-out sobs two days ago when I ordered five cases of disposable diapers from a mail-order maternity store and they offered to throw in a sixth case for free. It's things like that that make me think my kid is doomed.

But it will be what it will be.

Chapter 40

Brenda Joiner drives me back to Sorenson and my cottage. It's a quiet half-hour ride, and we're pretty comfortable with the silence at this point. Brenda and I have spent a lot of time together riding around over the past four months. For a while Hurley tried to be my escort all the time, but the issues with Emily put a serious crimp in that, leaving us at the mercy of Brenda, Junior, and two other uniformed cops who have picked up shifts that we pay for. The expense has added up over time, and I don't know how much longer we can continue to do it. I would have insisted that we stop it months ago, but the phone calls have continued to come, and everyone pretty much agrees at this point that Roscoe Schneider wasn't working alone. It isn't easy living under this shadow. My nerves are frayed enough already just from the pregnancy and the situation with Hurley and Emily. Add to that the constant feeling that someone out there wants me dead, and it's a wonder I have any sanity left at all.

We arrive at the cottage a little after four in the evening. It's a beautiful fall day, with a sky as blue as

Hurley's eyes and the faint smell of wood smoke in the air. My reinforced hearse is parked in its usual spot; I haven't been able to drive it much lately since I'm never allowed to go anywhere alone. A few times I've insisted and had one of the cops guarding me ride along, but for the most part it's just as easy to let them drive me, especially now that I can barely fit behind the wheel. The repair shop did a great job. The hearse looks as good as new, and you'd never know it had ever been smashed, dented, and shot up.

"Is Izzy home?" Brenda asks as we get out of the car.

"No, he's still at the office. He doesn't usually get home until five-thirty or so. And it's Tuesday, which means Dom is downtown with his acting group rehearsing. So it's just you and me. Want to come in for a cup of coffee?"

Brenda makes a face. "Is it that decaf stuff you usually drink?"

"I have a stash of the leaded variety in the back of one of my cupboards. I sneak a real cup every now and then. Don't tell on me."

"I won't."

I unlock the front door, and as soon as I'm inside I punch in the code for the security system. Then I drop my purse on the couch and head for the kitchen.

That's when the first pain grabs me.

"Ooh," I say, grabbing my tummy and nearly doubling over.

"Are you okay?" Brenda asks.

The pain passes, and I straighten up. "I think so. But either Junior just kicked much harder than usual or that was a contraction."

"Is it time?" Brenda asks, her eyes wide.

"Let's wait and see." I head the rest of the way into the kitchen and grab two mugs, then I reach up and open the cupboard where my real coffee is hidden. Another pain rips across my belly, and this time when I touch it, it feels as hard as a rock.

"Wow," I say when the pain passes. "Definitely a contraction." I turn around and walk back into the living room and plop down on the couch. "The coffee might have to wait."

"Maybe we should head to the hospital," Brenda says, looking a little scared.

I shake my head. "It's early yet. Typically first babies take hours to come. Let's just monitor the pains for a bit and see how often they come."

Two minutes later another pain hits me. I breathe through it, and when it finally lets up I say, "Okay, maybe we should go now. Can you grab the bag I have packed at the foot of my bed? I think I need to pee first."

I hit the bathroom and try to pee, but I'm so afraid of another pain coming that my bladder balks at doing anything. After a couple minutes of trying, Brenda yells through the bathroom door. "Are you okay in there?"

"I'm okay." I give up, flush out of habit even though there is no reason, and waddle back out into the living room. Brenda is standing by the door with my suitcase in her hand. Hoover is sitting between us, looking at me with this pleading expression.

"Oh, hell," I say. "I forgot to walk Hoover. Can you take him outside for a quickie?"

Brenda gives me a look of impatience. "Are you sure we have time for that?"

"We have plenty of time," I tell her, hoping I sound convincing, because I really have no idea.

Looking exasperated, Brenda drops the suitcase, grabs Hoover's leash, and hooks him up. "Come on, boy, let's go. And do your business fast."

She heads out the door, leaving it open. I pace the floor a couple of times and debate whether or not I should call Hurley yet. Finally I decide to go ahead and do it. I take my phone out of my purse and speed-dial his number. Clearly he was waiting for the call because he answers with, "Is it happening?"

"I think so. I'm having pains about"—I stop and grit my teeth as another one rips through me.

"Mattie? Mattie? Are you there?"

"Just a minute," I seethe. I puff my way through it, and when I can breathe halfway normally again, I say, "Sorry. I had a contraction."

"I'll be right there."

"No, Brenda is here. She's going to drive me to the hospital. Meet us there."

"Will do."

Brenda comes back inside with Hoover and lets him off his leash. I tell him to stay, arm the security system, and then head out the door with Brenda behind me carrying my suitcase. As I open the car door and toss my purse onto the floor, I feel this sudden warmth between my legs. Then I feel wetness. When I look down, I see that the entire inside portion of my pant legs is soaked.

"Damn!" I mutter. "I had to pee but couldn't, and now I've wet myself."

Brenda tosses my suitcase in the backseat of her car and says, "That's okay. Let's go." She heads for the driver-side door.

"I don't want to show up at the hospital having peed myself. Let me go in and change real quick."

Brenda stares at me over the roof of the car, looking like she wants to kill me. I ignore her and head back inside. I unlock the door, leaving it open, and make a lumbering dash into my room to grab some clean pants. Then I head for the bathroom so I can clean up. As I pull down my pants, a smell hits me, one that takes me back to my nursing school days. That's when I realize I didn't pee myself. The liquid isn't urine, it's amniotic fluid. My water has broken.

I kick off the wet under and outer pants and pull on dry ones. I have my slacks halfway up my legs when another pain hits. This one is even harder than the one before, and I have to grab the edge of the vanity to keep from sinking to my knees. It seems to last forever, and I keep expecting to hear Brenda's frantic voice yelling at me to hurry up.

Instead I hear a gunshot. And a few seconds later I hear another one.

Panting and still bent over, I pull my pants the rest of the way up and reach over to open the bathroom door. When I look toward the front door my heart leaps out of my chest as I see a figure come running through it. In the next second I realize it's Brenda, but before I can say a word, she slams the front door shut and throws the locks.

"Brenda?" I say, wondering what the hell is going on.

"Hush, and stay where you are," she says. She takes her phone out of her vest pocket and starts to dial, then curses and throws it on the couch. "He hit my phone, damn it!" she says.

"Who hit your phone? Did I just hear gunshots?"

"Where's your phone?"

I look around the bathroom as if I expect to find it there. Then I remember tossing my purse on the floor of the car. "It's outside in the car," I tell her. And then another pain comes.

This one is much worse than the ones before, and this time it does take me to my knees. I grit my teeth and try to breathe through it, but the pain is too great. I finally let out a yell.

Brenda looks over at me with a panicked expression. "Are you okay?"

I shake my head, unable to speak for a few seconds. As the pain finally eases, I sit down on the side of the bathtub. "What's going on?" I ask Brenda.

"There's a man out there in the woods who shot at me. I think it might be your caller. If it hadn't been for my vest, I'd be dead right now."

I don't know what's worse, the panic I feel about Brenda's information or the panic I feel about the pressure that's building between my legs.

"Don't you have a radio or something?" I ask Brenda.

"I'm not on official duty. All I have is my cell."

I look around the bathroom, hunting for a weapon. There is a pair of scissors on the vanity, the ones I use to trim my hair in between visits to my hairdresser, who happens to work out of the basement of a funeral home. For a second I see her in my mind's eye fixing my hair the way she always does—with me lying on an embalming table—only this time I'm really dead, not just pretending the way I have at times in the past. I shake off the morbid thought and start to grab for the scissors. Then I realize that the scissors are useless against a gun. In fact, pretty much anything I have in the house that could be used as a weapon will be useless against a gun. So I switch my strategy and quit weapon hunting and start looking for a place to hide. A second later it's a moot point because two gunshots hit the front door right where the locks are.

Brenda dashes over to the bathroom, says, "Stay in here and stay quiet," and then she shuts the door.

I reach over to lock it, but I have to stand to get to it. When I do, another pain hits, and my mind becomes singularly focused on that. In an effort to obey Brenda, I grab a washcloth and stick it in my mouth, biting down as hard as I can to stifle the scream that wants to come out of me. Somehow, in the midst of my pain haze, I manage to stand, take a tiny step, and throw the lock on the door.

I hear glass breaking beyond the door and two more gunshots. The pain is so severe I'm afraid I'm going to pass out or rip in two. The pressure between my legs is immense now, and I know that the kid is going to be here any moment, like it or not. I wait for the pain to ebb, but this time it won't. Somehow I manage to take my pants off, and then I pull a towel off the rack and lay it in the tub. I hear yelling, another gunshot, more yelling, and some pounding noises, but they might as well be in another universe. For me the only thing that matters is the pain and a sudden overwhelming urge to push.

I slide myself down into the tub. I try the breathing techniques I learned in the birthing class. I tell myself not to push, not yet, not here. But the urge is too strong. Finally I can't take it any longer. I rip the washcloth from my mouth, bear down, and push as hard as I can while letting out a mighty yell.

There is a thundering crash just beyond the tub

that makes the floor beneath me shake, and the bathroom door flies open. I wonder if I'm about to die, and for one desperate, insane moment I hope I am because it would make this god-awful pain go away.

Someone appears next to the tub, and I turn to face this person who has haunted and hunted me for the past four months, this person who wants me dead. But the face I see is Hurley's.

"Shots?" I manage through clenched teeth.

"We got him. It's okay," Hurley says. "Is the baby coming?"

Through my clenched teeth, I hiss a *yes*, and then suddenly the urge to push abates. The pain is still intense, however, and I start panting, trying to get through it.

Hurley yells out, "Brenda, call an ambulance." Then he looks back at me. "What can I do?"

Between pants, I say, "Wash your hands. More towels."

Another urge to push starts to build, and I try to breathe through it. But it's too strong, and before I know it I'm pushing. I grunt and groan as my body strains to expel the child within me, but after a minute or so the urge subsides.

"I think I saw the head," Hurley says, staring between my legs as he dries his hands. "Lots of hair. But it's bloody and really wet. It's kind of gross. Is it supposed to look like that?"

"What did you expect, Hurley?" I snarl. The pain has stolen any last vestige of politeness or patience I had in me. "Did you think this was going to be all magic, and fairy dust, and rainbows?"

I thought Hurley might look wounded, or snap

back at me, but instead he smiles and says, "Hell, yes. And unicorns, too."

I shake my head. "Leave it to you to get a phallic symbol in there somewhere."

Someone else comes through the bathroom door, and when I look past Hurley, I'm surprised to see Izzy.

"The security alarm went off, so the company called me," he says. "They called Dom, too." Then he looks down at me and says, "Ah, I see we are about to have a baby."

Hurley steps aside and waves Izzy closer to the tub. "Here, you're a doctor. You do this."

Izzy hollers out to the living room, "Dom, get my scene kit from the car, please." Then he turns to the sink and starts washing his hands.

"What do you need your scene kit for?" Hurley asks, looking worried. "Is something wrong with the baby? Is something wrong with Mattie?"

Izzy takes a towel to dry his hands and says, "I want it because there are gloves in it and other things I can use."

Hurley moves to the top of the tub by my head and takes hold of my hand. I'm sure he's about to regret it because another urge to push comes and I lean forward, pull my legs back, and bear down as hard as I can. In the process I squeeze Hurley's hand into pulp. After pushing as long as I can, I snatch a breath and push again.

When I'm done, I fall against the back of the tub, hot, sweaty, and exhausted.

Dom appears and hands Izzy his scene kit. Then he looks at me with a huge smile on his face. "It's finally coming," he says, clapping his hands together with giddy excitement. Then he glances down at my nether parts. Seconds later there is another crash as Dom passes out cold.

"Bob! Brenda!" Izzy yells as he's donning his gloves. "I need some help in here with Dom."

Bob Richmond enters the bathroom, stepping his way around Dom's prostrate body. He bends down and grabs Dom beneath both arms to lift him, but then he glances over into the tub and freezes. He is staring at my crotch, and I could care less. Everyone in the room is staring at my crotch, and I could care less. I just . . . want . . . this . . . kid . . . out!

I feel another urge to push start to build, and I brace myself and give it all I have. I feel something pop and hear Izzy say, "Atta girl, there's the head. Now give me one more good push. Give it all you got."

I suck in another breath and give it what I have left, which is enough. Seconds later the pressure and pain is gone, and I feel a warm gush of fluid along my thighs and butt.

Izzy smiles and says, "It's a boy."

The next thing I hear is the sweetest sound I could possibly imagine, the first cry of my newborn son.

Richmond says, "Holy cow! That was amazing!"

Izzy ties off the umbilical cord with dental floss from my sink and then cuts the cord in two. He wraps my son in a towel, wipes the goo off his head, and hands him to me. Holding that tiny life in my arms is the most amazing experience I've ever had. His face is exquisitely perfect.

I look over at Hurley and see tears coursing down his face. I give my son a kiss on the forehead and then hand him over to Hurley, who takes the tiny bundle as if it's the most precious, fragile thing in the world.

"Wow," he says, looking down at that tiny face. "Hello, Matthew Izthak Hurley. Nice to meet you. I'm your dad."

I'm smiling so big my face hurts, and for a few seconds nothing else in the world, nothing else in my screwed-up life matters except this moment, these people, and this wonderful new life that has come from me. I can't imagine ever feeling more joy.

And then I'm proven wrong when Hurley leans over, kisses me on the forehead, and says, "I love you, Mattie Winston."

Chapter 41

The EMTs arrive in time to bundle us up and take us to the hospital. Both Matthew and I check out fine, but we are asked to stay an obligatory twenty-four hours just to make sure. A parade of visitors wades through my room throughout the evening, and even my mother manages a visit, though she arrives wearing a mask and gloves. Dribs and drabs of what went down at the cottage are revealed to me as the night progresses—we arrested the shooter, it looks like he's been stalking you for a while, he has a phone that matches up with the last weird call you got, we found receipts in his car for other burner phones—but it's not until the next morning that I get the full story. Richmond, Hurley, Junior Feller, Brenda, and Izzy all enter my room just after eight.

"Little Matthew is sleeping like the proverbial baby," Izzy tells me. "We just came from the nursery. He's adorable."

"Yes, he is," I say, smiling. I had told the nurses last evening that I wanted Matthew in the room with me, and they complied. I spent the night nursing him—

or at least trying to—and waking up every hour to stand next to his bassinette and just stare at him. It was only when I went to shower this morning that they finally took him back to the nursery. I had hoped Hurley might be able to spend the night, but Emily, upon hearing that the baby had arrived, predictably created a crisis by calling Hurley and threatening to run off with her new boyfriend. Hurley wanted to ignore her, knowing it was most likely an empty threat, but I finally convinced him to go, to reassure her that she was still important to him. I also made it clear to him that we were going to get her some counseling, even if we had to hog-tie her to do it. This time he didn't balk or argue with me.

"How's Dom doing?" I ask Izzy.

"He'll be fine," Izzy says with a smile and a shake of his head. "They checked him out in the ER last night. He has a small cut on his head that took two stitches, but other than that he seems to be okay. He's home resting so he can come over and help with little Matthew as soon as you come home. He's so excited you'd think he had the kid."

"I'll be happy to have the help," I tell him. Then I turn to Richmond. "Any more news on this shooter?"

Richmond nods. "We know who he is."

"And it's someone you know," Hurley adds.

I'm sure they're going to say it's my father, and I brace myself for the news. But I'm wrong.

"It's Luke Nelson," Hurley says.

It takes me a moment to place the name, and then it all comes back to me. "You mean that raping shrink who came to town last fall?"

"One and the same," Hurley says. "He's been on the run and hiding out ever since you busted his little sex scam, and he blames you for everything that's happened to him. He knew Schneider because the two of them spent several years together in the same foster home in Florida with parents who abused them. Because of that they bonded and stayed in touch over the years. So when Schneider got out of prison, Nelson offered him money to kill you. When he found out that Schneider failed and you killed him, Nelson became focused on revenge. He's been spying on you for months, just waiting for a chance to catch you exposed and vulnerable. If it hadn't been for the security detail we had on you, I suspect he would have tried something, and likely succeeded, months ago."

"So he's the one who's been making all the phone calls?"

Richmond nods again. "We were able to trace the phone he had on him to the last call you got, and when they followed up on the receipts for the other phones, they coincided with other calls you received."

"I remember Nelson saying he was from Florida," I say. "I should have made that connection, but it's been almost a year since all that happened. He wasn't on my radar."

"He wasn't on anyone's radar," Hurley says. "We're lucky we caught him when we did."

I'm relieved that the mystery is solved, and even more relieved to know that it wasn't my father hunting me down and trying to kill me. But I'm also a little disappointed to know that it wasn't him who was calling me. Despite that, it still seems certain that he was the one peering through my cottage windows that night. Luke Nelson is blond, blue-eyed, and fair-skinned, whereas my father is dark-haired, brown-eyed, and ruddy in complexion. So perhaps he is still in the picture.

Junior, Brenda, and Izzy all congratulate me and then depart for their respective jobs, leaving me with Hurley and Richmond. The two men exchange a look, and then I see Richmond nod at Hurley. Then Hurley looks back at me and says, "There's something else we should tell you."

"What now?" I ask. I don't like the look on his face or Richmond's.

"Luke Nelson was shot as he was trying to break into your cottage. By the time the cops arrived, he was already down."

"So?" I say, confused as to why this is important.

"So, none of us shot him," Hurley says.

I contemplate this for a second. "Who did then?"

Hurley shrugs. "We don't know. Apparently you have a guardian angel. At first, we thought maybe David or someone from his place had come over through the woods when they heard the shots, but David and Patty were both in Chicago for the day. Brenda was inside with you. We ran ballistics on the bullets that hit Nelson, and they aren't a match for any of our guns."

"Bullets? Plural?" I say.

Hurley nods. "He was hit twice, once in the arm and once in the groin."

I can't help but feel that the shot in the groin is poetic justice, knowing what I do about Nelson.

Richmond adds, "The arm shot was a through-and-through, and we found the bullet embedded in your door frame. Based on Nelson's injury and where he told us he was standing at the time, we calculated a trajectory for the shots and determined they came from the woods."

"You didn't find anyone in the woods?"

Hurley shakes his head. "According to Nelson it was a bear in the woods who shot him."

This makes me smile. I have a strong suspicion who the bear was, but I decide to keep it to myself.

"What's going to happen to Nelson?" I ask.

"He won't see the light of day for years to come, if ever," Richmond says. "When they're done filing charges against him here, he's wanted for a host of them in Florida. In fact, they suspect he was Schneider's partner in the liquor store robbery. Not sure if they'll be able to prove it, but they have enough other stuff on him to put him away for a long, long time."

Richmond excuses himself after that, and moments later the nurse brings Matthew back into the room. I watch Hurley pick him up from the isolette and stare down into his face as he holds him in his hands. Hurley has the sweetest, gentlest smile I've ever seen on him, and I know he is going to make a great father.

As if he has read my mind, Hurley glances over at me and says, "We'll make this work somehow, Winston. With time, we'll make it work."

I nod and smile at him, hoping he is right, though I have a feeling the forks aren't done messing with me yet.

But for now, for at least this moment in time, life is perfect.